Day of the Dead

Nicci French is the pseudonym for the writing partnership of journalists Nicci Gerrard and Sean French. The couple are married and live in Suffolk. There are eighteen other bestselling novels by Nicci French, all published by Penguin. *Blue Monday* was the first thrilling story in the Frieda Klein series, followed by *Tuesday's Gone*, *Waiting for Wednesday*, *Thursday's Child*, *Friday on My Mind*, *Saturday Requiem* and *Sunday Morning Coming Down*.

Twitter@FrenchNicci

www.niccifrench.co.uk

http://www.facebook.com/NicciFrenchOfficialPage

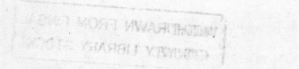

Day of the Dead

NICCI FRENCH

MICHAEL JOSEPH
an imprint of
PENGUIN BOOKS

MICHAEL JOSEPH

UK | USA | Canada | Ireland | Australia
India | New Zealand | South Africa

Michael Joseph is part of the Penguin Random House group of companies
whose addresses can be found at global.penguinrandomhouse.com.

First published 2018

001

Copyright © Joined-Up Writing, 2018
Map of the Rivers of London © Maps Illustrated, 2018

The moral right of the authors has been asserted

Set in 13.5/16 pt Garamond MT Std
Typeset by Jouve (UK), Milton Keynes
Printed in Great Britain by Clays Ltd, St Ives plc

A CIP catalogue record for this book is available from the British Library

HARDBACK ISBN: 978–0–718–17968–7
TRADE PAPERBACK ISBN: 978–0–718–17969–4

www.greenpenguin.co.uk

To Edgar, Anna, Hadley and Molly

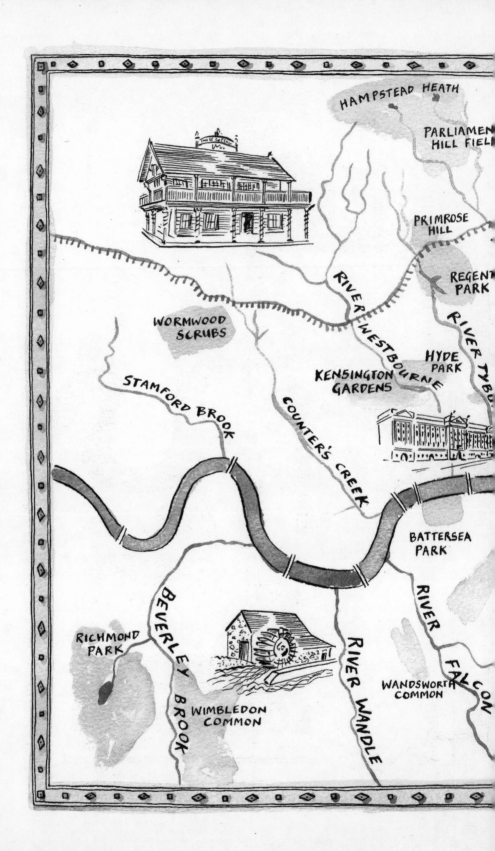

HAMPSTEAD HEATH

PARLIAMEN
HILL FIEL

PRIMROSE
HILL

REGENT
PARK

RIVER WESTBOURNE

RIVER TYB

WORMWOOD
SCRUBS

HYDE
PARK

KENSINGTON
GARDENS

STAMFORD BROOK

COUNTER'S CREEK

BATTERSEA
PARK

RIVER FALCON

BEVERLEY BROOK

RICHMOND
PARK

RIVER WANDLE

WANDSWORTH
COMMON

WIMBLEDON
COMMON

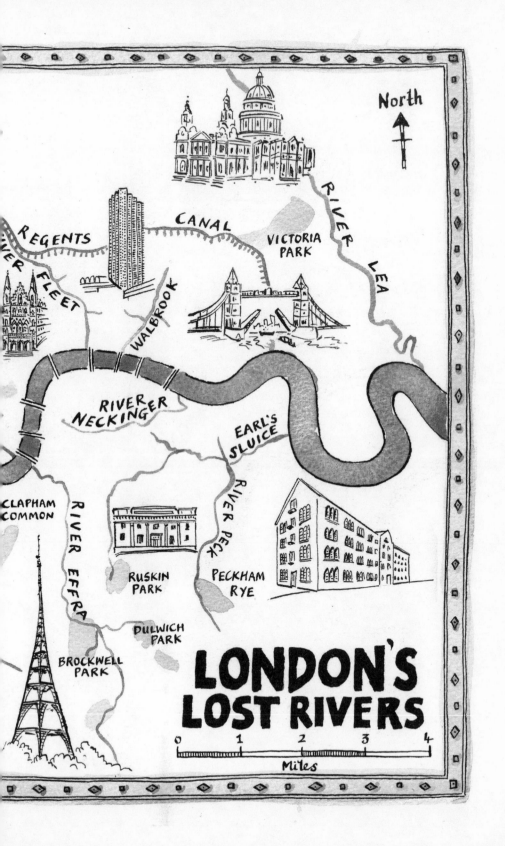

North

RIVER LEA

REGENTS

RIVER FLEET

CANAL

VICTORIA PARK

WALBROOK

RIVER NECKINGER

EARL'S SLUICE

CLAPHAM COMMON

RIVER EFFRA

RIVER PECK

RUSKIN PARK

PECKHAM RYE

DULWICH PARK

BROCKWELL PARK

LONDON'S LOST RIVERS

0   1   2   3   4

Miles

One

It was a Monday morning, it was bright, it was warm, too warm for late autumn, and Charlotte Beck was about to experience the one really dramatic thing that would happen to her in her entire life. She wasn't ready for it. She didn't feel ready for anything.

She was manoeuvring a chaotic little group up Heath Street, as she did every weekday. She was steering a buggy containing ten-month-old Lulu. On her left side two-and-a-half-year-old Oscar was pushing himself on a little scooter. Round her right wrist was one end of a dog lead and the other end was attached to a black Labrador puppy called Suki. Everything looked like it was in fog, but it wasn't real fog. It was the fog of tiredness that had hung stolidly over Charlotte's world for the previous six months. Lulu didn't sleep at night. She shouted and she screamed and nothing helped, nothing that Charlotte tried, nothing that the experts recommended.

Instead Lulu slept during the day. She was asleep now, contentedly under a blanket in her buggy, a dummy lodged in her mouth. Every so often, Charlotte leaned over to peer at her. She looked peaceful and angelic. It was difficult to believe that that smooth little face with its long eyelashes and pink cheeks could do so much damage to a grown woman. Charlotte felt so tired that it hurt. Her eyes were stinging with it, her skin felt stretched, her joints were aching. She was only thirty-one. It couldn't be arthritis, could it? Could lack of sleep damage your bones? It felt like it.

I

As her little caravan of chaos made its way up the hill, Charlotte was aware of so much that could go wrong. Suki wasn't properly trained yet. Charlotte had meant to teach her to sit and to beg and just generally do what she was told but she hadn't had the time. There'd been so much else to do. She might suddenly bolt towards another dog, or away from another dog, and drag them all into the traffic. Admittedly she was only a small puppy but she was more than a match for her owner. And Oscar on his scooter was a permanent danger to himself and to others. For the hundredth time Charlotte told herself that she really ought to buy him a helmet. What would happen if he came off it and landed on his head? What kind of a mother was she anyway? She wearily imagined the potential news headlines: 'Family Dragged Into Traffic by Dog'; 'Tot Dies in Scooter Crash. Mother Arrested'.

This morning the shops felt like a series of rebukes. She passed coffee shops with pairs of young mothers sitting and talking, as if motherhood was an easy and enjoyable lifestyle choice. The thought of even trying to sit in a café with Oscar and Lulu and Suki gave Charlotte the beginnings of a migraine. She passed a toddlers' clothes shop called Mamma Mia. Oscar stopped his scooter by ramming into the glass window.

'Is that a robot?' he asked, staring at the silvery, dead-eyed, child-sized dummy, wearing a jacket that cost £87.50.

'No,' said Charlotte. 'It's a . . .' She hesitated. How to explain? 'It's a sort of doll for wearing clothes.' Behind the shop dummies, Charlotte saw a woman wearing a pink Puffa jacket with two children, a boy who looked the same size as Oscar and a girl a few years older. The girl had blonde hair tied in a ponytail. Charlotte felt as if she was looking at a performance by people who knew how to be a family and had the money to get it right.

They proceeded up the street. They were heading for the top of the hill, the Whitestone Pond, Hampstead Heath. It always felt to Charlotte like it was breaking out into the light, escaping the murk below, the traffic and fumes of the four-wheel-drives taking children to one of the dozens of little private prep schools dotted around Hampstead. She paused again outside a dentist's surgery. When did children first need to go to the dentist? She looked at the glass sign outside, with a list of the services they offered. 'Celebrity Smile Portfolio'. That sounded like something she could use. 'Turn Back Time Treatments'. Even better. She thought of herself ten years ago – was it really that long? – at university. Those Friday and Saturday nights, the late mornings. Nobody to feed. Nobody to worry about except herself and the occasional flatmate taking the last of the milk. She caught sight of herself in the mirror. What would twenty-one-year-old Charlotte Beck make of thirty-one-year-old Charlotte Beck, sleep-deprived, hair unwashed and – she suddenly noticed – with a stain on the front of her shirt? She pulled up the zip of her jacket so that it couldn't be seen.

They continued up the hill.

'Where are we going?' said Oscar.

'Where we always go. To the pond. Maybe one day we'll get a boat.'

'What sort of boat?'

'A little sailing boat.' It sounded a bad idea as soon as the words were out of her mouth.

And then it happened.

A flash of silver as the car passed her, heading down the hill.

Too fast, she thought, and turned to Oscar and the buggy and Suki. She wasn't looking in the right direction, but she heard screams and then a scraping sound and then the sound of bumping and metal and then shattering glass. She stared back down the hill. She had difficulty in making sense of what she was seeing because everything was suddenly different. Nobody was moving and the world had gone silent, except that a bell was ringing somewhere, a burglar alarm or a fire alarm. Improbably, as if in a dream, the silver car that had passed her was now wedged into a shop window. It was almost the whole way in. A white van coming up the hill had stopped in the middle of the road and the driver had got out but he wasn't doing anything, just standing and watching.

Charlotte felt as if normal life had cracked and she had stepped through the crack and everything was different and nothing made sense. She started walking slowly towards the devastation and then stopped. She had Suki; the lead was fastened to her wrist. But she had forgotten her children. She stepped back and took hold of the buggy. Lulu was still fast asleep. Oscar was gazing at the crashed car, his mouth open, like a caricature of surprise in a storybook.

'Come,' Charlotte said to him, then awkwardly took his right hand in her left and steered the buggy with her other, which was also attached to Suki's lead. As she got closer, she could see that some people were just standing and staring. Two women had come out of the café. There was a postman. No. Charlotte mentally corrected herself: it was a post*woman*. She had her funny red trailer and she was holding a package in her hand. Next, Charlotte saw figures lying on the ground. Why was nobody helping them? Who was in charge? She looked around. What she wanted was people in uniform to appear and take over and put up tape and tell everyone to keep on the other side of it. But there was nobody. Just ordinary people who didn't know what to do.

Two young women were standing next to her. One had a leather bag over her shoulder.

4

'Have you got a phone?'

The women looked puzzled and Charlotte repeated the question. One woman raised her hand to show the phone she was holding.

'Ambulance,' said Charlotte. 'Nine nine nine. Call it now.'

She looked at the other woman, then gestured at her children. 'Take care of them,' she said. 'One minute. I'll be back.'

Charlotte took Suki's lead off her wrist and gave it to the still open-mouthed Oscar. 'Look after Suki for one minute. Can you do that?'

He nodded solemnly. Charlotte turned round and walked towards the car. A person was lying half on the pavement, half on the road, splayed out. One leg was bent in a way that seemed wrong. Charlotte knelt down beside the woman and gazed into her eyes. Her mind was a blank about what you were meant to do. Were you meant to move them or not to move them?

'How are you?' she asked.

'My leg,' said the woman. At least she could talk.

'Anything else?'

'My husband. Where's my husband?'

'The ambulance is coming,' said Charlotte, hoping it was true. She walked round to the other side of the car. An old man was lying on his back. He was staring up at the sky without blinking and without seeing. It was the first dead person Charlotte had ever seen.

She stepped towards the car. She could see a slumped figure inside. She couldn't make out whether it was male or female. She was going to open the car door when she heard a sobbing sound. She turned her head: it was coming from inside the shop. She stepped in through what had been the shop window. She heard the crunch of the glass under her

5

feet, looked down and realized this was Mamma Mia, the children's clothes shop.

She walked further in and saw a figure lying on the floor half under the front wheels of the car. As she bent down towards it, the figure groaned and moved, and suddenly she felt a warm splash on her and saw that it was a woman and there was blood gushing from her shoulder or near her shoulder. It came in spurts, as if someone was blowing it out, then breathing in and blowing it out again. The woman was staring up at her, looking directly into Charlotte's eyes. Charlotte had an impulse to run away and let someone else deal with this.

She had a dim memory of what one should do. Press on something. That was it. But where? She pushed her fingers over the wound but the blood bubbled through them. It wasn't working. Then she moved her hand slightly down from the wound and pressed again, really hard. The flow of blood stopped, as if she had stepped on a garden hose. She pressed even harder and the woman gave a gasp.

'Am I going to die?' she said, her eyes flickering.

'There's an ambulance coming,' said Charlotte.

'Joey,' said the woman. 'And Cass.'

Suddenly Charlotte realized that this was the woman she had been looking at through the window, and then she wondered where the woman's children were.

'I'm sure they're safe,' said Charlotte.

She glanced around, almost frightened of what she might see. There to one side were the two children, slumped on the floor, glassy-eyed with shock. Charlotte felt she should do something but was scared to move her hand. Suddenly there was a bustle around her, uniforms, young men and women in a blur. Someone shouted questions at her but she couldn't think. She was pulled away from the woman, who

6

disappeared under a scrum of paramedics. Charlotte stepped back, the glass still crunching under her feet. She looked at the two children still slumped on the floor and held out her hands helplessly.

She remembered her own children and made her way gingerly through the wrecked shop. People in uniform were everywhere. Some of them looked at her curiously. She stepped outside and felt the sunshine on her and heard sounds of gasping. She was puzzled and wondered what it was about, and then she looked down at herself, soaked with red, and understood it was about her.

Two

Constable Darren Symons had been in his job for just over two months. The most serious accident he had attended up to now was when a young man had been knocked off his motorbike by a cement mixer. He hadn't died, though, just broken his leg. This was something else. He gazed around at the carnage with a kind of awe. It was like a fever dream: the blue lights flashing, the silver car inserted into the shop, the shards of shattered glass glinting on the pavement, the body still trapped in the crumpled vehicle. It didn't look real, no more real than the child-sized mannequin standing placidly amid the wreckage of the shop. He saw a body being lifted onto a stretcher. Two small children were being led to a waiting car by a female officer. He saw blood on the pavement. He heard someone crying, high and loud.

'Constable Symons. *Darren.*' He blinked and turned to his senior investigating officer, who gestured around them. 'Witnesses. Get their names. Before they vanish.'

He nodded and took out his notebook. His pencil wobbled on the paper as he wrote the date: 3 October 2016. He looked at his watch and added the time: 09.11. There was a throng of people behind the cordons and tapes, and more people flowing up the hill, as if they were on their way to a concert. How did they hear so quickly? He looked up and saw faces in the windows of the houses.

A woman was sitting on the pavement covered in blood, holding a lead at the end of which was a little dog; every time it strained forward her body jerked after it. Why was no one attending to her? He approached cautiously, as if she was a bomb that might explode, and she looked up. Her face was white with shock but she seemed unharmed. In the buggy at her side was a baby, improbably asleep in all the hubbub, a dummy planted in its mouth and its eyes flickering in its dreams. A tiny boy in striped dungarees was jumping on and off the pavement, his cheeks hectic.

'Are you injured?' Symons said.

Behind them, he could hear the whine of a saw: they must be cutting the body out of the car.

'Me? No. I just . . .' She tailed off. 'I feel a bit sick.'

'That's blood!' roared the boy. 'Bloody blood.'

He hopped back and forth, panting with the effort, his face screwed up with effort and his eyes gleaming.

'Can I ask you a few questions?' asked Constable Symons. 'About what you saw.'

'I didn't see anything.'

'You're covered in blood.'

She looked down at herself, dazed. 'It's hers. Will she die? Where are her children?'

'Who?'

'The woman in the shop. I tried . . .'

'I don't know anything about that,' he said. 'If you could tell me what you saw.'

'It went smash-bang,' shouted the boy. 'On our way to the pond. We're going to buy a sailing boat soon.'

'Let's begin with your name.'

'My name is Charlotte Beck,' said the woman. She started to weep, her thin body shaking, her face streaming with tears.

He sat down on the pavement beside her and put his hand on her shoulder. The little boy stopped jumping and crouched beside her.

'It'll wash off,' he said. 'Mummy. Don't cry.'

*

9

'I was in the stockroom,' said the owner of Mamma Mia. Her voice cracked. She kept touching her face, her body, with her hands, as if checking for damage. 'I was looking for –' She stopped. 'I suppose it doesn't matter what I was looking for.'

'So you didn't see anything?' Constable Symons asked.

'I thought it was an earthquake. Or a bomb. I thought I was going to die.' She stared at him. 'I crawled under the table,' she said. 'I didn't try to help, I just hid.'

'That's only natural,' he said.

'There was someone in the car with him.'

'Really?'

'A man. Wearing a hat, I think. It happened so quickly, but I think I recognized him. Has he disappeared? That's strange, isn't it?'

'There was something strange about it.'

Symons looked at the man. He was strongly built, hair cut short, jeans and a thick green jacket. 'Of course it was strange,' said the officer. 'Car driving into a shop. You don't get stranger than that.'

'I don't mean that. The car didn't look like it was being driven. It was more like it was just rolling down the hill, out of control.'

'Rolling? What do you mean?'

'I'm just telling you what I saw.'

'Can you give me a name and number?'

'McGill,' said the man. 'Dave McGill.' And he recited a phone number.

Symons was trying to concentrate. The sun was so sharp and the noises so persistent, that alarm still going off, the whine of the saw, horns blaring from the bottom of the road and in the distance the sound of the sirens. He peered at the woman facing him, whose name was Sally Krauss and who was visibly trembling, holding her shiny brown bag to her chest, like a shield.

'He had a bald head,' she said. 'He was hunched over. Probably had a heart attack. It happened to my uncle. He drove straight into a tree. Sudden heart attack. They said he probably didn't feel a thing.'

Symons looked down at his notes. Everybody had seen something different. He sighed.

'My name is Adrian Greville and I saw everything,' said the man with a moustache as thin as string on his upper lip. 'It was coming straight at me. It missed me by this much.' He held up a thumb and forefinger to indicate the narrowness of his escape. 'It went into this old couple. I saw him fly up in the air. I saw his face. I could swear he was looking straight at me. Poor guy.'

'Did you see the driver at all?'

'Completely. He was sitting there gripping the steering wheel. He was smiling. It was no accident. He meant to do it.'

Some of the witnesses seemed reluctant to leave. They hovered around in groups, talking to each other. One of them, the one in the green jacket, the one who had noticed something odd about the accident, that the car seemed to have been rolling down the hill, sat on the pavement beside the blood-soaked Charlotte Beck. Her little boy sat beside her sucking the lollipop a police officer had given him and the baby slept in its buggy. She looked at the man with a dazed expression. 'I should go home,' she said.

'I saw what you did.'

'I just did what anyone would have done.'

'Except no one else did. They'll probably give you a medal.'

He stood up and held out his hand to help her from the pavement. 'Here,' he said. 'I'm Dave. I'll walk you home. Let me push the buggy.'

In the shattered space of what had once been Mamma Mia, a group of white-suited scene-of-crime officers lifted the body of a man clear from the car. He was middle-aged, with close-cropped hair, a mole on his right cheek. He was dressed in grey trousers and a grey-and-white checked shirt, trainers, a watch with a metal strap. His skin looked chalky, the eyes opened wide in a stare of fixed surprise.

They laid him on the stretcher. His arm dangled down and one of the officers lifted it on to his chest.

'There's not much blood,' she said.

As they moved the body away, one of the officers bent down and reached forward, trying to avoid the glass and the jagged metal.

'Got it,' he said, holding up a wallet.

Sergeant June McFarlane flicked through the wallet, ignoring the cash, the credit cards. She removed a driving licence. The fuzzy pixelated photograph was clearly of the man in the car.

'Geoffrey Udo Kernan,' she read aloud. 'Ten Motherwell Road, RM10 9BB.' She looked round at Symons. 'You know where that is? Is that out of London?'

'It's Romford, I think. Depends what you mean by out of London. Do you want me to arrange for someone to go there?'

McFarlane shook her head. 'We'll go ourselves. Right now.'

Symons looked doubtful. 'It's a long way.'

'Doesn't matter. There are people dead here, people injured. We need to do this ourselves.'

It was half past three in the afternoon. The sun was already low in the sky. The road was still cordoned off and guarded, police cars and vans stationed across it. But the crowds had gone, the car had been towed away, the glass had been removed. The forensic team were hard at work, taking photographs, measuring skid marks, collecting pieces of ripped metal, following the rules and giving everything an order and a meaning. Mamma Mia was just a jagged hole.

Meanwhile, McFarlane and Symons were on the North Circular, stuck in traffic. They had checked on the satnav. Symons hadn't been entirely right. Kernan's home was more Barking than Romford, but it wasn't any closer.

'It's the wrong time of day to be driving,' said Symons.

'When's the right time?' said McFarlane. 'Maybe about three in the morning.'

They'd had time to check Kernan's name on the police computer. Nothing. Symons started talking about the crime scene, about what might have happened, but McFarlane stopped him.

'Let's wait and see,' she said, and for the rest of the journey they talked about other things. The drive took over an hour before they turned off the North Circular on to the Barking bypass and off that to Motherwell Drive, a road of post-war pebble-dash, two-up-two-down terraced houses. They sat still in the car.

'It's always a strange moment,' said McFarlane, 'when you're about to ring on the door and ruin someone's life.'

'Maybe he lived alone,' said Symons. 'Or maybe nobody's home.'

'We won't find out sitting here,' said McFarlane, and they both got out and walked up the little path. They stopped next to a grey Peugeot hatchback that was parked on the driveway.

'Looks like somebody's home,' said McFarlane; she pressed the doorbell and they heard a distant chime. There was the sound of movement and footsteps and then the door opened. The woman was dressed in loose jeans, a white blouse and a turquoise cardigan that June McFarlane noticed had small holes on one sleeve. Moths. But mainly they saw her face, pale and anxious, which made her dark hair seem almost black by contrast.

'Do you know Geoffrey Kernan?' asked McFarlane, and Symons felt his stomach lurch at what was about to happen.

'He's my husband,' she said.

'May we come in?'

At first they just sat awkwardly in the front room, and watched Mrs Kernan as she cried. McFarlane leaned forward slightly and handed her the tissues she had ready. Symons went into the little kitchen, found a jar of instant coffee and made a mug for each of them, adding several spoons of sugar for Mrs Kernan. McFarlane sat next to the woman and made her drink it.

'I can't believe it,' said Mrs Kernan. 'I can't believe it. I keep thinking I'm going to wake up.'

'I'm so sorry,' said McFarlane.

'I thought something had happened. But not this.'

'What do you mean? Why did you think something had happened?'

'I reported him missing.'

McFarlane looked at Symons with a puzzled expression. 'I thought you said . . .' she began.

'I checked,' he said. 'There wasn't anything.'

She turned to Mrs Kernan. 'When did you report this?'

'Three days ago. I went into the police station and said he was missing.'

'Did you make a statement?'

'They weren't interested. They said he had probably just gone away suddenly. That people do that.'

'So you didn't make a statement?'

'They just sent me away. They weren't interested. They said, "Come back in a few days if he still hasn't come home." And now . . . now . . .' And she started crying again.

'Mrs Kernan, did you –'

'I knew he wouldn't do that.'

'Do what?'

'I went over to see my sister and when I got back he wasn't here. I thought he'd gone for a walk or met a friend some-where. But it got later and later and he wasn't answering his phone and then he didn't come back at all. I waited the whole of the next day and then they called from his work and asked why he hadn't been in touch and then I went to the police.'

'Do you have children?'

The woman wrapped her arms around her body for com-fort. 'Ned. He's at university. I have to tell him. It's his first year. He's only just started. I didn't tell him about Geoff going missing. I didn't want to worry him. And now . . .' She dabbed at her face with the tissue. Her eyes looked sore.

'Was he close to his father?'

'They argued a lot. But that's because they were so like each other.'

'What work did your husband do?'

'He's in sales.'

'Sales of what?'

'Sanitary supplies. For companies. He drives around a lot.' She blinked. 'Drove. It's the first time I've said it like that.'

'Yes,' said McFarlane. 'That's hard. Is that your car outside?'

'It's his car. It's actually the company car.'

'Does he have another? A metallic silver-grey Nissan?'

'No, we only have one.'

'This incident happened in Heath Street, Hampstead. Would your husband have had any business or personal reason to be there?'

'He drove around all the time for his work, all over the country. I don't know anything special about Hampstead.'

'Maybe he has a business acquaintance there. Or a friend.'

'What do you mean, friend?'

'He might have had an appointment with someone.'

'Not that I know of. What was it that happened?'

McFarlane gave an account of the crash.

'Did anyone die? I mean, apart from Geoff.' She took a violent hiccuping breath as she said the name.

'One person died at the scene. There are other casualties, some severe.'

Mrs Kernan took a tissue from her pocket and blew her nose.

'Mrs Kernan, I know this is a terrible time. But I need to ask certain questions.'

'What kind of questions?'

'Were there any problems between you and your husband?'

'What do you mean?'

'Marital problems.'

'No. Nothing like that.'

'Your husband must have been away a lot. Was that difficult?'

'Sometimes. We got through it.'

'How were things at work?'

'Fine. The usual. Too many hours, not enough money.'

'Was there anything recently?'

Mrs Kernan shook her head. Her expression had been dull with grief but she suddenly changed and looked suspicious. 'What are you saying?'

'I'm not saying anything.'

'Do you think he did this to himself?'

The phone rang and Mrs Kernan got up to answer it. McFarlane took the mugs back into the kitchen and washed them. Looking out of the window, she saw a robin perched on a spade that was sunk into the soil. Beyond that the garden was like a miniature building site, with large paving slabs stacked at the end.

'That was Geoff's idea,' said a voice behind her. Mrs Kernan had come into the kitchen. 'He said it would be nice for having barbecues.'

'Do you have someone who can come and be with you?'

'I could ask my sister.'

'Good.'

When they were in the car again, they sat in silence for a time.

'I think she was holding something back,' said Symons. 'I think they had problems.'

'Everyone has problems,' said McFarlane.

'But it's all obvious, isn't it?'

'Is it? Good. Explain it to me.'

'Geoffrey Kernan, pressured at work, unhappy in his marriage, he finally cracks. He walks out on his life, spends a couple of days wandering around, deciding what to do about everything. Then he gets in a car and ends it all. Simple.'

'In *a* car. Not his own car.'

'There's no law that says you need to use your own car.'

'And in Hampstead, an hour-and-a-half drive away?'

'He wanted a hill.'

'Why does he need a hill? He's in a car, not a shopping trolley.' The two officers looked at each other. 'Well,' she carried on, 'it'll all be solved tomorrow. In the meantime, check the car he was driving.'

Dr Jane Franklin, consultant pathologist, looked down at the body of Geoffrey Kernan, then across at a group of students, masked and gowned in green.

'Did you read the notes?'

There was a murmur.

'Well?'

'Car accident.'

'And?'

'Possible heart attack.'

'Anything else?'

'Or stroke. Or suicide.'

'The problem with police reports,' said Dr Franklin, 'is that they get in the way of your eyes. Forget what you've read. What do you see here?' She gestured with a scalpel at the ravaged face and forehead. 'You.' She pointed at one of the pale-faced students.

'Er . . . fracture to the –'

'Stop,' said Dr Franklin sharply. 'Let me rephrase the question. What *don't* you see?'

There was more murmuring but no actual words.

'Have any of you ever had a head injury? Banged your nose? What do you get?'

'Blood?' ventured one student, in a quavering voice.

'Yes. Blood. Lots of it. There's no blood in these wounds at all. Which means?'

'That the heart wasn't beating.'

'In other words?'

'He was already dead.'

'Exactly.'

'But how can a dead person drive a car?'

'We're pathologists,' said Dr Franklin. 'We don't look at the reports. We look at the body.'

'I checked the registration,' said Symons. 'It belongs to a Mr Alexander Christos from Didcot.'

'Is he a friend of Kernan's?'

'It was a bit complicated. I talked to the local police and they contacted Christos.'

'Give me the uncomplicated version.'

'The car must have been stolen.'

'Stolen?'

'Christos is on holiday in the Canary Islands. As far as he's concerned, his car is parked outside his house.'

McFarlane frowned, irritated. 'What's going on here? This toilet salesman goes all the way to Didcot, steals a car, then drives it to Hampstead to kill himself.'

There was a knock at the door and a young officer appeared. 'There's a call for you. It's Dr Franklin. She wants to talk to you.'

Dr Franklin met McFarlane at the door to the examination room. 'Are you comfortable seeing the body?' she said.

'I was there at the scene.'

'Even so. Some people find it difficult when they've been cut open. I want to show you something.' She led McFarlane across to one of the slabs and pulled back the sheet. 'Have a look at this.' She was pointing with the tip of her scalpel to the incision in the middle of the dead man's neck. 'See that?'

'The hyoid,' added her assistant, looking at the delicate bone in the shape of a horseshoe. 'It's broken.'

'So what? He was in a car crash. Lots of things must have been broken. I've heard about the hyoid bone. It's an indicator of strangulation. But it's not a hundred per cent accurate.'

'Yes, but it's accurate the way we need it to be.'

'What does that mean?'

'Strangulation breaks the hyoid bone in about a third of cases. But when the hyoid bone is broken, it always means strangulation.'

'But he was in a car crash.'

'That's the other thing. He was already dead.'

'You just said that,' said McFarlane. 'From the strangulation.'

'No, I mean really dead. So that the severe facial injuries, here and here—' she pointed at the crushed skull, the caved-in cheekbone – 'didn't bleed.'

'So Kernan didn't die at the scene.'

'No.'

'Do you have a time of death?'

'Do you know what I hate?'

'Lots of things, probably.'

'Yes. But what I really hate is when people have watched crime shows on TV and expect me to say that the victim died at two thirty-two in the morning two days ago.'

'I don't get to watch much TV. And I'm a police officer so I know those things are fiction.'

'Good. So, do you know where Kernan died?'

'Not as yet.'

'Do you know where his body was kept?'

'No.'

'Do you know the ambient temperature? The humidity?'

'I get the point. But could it have been two or three days before?'

Dr Franklin wrinkled her brow. 'Yes,' she said finally. 'It could have been two or three days. It could also have been longer. Much longer. Or shorter. But it couldn't have been less than several hours before the incident.'

'I see,' said McFarlane, who didn't.

'If this was TV, the pathologist would now go out and interview witnesses and solve the case herself.'

'I wish you would.'

Darren Symons blew his nose and wiped his eyes, then put a throat lozenge into his mouth. The day had gone on too long. The horrible excitement it had delivered had leaked away and now he just wanted to go home, order a takeaway, watch some TV, go to bed.

'I've got one question,' he said.

'Just one?' said McFarlane.

'It's quite long, though. How did a salesman from Barking go missing for several days, get murdered and end up in a car out of control down Heath Street? Or maybe I mean why.'

'The good news is we don't need to find out. It's become a murder investigation, way above our pay grade. Someone else has to deal with Geoffrey Kernan now.'

Three

Simon Tearle, visiting senior lecturer in criminology at Guildhall College, University of London, poured two mugs of coffee from his cafetière. To one he added a teaspoon of honey, to the other a splash of half-fat milk. He took them over to his desk. When he told his students that his door was always open to them, he hoped they wouldn't take him literally. But Lola Hayes had taken him literally and he handed her the white coffee. This was the day when he had a few minutes alone, where he could do anything he wanted. He could go online, do the crossword, stand in the window and look out on Russell Square. Tantalizingly, he could glimpse the square behind Lola's head, the golden leaves of the plane trees.

Tearle sipped at his coffee and looked at his student. Lola Hayes's face was round, pale, freckled, with large grey-green eyes. Her hair was soft and brown. She seemed to have no hard edges anywhere. She examined his office with an eager interest, as if she was fascinated by his choice of pictures on the wall, the objects on his desk.

'So?' he said.

'What?'

'Your coming to see me. Is something the matter?'

'My mind's a complete blank,' she said.

'About what? About why you're here?'

'About the dissertation. I can't think of what to write about.'

Dissertation. The very word made Tearle shudder. By the

end of the first term of the second year, each student had to have written a ten-thousand-word dissertation on a subject relevant to the field of criminology. Ten thousand words. Tearle had fifteen students. Fifteen times ten thousand added up to a hundred and fifty thousand words. Tearle would have to read every one of those words, write comments and award marks.

'So what are your friends doing?'

Lola's nose wrinkled in concentration. 'I think Ellie's writing about historical sexual abuse.'

'That's interesting.'

'Yes, but it's such a big subject. And Ellie's already doing it. And Rob's doing something about DNA.'

'Which is also interesting. And important.'

'I'm terrible at science. That's why I chose criminology.'

'Actually, we do think of criminology as a science. The clue is in the "ology".'

'It's just that I don't understand the chemistry bit.'

Tearle was silent for a moment. 'Lola, do you think that criminology is a good fit for you?'

Her eyes widened in alarm. 'Totally,' she said. 'I've had a really great time doing it.'

Tearle had been hoping for 'inspiring' or 'stimulating' rather than 'a great time'. He tapped on his keyboard, calling up her last year's marks. He raised his eyebrows in surprise. 'In fact, you've been doing well. Very well.' Lola's face flushed red. 'All right, Lola, are you interested in something historical?'

'I'd rather do something current.'

'Philosophical?'

'Not so much.'

'What about a person?'

Lola's expression instantly changed. Finally she looked

alert, engaged. 'Exactly. I'd much rather write about people than ideas or science.'

Tearle suggested a series of names: a lawyer who had chaired a public inquiry; a home secretary; a police commissioner; a campaigner. None of them seemed to raise much interest. Why was he doing this? They were supposed to be grown-ups. Couldn't she find her own subject? But he needed to come up with something, if only to get Lola out of his office. Then an idea occurred to him. He walked over to his filing cabinet and pulled open a drawer. He flicked through the different categories until he found a file of random press cuttings he kept. He dumped them on his desk and started leafing through them: trial reports, interviews with crime victims, surveys on crime rates, nothing seemed quite right. Then one news story caught his eye.

'You want a person?' he said. 'Here's a person. Have you heard of Frieda Klein?'

'No.'

Tearle took a deep breath. Yet again he wondered if any of his students actually knew anything at all about their subject beyond what he spoon-fed them. 'Frieda Klein is a psychotherapist. About ten years ago she suspected that one of her patients was involved in the Matthew Faraday kidnapping case. You remember that?'

'I would have been a child.'

'Anyway, after that she somehow ended up as a sort of informal, unofficial consultant to the police. She was involved in the Robert Poole murder and the Lawrence Dawes case. Things got a bit complicated. You may have read about her being arrested. More than once, I think.'

'No, I didn't.'

'Lola, you're studying criminology. You're meant to know this sort of thing.'

'It wasn't on the course.'

'She was involved in the Hannah Docherty case. You must have seen that.'

'It sounds familiar,' said Lola, without much conviction.

'Or, more recently, in the copy-cat cases down in Silvertown.'

'Ye-es.'

'Well, now's your chance to find out about her. Analyse her. Unpack her. Deconstruct her.'

'What should I say?'

'That is up to you. Just ask questions. Why would police need the help of a psychotherapist? Is crime investigation actually a form of therapy? Does it represent a failure of policing?'

'How do I start?'

'You start by starting,' Tearle said, sounding more cross than he meant to. He calmed himself down. 'Go to the library, look her up, read academic papers she's written or that others have written about her, go through the press cuttings. She's left a bit of a trail, over the years.'

'Great,' said Lola. 'Can I keep this newspaper?'

'Sure.' Lola was getting up to go when Tearle remembered something. 'There's someone in the university who knows her. Or certainly knows about her. Professor Hal Bradshaw down in Psychology.'

'I know him,' said Lola. 'I've seen him on TV.'

'The psychology world is quite a small one. I think they've crossed paths a few times.'

Five minutes later, Lola was three floors down knocking on a door that had Hal Bradshaw's name on it.

'Come,' said a voice.

She opened the door and walked inside. Coming from

Simon Tearle's office, she felt she had stepped into an entirely different world. Tearle's room had been lined with books and every surface had been strewn with papers and journals. This room was completely bare, the walls undecorated and painted a blue that was so white it was almost grey. The room contained no books, no furniture, except for a desk and two chairs. On the desk were a laptop computer, a pad of paper and a pen. The man behind the desk looked up at her. Lola was so struck by his spectacles – the frames were under the lenses rather than above – and by his tie, speckled yellows and oranges and blues, that she scarcely saw the person behind them.

'Yes?' he said.

Lola's words poured out in a rush. 'This is completely out of order, barging in like this without warning, but my supervisor is Simon Tearle and I was just talking to him and I think I might be doing my dissertation on this woman called Frieda Klein and he said you know her and I wondered if I could have a quick word with you about her.'

Bradshaw frowned, but then gestured Lola to sit in the chair opposite his desk. She could see him properly now. He was beautifully groomed, his face smooth, his short hair immaculate. Here in his office, at work, he looked precisely as she'd seen him on television under the bright studio lights.

'Frieda Klein,' he said slowly, as if savouring the sounds of the words over his tongue.

'Have you met her?'

'Yes.'

There was a pause.

'I was hoping you could tell me something about her. Steer me in the right direction.'

'You're studying criminology, no?'

'Yes.'

'So presumably you've read how criminal investigations attract fantasists, charlatans, the mentally disturbed?'

'Are you talking about Frieda Klein?'

'I just mean that you should approach the subject of an amateur insinuating herself into police operations with a certain objectivity.'

'I thought she'd been involved in solving some cases.'

Bradshaw gave a sad smile. 'The main advice I would give you is to be careful of taking Frieda Klein at her own valuation. If you do your research properly, you may well come to see Klein as someone who has left a trail of havoc behind her.'

'It sounds as if you really don't like her.'

Bradshaw shook his head. 'I'm a scientist. I just analyse the data. If people choose to see her as a fraud and a busybody and a menace, then that is a matter for them. Or for you.'

Four

'Where's this one from? Go on, have a guess.'

Dan Quarry picked up the freshly filled glass of whisky, sniffed it and took a sip. He'd been off the drink for several months now. He'd promised his wife. But this was a special occasion. And going out with his new boss was part of the job. It was compulsory. He smelt it and tasted it again. This was the fourth – or was it the fifth? By now they all seemed the same.

'Scotland?' he said.

Detective Inspector Bill Dugdale looked disappointed. 'Scotland? I wouldn't have asked you if it was from Scotland. This is Japanese. Nice stuff. Smooth. A bit of class.'

'I didn't know they had whisky in Japan.'

'You've got a lot to learn, Quarry. About policing, about whisky.' Dugdale raised his glass. 'Here's to guilty verdicts.'

Quarry drained his glass. The verdict had come in just after three that afternoon. Guilty on all charges. They'd headed straight for the pub, the detectives and the uniforms. There had been a few hours of laughter and backslapping and mocking jokes about the failed defence strategy. Then Dugdale had nodded at his new colleague and they'd walked over to a members-only bar just off Tottenham Court Road. Dugdale had called it a whisky-tasting, as if it were a scientific experiment.

'Whenever we get a good result,' Dugdale had said, 'I taste half a dozen whiskies I've never tried before.'

Half a dozen, thought Quarry. That meant there was one,

or even two to go. He looked at his new boss. He had a large head, close-cropped, and a face that was round and soft and pouchy and flushed, with soft-grey eyes. But Quarry's previous boss, down in Camberwell, had told him to watch out for him. Dugdale's previous assistant had been got rid of very suddenly. Nobody would tell Quarry exactly why, but it made him nervous. He had seen hints of what happened when his boss wasn't pleased.

'So which is your favourite so far?' Dugdale asked.

Quarry tried to remember them. There was the one that was caramelly and sickly. There was the one that smelt like the stuff you dabbed on cuts and scrapes. There was the one that Dugdale had told him was cask strength: 'You'll want a spot of water with that one, lad.'

Quarry's honest answer would have been: none of them. He didn't like whisky. He didn't really like this part of being a detective, the drinking, the joshing, the camaraderie, pretending everything was all right when it wasn't. He looked around the small upper-room bar they were in. There was a masonic atmosphere of men in suits, huddled, drinking, in conversation, doing deals, making contacts, networking. What would they make of him? He looked at himself in the mirror behind the bar and saw a face he barely recognized as his own, pale, unshaven, not quite at ease. What Quarry really felt like was a cigarette, outside, on his own, and a chance to think. But he had to make a choice. The Japanese was least like whisky, almost as good as not having whisky at all.

'This one,' he said. 'It's . . .' he searched for a word '. . . unassuming.'

'Unassuming,' said Dugdale, with a guffaw. 'I like that. Unassuming. Good choice, though. I think you'll like this next one.'

But before he could order it, his phone rang. Dugdale showed some irritation, but within a few seconds his entire face seemed to change, to harden. He asked a few curt questions, but mainly he just listened. When he replaced his phone in his pocket, he was lost in thought, as if he had forgotten that Quarry was there. Then he looked round.

'We'll have to save the bourbon until next time,' he said.

'I'm sorry to hear that.'

Dugdale gazed at him with narrowed eyes. Quarry felt a nervous twinge. Had he sounded sarcastic?

'That car in Hampstead, ran down Heath Street out of control, killed a man, another dead body inside. Did you read about it?'

'No,' said Quarry.

Dugdale seemed disapproving, as if he thought Quarry should know, as if it was a part of his job to know. 'It's our problem now,' he said.

At ten the following morning Quarry was sitting opposite Dugdale's desk, a file and a notebook precariously balanced on his lap. Dugdale took a carton of milk from the tray and poured some into his coffee.

'You're not having one, Dan?' he said.

Quarry shook his head. 'I've had too many already.' He had been in the office reviewing the material on the case since before seven.

Dugdale chuckled. 'You look like you had a few too many last night as well.'

Quarry thought of various answers he could make to that but he kept them all to himself.

'I'm assembling a team,' said Dugdale. 'But before we get them together, we should be clear about where we are.'

'That's why I came in early.'

'So where are we?'

'I read through the interviews with the bystanders,' he said.

'Waste of time,' said Dugdale. 'They all saw something different. Someone said there were two people in the car. Someone else saw him gripping the wheel and smiling.' He took a gulp of coffee. 'Sometimes I wonder why we even bother talking to eyewitnesses.'

'The car was stolen in Didcot,' said Quarry. 'The owner's on holiday. That's why it hasn't been reported.'

Dugdale frowned. 'Are you sure the owner's on holiday? Has anyone checked?'

Quarry looked down at his notes. 'They checked. He's in the Canaries.'

'Lucky bastard,' said Dugdale.

'Not that lucky,' said Quarry. 'His car's been stolen.'

'Forget all that crap,' said Dugdale. 'Let's start with what's important. A car goes out of control down a London street. The only person in it is a man who's already dead. Murdered. Was he even sitting in the driver's seat?'

There was a pause.

'I'll check,' said Quarry.

'The witnesses to the car going through the shop window don't matter now. We know what happened. What matters is what happened at the top of the hill. Those are the witnesses we need.'

'As far as I can see, the police only interviewed people at the actual scene of the accident.'

'We're the police. We can find witnesses. Whoever did this drove the car from a place unknown to the top of Heath Street. He or she must have exited the vehicle and arranged for it to proceed down the hill. It's the sort of thing someone would notice.'

'If they did, then we don't know about it.'

'So it's up to us to get hold of them. And it may have been caught on CCTV cameras.'

'We don't know exactly where it happened.'

'Then go there and find out.' Dugdale rubbed his face. 'You kill a man, put him in a car and send him down a hill into a bunch of innocent people. What's that about?'

There was a long pause.

'Do you want an answer to that?' said Quarry.

'What I want is some pictures. Or a witness. But you can do that later. First we need to see the widow. We need to tell her that her husband was murdered.'

Five

A little more than an hour later the two detectives were in Barking, on Sarah Kernan's doorstep. Dugdale pressed the bell and stood back. The door opened on the unshaven face of a young man. He was wearing pyjamas and his hair was sticking up in tufts. Dugdale looked puzzled.

'You must be Ned Kernan,' said Quarry. 'You're the son, aren't you?'

'Who are you?'

Dugdale held up his ID. 'We need to talk to you and your mother.'

They entered the kitchen to find Sarah Kernan sitting at the table, also in her nightclothes, a striped towelling robe over a blue cotton nightdress, cheerful slippers on her feet. Another woman was standing at the sink, her back to them.

'Mum, it's the police again.'

She put her hand to the neck of her robe. 'I didn't know. I'm not dressed yet.'

'That's all right,' said Dugdale. 'There is something that we need to tell you.' He nodded at Ned. 'You might want to take a seat.'

'My husband's dead,' said Sarah Kernan, her voice high and wavery. 'What else do you need to tell me?'

'Do you want me to leave?' said the other woman.

'No. Stay.' Sarah Kernan put out a hand and clutched her arm. 'This is my sister, Peggy.'

'Yes, I can see that,' said Dugdale.

'You're not the same police.'

'We've taken over the case. That's what I need to tell you: your husband was murdered.'

He looked intently from her face to that of the son, watching their first reactions. Behind him, standing by the door, he was aware of Quarry doing the same. He'd said on the way over that you needed to be alert at the first instant when they hear the news. You'll never catch them that unguarded again. All he saw was bewilderment. Sarah Kernan gave a small cry, like an animal in pain. Her son just looked stunned. The sister put a hand to her mouth and her eyes grew round.

'How can that be true?' Sarah Kernan said at last.

'Who did it?' cut in Ned Kernan. His voice was gruff. Dugdale saw the effort he was making to be manly, while his eyes were the eyes of a child, and full of fear.

'We're just beginning the investigation,' said Dugdale. He wished he could say something more positive, make a promise.

'So he didn't leave me. I knew he wouldn't leave me.'

'All we know so far,' said Dugdale, 'is that you reported him missing three days before his body was found in a car in Hampstead.'

She nodded.

'September the thirtieth,' said Quarry.

'I suppose so,' said Sarah Kernan. 'Peggy, was it then?'

Peggy nodded. 'Yes. That would be right. Do you want tea?' she added.

'No, thank you,' said Dugdale.

'Splash of milk, no sugar,' said Quarry, and he drew up a chair and sat beside Ned. 'This has been a shock to everyone.'

'You reported him missing,' continued Dugdale, 'but were told it was probably not a police matter. Is that right?'

'I should have insisted. I knew it wasn't right.'

'Don't think of it like that,' said Dugdale. 'You couldn't have known.'

'We'd been squabbling a bit,' said Sarah Kernan. 'It was so hard to be just the two of us with Ned gone.'

'Mum,' said the boy, his face wrinkling in distress. 'Don't.'

'Now it's too late to make it better.' She put her hands over her face.

'We need to find out what happened to your husband, and to do that we need to ask you questions,' he said mildly. 'Are you up to that?'

She removed her hands and nodded.

Quarry watched as slowly, patiently, Dugdale extracted information from her. Her husband, as they already knew, was a rep for a sanitary supply company – toilet paper, soap, paper towels – and spent much of his time in his car. She worked in a garden centre, although she didn't know much about plants. Before that, she had been a PA in an architect's firm, but that had gone bankrupt a few years ago. They had been married for twenty-seven years, and Geoffrey Kernan's mother was still alive. He had an older brother, to whom he was not close. Sarah Kernan told them he had been worried about work recently, and been working harder than ever.

'Everyone's having a hard time,' she said. 'I've been in and out of work myself.'

She said he had no enemies (they all say that, thought Dan Quarry, looking at her startled face, at the son's blotchy one), and she couldn't think of a single reason why anyone should have killed him.

'He's just Geoffrey,' she said. 'Or Udo.' She gave a snuffling laugh.

'Udo?'

'His middle name. He said there was a part of him, a secret

35

part, that wasn't boring, English Geoffrey, but more mysterious Germanic Udo. It was like a family joke.'

'I see. But whichever one, you can't think of any reason why he should have been killed?'

'No. He got angry sometimes, irritable. But everyone does, don't they?'

Dugdale asked her about the past few weeks, who her husband had seen, what he had done, anything that stuck in her mind.

She frowned, staring down at her cooling tea. 'We saw Peggy,' she said. 'And he went to the pub last Saturday, but not for long. He wasn't here that much because he was working.'

'Where was he working?'

'I don't know exactly. But it was round here – Essex and London, I mean. Sometimes he goes as far as Derby, Sheffield, and a few weeks ago he had to go to Cardiff. But not the last week. And when he wasn't working, he spent most of his spare time in the garden, digging up plants and things. We're having a patio laid and so everything needs replanting.'

They all looked out at the cratered garden.

'The man who's doing it only comes in when he feels like it. So it's been a bit of a slow process. It made Geoff mad.'

'What else made him mad?'

'I did sometimes,' said Ned. He aimed at a laugh, but it wobbled, came out as a broken guffaw. 'He thought I drank too much. And didn't work hard enough. He didn't know why I had to go to university and build up debts. He thought I should learn something proper, do an apprenticeship.'

Dan Quarry tapped him on the shoulder. 'Fathers and sons,' he said amiably. 'Don't you go beating yourself up.'

Dugdale stood. He was bulky but surprisingly agile. 'So, Mrs Kernan,' he said. 'There are things I'll be wanting from you. A diary of the last few weeks. If you don't have things written down already, do you think you can write them out for me as best you can remember? Everything you remember. Names of everyone he saw, everything he did, places he went to.'

She nodded.

'And then I'm going to want all his correspondence, his bank details, bills, things like that.'

'Why?' demanded Ned.

'Just routine stuff,' said Dugdale. 'I assume he has a computer.'

'A laptop.'

'I'll be needing that.'

Sarah Kernan stared at him, stricken. He saw there were stains on her towelling robe.

'The car outside, is that the car he normally drove?'

'Yes. We've just the one.'

'Then I'll need to take a look at that. If you could give us the keys.'

Without a word, she stood up, went over to a hook near the garden door and brought down a bunch of keys.

'We'll do our best not to be intrusive,' he said. 'But this is a murder case.'

He nodded at Quarry.

An hour later, Dugdale and Quarry left the house, carrying boxes of letters, receipts, bills, invoices. They'd taken his computer, together with the small notebook in which, Sarah Kernan said, her husband had written down his various passwords. They also had his satnav, along with the log he had made of all his journeys, with mileage written down alongside each.

As they got into the car, Quarry looked at his phone. Six

missed calls. All from his wife. Soon to be ex-wife. He'd call later. When he was alone.

'Everything all right?' asked Dugdale.

'Fine,' said Quarry, starting the car.

For a few minutes they didn't speak. The two men were thinking hard, about different things.

'You can look through all this stuff,' said Dugdale.

'What?' said Quarry. His mind had been on the call he'd have to make later to his wife.

'The stuff in the boxes. I want you to go through it.'

'Am I looking for anything in particular?'

'An ordinary man disappears for no reason so look for something out of the ordinary.'

'They were arguing,' said Quarry.

'Everyone argues,' said Dugdale. 'Even married couples. Maybe especially married couples.'

Quarry didn't answer.

'Any other thoughts?' asked Dugdale. 'What do we know?'

'Nothing,' said Quarry.

'Really?' Dugdale raised his eyebrows.

'The killer wanted to be noticed,' Quarry said hesitantly.

'That's possible.' He nodded at him. 'Most murderers try to hide the bodies. They bury them.'

'So I'll go through his bank statements.'

'There's another thing,' said Dugdale. He held up the sat-nav. 'Try the recently found destinations. See where Geoffrey Kernan was in the last days before his death.'

'His wife said he drove all over the place.' Quarry laughed. 'I might end up in Scotland.'

'But she said he was in the London area in the final week.'

'Right. How far back shall I go?'

'Let's see how you get on.'

'What are you going to do?' asked Quarry.

'Before anything else, I'll have a look at what's on his computer.'

Back at the station, Quarry made an excuse and walked out to the car park. He needed a cigarette. He lit it and took several drags. Then he pulled his mobile from his pocket and turned it on. Several texts pinged on to the screen, and more notifications of missed calls. He was about to turn it off again when it rang. Maggie's name appeared, as if she knew he was there.

'Fuck,' he said, but he answered it anyway. 'I'm in the middle of something.'

'This won't take long.' Her voice was clipped. For a second, he remembered how she used to talk to him, as if she were about to laugh, as if there were a secret joke just the two of them shared. She used to call him Danny, the only person apart from his mother who called him that.

'Go on.'

'You know why I'm ringing.'

'I'll get it to you soon.'

'That's not good enough. I need it now. It's part of our agreement.'

'I said I'll get it to you.'

'I can't go on borrowing from my dad.'

'Maggie, I've explained to you –'

'This is your daughter. Never mind what else you did, what you did to me, this is Lucy we're talking about.'

'I'll get it.' He wanted to shout but he made himself speak calmly. 'By the end of the week. I promise.'

'I'll call my solicitor. I don't want to but I will. And, Dan?'

'What now?'

'I don't want to do this, you're her father, but I'll stop you seeing her. If you can't even pay that bit of money towards her upkeep, you don't deserve to see her.'

After the call ended, he felt winded. His legs were trembling. He was leaning on the door of a police car. He had a sudden impulse to punch the window, see if he could smash it with his fist. The pain of it, the blood, would drown out everything else. He shook another cigarette loose from the pack and lit it, sucking the smoke deep into his lungs.

Dugdale pulled on gloves, lifted the lid of the computer and turned it on. The screen glowed. Icons sprang up. He typed in the password that Sarah Kernan had given him, then opened up the emails. Geoffrey Kernan hadn't been much of a correspondent. There were online orders. Nothing interesting: light fittings, paint, ink cartridges. There were a few emails from his son, but they seemed to be about practical things. The 'sent' box was, at first glance anyway, equally uninspiring.

Dugdale clicked on the browser and opened History. He frowned, clicked again, sat back in his chair and scratched his head. There was nothing at all: the history had been erased. He stared at the computer as if it could give him an answer, then closed it, stood up, and delicately picked it up in his gloved hands. What had Geoffrey Kernan wanted to hide?

Six

Lola sat in the library. Her eyelids felt heavy. She had been there for nearly three hours. At first it had been interesting because she had simply gone through newspaper cuttings about Frieda Klein. Many of them had been written by a crime correspondent called Liz Barron, who seemed to be the Frieda Klein expert. Frieda Klein, she wrote, 'is a woman who is drawn to violence, darkness and death'. Lola looked at all the photographs of Frieda Klein over the years and thought Liz Barron might have a point. She never smiled. She had dark hair and dark eyes and she stared out of the newspapers as if she was challenging you.

Lola had made a timeline for all the cases that Frieda Klein had been involved in. It started in 2010 and continued up to the present. It had got a bit complicated, and she'd had to add lots of arrows and circles. There was the case Professor Tearle had mentioned, of the little boy who had been abducted by Dean Reeve. Of course Lola had heard of Reeve, everyone had heard of him, though she was hazy about the details: he was more like a bogeyman, a name that sent shivers up your spine. There was a dead man who'd been found naked on the couch of someone called Michelle Doyce, who was obviously mad and had tried to feed him while he sat there rotting. There was a woman who'd been found dead in her own home, and a case of missing girls that made Lola feel shivery and sad. There was another girl, the following year, who'd been raped and murdered. There was Hannah Docherty, locked away in a hospital for the criminally insane.

There was Daniel Blackstock, and the whole media furore when it had at last become public knowledge that what Frieda Klein had always insisted on was true, and that Dean Reeve was alive. Lola stooped over the papers, chewing the end of her pen. Reeve had killed his twin brother, he had disappeared from view, but all these years he had been following Frieda Klein, stalking her, like her obsessive enemy and creepy lover. It made Lola feel a bit spooked just thinking about it.

She tried to make it simpler by colour-coding events. She highlighted deaths in orange, arrests in blue, everything connected to Reeve in green. It was a hopeless mess now, a smudge of colours and criss-crossing lines and exclamation and question marks everywhere. But this wasn't what Professor Tearle was after. Deconstruct her, he'd said. Unpack her. She half remembered him asking if a crime investigation was actually a form of therapy. What had he meant by that?

That was when it became hard going. She didn't know why people had to write as if they were tying things up in barbed wire. She had tried to read a paper that Frieda Klein had written on the concept of personality, but had got hopelessly stuck at the first page, with its discussion of pronouns, though she liked the quotation from George Eliot: 'It's never too late to become the person you might have been.' She wrote it down and circled it several time. It appeared Hal Bradshaw had written on Frieda Klein several times. If Liz Barron was the reporter of her external life, Professor Bradshaw had made himself the expert on her inner one. Lola copied some of his terms into her notes: narcissism, self-dramatization, auto-delusion. Bradshaw argued that she craved celebrity and was hollow at her centre. Lola took the Mars bar from her bag. While chewing slowly, she stared at the words in front of her, by a postgraduate student who had written a paper on 'Dr Frieda Klein and Shattered Autonomy'. She took another bite and now somehow there was chocolate on the paper. Shattered autonomy. That didn't sound good.

She looked around at the other people, working away, bent over their tablets or notebooks. It was too hot in here. She pushed her trainers off her feet and wriggled her toes. She let her eyes close, just for a moment. The image of Professor Bradshaw floated through her mind, with those under-framed spectacles, and her head lolled.

'Lola!' A loud whisper. She jerked awake, saw her friend Denzil grinning at her.

'I was just thinking about something,' she said.

'You were snoring.'

'Loudly?'

'Come and have a drink.'

Lola rose with alacrity, pulling on her trainers, picking up her jacket. 'You bet.'

'It's all rubbish,' she said, over her second glass of wine. 'She's seen such awful things. She was raped. Her ex was killed. She's being stalked by a psychopath. Can you imagine? And all these academic papers do is talk about, I don't know – *confabulation*. I'd like to know what it feels like to be her, caught up in all this violence.'

'So what are you going to do?'

'I'll have to cobble something together. Ten thousand words isn't that long.' She wrinkled her nose. 'None of the pieces I've read seem to get me anywhere.'

'Is she alive?'

'Yes.'

'In London?'

'I think so.'

'Well, then.'

'What do you mean?'

'Go and see her.'

'Is that allowed?'

'Why not? You can get her to do your work for you.'

Lola thought for a moment. Seeing Frieda Klein. Talking to her. Suddenly it sounded easier than reading about her.

Dear Frieda Klein, I hope you don't mind me contacting you like this, out of the blue. My name is Lola Hayes and I'm a student of criminology . . .

But the email Lola sent to the address she found in the British Association for Counselling and Psychotherapy register bounced straight back: 'Your message cannot be delivered to the following recipient'. There was no phone number to call and, of course, she was ex-directory.

Lola looked at the photos of Frieda Klein with her unsmiling mouth and her clear gaze; she looked at her notepad with its barely decipherable scrawls. She knew from the cuttings that she had a house in Saffron Mews, just off Tottenham Court Road. According to Google, that was about eight minutes' walk from where she was sitting.

Lola buttoned up her jacket. Her mother always said there was no time like the present.

Lola liked the look of the little house in Saffron Mews. It was narrow, squeezed between lock-ups to the left and council flats to the right, and had a blue door. Standing back on the cobbles and tilting her head, she could see there was a skylight in its roof. It looked cosy, she thought, and felt a stab of homesickness. She had grown up in Herefordshire, the only child of parents who had both been in their forties when she was born, and as soon as she had left for university, they had sold their house and moved to Spain, near Málaga. The last time she'd been there she'd got such bad sunburn that there were even blisters behind her knees. After what had happened this summer, with the referendum, perhaps they'd be coming back again, but for now, she had the feeling of being without a real home.

There were no lights on and the shutters on the ground-floor window were folded shut on their hinges. That could mean someone was at home, or that they weren't. She went to the door and knocked on it firmly, waited, knocked again. Once it was clear no one would answer, she stooped and tried to peer in through the letterbox. She saw a wooden floor, letters stacked neatly on a ledge, a coat hanging from a hook and, straight ahead, the stairs going steeply up.

She pressed her face to the narrow strip of window between the shutters and squinted into a small, book-lined room. Just beneath the window there was a chess table, with the pieces arranged irregularly over it. Lola had never learned to play chess, but she recognized that someone was halfway through a game. At the other end, two chairs sat in front of a small fireplace. The fire was laid, waiting for a match to be put to it. There was a pot plant with orange flowers on the little table, a book with a plain green cover beside it. The room was immaculately clean and tidy.

Lola straightened up and turned away. No one was in. She would have to find Frieda Klein another way.

Dan Quarry stayed late, working his way through the papers. He hated this side of police work, but for the moment it felt like a welcome escape. If he wasn't doing this he would be at home with the TV, a frozen meal, a few cans of beer. He'd put the bank statements in order, which Geoffrey Kernan hadn't bothered to do, and now was going through each one. So far, he hadn't found anything. He looked at the clock on the wall and gave himself half an hour more. Then he'd get a sandwich from the canteen and continue. This was going to take a long time.

Bill Dugdale took the free London paper that was being held towards him as he entered the Underground station and opened it once he was on the train. The mayhem in Hampstead was on the front page, mostly in pictures. Geoffrey Kernan's murder was on page three, next to a photograph of him that must have been taken years ago. There was a photo of Dugdale as well, taken at the press conference just a few hours ago. His shirt was only half tucked in; he looked large and dishevelled.

He turned the paper over so he could only see the sports headlines on the back. Two days in, and he had almost nothing.

Seven

It was a complicated Underground journey to Swiss Cottage. After leaving the station, Lola kept needing to check her phone. But it was better than sitting in a library. Finally she found herself in front of an industrial-looking building that felt out of place in this upmarket residential area. She looked at the brass plate next to the door: The Warehouse. She looked up at the building. Well, it did look like an old warehouse, although a warehouse that had been spruced up with bright colours around the windows and a colourful abstract tiled frieze running the length of the façade just under the roof. She pushed the plate-glass door open and stepped into a small foyer, all wood and bright cushions and a comfy sofa, and a woman of about her own age sitting behind a desk staring down at her phone. She looked up.

'I'd like to see Frieda Klein,' said Lola.

'Do you have an appointment?'

'Not exactly,' said Lola. 'I mean, no.'

'Take a seat, please.'

Lola sank into the soft, off-white sofa and realized she hadn't thought of what she would say to Frieda Klein when she met her. Perhaps they could just have a chat and she could get a few tips for her dissertation. A woman came down the stairs, her shoes clattering on the hard floor. She talked to the person at the desk, then looked round at Lola. She had dark hair and dark eyes; her fingers glittered with rings; she was dressed in a white blouse and an almost startling long skirt, striped amber and blue and red. She walked over and sat down beside Lola.

'You look different from your picture,' said Lola.

'What picture?'

'In the newspaper reports. But it's good of you to see me.'

The woman gave a puzzled frown, and then her face relaxed into a smile. 'You think I'm Frieda Klein?'

She was speaking in a foreign accent. Was it Spanish? Was Frieda Klein Spanish? None of the newspaper articles had said so.

'Aren't you?' she asked doubtfully.

'I'm a colleague of hers.' There was a pause. She seemed to be waiting for Lola to speak, but Lola couldn't think of anything at all to say, so she continued, talking in a soothing tone, 'If you want to be seen by Dr Klein, it's usual to get a doctor's referral.'

There was another pause.

'I'm not exactly a patient,' said Lola.

'Then who are you?'

'I'm a student.'

'For training and internships you make an application. You don't just turn up.'

'I'm not that sort of student. I just want to talk to Frieda Klein.'

'Many people want to talk to Dr Klein.'

'I'm doing a dissertation. I wanted to ask her some questions.'

'What is the dissertation about?'

'It's about Frieda Klein.'

'What kind of student are you?' Suddenly her tone wasn't so friendly.

'I'm a criminologist. I was told she'd be an interesting subject.'

The woman stood up. 'No,' she said.

'No what?'

'Dr Klein isn't here.'

'Do you know when she'll be back?'

'She's away.'

'What? On holiday?'

'That is not a concern of yours.'

'Do you have a number for her? An email?'

'She is a private person.'

'Look, I've read about her in the newspapers. The one thing she is not is a private person.'

'You need to leave,' said the woman, her tone angry.

A young man joined them. He was tall and rangy, and wore loose silky trousers, a cardigan Lola wouldn't have minded owning herself, and heavy boots. His light-brown hair was tied back in a ponytail. Lola saw he had several piercings.

'Can I help?'

'No. This young woman's just on her way out.' She glared at Lola before turning away.

'She's not very friendly,' said Lola.

'She sees it as her job to protect everyone.'

'Are you a patient?' asked Lola.

'I work here.'

'Are you a psychoanalyst? You don't look like one.'

'And what do psychoanalysts look like?'

'Oh, I don't know. Older than you. And more severe, with a beard and glasses, and . . .' She looked at him dubiously. 'Not dressed like you.'

He laughed. 'You mean, we should all look like Freud?'

'What's your name?'

'Jonah Martin. What's yours?'

'Lola Hayes. Do you know Frieda Klein?'

'I'm afraid not. I only started work here last week. Of course I know of her. She's part of the fabric of this place.'

'Do you know how I can find her?'

He shook his head. 'No. And if I did, I probably wouldn't tell you.'

A minute later Lola was outside on the pavement, with no apparent way of reaching Frieda Klein. Ten minutes later, as she was making her way back to the Tube station, her phone rang. It was Hal Bradshaw.

'Oh!' she said, startled. 'Have I done something wrong?'

'Not at all.' He gave an easy, practised laugh. 'I was just following up on our conversation about Frieda Klein.'

'Really? Well. That's very kind of you.'

'How are you doing?'

'Not well. I've just been to her clinic in Swiss Cottage. She seems to have gone away and it doesn't seem possible to contact her.'

'Really? That's interesting. In that case, I've got another suggestion. She was trained by Dr Reuben McGill. He used to be famous, or notorious. He's always been one of Frieda Klein's friends and he lives in Primrose Hill. You could walk there.'

'What? Now?'

'Yes, now. He knows her secrets. As much as anyone does. Go and see him, then ring me and let me know what happened.'

He gave her the address. Lola felt uneasy about this scheme and she was still feeling uneasy twenty minutes later when she rapped on Reuben McGill's door. There was a shuffling sound from inside and then it opened to reveal a rumpled figure. He was in his sixties, with untidy, curly grey hair, bags under his eyes, unshaven. He wore a checked shirt and his feet were bare. Lola said she wanted to meet Reuben McGill.

'That's me.'

As Lola explained why she was there, his expression grew more and more suspicious. When she was finished, he gave a grunt. 'How did you get this address?' he said.

For reasons she didn't quite understand, Lola was suddenly tempted to make something up. But she couldn't think of anything, so she stuck with the truth. 'Professor Hal Bradshaw gave it to me.'

She thought he might react blankly or with irritation. What she hadn't expected was a wheezing laugh.

'Hal Bradshaw,' he said, as if the name itself was funny. Then the laugh turned into a cough. He waved her inside. With some trepidation she followed him into his front room. It was a bit of a mess in there, with books and bottles and coats everywhere. A tortoiseshell cat lay asleep in the armchair.

'Josef,' Reuben shouted, while still looking at her. 'You need to come and see this.'

Lola heard the thumping sound of feet on the stairs and a man came into the room, dark-haired with brown, soulful eyes. He wore a T-shirt, paint-spattered jeans and rough boots, which looked wrong indoors.

'She's a student,' said McGill. 'And she wants to write about Frieda.'

'Strange,' said Josef.

'And she was sent here by Hal Bradshaw.'

Now Josef smiled as well. Lola was confused. What was so funny about Bradshaw?

'Can we get you a drink?' said McGill.

'You mean like tea?'

'I was thinking something a little stronger.'

'It's a bit early in the day.'

'I thought that's what you students did.'

'Not all the time.'

'So you're a friend of Hal Bradshaw's?'

'I'm not a friend. I've only met him once. My supervisor told me that he knew Frieda Klein. I went to see him and he pointed me towards you.'

McGill smiled again.

'Is something funny about this?' Lola asked.

'Have you seen *Road Runner*?' McGill asked.

'I don't think so,' said Lola.

McGill looked over at Josef. 'Have you?'

'*Road Runner*?' said Josef, thoughtfully. 'Is a car?'

'This is hopeless,' said McGill. 'It's a cartoon. You should see it, both of you.' He looked disconsolate. 'Well, the road-runner is a kind of bird and there's a coyote that keeps trying to catch the roadrunner with more and more cunning plans and keeps failing. This would make more sense if you'd seen it, but if you had, and you knew Bradshaw the way we do, you'd realize that Bradshaw is like Wile E. Coyote. And Frieda is like the roadrunner.' There was a pause. 'You should watch it. It's funny. It's probably on YouTube.'

Another pause.

'I'm not out to get Dr Klein,' said Lola. 'I just want to write about her, about what she's done.'

McGill and Josef looked at each other.

'The point is moot,' said McGill. 'She's away.'

'I know she's away,' said Lola. 'I went to her house. I've just been round to the Warehouse where this woman treated me like I was a criminal.'

'Yes,' said McGill, cheerfully. 'Paz is a dragon.'

'What's the big problem? Why can't I just phone her? If she's away, I can email her or whatever she uses. I just want to ask her a couple of questions.'

'Not so easy,' said Josef, shaking his head.

'Can you at least tell me why you won't tell me anything?'

'That would be telling you something,' said McGill. 'Look, Layla –'

'Lola.'

'We've done you the courtesy of speaking to you. I think it would be easier if you found another subject for your dissertation.'

'But now you've got me all interested,' said Lola.

As she left the house she met a young woman coming in. She had spiky black hair and kohl-rimmed eyes and was wearing clumpy boots and a black leather jacket. Lola thought she looked rather scary, but the young woman smiled at her and her face behind its make-up seemed suddenly vulnerable and sweet.

'Hi,' she said.

'Hello, Chloë,' called Josef, from inside the house.

So that was Frieda's niece. Lola had read about her in the newspaper cuttings. She might be a good person to talk to. She turned, but as she did so, the front door closed.

Lola met Liz Barron in her newspaper office in Canary Wharf. She was on the eighteenth floor. From her desk, Lola could look across the Thames at the Millennium Dome. It was like a white spiky tortoise in the bright afternoon sun. She had to force herself to turn away and concentrate on the gleaming, smiling figure opposite her. She had shining hair and glossy lips and a look of implacable friendliness that Lola found unsettling.

'I went through the newspaper reports on Frieda Klein,' Lola said. 'You seem to have written about her more than anyone else.'

'For my sins,' said Barron. 'Most doctors love the attention. You can't keep them off the TV or out of the papers.
But there was a mystery about Frieda. I interviewed her, I
probed her, but she was always uncomfortable in the
limelight.'

'Then why was she there?'

Barron shook her head. Her hair swung from side to side.
'Maybe you'd need to be a psychologist to answer that question, but I did my best. I always thought there was a darkness
about her, something that drew her to what she most feared.
I've written about that. I did a long feature about women
being drawn to darkness and violence.'

'Yes. I saw it.'

'It got a terrific response.'

Lola nodded in a noncommittal fashion. She wasn't drawn
to darkness and violence herself.

'I wonder what will become of her,' said Liz Barron.

'In what way?' Lola asked.

'She got involved with the Hannah Docherty murders.
That ended badly. Then there was the Daniel Blackstock
case. I knew him. It happened under my nose. What I'm trying to say is that I think Frieda is in a bad way.' She looked at
Lola thoughtfully. 'And you're writing about her for your dissertation. Interesting. What did you make of her?'

'I haven't been able to find her.'

'What do you mean? Don't you have her address?'

'There's nobody at her house. The mail's piled up. I went
to her work. They said she's gone away, can't be reached, they
don't know when she's coming back.'

'Really?' Liz Barron's eyes gleamed. She picked up a pen
and wrote a note on a pad in front of her. Then she looked
up. 'So what else do you want to know?'

*

When they had finished, Liz Barron walked Lola back to the lift. She pressed the button, then pressed it again. She gave Lola a winning smile.

'If you find out anything interesting, you must let me know,' she said.

'I don't think that will happen,' said Lola.

Still the lift didn't come. Barron pressed the button again. 'I always have the illusion that if you push the button over and over again it might hurry the lift along.'

Finally it did arrive. Lola stepped inside. As the doors started to close, Barron put out her hand to block them.

'What?' said Lola.

'It's just that when people get involved with Frieda Klein . . .'

'Yes?'

'I don't know. Just watch out, that's all. And keep in touch.' She withdrew her hand as the doors closed.

Eight

Larry Phelps was about six foot five inches tall and very spindly. He reminded Dugdale of a tree that had grown too quickly towards the light. Even when he was sitting down, he was tall, with thin wrists and sharp bones and a high forehead. He pushed his glasses back over the bridge of his bony nose and leaned forward.

'We have a problem,' said Dugdale. 'We have a computer. It belonged to a murder victim. We're interested in his browsing history. But he seems to have deleted it. Is there a way of recovering it?' He pointed at the laptop on the desk.

Phelps flipped it open.

'Is that something you could do? You could take it away if you wanted. I know it might take some time but the sooner we get it the better. If it's possible.'

Phelps looked up from the computer. 'Could you get me a coffee?' he said. 'Milk and two sugars.'

'Of course.'

'I mean, like, now.'

Dugdale flexed his jaw and went very slightly red. Any of his subordinates would have been alarmed by this but Phelps just went on looking at the screen and tapping on the keyboard. In the police, there were people who asked for coffee and people who fetched coffee, and Dugdale was in the first group. But he swallowed and stopped himself saying what he wanted to say. He left the room and walked across the office to the coffee machine and pressed the button for a white coffee and a black coffee for himself. He found two packets of sugar and made his way back to his office. Phelps was sitting with his arms folded, looking up at the ceiling.

'Is it going to be a problem?' said Dugdale.

'I've got his full search history.'

'I thought he'd deleted it.'

Phelps took the coffee and moved his chair away from the desk. 'Hiding your search history by deleting it is like . . .' He took a sip of coffee. 'It's like when me and my three-year-old daughter play hide and seek and she puts her hands over her face and thinks I can't find her. There's a list of URLs on the screen.'

Dugdale stepped forward.

'Hey! Stop!'

'What?' asked Dugdale, startled.

'You want to hide the information on that computer so that it can never be found? Just spill that coffee over it.'

'All right, all right,' said Dugdale. He carefully placed his coffee on the other side of the desk. 'Did you see anything interesting?'

'I thought you were looking for porn. Child porn, animal porn, some kind of porn.'

'Isn't there any?'

Phelps shrugged. 'Odd bit here and there. Nothing out of the ordinary. But have a look at his recent searches.' Larry Phelps unfolded himself from the chair. 'I'll leave you to it.'

When Phelps had gone, Dugdale sat down in the chair and looked at the screen. There was a window open with a list of web addresses. Weather, sport, online stores. But Phelps had mentioned searches. What had he meant? Dugdale clicked on the most recent ones and then he knew, and he read the name aloud: 'Detective Inspector Malcolm Karlsson.'

He sat very still. What was that about? Why was this sales-man searching for information about a police detective?

Dugdale knew Karlsson a bit. They'd run into each other at functions from time to time. They'd been on a training course together. There was something a bit out of the ordinary about him. He wasn't a team player, he wasn't a back-slapper, not one of the guys. Clever, though. He'd been involved in some high-profile cases over the years: the one where Dean Reeve abducted that little boy, for instance, or the strange affair when a dead man had been found rotting on the sofa of a madwoman. And, of course, he'd teamed up with Frieda Klein; people used to say he was smitten with her, though they would never have dared say it to his face. Dugdale ran a finger round the inside of his collar. Why was Kernan interested in him, though? He sat for a moment, scowling in concentration, then went to the door. Quarry was on the phone having a muttered conversation. Clearly something private. Dugdale stood there until Quarry noticed him and became self-conscious. He put the phone down.

'Everything all right, Dan?'

'Fine,' said Quarry, abruptly.

Dugdale explained about the search history.

'Get in touch with Karlsson, find out if he's got any history with Kernan. I'll phone Mrs Kernan about him. Remember her first name?'

'Sarah,' said Quarry.

'Good,' said Dugdale. 'I'm bloody awful with names.'

When Sarah Kernan answered the phone, Dugdale dutifully asked about her state of mind, whether she was sleeping, about some counselling she'd been receiving, but then turned to the job in hand.

'We've been checking your husband's computer and one of his searches was for a senior detective called Malcolm

Karlsson. We were wondering if you could throw any light on that.'

'I've never heard that name.'

'Did your husband have any dealings with the police in the last month or so?'

'I hadn't heard anything. Do you think he was in some kind of trouble?'

'There's no record of that. Could he have witnessed something?'

'I don't know. He didn't always tell me things.'

'But if your husband did the online search, he had to have known Karlsson's name. And he had to have had a reason.'

'All I can say is that I never heard the name. Maybe he was a client.'

Dugdale didn't think a senior detective was likely to be involved in the purchase of toilet supplies. 'Could he have had something he wanted to tell Karlsson?'

'I don't know, I don't know anything. Wouldn't he just have called the local police station? Or dialled nine nine nine?'

Something else occurred to Dugdale. 'Did your husband take the laptop with him on jobs?'

'I'm sorry, I don't know much about my husband . . . my late husband's . . .' She gave a stifled sob.

'I'm sorry. This must be very difficult for you. If you want to do this another time . . .'

There was a cough and snuffling. Dugdale suddenly wished he'd asked some female officer to make this call. Women were better at this sort of thing. Empathetic. Tolerant. Patient.

'No, I want to help.'

'Did he share his computer with anybody?'

'I've got my own computer. And Ned's been away at university until this happened.'

Dugdale heard the sound of nose-blowing. 'But the computer was lying around, people could have used it,' he continued.

'He kept it up in his den. Nobody goes there.'

'With the door locked?'

'No. But nobody comes here. Just a friend of mine for tea sometimes. And my sister.'

Dugdale knew when he had hit a wall, when there was nowhere else to go. He asked her to ring him if she remembered anything. She probably wouldn't. He put down the phone and frowned, drummed his fingers on the desk. He knew there was something, but he hadn't got it.

While Dugdale was finishing his call to Sarah Kernan, Quarry was walking along Lincoln's Inn Fields. He'd been told that Karlsson was having a meeting in a pub called the Admiral Hood. It was early evening and the bar was crowded with escaped office workers. A large bald man in a grey suit was sitting alone at a table with a pint of beer reading the evening paper.

'Are you Malcolm Karlsson?' Quarry asked.

The man looked up with an irritated expression.

'Over here,' said a voice from behind him.

Quarry turned round. A man was gesturing towards him. He had short dark hair, an alert, slightly ironic expression. Despite the suit and the tie, he didn't quite look like a detective. More like a teacher, perhaps. He was sitting with two women. One was younger, with a stern jaw, her brown hair tied austerely back, her eyes regarding him suspiciously, almost with hostility. She was wearing dark, loose-fitting trousers and a brown jersey. The other was more expensively dressed, her hair falling round her face, bangles on her wrists and earrings in her lobes, her lips glossy; even from where

Quarry stood he could smell her perfume. They made an awkward-looking group, obviously not friends but not business either. Even within a few seconds, Quarry could sense a tension between them.

'This is my colleague, Yvette Long,' said Karlsson. 'And this is Liz Barron. A journalist. Is this about work?'

'Yes.'

Karlsson looked at Liz Barron. 'Could you give us a moment?'

Barron pulled a face, almost a pout, got up and moved across the room and stepped out of the saloon door.

'There aren't many crime correspondents left,' said Karlsson, 'but Liz Barron is a crime correspondent. She has a nose for the job. And,' he added, 'she always seems to know where to find us.'

'You make that sound like a bad thing.'

'Well, what is it they say about news? It's something that someone doesn't want you to print. So what do you need me for?'

'Did you hear about the car crash in Hampstead?'

Karlsson looked puzzled, but then Quarry described it in more detail and Karlsson nodded. 'I read something about it.'

'It's now a murder case.'

'And?'

'Do you mind if I get a drink?' asked Quarry.

'I'll get it for you,' said Long, abruptly, and on Quarry's instructions went to the bar for a gin and tonic and a packet of salt and vinegar crisps. When she returned, he drank half of the gin straight away.

'The victim was a salesman called Geoffrey Kernan. Did you know him?'

Both Karlsson and Long looked surprised.

'What do you mean?' said Karlsson.

'There are some strange things about the case. He was in a car, alone, when it ran into some people. But he was already dead. The car was stolen. And there's another thing. A few days before, he was searching for you on his computer.'

'There could be another Malcolm Karlsson.'

Quarry took a piece of paper from his pocket, unfolded it and laid it on the table. Karlsson put on reading glasses, picked it up and looked at it.

'That's a list of what he found. It's basically what you've been up to in the last year or two.'

'What was the name again?' said Karlsson.

'Kernan. Geoffrey Kernan.'

Karlsson looked at Yvette Long. 'Mean anything to you?'

She shook her head. 'I'll check in the office,' she said. 'Ask around. But I don't remember the name.'

Quarry took a photo from his pocket and handed it to Karlsson. He and Long scrutinized it.

'I don't know what to say,' said Karlsson. 'I'd like to help in some way but I can't think of anything.'

Quarry gave Karlsson his card. 'If you do,' he said, and stood up.

'If you pass Liz Barron,' Karlsson said, 'you can send her back in so we can politely tell her we've nothing to tell her.'

Quarry made his way out of the bar. Out on the pavement he saw Liz Barron smoking a cigarette. He nodded at her. 'They're ready for you inside,' he said.

She seemed in no hurry to finish her cigarette. 'What did they say about me?' she said. 'Nothing good, I trust.'

'We had other things to discuss.'

'Anything interesting?'

'Just an ongoing inquiry.'

'His inquiry or yours?'

Quarry frowned. 'I can refer you to the press office, if you want.'

Barron opened her purse and took out a card. Quarry couldn't suppress a smile.

'Is something funny?' Barron said.

'We're all exchanging cards,' said Quarry. 'I just gave mine to Karlsson.'

'So we're all getting to know each other.'

He looked down at the card. 'What's this for?'

'I'm always interested in . . .' She paused. 'Well, in interesting things. I'm very discreet. And my arrangements are strictly professional.'

'Professional?'

'I'm always willing to pay for people's time.' She waited again, but Quarry didn't reply. 'To cover expenses.'

'I guessed that was what you meant.'

'We should meet for a drink some time. We can probably help each other.'

Before he could reply, she had tossed her cigarette on to the pavement and walked back inside. He heard a message ping on his mobile: that would be Maggie again, he thought.

Nine

Quarry got into his car and plugged in Geoffrey Kernan's satnav. There was a delay as the device booted up and then there was an assertive female voice: 'As soon as possible, make a U-turn.' He smiled grimly. Another disapproving woman telling him what to do. Following the instructions, she took him north and out of London to a large bathroom shop on the outskirts of Maldon, a primary school in Ingatestone, a Travelodge near Stansted airport, two pubs, the garden centre where Kernan's wife worked, a new estate under construction, a furniture store and an optician's. Almost everyone recognized Geoffrey Kernan, and knew that he had been murdered; they said he had been there in the week leading up to his disappearance. Sometimes Quarry had to knock on several doors, holding up his ID and Kernan's photograph, before he found the right place: a woman who was having a new bathroom installed, or a couple who had sold him an almost-new microwave on eBay.

A number of the addresses were much further away, up near Coventry or Bristol or Norwich. Kernan had been covering a lot of miles. Quarry made a note to check these with the man's employer. There was a house in West Ham, near the football ground, where nobody answered the door. He made a note to come back later. There was the park over at Beckton: probably Kernan had gone for a walk. Did he have a dog? Quarry was sure he didn't. The most recent destination was the closest to Kernan's house. He drove over the bypass on to a road leading into an industrial area. The screen of the satnav showed that he was near the river but he would never have known it. He drove past builders' yards, a bus depot, a timber yard, a recovery centre piled high with cars that were far beyond recovery. There was a café operating out of a caravan, a heavy-equipment depot and a vast waste-management centre. The voice announced that they were reaching their destination. He pulled the car off the road onto the rough verge. Improbably there was a terrace of three houses. One was boarded up. It looked like a forgotten remnant, perhaps a survivor of the Blitz that had set this whole area on fire.

When Quarry got out of the car he became aware of the noise of the lorries and the diggers. And then there was the smell, which he could almost feel, the sour reek of the garbage. It wasn't just one bad smell but layers of them, industrial and organic, sour and sweet, bitter and acrid.

He walked over to the strange fragment of a housing terrace. The first house was clearly empty. He walked up the steps to the middle one. There was no bell or knocker, so he rapped on the door with his fist. It was opened by a man who looked barely awake. He wore dusty, stained jeans, a grubby T-shirt, and all of his exposed skin below his head was covered with tattoos. He had piercings in his ears, nose and lips. Quarry held up his identification. 'Do you know a man called Geoffrey Kernan?'

'No.'

'You said that very quickly. Have a think. Geoffrey Kernan. Geoff, maybe.'

'Never heard of him.'

He took a picture from his pocket and showed it to the man. 'That's Kernan.'

The man shook his head.

'Do any other people live here?'

'A few. People stay here when they're working.'

'Can I talk to them?'

'They're out.'

'Do you know when they'll be back?'

'I don't know. An hour maybe.'

Quarry went to the little caravan and bought a tea. The woman behind the counter was dark-haired, pale. Her accent was eastern European, probably Czech, Quarry thought. They chatted casually, but when Quarry asked about the people in the house opposite, who they were, what they did, she went quiet. He was used to that. People were worried now about whether you were from the council or immigration or the police. He thought of telling her that he didn't care whether they were here legally or not, but he didn't bother. She wouldn't believe him.

After he had finished the tea, he walked around aimlessly. He found a path leading towards the river and looked across at Thamesmead and at the huge flood barrier across the creek on his right. He had lived in London all his life and all of it was new to him. Finally he walked back to the house. Two men had arrived from work, dusty and sweaty in their yellow high-visibility jackets. Suspiciously and reluctantly, they looked at Kernan's photograph and said they didn't recognize him. He didn't know whether they really hadn't seen him, whether they had seen him and were lying, or whether they just had a policy of pleading ignorance to everything as a way of staying out of trouble.

Back in the car, he went through his notes and felt dissatisfied with his day. Sometimes finding nothing was as useful as finding something. Not this time.

Ten

Twelve years ago, Neil Morrell had been a solicitor, in a small practice, with a pension, a fiancée who worked in the City, a house in Camden and a drug habit. Now he was no longer a solicitor; he had no pension, no fiancée, no house – and no drug habit. He didn't even drink caffeine. Instead he worked as a park warden on Hampstead Heath for four days a week; the other three days he spent as a yoga instructor. His hair was long, tied back in a silver ponytail; he had a thick beard and on his upper left arm was a tattoo of a tree. He said that trees had saved his life. He sometimes spoke to them, stopping by the old oak tree that had been split by lightning many years ago but had survived, or the willows down by the ponds, patting their trunks, squinting up to make sure that none of the branches were dead, or leaves showing signs of blight.

He knew the Heath like the back of his hand. When it was being dug up by those terrible machines to stop the flooding, he almost felt physical pain. He loved it in all seasons, but autumn was his favourite: the soft, rich colours, the smell of decay, the leaves making a rustling sound as he walked slowly through them.

On this particular morning a thin drizzle hung over the landscape, like a mist. There weren't many people around, just a few runners and the odd dog-walker. Neil Morrell made his way up the hill towards Whitestone Pond, doing his rounds. He hadn't been there for a few days. Before he reached the top, he stopped and gave a sniff. There was a smell of smoke: probably a bonfire in someone's garden, and sure enough, when he came out of the trees he could see a thick plume of smoke curling up into the sky.

As he made his way up the slope, the hollow came into view, a place that used to be a pond and was still damp underfoot even during the driest summer. This year, the council had designated it as the site for the 5 November bonfire, though Neil thought it daft to have a bonfire on such a spot: people would trample it into a muddy bog and it would take months to heal. They had been collecting the wood for weeks, building a wigwam of branches that was already a good size. But now, a month before its time, someone had obviously set fire to it.

'Scamps,' Neil said, his brows creased in disapproval. It was probably a group of teenagers playing a prank and ruining the fun for everyone else.

Flames were licking up one side and billowing out. In spite of the drizzle, the fire was taking and he could hear a crackling sound. He sighed and pulled out his phone to call the office, then went down into the hollow to see if there was anything he could do.

He saw as he approached that they had even made a Guy. A figure in thick pale-blue clothes, like a uniform, was propped up against the branches, flames curling round it so that its outline wavered although it wasn't yet alight. A whooshing sound made him start as a rocket suddenly exploded out of the fire, scattering petals of brightness as it went. Then another. He went nearer, his feet sinking into the soft ground. The Guy slipped as a branch it was leaning against caught and crumbled into flame and ash.

Nearer still. And then he was running, slipping on the wet grass, breath catching in his throat. The effigy had a face, melting in the heat, whose eyes were wide open and staring at him.

*

68

Ten minutes later the hollow was filled with police officers and paramedics. The fire had been put out, the body pulled from it. Constable Darren Symons was there again. He still had a cold, and had developed a nasty chesty cough. His eyes watered as he gazed around the scene. A smoking bonfire, a body lying on the grass where the park warden had dragged it, its arms and legs trussed. Constable Symons could see tufts of singed hair on a pale skull. It was dressed in a kind of canvas that had blackened but not caught fire. He couldn't tell if the figure was a man or a woman. He remembered in school history lessons learning about people who had been burned to death as heretics: he had always thought it would be the worst way to die. Even worse than drowning.

On the road above him, behind the police officers who had been stationed there, several figures were peering down at the scene. He was supposed to be putting tapes up, while the drizzle hardened into rain and the ground turned to sludgy mud. He looked across to the man, a couple of feet from him, who had found the body. He was talking to one of Symons's colleagues but he wasn't looking at her; instead he kept his eyes fixed on the wooded horizon. Every so often he would blink rapidly, his eyes a curious mottled grey. He had burned his hands getting the body out of the fire and they were wrapped in bandages, so that he looked like an old boxer.

'Here comes Eeyore,' said a voice behind him.

Symons turned to see DCI Dugdale and DC Quarry making their way down the slope. Dugdale wasn't hurrying, but his head twisted this way and that, taking everything in. As he came on to the level, a last firework that must have been smouldering in the ruins of the fire exploded in a shower of colour.

Dugdale looked around. 'People have been walking all over my crime scene.'

'They thought it was just a fire, sir.'

'I don't care what they thought. I care what you do. Find some tape, seal off the area.'

He walked across to the body and bent over it, his expression impassive. The corpse's eyes were open. They seemed to be staring at something beyond them.

'Any chance it could be an accident?' said Quarry. Dugdale looked round at him sharply but he continued. 'On drugs, make a fire, fall into it, die. I've read about it.'

'The victim's legs and arms are tied. We're five minutes' walk from the Kernan scene. But if you want to show it's an accident, please go ahead. Anything to get it off our plate.'

Simon Tearle was listening to a Bach cantata on headphones when his door opened and a head poked round.

'Yes?' he said.

'I knocked,' said the young woman. 'You probably didn't hear.'

He pulled off the headphones.

'It's Polly, isn't it?'

'Lola,' she said. 'Lola Hayes. I came to see you a few days ago.' She waited for him to remember, then added, 'About my dissertation. You suggested Frieda Klein.'

'That's right.'

'The thing is, it's not going very well.'

He sighed. 'Come in. Tell me the problem.'

She took a seat. He looked at her, in her buttercup-yellow skirt and her red duffel coat, her eyes large and trusting, and thought how young she seemed for her age.

'You said I should deconstruct her,' Lola said. 'Dismantle her.'

'Did I?'

'So I tried to see her, and some of the people who know her.'

70

'That's probably not necessary. You're not on a journalism course.'

'Nobody could tell me anything, really. So here I am.'

'With a dissertation due in two weeks' time.'

'I know. What shall I do?'

'Make a plan.'

'That's all very well,' she said.

He could hear the cantata still coming from the headphones on the desk and tried to hide his impatience. 'What have you found out so far?'

'That she's been involved in lots of scary things, that her lover was killed and she was injured, that she loves walking – she's got a thing about following secret rivers. That she –'

'Stop right there.' Simon Tearle held up a hand.

Lola stopped.

'Psychogeography.'

'What?'

'The effect of the environment on the emotions and behaviour of individuals. Look at Frieda Klein's experience in one or two of the key cases she was involved in through the lens of her urban surroundings.'

'Really?' Lola wrinkled her nose doubtfully.

'Go and explore. Follow in Frieda's footsteps. Radical wandering.'

He replaced his headphones, leaned back and closed his eyes. He heard the door click shut.

Dugdale sat at his desk with the preliminary results from the autopsy in front of him. He'd had very little sleep, but he had just had a shower and put on a clean shirt: that always helped. He glanced across at Quarry. He looked tired. Worse than tired. That morning several newspapers had carried ominous stories about 'The Hampstead Murders'.

'Is it the same killer?' asked Quarry.

Dugdale stared down at his breakfast, a bacon and tomato sandwich with tired shreds of lettuce trailing from it. 'Let's think about that, shall we?'

Quarry looked blank.

'How they are similar?' said Dugdale.

'Are you wondering or asking?' said Quarry.

'I'm asking.'

'Location.' Quarry could feel his mobile ringing in his pocket once more: Maggie, he thought. He tried to concentrate.

'We've already agreed. Anything else?'

There was a silence. Then Quarry added cautiously, 'They're both out of the ordinary.'

'That's true. It doesn't take us very far but it's true.'

'Both planned.'

Dugdale nodded unenthusiastically.

'Apart from that, they're completely different. They're a week apart. Geoffrey Kernan lived in Barking, Lee Samuels in Royal Oak. Kernan was forty-seven, Samuels thirty-two. Kernan sold toilet supplies, Samuels was an engineer, currently out of work. As far as we can tell, they had no connection to each other. No shared interests, no friends in common.'

'You're missing something,' said Dugdale. He passed a piece of paper across. 'Look at the words I've highlighted.'

'Modacrylic fibres,' Quarry read. 'I've no idea what that is.'

'It was found attached to Samuels's skin. Around the legs and torso and even his face. I called Forensics. It's a fabric used in work clothing, linings of coats, rugs.'

'I've still no idea.'

'Look at the other highlighted words.'

'Flame-resistant.'

'Yes. He was wrapped in flame-resistant fabric.'

'So he wouldn't burn?'

'That's right. But why?' He waited a couple of seconds, then continued, 'Why do you put a body on a fire? To get rid of it, dispose of the evidence. Right?'

Quarry nodded.

'But Samuels was put in a fire in protective garments, meaning he wouldn't quickly be burned. Why?'

'Someone wanted him found?' suggested Quarry.

Dugdale slapped his desktop irritably. 'We now know he was killed at least a week ago. We also know his girlfriend reported him missing on September the twenty-ninth, but it wasn't taken very seriously. So?' He looked at him, his eyebrows raised.

'So whoever killed him waited before displaying the body,' said Quarry.

'That's right.'

There was a long pause.

'Is it all right if I say something? It's probably meaningless.'

'You can say anything here.'

Quarry hesitated. He wasn't sure if his boss really meant that. 'Normally if you put a body on a fire, it's to dispose of that body. But we think he did this as some sort of display.' Dugdale didn't reply, so Quarry went on, 'But if you go to the trouble of protecting the body, that's not just a display. If they hadn't done that, it might have been difficult to identify the body. But maybe it was important that we identified it. Maybe that's part of the point.'

Dugdale frowned. He was fidgeting with his pen.

'Just like Kernan,' said Quarry.

'Just like Kernan.' Dugdale nodded approvingly.

'So it *is* the same killer.' Quarry felt a jolt of excitement. This could be big, the kind of thing that made a career.

'It's possible,' said Dugdale, finally. 'It's definitely possible.'

'This is going to be big, isn't it?' said Quarry. He'd had another idea. Something he should do. But this time he didn't share it with his boss.

'I'm only going to tell you things that you'd find from other officers.'

'Of course.' Liz Barron gave Dan Quarry her most engaging smile.

'I'm not going to do anything that would compromise cases.'

'I wouldn't expect you to. The way I see it, we're just making each other's jobs a little bit easier. Everyone wins and no one loses, right?'

'Right.'

'You can give me advice, steer me in the right direction, keep me one step ahead of the competition.' She patted Quarry's shoulder. 'Don't look so anxious.'

'If it were ever to get out . . .'

'This is my job. It won't get out.' She sat back. 'And, of course, in return for your help, we'll cover your expenses.'

Quarry winced. That was why he was doing it, why he *had* to do it, but he didn't like it being said out loud.

She nodded at him, her glossy hair swinging, then dipped her hand into her bag and pulled out a notebook. 'I think we understand each other, Dan. Now, there's something I'm interested in following up. Perhaps you can help me.'

Eleven

Lola overslept. And she had to have breakfast before she started out: it was her favourite meal of the day. She put a teabag in a mug, poured boiling water over it, then washed up a dirty pan that was in the sink from last night and made herself a poached egg on a toasted, thickly buttered muffin.

Then she rummaged around at the bottom of the wardrobe and found the old pair of walking shoes that used to belong to her flatmate Jess before Jess's feet had had a growth spurt. Lola wasn't sure that she'd ever actually worn them herself, but she thought she ought to dress for the task ahead. She saw that the sky was overcast; rain might be coming.

She had made some very basic preparations. She had googled psychogeography, just to make sure she wasn't getting it wrong. It was, she discovered, about playfulness, about drifting around urban environments, about getting away from your normal routes, about opening yourself up to randomness. It sounded perfect, nothing like work at all. She'd even thought of inviting a couple of friends along. They could make a day of it, grab a coffee, a sandwich, end up with a drink at a pub. But then she read an article that to achieve this new awareness it had to be done alone. That made sense. Lola could imagine that if she went with friends like Ellie or Ben, they'd just spend the whole day talking and wouldn't even notice where they were going. The question was, where to go. Lola had flicked through her notes on Frieda and saw that the River Lea and the Regent's Canal in East London came up several times. She consulted the map on her phone.

It looked like a good starting point. She found a pen and a notebook that would fit in her jacket pocket, and that was all she needed. She took a bus over to Clapton Pond, walked through the park and there, almost like magic, was a river. She had never seen it before, never even heard of it.

Everything Lola saw was new and surprising. From the right a boat with – she counted them – eight rowers and a cox, just like the Boat Race, came towards her. A voice shouted and she looked round and stepped back. A man was cycling alongside the boat, shouting instructions. On the western bank of the river there were gleaming new apartment buildings, on the other side, trees and scrubby grass as far as she could see. Just a few yards away from her, two white swans and four mangy little grey ones were pecking at something in the water. What were they called? Swanlets? Lola looked at her phone again and scrolled on the map, this way and that. She saw that if she turned left, the river would take her through Tottenham and Enfield, past reservoirs and lakes and then gradually and messily out of London. But she had to turn right, heading back into town. She walked past a row of houseboats. On one of them a woman with long hennaed dreadlocks was stacking firewood on the deck. Lola and the woman got into conversation. Lola asked how she kept the boat warm, and washed and cooked, and whether the boat leaked.

The woman mainly laughed at her questions. 'You get a new kind of rhythm,' she said. 'You manage.' She talked about what it was like on summer evenings, putting out chairs on the path, having a barbecue, drinking with friends until the dawn came up over the marshes. Then Lola talked about how she was following in the path of a female psychotherapist who investigated crimes and that one of them had taken place here.

The woman frowned. 'I think I remember that one,' she said. 'It was a guy and a girl who lived in one of the boats just along here. I can't remember the details. It just became one of the stories people tell each other.'

Lola took a photograph of the woman outlined against a wall on the other side of the river. It had a huge mural of a sort of devil with a vast open mouth and ferocious teeth.

As she walked along the river she nodded at dog-walkers and runners and cyclists. She stopped and talked to a man in a yellow reflective jacket who was pushing a trolley along, picking up rubbish. For a mile or so she could almost have been in the countryside. Then she passed under what looked like a motorway, feeling the rumble of the lorries overhead, and emerged into the beginnings of the Olympic Park. She turned off the River Lea onto a canal that took her along the edge of Victoria Park. On the other side, terraced houses with gardens bordered the water. Lola almost felt envious: it would be like living on the canal, but you could have a proper bed and a bath at the end of the day.

The little canal joined the Regent's Canal at the end of Victoria Park and there Lola turned right, still with the park beside her; she saw a young woman struggling with five dogs of different kinds, the leads all entangled. Lola took the leads one by one and helped her to get free. It turned out that, no, they weren't her dogs. That was her job, taking dogs for a walk every day.

'Is that a real job?' Lola asked.

The woman looked a little offended and the dogs dragged her away into the park. Mainly, the towpath was lined with houseboats, but Lola reached a clear patch where three men had taken advantage of the space and were sitting fishing, each separated from the other by just a few paces. Lola took up position between the first two. On her left was an old man with a shock of white hair, a woolly hat and a bulky jacket. He was so enormously fat that Lola couldn't see how his little camping stool could possibly bear his weight. On her right was a man who looked like his opposite in every way. He wore black workman's boots, black jeans and a checked shirt, rolled up to the elbows. He was lean, tanned and his hair was cut very short. While the fat man was muttering to himself, or to the water, the lean man just looked straight ahead in total concentration.

'What sort of fish do you get?' Lola asked.

The fat man sniffed.

'Get some tench,' he said. 'Some bream. Got a ten-pound carp once.'

'Do you eat them?'

'Eat them?' The man gave a deep laugh that seemed to come from far inside his belly. 'What do you think, mate?' He looked across at his companion, who gave a shrug. 'I've heard there's a Korean place down in Bermondsey that'll cook anything you bring them.'

Lola wasn't sure how to respond to that. Was it a racist comment or was it not a racist comment? She responded, as she generally did when she was confused, by talking about herself in a slightly uncontrolled way, saying, as she had said to the woman on the boat, that she was following in the footsteps of a psychotherapist who investigated crimes. Both of the fishermen looked round at her curiously.

'What's her name?' said the lean man.

'You probably wouldn't have heard of her,' said Lola.

'Murders?' said the fat man.

'Some murders,' said Lola.

'I've had some strange things on the end of my hook,' said the fat man. 'Sometimes it's eels. I used to like an eel. But once I got a bit of wood with nails in the end and barbed wire.'

78

'A fence post?'

'No, for hitting someone with.' The man resumed his deep, throaty laugh.

'What sort of jobs do you do?' asked Lola. 'That give you time to fish here in the day.'

'We come here to get away from questions like that,' said the lean man.

'My mistake,' said Lola. 'Mind if I get a picture?' She brandished her phone.

'Flattered, my love,' said the fat man. 'Mind you get my good side.'

'Want to be in it?' said the lean man.

She handed her phone to him and she knelt beside the fat man and put her hand on his ample shoulder.

'Do you want the water or the path in the background?'

'You decide.'

The lean man examined Lola's phone.

'Do you want me to show you how it works?' said Lola.

'I can do it.'

He took the picture and one for luck, and handed the phone back to Lola. Then she took a photograph of the two men.

'Don't steal our souls,' said the lean man.

'I'll try not to.'

Further down the bank, Lola talked to a group of people her own age, who were sitting on a houseboat having an impromptu music session. She talked to a group of small children who were carrying balloons and whose faces were all painted as different animals. She talked to a man who was paddling down the canal on what looked like a giant surfboard. He told her he was on his way to Limehouse. She stopped at a café with tables on the towpath, drank a flat white and ate a piece of carrot cake. The waiter was from Peru and the woman behind the counter was from Sweden.

She wanted to ask them whether they were worried about being expelled from the country but felt it might be a sore point with them. She wouldn't be a good reporter, she thought. She found it too difficult to talk to strangers.

As she approached Islington, the houses became noticeably smarter, the office blocks more elegant, the crowds on the towpath denser. When she arrived at the end of the path where the tunnel disappeared under the hill at the Angel, she looked at her phone. She had taken over eighty pictures. Maybe she could just present her dissertation as an exhibition of pictures. As she walked up the steep slope that led away from the canal, she thought: had that walk brought her closer, in some spiritual way, to Frieda Klein? She felt doubtful. She'd almost forgotten about her.

When she got home, her flatmate, Jess, was sitting at the kitchen table in her dressing-gown with a towel round her head. Her face was pink and smooth from the bath. She was going to a party in Mile End. She poured Lola a mug of tea.

'Next year we should look for somewhere east,' she said. 'We spend half our time travelling there and the other half travelling back.'

'I've just come from there,' said Lola.

'How did it go?'

Lola took out her phone and swiped through the pictures she had taken and talked about them.

'There are some really creepy people on the canal, aren't there?'

'They weren't creepy,' said Lola. 'They were nice. If you just talk to people, everyone's the same, really.'

'Well, that's not true,' said Jess. 'Anyway, you wanted it to be creepy, didn't you? Isn't your dissertation about murder and kidnapping?'

'I'm not sure what my dissertation's about. I was just trying to get into Frieda Klein's head, walk where she walked,
see the people she saw, feel what she felt.'

'And did you?'

'I don't know. I don't know enough about her. Maybe I
need to be a bit more specific. I should find the actual places
that are most important to her.'

'Have you been to her house?'

'Yes, I looked through the window.'

'Did you learn anything?'

'It was in this little mews street just off Tottenham Court
Road and Euston Road. It felt like a little quiet island in the
middle of town.'

'What about her work?'

'I didn't get anything from that. They wouldn't let me past
Reception.'

'What about where she was born?'

'That was out of London somewhere. I can't be bothered
with that.'

They sipped their tea.

'Graves,' said Jess.

'What?'

'That's about the only emotional thing I do with my
family. We go to my grandmother's grave up in Lough-
borough. My uncle's buried there as well. He died in a car
crash. We go there once a year. On my gran's birthday. Well,
almost every year. I didn't go this year. It was during term
time.'

'I can't go to Frieda Klein's grave. She's still alive. At least
I assume she is. Nobody seems to know where she is. Or if
they do, they won't tell me.'

'I didn't mean her grave. But everybody's got someone
they miss. Is anybody connected with Frieda Klein dead?'

'Are you kidding?' said Lola. 'You should read what I've read. It's like a war zone.'

'So there must be someone,' said Jess. 'Someone special.'

Lola thought for a moment. 'Maybe,' she said.

At Olivia Klein's house in Islington, a drinks party was ending, just a few people left, empty glasses and bottles standing on every surface. Olivia picked up a bottle and shook it to see if there was anything left in it, then tipped the last of the sparkling wine into her glass. She wore a red dress and high black shoes that were beginning to pinch her toes horribly.

'Fifty,' she said bitterly. 'I'm *fifty*!'

'How does it feel?' asked the young man with tawny hair and a flowery shirt who stood by her side.

'I'll tell you what it feels like, Jack. Like a scandal. Like a bad joke that's been played on me.'

He looked at her. He always had the feeling that Olivia was about to unravel: her hair escaping from its clips, her clothes somehow temporary, her make-up often smudged, her mood skittering from euphoria to despair. He was trying to think of something comforting to say when Chloë came towards them.

'I've put some pasta on,' she said. 'And Josef has made a spicy sauce. You should probably have something to eat.'

'A scandal,' repeated Olivia. 'An outrage.' She glared from her daughter to Jack and back again. 'It feels like yesterday that I was your age and life was in front of me.' Jack saw with alarm that tears were standing in her eyes. 'Why did you two ever break up,' she said, her voice wobbling.

'Mum. Don't. Come and eat something.'

'You were so sweet together.' Olivia sniffed. 'Even if Frieda didn't like it that the student she was supervising was going out with her beloved niece. And that's another thing.'

'What?'

'I thought she'd come.'

'Frieda?'

'Why isn't she here?'

'You know why.'

'I thought she'd make an exception. I'm *fifty*.'

'Pasta,' said Chloë, encouragingly. She took the glass out of Olivia's hand, put it on the mantelpiece and pulled her towards the kitchen.

'Where is she?'

'I don't know. No one knows.'

'I bet Josef does.'

'I not know,' said Josef, from the stove where he was stirring a pungent tomato sauce.

'Well, I wish she was here. It's not the same without her.'

Twelve

Lola was surprised when the woman in the little hut at the entrance said it was four pounds to enter. 'I've never paid to go into a graveyard before,' she said. 'What if I want to visit the grave of a relative?'

'Do you?'

'No. But just suppose.'

'Then you don't pay.'

The woman was quite old. She had beautiful blue eyes in a face of folds and creases, silver hair. Lola assumed someone she loved was buried in the cemetery and that was why she worked there. She wanted to ask her, but there were people waiting behind her, so she paid her four pounds, took a map, and went in.

She was glad she had done a search on the Highgate Cemetery website before coming because she wouldn't have known where to start. She stood at the top of the main avenue and saw graves spread out in every direction, up grassy banks, beneath the trees and in thick tangles of undergrowth. Like a city, she thought, and a small shiver passed through her. She knew that Alexander Holland, known to his friends as Sandy and once the lover of Frieda Klein, was buried in the eastern half of the cemetery, next to some railings, and she looked at the map to find which way she should go.

It was a damp, foggy day, wet leaves underfoot and the light muted. There were few people around, though a middle-aged man was carefully tending a plot, picking out weeds. It took Lola some time to get to Sandy's grave because she kept getting diverted, now by a broken angel, now by an inscription. Some of the stones were new but some had almost disappeared beneath the ivy and their lettering was rubbed away; nature was taking over. Some of the thousands of people buried here had died old, but others were barely out of babyhood. She didn't know why she had never come here before: you could spend days, she thought, just wandering around among the stones and brambles, mouldering figures leaning towards you out of the undergrowth. She passed a couple, hand in hand, and wondered if they were tourists, or perhaps they had a child buried here. She nodded at them and said good morning, hoping they'd stop so she could talk to them, but they walked past without slowing.

She did at last find Sandy's grave, a simple low headstone set between two larger memorials. The inscription just gave his name and his dates. There were two miniature cyclamen growing there and someone had put a beautiful round stone between them. She took several photos, zooming in, crouching down to get a clearer view.

Lola stayed by the grave for a few minutes. She wondered what she should do next. How could she turn this into a dissertation? She gazed around her. There was a woman sitting on the bench nearby. She had short silver hair and tortoiseshell spectacles, and she was reading a book. She looked intellectual and forbidding.

'Hello,' said Lola, approaching her.

The woman looked up from her book. 'Yes?'

'Can you tell me where Karl Marx is buried? I can't go without seeing him.'

The woman pointed back up the hill.

'It's my first time here,' said Lola. 'I can't believe I've never come before. It's amazing. Spooky – but in a good way. Don't you think? Do you come here often?'

'No.' The woman closed the book and slid it into her bag, then stood up.

'I'm only here now because my tutor suggested I come. Oh, look, there's a wren in the bush. I love wrens. And blackbirds. Except I always feel the female blackbird has a raw deal, being brown. That way?'

She walked back up the hill, the way the woman had pointed. Sure enough, there was Karl Marx's bust staring down at her, enormous and solemn. Lola found the sight unexpectedly funny. She took a photo with her phone, then another of the view down through the graves in the dim light. She slid her phone back into her pocket, frowned, and an idea slid into her mind like a cold blade. She turned to run back to the entrance. The main avenue was empty. She dashed out of the gate and looked up and down the hill. In the distance, she could see a figure walking swiftly away and she sprinted towards it.

'Excuse me,' she said. Her voice came out in a gasp.

The woman with silver hair who had been sitting on the bench turned. 'Can I help you?'

'Well, yes. Yes, you can.'

The woman waited.

'You're Frieda Klein.' Her certainty wavered. 'Aren't you?'

'No.' The woman's expression didn't alter.

'Are you sure?'

'Quite sure,' the woman said drily. 'My name's Ursula Edmunds.'

'I've been looking for someone called Frieda Klein and it would have helped me a lot if it had been you. I'm doing a dissertation on her, you see, except it's not going very well.'

'Good luck,' said the woman, and walked away.

Lola hesitated, confused, then hurried after her.

'It's you,' she said. 'I know it is.'

The woman turned towards her, her eyes stern behind her glasses. 'Which way are you going?'

'This way,' said Lola, eagerly.

'Good. Then I'll be turning off here.'

'I'll come with you, then. I'm not really going anywhere.'

'That wasn't the point.'

'Now I know you're Frieda Klein. Professor Bradshaw said you were difficult.'

'What's your name?'

'Lola Hayes.'

'Are you listening to me, Lola?'

Lola nodded several times.

'Go away.'

'Oh.'

'Go away right now. Do you hear me?'

'Well, I hear you, of course. I can't help but hear you. Why have you dyed your hair?'

'You seem to have difficulty in listening to what is being said to you.'

'That's what my father always says. Do you miss him very much?'

'What?'

'Do you miss Sandy? Is that why you go and sit by his grave? What happened to him was awful. I think that's why I'm finding it hard to write my dissertation. My tutor says I should deconstruct you, whatever that means, but instead I keep imagining what these last years have been like for you. How scary, knowing that Dean Reeve is still out there.'

'Stop right there.' She faced Lola. Her face was pale and her eyes glowed.

'You are Frieda, aren't you?'

'Why are you doing this?'

'I knew you were,' said Lola, and impulsively she put her arms around the woman as they stood together on the pavement. 'You poor thing. Everything you've been through. You must feel so sad and alone.'

But Frieda Klein pushed Lola away. She looked at her steadily and Lola had the strangest feeling of being looked not at but into, a gaze going right into her most secret part.

'Do you realize what you're doing?' said Frieda, softly. 'Getting involved in my life is a dangerous thing to do.'

'It's just for a dissertation.'

'You've been talking to people I know, looking for me.'

'And now I've found you.'

'You won't find me again. And you must never tell anyone that you did so once.'

'I don't understand.'

'You don't need to understand. Leave me. Forget you met me. Stop trying to find out about me.'

'Shall we have coffee together first?'

For the first time, Frieda's face lost its stony expression. Lola thought she was trying not to smile.

'You really are persistent, aren't you? All right, come with me.'

'You saw Hal Bradshaw,' said Frieda, as they sat with their coffee. She thought how young Lola seemed, with her soft round face and the scattering of freckles on her nose.

'Yes.' Lola glanced at her doubtfully. 'I don't think he likes you very much.'

'I don't think he does.'

'I met the journalist Liz Barron as well.'

'You have been busy.'

'And your friends Reuben and Josef.'

Frieda winced slightly. 'You saw them?'

'Yes. I went to Reuben's house. They didn't tell me any-thing, though.'

'I see.'

'Your niece was there too.'

Frieda looked away from Lola, out of the window. 'Did she seem all right?'

'As far as I could tell. Haven't you seen them recently? Why is that?' She leaned forward and said, in a loud whisper, 'Are you in disguise?'

Frieda drew back, frowning at her. 'Why did you go to the cemetery?'

Lola told her about Simon Tearle. 'I'm following in your footsteps.'

'You mustn't do that.'

'It's been quite fun.'

'I'm serious. You must stop.'

'I've been to bits of London I didn't even know about. The cemetery – and then I walked along the River Lea as well. It made me think I'd quite like to live on a houseboat – maybe not in the winter. There was one with a whole garden on its roof. Look.'

She took out her phone and started scrolling through it.

'Here,' she said. 'Isn't this great?'

Frieda glanced down. For a few seconds she sat absolutely still. 'Give that to me.' She took the phone.

And then she saw him.

He was looking at her, thinner than she remembered, with his hair cropped very short but with the same smile. A man who sat fishing on the riverbank, a few yards from the spot where he had killed his twin brother. A man like her shadow, a man like a ghost.

'What have you done?' she said to Lola.

'Me?'

'Yes, you.'

'I don't know what you mean, I just –'

'This is Dean Reeve.'

There was a silence. Lola's mouth was open and her eyes were wide.

'You're joking,' she said at last.

'You're not safe.'

Lola gave a nervous little laugh. 'But you're the one he's after.' She looked into Frieda's eyes. 'Anyway, he doesn't know who I am. Is it really him? You're sure?'

'Yes.'

Lola put a hand to her mouth, incredulous. 'I spoke to him. I feel dizzy. I'm in shock.'

'What did you say to him?'

Lola gestured helplessly. 'I can't answer that because it wasn't important. He didn't make an impression on me. I just chatted with people as I walked along. It's called psycho-geography. What that means –'

'I know what it means,' Frieda said, so sharply that Lola was surprised into silence. Frieda picked up a packet of sugar and rotated it between her fingers. 'You might have got away with it,' she murmured, as if to herself. Once again, she raised her eyes and looked at Lola directly. 'So. You talked to the people you met?'

'A bit.'

'Did you mention my name?'

'No. I didn't think they'd have heard of you.'

'What did you say about what you were doing?'

'Not much. Just a few vague things.'

'Lola,' said Frieda, in a gentler tone, 'I'm not trying to catch you out. But this is serious. We need to know where we are – especially where *you* are. You just need to tell me what happened.'

'All right,' said Lola. 'I just said to some of them – not all of them – that I was following in the footsteps of a woman, a psychologist or psychotherapist, I think I said. Yes, I did. Who investigated crimes and walked around London on her own. That's all.'

Frieda picked up Lola's phone and flicked through the photographs, then stopped. 'This one,' she said, and handed the phone back to Lola. Lola looked at it. It was the picture of her and the fat fisherman.

'What about it?'

'You're in the picture. Who took it?'

'He did.'

'Dean Reeve.'

'All right, Dean Reeve took the photo.'

'How long did he have your phone in his hand?'

'I don't know. He just took the photo. I mean, he had trouble getting it to work. Everyone does with other people's phones.'

'What could he find out from your phone?'

'Nothing much.'

'Your number? Your name maybe?'

Lola chewed a strand of hair, thinking. 'Maybe,' she said. 'They come up as soon as you press on my contact list. Though he didn't have that much time. Look. I'm sorry if I messed things up. If you think it's a problem, I'll just give up doing this stupid thesis and go back to my supervisor and get a new subject and act as if none of this ever happened.'

Frieda shook her head. 'Don't you understand anything?' she said. 'Haven't you been reading up about me? People who cross Dean Reeve's path get killed. There's a bit of me that wants to just get up and walk out and leave you to deal with this.'

'Fine,' said Lola. 'Why don't you? I'm sorry I got mixed up with you. I'll just find something else to write about.'

'Something else to write about? None of that matters. That's all done. Don't you realize you've left your old life behind?'

'*What?*'

'You have to accept that.'

'I don't know what that means.'

'It means that you can't go home. You can't go anywhere you normally go.'

Lola had gone very pale and she was breathing in short gasps. 'That's just stupid.'

Frieda reached across and put her hand on Lola's. 'Look at me. You need to stay calm. But you have to listen to me.'

Lola picked up the phone and stared at the photo of Dean Reeve. Frieda could see that she was wondering if it could actually be true. Could she trust this woman? She waited for her to speak.

'I can't just walk out on my life,' said Lola. 'People will miss me. They'll call the police.'

'It won't last for long,' said Frieda. 'He's reaching the end. One way or another.'

'The end?' Lola's expression was startled. 'What end?'

'Of his journey.'

'And while he's getting to the end of his journey, whatever that is, what am I meant to do?' said Lola. 'Wander the streets until somebody catches him?'

'Go and stay somewhere. Somewhere you've never been before.'

'Where? With what? I've got about thirty pounds in the bank. Can't I just go to the police? I can show them this picture of Dean Reeve and I can say that you think I'm in danger and then . . .' Lola obviously didn't know how to finish the sentence.

'Yes,' said Frieda. 'And then?'

'They're the police,' said Lola. 'They'll put me under protection and then go and find him and arrest him.'

'The police have been failing to find him for years,' said Frieda. 'And when he wants to kill people, he kills them.'

'Can I go with *you*?' Lola said.

Frieda blinked. 'With me?'

'Yes.' Lola's face had brightened.

'Certainly not.'

'Why?'

'For a start, this is all about me. I wish it wasn't but it is. The further you are from me the better.'

'Where better to hide than with someone who's hiding? I don't know how to do this. You do. If I'm on my own, I'll just do something stupid. I always do. It would just be for a few days. That's what you said. I'll be safe with you.'

Frieda drummed on the table with her fingers.

'What?' said Lola. 'Say something.'

'I don't know.'

'It would be fun,' said Lola.

'Fun.'

'You say it like it's a dirty word.'

Frieda smiled slightly. 'You don't know what you're getting into,' she said.

'But you'll protect me?'

Frieda looked full on at Lola. Those eyes again. 'You'll do what I say.'

'Yes!'

'You won't lie to me.'

'Of course I won't.'

93

'There are different ways of lying. It won't happen the way you expect. It'll seem like the right thing to do, but it won't be.'

'I don't understand.'

'You don't need to,' said Frieda. 'That's why we have rules. That's why we make promises.'

'All right, I promise. But you'll protect me? For a while.'

'We'll give it a try.'

Thirteen

The two of them walked out of the café and Frieda told Lola to wait while she went into a newsagent's. She emerged and handed Lola an Oyster card.

'Don't do anything that can be traced,' she said.

'Isn't that going too far?'

'Let's try that for the moment,' said Frieda. 'Going too far.'

'Am I really doing this?'

'I don't know. Are you?'

'I've got nothing. My passport, my laptop, my clothes. Everything. It's all back in my flat.'

Frieda nodded. 'All right,' she said. 'We'll go there. Five minutes. Take what you can carry in one shoulder bag. Where do you live?'

'I'm sharing a flat just off Holloway Road.'

'Good. We can walk.'

'Can't we take an Uber?' Lola saw Frieda's disapproving expression. 'I forgot. Walking is what you do.'

As they crossed Junction Road and went through Tufnell Park, Frieda didn't speak. She just strode so quickly that Lola almost had to run to keep up with her.

'The funny thing,' said Lola, 'is that I'll probably never know whether this was the right thing to do.'

'I think you'll know,' said Frieda.

After twenty minutes' walk, they were standing in front of a large, dark-bricked terrace house, almost in the shadow of Holloway Prison. Frieda looked around. She couldn't see anybody. Not that that meant anything.

'We're on the second floor,' said Lola.

'We?'

'My flatmate, Jess. She's probably my best friend as well.'

'Make an excuse for going away.'

'Do you want to come up and meet her?'

'Of course I don't.'

'You'd like her.'

'I'll stay here,' said Frieda. 'Remember. Five minutes.'

It was closer to ten minutes later when Lola re-emerged with a bulky canvas bag over her shoulder. Frieda immediately set off in the direction of Holloway Road.

'I was talking to Jess,' Lola said. 'I said I was going away to work on my dissertation and that I wasn't sure when I'd be back, but it'd be several days at least, maybe more.'

'Was she all right with that?'

'Jess is all right with everything.'

They jumped on a bus in Holloway Road. At Camden Town they changed to another bus. At first Lola recognized the areas they were passing through, Chalk Farm, Swiss Cottage, but then they changed buses again and she stared out of the window at residential streets and busy roads and warehouses and she felt like she could have been in any city. It seemed as if she had gone into another world, another life, and she wanted the old one back. It must have shown on her face because Frieda looked at her with concern and gave the first smile Lola had seen from her. She put her hand on Lola's arm. 'You just need to trust me,' she said.

For a moment Lola felt a wave of relief and then the wave seemed to recede. It was a physical feeling. Trust. It was so easy to say that. But how did you know who to trust? She wished she had paid more attention while reading through the files and press cuttings. She remembered enough to know that people close to Frieda Klein, people associated with her, people who had just crossed her path, had got killed. But had they trusted her or had they failed to trust her?

She was woken from these confused thoughts by Frieda's voice. 'This is where we get off.'

They walked through various residential streets and arrived at a warehouse that had been turned into apartments. Frieda stopped outside a black front door, took out her key, unlocked it and they stepped inside. It didn't feel like a home at all. There was a smell of paint. The floor was wood; the walls were painted white and entirely bare. The living room, which was also the kitchen, contained a wooden table and chair, a sofa and nothing else. The only brightness came from the large windows in the far wall and Lola stepped forward to look out.

'Wow,' she said.

She was staring down on the dirty grey water of a canal. On the far side was the towpath. There was a woman pushing a buggy, an old man with a dog: the normal life she was now seeing through glass.

'You like canals,' she said. 'You and Dean both.'

Frieda showed Lola round the spartan flat. There was one bedroom, but the sofa in the main room pulled out into a bed and there was a spare set of sheets. Frieda went over to her computer and Lola saw her face clench as she looked at the screen. Then she filled a kettle with water, before gesturing Lola to sit down.

'Ground rules,' she said. 'Number one. Don't communicate with anyone.'

'What? What about on Facebook?'

'No. Later you should go to a café and put up a post saying you're going off radar because you're working on your dissertation, so nobody will worry or try to track you down. Then that's it.'

97

'Seriously?'

'You don't use your card. You don't email anyone. You can go online and read things, research your dissertation if you want, watch a film. But there can be no output from you. Give me your mobile.'

'Why?' asked Lola, but she handed it over.

Frieda opened the window and, before Lola had time to realize what was happening, dropped it into the canal beneath.

'My phone!' she yelped. 'I've only just got it. What do you think you're doing?'

'I'll buy you a pay-as-you-go tomorrow. When this is all over, I'll get you a new one.'

'Now I won't even know what time it is. I don't have a watch. Or, at least, I do. I've got a nice one, my gran gave it to me when I turned eighteen, but I left it in the flat.'

'You can ask me the time.'

'That's not the point. Anyway, this seems extreme to me. Honestly, do you really think it's necessary?'

'I wish it wasn't. But, you see, you've already stirred things up.'

'What do you mean?'

'If you go and talk to someone like Liz Barron, what do you think she's going to do about it?'

'The journalist?'

Frieda pulled her laptop towards her and read aloud from her screen: '"Fears are growing for the safety of troubled therapist Frieda Klein, forty. She has not been seen since her controversial role in the Daniel Blackstock murder case. Close friends have expressed concern . . ." And so on and so on. Barron just did what you did, bothered my friends and bothered my colleagues, but she got more out of them than you did. Or probably she just made it up. I can't imagine Paz expressing concern to Liz Barron.' Frieda scrolled down the article. 'You're mentioned too. Though not by name. "Dr Klein's disappearance came to light when a student studying Klein and the Dean Reeve case could find no trace of her at her home or at her work."'

'That's not true,' said Lola, indignantly.

'It doesn't matter. What matters is that Dean Reeve will read it. He doesn't like it when people think they can get the better of him.'

Lola stared at her with the scared eyes of a child.

'I've seen what he does to them,' said Frieda, going over to the boiling kettle.

'Don't say that.'

'Why?' said Frieda. 'Do you want me to say that I'm sorry and I didn't mean to frighten you? Because I absolutely want to frighten you.'

'All right, I'm frightened. I'm frightened and I'm hungry.'

'I can help with the hunger. Hold on to the fear.'

After they had eaten, Frieda sat at her computer. Lola put on her flannel pyjamas, then sat on the sofa-bed. Everything felt very quiet. She looked at Frieda and Frieda seemed to sense her gaze. They stared at each other in silence for a moment.

'Do you mind if I ask something?' said Frieda.

Lola just shrugged.

'It's difficult to walk out on your life,' Frieda said. 'I know, because I've done it. I've done it more than once. You hurt yourself and you hurt other people. But you've just done it.'

'What are you saying?'

Frieda gave a faint smile. 'You don't seem like someone who can disentangle herself so easily. What about your family? What will they say?'

'There's just my parents. They've moved to Spain. They've

got a house in Málaga. I hardly ever talk to them. Or, at least, I do. I call them up but they don't seem to notice if it's been a day or a week since we last spoke. I don't think they miss me. I sometimes think –' She stopped and looked down at the floor, blinking rapidly.

Frieda regarded her thoughtfully. Then she asked, 'What about friends? They might get upset. They might even report you missing.'

Lola suddenly felt her heart beating hard in her chest. She started to speak but she found it difficult to put into words. 'I don't know,' she said. 'Last year I had a really intense time. Maybe too intense. I've got friends, I guess. I always have. Lots of friends in a way. But I pulled back from them a bit. I mean, I still go out and have fun and get drunk and giggle and dance and all that stuff. Good-time Lola. But it's been a bit of an act in the past few months. I don't talk to them like I used to. You know. Talk about anything that really matters. It's all just ...' she waved a hand in the air '... stuff. The chats. My father always says I can talk for England. People probably like having me around, but maybe they wouldn't really notice if I wasn't there.'

'You're telling me that both your parents and your friends aren't attending to you?' Frieda's voice was soft.

Lola flushed. 'They probably would if I asked them – or, at least, my friends would. But I needed ... I needed some space, some time. I think if I let people know I've gone away to write my dissertation, nobody will try to track me down. I mean, they know I'm in a bit of a pickle over it. So I'm OK for a week or two anyway.' There was a long silence; Frieda's dark eyes were on her. She forced a little laugh. 'You probably think I should be coming to see you as a patient rather than, you know, whatever this is.'

'This will pass,' said Frieda. 'It's serious. Very serious. But it will pass. Then you can go back to your life and deal with things. Maybe I could be of some help.'

'Yeah, whatever,' said Lola. She got up and rifled through the bag she'd brought from her flat, lifting out the clothes and toiletries before she found what she wanted.

Putting the harmonica to her lips, she gave a loud blast on it. That did the trick: Frieda looked up, startled.

'What are you doing?'

'Playing my harmonica,' said Lola, cheerily. 'Or, rather, making a sound on it. I don't know how to play. Not yet.'

'Your harmonica.'

'Someone gave it to me on my birthday, but I haven't got round to using it before. I thought it would be a good time to learn.'

'You did, did you?'

'It can't be that hard.' Lola looked at the little silver bar doubtfully. 'I don't have any instructions. I'll find something on YouTube.'

She put the instrument to her mouth and blew once more, this time emitting a high, brassy shriek. Frieda winced.

Fourteen

Liz Barron sat in the bar and nursed her gin and tonic, her third of the evening. Or was it her fourth? After the first she had felt sharp and clear and exaggeratedly alert. From the moment she had talked to that student, she'd had the nerve-tingling sense that she was on to a story that nobody else even suspected. But then she had used the second and the third and then maybe the fourth, if there had been a fourth, to calm her down, relax. Recently she'd been doing that more and more. Self-medication.

She fished the slice of lemon out of the tumbler and slid it into her mouth. Frieda Klein had been her subject for years now. She had interviewed her, door-stepped her, researched her life, spoken to her friends and to her enemies. And Frieda Klein had disappeared and nobody would tell her why. Malcolm Karlsson hadn't been any help at all, and his sour-faced sidekick had been even worse.

What was more, she had tried to find Lola Hayes but her friends and tutor said she had gone away recently, to write her dissertation. Nobody seemed to know where she was. But Quarry might be useful. She gave a small smile and lifted her glass again, only to find it empty.

'Would you like another of those?'

She looked round, tried to focus her blurred vision. A man whose face had a windblown, outdoor look seemed to be smiling at her; she squinted at him.

'Why not?' she said.

He went to the bar to order and she watched him from

behind. He was lean and, though he wasn't tall, he looked powerful. His arms were thick.

'Here.' He put it down in front of her, along with a pint of beer for himself.

'Thank you. I'm Liz.'

'Graham,' he said. 'I was half scared to approach you.'

'Scared?' She gave a low laugh. 'I don't think I'm that scary.'

'You looked deep in thought.'

'I was.'

She took a deep swallow of her drink and felt it slide down her throat, clean and viscous. Her bones felt soft and her thoughts swam in her head.

'Are you going to tell me why?'

'I don't know.' She looked at him and took another sip. The bar was almost empty. 'That depends.'

'What does it depend on, Liz?'

'How quickly I drink this.'

They both laughed. He lifted his beer but didn't drink any.

'I don't want to pry,' he said. 'Perhaps it's personal. Maybe you were thinking of a man.'

'Wrong!' She leaned forward. 'I was certainly not thinking of a man. I was thinking of a *woman*.' She sipped her gin. It seemed to be almost all gone. 'Not in a personal way,' she added.

'Then how?' said the man. His voice was soft, almost caressing. 'Tell me.'

'I haven't really got anything to tell. Not yet. I'm a journalist and I've got a hunch I might be on to something. Or, rather, someone.'

'This woman.'

'Yes. Do you ever have the feeling that there's something you want, just out of sight and out of reach, and if you're careful and clever, you'll be able to get hold of it?'

The man nodded. 'I do,' he said. 'I like to fish. I sit by the water and I wait. I can wait all day. I wait until the line twitches. Even the smallest tug and I feel it. I'm a patient man, Liz.'

Her mobile, which was lying screen down on the table, started to rattle and she turned it over. It was a text from Dan Quarry and she gave a small smile of satisfaction.

'Good news?' asked the man.

'I've been fishing too,' she said. 'This is the tug on the line.'

He chuckled, watching her intently.

'I should go,' she said, looking at her watch. 'I can still get the last train.'

She stood up, surprisingly steady on her feet, and he rose too.

'I'll walk you to the station,' he said. 'It's dark out there. Dark and cold.'

Fifteen

Dugdale stared round the room at the start of the daily meeting. 'Let's have a round-up, starting with Lee Samuels.' He turned to the young detective who was newly recruited to the team. 'Malik. What have you got?'

The detective glanced down at his notes, gave a small cough. 'I talked to his girlfriend and she said he'd been rather depressed recently. He was out of work and drinking a bit too much. It seems he flew off the handle with her quite a bit.'

Dugdale felt a flicker of interest. 'How badly?'

Malik shook his head. 'To kill him, take the body to Hampstead Heath, put it on a bonfire? She didn't seem quite the type. Too small for a start.'

'You never know. Anyway, go on.'

'His parents both live in Derby. They don't know much about his life since he moved to London. He was last seen on September the twenty-sixth, when he had a drink with friends at a pub in Royal Oak, and he was reported missing on September the twenty-ninth , so he must have been killed, or at least taken, between those two dates.'

'Anything more?'

'The autopsy shows that Samuels was strangled,' he said. 'Like Kernan. Probably with thin wire, though. There was no evidence of significant decomposition before the body was placed on the bonfire. The site was muddy and by the time Forensics got to it –'

'I know, I know,' said Dugdale. 'Total disaster. So were any traces found?'

The detective looked back at the notes. 'There were grooves nearby, but the man who built the fire confirms that he transported much of the wood by wheelbarrow so they probably come from that.'

'Anything from CCTV, Kevin?' asked Dugdale, to a sandy-haired detective on his left.

'We've looked at all the cameras in the area, and they show us nothing remarkable – but, then, we don't know what we're looking for. There were hundreds of cars but we don't know where to start.'

'What else?' Nobody spoke. Dugdale sighed, scratched the side of his face and then said, 'All right. We're working on the assumption that Kernan and Samuels were killed by the same person. Let's turn to Kernan. Dan, what have you found out?'

'I've been through all the stuff we took away and there's nothing that leaped out. He didn't have money problems, he didn't seem to have any secrets.'

'You mean you didn't find any.'

'None that were apparent.'

'There's his searches on Karlsson,' said Dugdale. 'That's the one odd thing we've discovered.'

'Yes. But Karlsson was baffled,' said Quarry. 'He'd never heard of Geoffrey Kernan. He and his colleague are going to make sure there's no connection.'

He remembered Yvette Long looking at him with a kind of morose disapproval and felt shame flushing through him as he thought about his deal with Liz Barron. It was only temporary, though. A bad patch.

'Tell me when you've heard back from him. I'm wanting to ask you about the satnav but I guess, if there was anything, you wouldn't have kept me in suspense.'

Quarry shook his head regretfully. 'I've been everywhere

that he went in the week before he died,' he said. 'I mean everywhere that was on the satnav. It's not the same thing.'

'Did you specifically eliminate every address?' asked Dugdale, sharply.

Quarry flushed. He felt Dugdale was being harsher on him than on the others. 'I did what I could. A couple of people weren't at home. Sometimes it's difficult to identify the exact address.'

'Difficult?' said Dugdale. 'If they're nothing to do with the inquiry, prove it to me.'

'Yes, sir,' said Quarry, in a low voice.

Dugdale gazed gloomily at the men and women in front of him. 'So what have we got? We have a man strangled, then put in a car and sped down a hill. We have another man strangled, then put on a bonfire. But he was dressed in a non-flammable fabric so that he wouldn't be consumed by the fire. Both were displayed in public places. Probably the bodies were kept somewhere. There are no witnesses who are any use, no blood or traces or fingerprints to work with. The only thing we've found is that Kernan did multiple searches on DCI Karlsson. That must mean something.'

He stood up and pulled on a shabby overcoat. 'Off to meet the press,' he said, peering disconsolately at a rip in the coat's pocket.

'I usually put in more butter than that,' said Lola.

Frieda ignored her. She broke three eggs into the pan, then beat them with a wooden spoon.

'Scrambled eggs should be soft and buttery,' continued Lola. 'With *lots* of black pepper. You can never have too much black pepper. Don't you agree? I sometimes even put black pepper on strawberries. It's surprisingly tasty. Strawberries can be a bit boring on their own. Shall I butter the toast?' She pulled open the door of the fridge and put her head inside, then withdrew it with an almost-finished pack of butter and disappointment on her face. 'There's not much in here, is there? My friend Jess always says that happiness is a full fridge. Not for you, obviously.' She scraped the last of the butter on to two pieces of toast. 'If I went to see a psychotherapist, I'd just gabble to fill up the silence. Does that happen a lot?'

'Sometimes people can't stop talking and sometimes they can't start. I've had sessions in which nothing has been said at all.'

Lola pulled a face. 'I couldn't stand that. And not just with a therapist – I say whatever comes into my mind as it is, to whoever cares to listen. My mother says there's no gap between me having a thought and putting it into words. My dad's even ruder.' She gave a happy laugh.

'You probably have things you don't ever bring yourself to talk about.'

'I don't think so. I'd lie on your couch – do you have a couch? – and chatter away.'

'I don't have a couch. Perhaps we would think about what's behind the chatter, what it's trying to hide.'

'What if there isn't anything?'

'For instance,' said Frieda, 'when you talk about your parents, it's always the critical things they say about you.'

Lola wrinkled her nose. 'They think I'm a bit flighty. Scatter-brained.'

'And are you?'

'It's just my manner.'

'Exactly. And manner gets in the way of self-revelation. As you told me when you explained why your friends wouldn't miss you.'

'I was probably exaggerating,' said Lola, with an uncomfortable laugh. 'It had been a strange sort of day.'

'You didn't sound to me like you were exaggerating. You sounded to me like you were feeling hurt.'

'Well, I don't know about that. You shouldn't read too much into what I say.'

'That's my job.'

Frieda shared the eggs between the pieces of toast and they sat at the small table.

'You haven't put black pepper on it. Why do you call yourself Ursula Edmunds?' Lola asked.

'In order not to call myself Frieda Klein.'

'Well, obviously. I can see that. You've cut your hair and dyed it silver as well. And you wear those glasses. You don't look bad, actually.'

'Thank you,' said Frieda, drily.

'Though you probably look better as yourself. Of course, I only saw the photos of you. When you're being Ursula, do you feel different? Inside, I mean. Like when I'm in Italy and I wave my hands around and am more Italian. My inner Italian is released.'

'All right,' Frieda said. 'I'll tell you what you need to know.'

Lola leaned forward expectantly.

'I had to disappear, not because I was in danger from Dean Reeve but because everyone I was close to was in danger. I was cursed, like a plague-carrier, and I needed to remove myself.'

'But how? That's really hard, isn't it? How do you live without a bank card and things like that?'

'I have a bank card – or, at least, Ursula Edmunds does. She also has a birth certificate, a passport, a medical card, a National Insurance number, an account, a phone. And a key to this flat.'

'How did you do that?'

'I didn't. Someone did it for me.' Frieda frowned, thinking

of Walter Levin, with his pin-stripe suit and his frayed tie, smiling amiably but his eyes cold and watchful. 'I've worked with him. He's good at things like that.'

'He sounds like a spy.'

'Yes, he does.'

'Why Ursula Edmunds?'

'It's a name.'

'I wouldn't choose it. I'd call myself something dramatic. Scarlett Savonarola.'

'I didn't want to call attention to myself,' said Frieda.

'So you're like a ghost.'

'It's interesting you say that. I've always thought of Dean as a ghost.'

'Two ghosts then – doing what?'

'Looking for each other.'

'How are you looking?'

'Maybe looking is the wrong word. I'm waiting for a sign.'

'What kind of sign?'

'I'll tell you when I see it.'

'And I can help you?'

'The main thing is that you don't get in my way.'

Sixteen

The following evening, a middle-aged man wearing a bright yellow top and headphones was running along the canal towpath in the dusk and the rain. He dodged the cyclists, with their heads down and water streaming off their waterproof jackets, and the Canada geese and kept on, along the empty stretch ahead of him. Then his footsteps faltered. Something had caught his attention. He stopped, turned around.

Sure enough there was an object floating in the water. A log, perhaps, but it didn't look like a log. Or a large plastic bag, but it didn't look like a bag either, and then he saw that the thing had what appeared to be arms, lying slack along its length, and his world tipped. He looked around frantically for someone to take charge, he called out, his voice sounding feeble, but there was no one, just him and the object in the water, and the rain falling steadily.

He took several deep breaths, not quite believing he was going to do this, and climbed down into the water, which was cold and murky and probably full of rats and disease, and waded towards the thing. As he got nearer he saw strands of hair floating on the surface and white legs and a yellow dress with the buttons still neatly done up. His music was still playing in his ears. With a lurch of terror he put his hand out and grasped at the shoulder, and with his eyes half shut he pulled and the body turned. He saw a face. He started to shout for help as he towed her towards the bank, and then let her go. It didn't matter. There was no rush.

*

Frieda was lying on her bed, still dressed, her eyes open. Her mind was full of thoughts and she knew she would not sleep tonight. She got up and put her face to the window. In the dim light before dawn, she could see the canal beneath her and she let herself be drawn into its softly moving greyness. It was windless and quiet, everything holding its breath.

Then a scream cut through the silence.

She whirled around and ran to the living room. Lola, wearing her stripy pyjamas and her hair in pigtails, was huddled on the sofa-bed. She looked ten years old. Her face was stricken. Frieda crossed the room and put a hand on her shoulder.

'Tell me quickly.'

Lola stared at her with huge eyes. 'You were right.' She spoke in a hoarse whisper.

'What are you talking about?'

'I woke up and at first I couldn't remember where I was. I felt so odd and restless and scared.'

'You called out because you were scared?'

'No. I started browsing –' Lola broke off and started sobbing, pointing towards her computer. Frieda crouched in front of it. She had only to read the headline on the screen: 'Journalist's Body Found in Canal'.

'Liz Barron.' It wasn't a question.

'It was me, wasn't it?'

'No.'

'If I hadn't started poking around, this wouldn't have happened.'

Frieda sat down beside Lola. 'Listen. This wasn't you. This was Dean Reeve. You've stepped into his story and I'm sorry for you. I'll do my best to make sure you're not harmed. It's important that you try to keep your mind clear, alert. Do you understand?'

Lola nodded. Tears filled her eyes but she bit her lower lip and tried not to let them fall.

'Good,' said Frieda, nodding at her, and in spite of her terror, Lola felt a trickle of pleasure spread through her. 'Now I'm going to make you some tea and then we'll go.'

'Go where?'

'To where she was found.' Her face was turned towards Lola, but she seemed to be gazing inward. 'This is where it begins.'

It was getting light as they left the flat and set off along the canal, although the sky was cloudy and there was still a faint drizzle falling.

'Do you always walk this fast?' asked Lola, struggling to keep up.

Frieda didn't reply. Her expression was stern, intense.

'What are you hoping to find?' Lola waited a few seconds, then asked the question again, thinking that Frieda hadn't heard.

'I don't know.'

A man in a suit cycled past; then a young woman ran by. There were lights on now in some of the houseboats. Under a bridge, a man lay in a sleeping bag, only his hair showing.

At a bend in the canal, they came across police tape.

'It was here, then,' said Frieda, stepping over it.

'Won't we get into trouble?' asked Lola, but she followed Frieda and stopped when she stopped to stare out at the rippling canal, where rubbish and a solitary moorhen floated.

'What are you seeing?' asked Lola. 'Because all I'm seeing is the canal.'

'Look harder.'

'At what?'

'Tell me what's here.'

'The canal, the towpath. That's it.' Lola nodded energetically. 'So I met Dean by the canal, and you live by the canal
and Liz Barron's body was found in the canal.' She clutched
Frieda's arm. 'Does that mean he knows where you live?
Where *we* live?'

'You need to look more carefully,' said Frieda. 'What is in
front of you?'

'The canal,' repeated Lola. 'Water, rain. On the other side,
houses.'

'Go on.'

Lola rolled her eyes. 'A duck. Several ducks.'

'Yes.'

'Plastic bottles. Weeds. A pipe thing.'

'Right.' Frieda's voice was fierce.

'What?'

'That pipe, what is it?'

Lola stared at the thick metal pipe that ran like a bridge
over the canal. 'Sewage?' she said. 'Water?'

'Not just water, a river.'

'I don't get it.'

'In that pipe,' Frieda pointed towards it, 'runs the River
Westbourne.'

'Oh.' Lola blinked, then opened her eyes wide. '*Wow*. One
of your secret rivers, the ones you walk along.'

'Yes.'

'And you think that's why the body was put here?'

'I do.'

'My God. That's horrible. Really horrible. You're saying
Dean Reeve killed poor Liz Barron just in order to put her
body here as a sign. As if she was just an object, a *thing* that
was serving his purpose.'

'That's exactly what I'm saying.' Frieda's voice was low.
'Dean Reeve would know that over the years Liz Barron

showed a hostile interest in me. You've read her pieces.' Lola nodded. 'And she was starting again. So he's removing her and putting her body in a place that holds a particular significance for me.'

'This is really creepy.'

'He's very dangerous, Lola. You must never forget that, not for a minute.'

'Surely you have to tell the police.'

'I will. For what it's worth.'

'What happens next?'

'Not next. I think we need to find out if something happened *before*.'

Seventeen

'This probably doesn't mean anything,' said Karlsson, hesitantly. 'But it just might.'

Dugdale nodded. Karlsson was wearing a suit that might have been grey but might have been a mossy-green as well, and though he was tie-less and there was stubble on his cheeks, he made Dugdale feel slightly shabby.

'Tell me.'

'I've already spoken to Matt Selby. He's in charge of the investigation into Liz Barron's death, for the time being.'

'For the time being? I don't like the sound of that.'

'I wanted to speak directly to you as well. A couple of days ago, Liz Barron came to see me.'

'Why?'

'It's complicated. I've known her over the years, largely because of her persistent interest – that's putting it kindly – in Frieda Klein.' Dugdale nodded: everyone knew about Karlsson and Frieda Klein. 'She was trying to track her down, and failing. She thought I might be able to help her.'

'Did she now?'

'Yes. It was on the day you sent your officer round.'

'Dan Quarry?'

'That's it.'

'I don't see how this is connected to the recent murders.'

'It probably isn't. But, given that my name had come up on Geoffrey Kernan's computer, I thought you should know.'

'You mean,' said Dugdale, 'that you're connected to both Kernan and Barron?'

'It's a very loose connection. But, yes, that's what I mean.'

'Thank you for telling me.'

'As I said, probably nothing.'

'Probably,' said Dugdale.

Eighteen

Frieda made tea for herself and for Lola. She stood at the window, staring out, lost in thought. When her mug was empty, she refilled it and sat down and opened her laptop.

'Can I help?' said Lola.

'Don't you have your studies to get on with?'

'You mean my essay about *you*? I think I'm going to have to rethink that. You're looking for something. Can't I look as well?'

Frieda made up her mind. 'All right. This is what I've been pondering. If Liz Barron had been found in her home or on the street, then that would just be Dean Reeve doing what he does, punishing people who get in his way. But when he put her body where he did, he did something different. He was sending a message to me personally. One that only I would understand.'

'Can I make a comment?' said Lola. 'I mean I'd just like to raise something. For the sake of argument.'

'Go on, then.'

'Well, some people would say, not necessarily me, but I'm imagining them, some people would say that you're interpreting a tragedy as being all about you.'

'You mean *wrongly* interpreting?'

'That's what some people might say.'

'Go on.'

'And some people might also say that Liz Barron's murder might not have anything to do with Dean Reeve. Maybe it was a mugging that got out of hand. Maybe it was a jealous boyfriend.' Lola looked nervously at Frieda to see if she was angry, but she just seemed reflective.

'They might say that. So we test the idea,' she said.

'What are you looking for?'

'Murders. In London.'

'What?' said Lola. 'All of them? There must be thousands.'

'There are about a hundred every year. Sometimes a few less, sometimes a few more. And about a quarter of them are committed by friends or family.'

'That's a bit depressing.'

'But it's not surprising. They're the people who love us most and hate us most. Also, we're searching for bodies found recently, not more than a month or so.'

'I'll start looking,' said Lola, and soon there was the sound of tapping from her keyboard. 'Here's one. A teenager was stabbed outside a club in Streatham. He bled to death in the street. He –'

'No,' said Frieda.

'Sorry.' There was more clicking accompanied by the sound of Lola humming to herself. 'A few weeks ago there was a shooting in Tottenham. In a kebab house.'

'No.'

More clicking.

'Shit,' said Lola. 'This man in his fifties was stabbed to death on the Tube. A group of kids were picking on an old man and he intervened and one of them pulled out a knife and stabbed him.'

'That's very sad. But it's not what we're looking for.'

Lola continued talking as she clicked from page to page. 'I've always wondered if I'd get involved. If it works out, then you're a hero, but if you choose the wrong person and they pull a knife and they try to scare you with it but they nick an artery and then . . .'

'Quiet,' said Frieda.

'Sorry. I know I talk too much but –'

'I've found something. Hampstead murders.'

'I read about them. Well, I could hardly miss them. They were everywhere. So why are your murders better than my murders?'

Frieda scanned the article. 'A car plunged into a shop in Hampstead. The man in the car was already dead.'

'I know. Horrible.'

'Then a week later a body was found in a bonfire half a mile away on Hampstead Heath.'

'I'm sorry,' said Lola. 'I may be missing something. There's a body found in a canal, a body found in a car and a body found in a fire. Two are near each other but the third isn't. They don't seem to have much in common.'

'You've already said one thing,' said Frieda. 'Body.'

'Yes, but you're looking at murders. It's not exactly surprising that each of them involves a body.'

'I mean that in each case a dead body was staged in a particular way.'

'Is dumping a body in a canal really staging? Isn't that just one of the things that people do with dead bodies? Bury them. Burn them. Throw them in canals. Sorry. Am I sounding a bit negative? I don't mean to be.'

'Not at all. It's good to ask questions.' Frieda stood up. 'I need to go there,' she said. 'Are you coming?'

An hour later they emerged from Hampstead Tube station and turned right up Heath Street. They quickly reached the boarded-up shopfront of Mamma Mia, where they stopped.

'Must have been a bit of a bang,' said Lola.

Frieda looked up the hill. 'The car came from up there, rolled down the hill.'

'As I say,' said Lola. 'A bit of a bang.'

'Are you enjoying it?' said a woman's voice, from behind her. Frieda and Lola looked round and saw a woman pushing a buggy. On one side of her was a black Labrador puppy and on the other a very small boy. 'Has this become a tourist sight now? Shall I take a photograph of you both in front of it?'

When the woman saw Frieda's face, her expression softened slightly.

'It's not quite like that,' said Frieda. 'I've got a connection with someone who was involved in this.' She paused. 'Were you here when it happened?'

'Yes, I was,' said the woman, abruptly.

Frieda looked at her, at the two children and at the dog. 'I read about you,' she said slowly. 'In the news reports. Charlotte Beck. You were at the scene, you saved that woman's life.'

Charlotte Beck shook her head. 'I can't really remember the details of it. I just remember coming out of the shop with her blood on me and seeing the man's face and wondering why they hadn't covered him up.'

'Why are you here?' said Frieda.

'I've been back every single day since it happened. Sometimes twice a day. But Oscar doesn't mind. You saw it, didn't you, darling?'

Frieda looked at the little boy, who stared back at her.

'You can't imagine what it's like,' said Charlotte, 'when someone is bleeding like that on you. And you're trying to stop it. I see it when I close my eyes. I even smell it.'

Frieda could imagine what it was like, but she didn't reply. Instead she took a small notebook from her pocket and wrote on it and tore it off and gave it to Charlotte. 'I used to talk to people about things like this,' she said. 'This man's a friend of mine and he might be able to help you. In the meantime, try not to come here. You may think it's a help but it probably isn't.'

Charlotte looked at the piece of paper, then back at Frieda. 'What are you actually doing here?' she asked.

'It's complicated. If you feel you need help, call Reuben McGill on this number.'

As Frieda led Lola away up the hill, Charlotte was still staring at the piece of paper.

'Where are we going?' asked Lola. 'Haven't you seen what you came for?'

'That wasn't the important bit.'

'Two people died. That seems pretty important.'

Frieda didn't speak until they arrived at the top of the hill, the Whitestone Pond straight ahead of them, a view across London to their right.

'Nice spot,' said Lola.

Frieda turned around and looked back down the hill. 'Take the car out of gear just here, let it start rolling down the hill, step out of the door.'

'It could have hit anyone,' said Lola. 'Innocent children.'

Frieda turned left across the road, Lola hastening after her. They skirted the edge of the pond and crossed the road again onto the small edge of the Heath that dropped down and away from them.

'There,' said Frieda.

An area down in the gully was still cordoned off with police tape. A section of it had broken off and was flapping in the wind. Frieda walked briskly down towards it. There were still the remains of a bonfire, black on the turf.

'It looks like the day after Guy Fawkes night,' said Lola. She looked across at Frieda. 'If you wanted to do a fire as some sort of a sign, wouldn't you put it at the top of the hill where everyone could see it, rather than hiding it down here?'

'Put your hand on the grass,' said Frieda.

'What do you mean?'

'Just do it.'

Lola knelt down and touched the grass. 'It's wet.'

'Let's walk back up to the road,' said Frieda.

When they got to the pond, Frieda stood looking around.

'So are you going to tell me?' said Lola.

'What?'

'Well, for example, me having to touch the ground. What was that about?'

'Rivers,' said Frieda. 'Up here, where he let the car go, is where the River Fleet starts. It flows down through the Heath and then underground through London to the river at Blackfriars.'

'You mean Fleet as in Fleet Street?'

Frieda smiled. 'Yes. It goes past Fleet Street. And that dampness in the gully – that's where the River Westbourne starts, somewhere down in that damp hollow. It goes through Kilburn and Hyde Park and Chelsea, down to the river at Chelsea Bridge.'

'You think that's why he put the bodies there?'

'Yes.'

'To get your attention?'

'It's a possibility.'

Frieda turned and crossed the road and they walked back down Heath Street towards the Tube station.

'Do you mind if I ask a question?' said Lola.

'Anything.'

'Why did he choose the people he chose? I don't mean Liz Barron, I mean the other two.'

'I don't know.'

'But you think he chose them for a reason?'

'Perhaps.'

'Just one more thing. You think that this Dean Reeve put a dead body on the source of the River Fleet, right? And another dead body on the source of the River Westbourne, right?'

'Yes.'

'Then why did he put a second body on the Westbourne? Why one on one and two on the other?'

Frieda stopped suddenly and looked at Lola with a curious expression. 'Now that's a really good question,' she said. 'And I've no idea what the answer is. But there's a bigger question.'

'What?'

But Frieda didn't answer. She was striding ahead, so that Lola struggled to keep up with her. She had a stitch and her boots were pinching her feet. She'd had enough of walking, of staring at pipes and canals and boarded-up shops, of being hungry and cold and lost, of the whole psychogeography thing.

'Can't we have coffee first?' Lola said. 'Get warm. And that's another thing. I'm hungry. My blood sugar's low.'

'It's not far.'

'I've got blisters. Can't you slow down a bit?'

Nineteen

DCI Selby, in charge of the investigation into the murder of Liz Barron, squinted in puzzlement at the letter that had been delivered to the station earlier that day. It had no stamp on it and was hand-written, but its message was clear enough.

He sighed and picked up the phone. When he was put through to Bill Dugdale he came straight to the point. 'It's Matt Selby here. I've had an anonymous letter. It says that the person who killed Liz Barron was Dean Reeve.'

'What the fuck?'

'I know.'

'But why are you telling me?'

'This is the thing –' Selby's tone was almost apologetic '– it also says that Dean Reeve is behind your Hampstead murders.'

There was a pause. Selby could hear a snorting sound at the other end of the line.

'It's crap, right?' said Dugdale.

'Probably.'

Both men were silent for a few seconds, then Dugdale said, 'We get mad letters like that all the time.'

'Anyway, I thought you'd want to know.'

'I'd better take a look.' Dugdale sounded tired and gloomy.

'Someone's scanning it in right now.'

Dugdale ended the call and leaned back in his chair. He needed coffee. He needed something to eat. He needed a shower and a walk in the country. Anything but this. He remembered something Karlsson had said and made another call.

'Dan? You met Liz Barron.'

'Did I?'

The words were too loud and then Quarry gave several hacking coughs that sounded artificial to Dugdale. He frowned at the phone. 'Yes, you did.'

'Oh, yes, she was with Karlsson. *Met* is putting it a bit strongly.'

'It seems to me that when a high-profile journalist you recently encountered is found murdered, you would remember it a bit more clearly.'

'I do remember,' said Quarry. He gave his cough once more. 'I just –' He stopped.

'You should have mentioned it.'

'I didn't think it was relevant.'

'You should have mentioned it,' Dugdale repeated. 'You don't get to decide what's relevant.'

'I'm sorry.'

Dugdale squeezed the top of his nose between his thumb and forefinger and shut his eyes. 'One more thing.'

'Yes?'

'It's probably nothing.'

'OK.'

'I just got a call from Matt Selby, who's in charge of the Liz Barron murder. He's got a letter – likely a crank letter, mind – that says she was killed by Dean Reeve.'

'Fuck.'

'Quite. But this letter also says Reeve killed our two.' He heard Quarry's excited intake of breath and frowned. 'I said it was probably nothing.'

Half an hour later, there was a knock and Phelps put his head around Dugdale's door.

'Yes?'

'Something you might be interested in.' The words were

casual but Phelps looked excited. There were small blotches on his pale, thin cheeks.

'Take a seat. What is it?'

'Your man went missing on September the twenty-ninth.'

'He was reported missing then. He was last seen on September the twenty-sixth.'

'OK. So I've been going through the computer.'

'Yes.'

'The last searches were done on October the first and second.'

'What?'

'I said –'

'I know what you said.' Dugdale rose from his chair, suddenly not tired any longer. 'Get me Quarry. And a car.'

'I don't understand,' said Sarah Kernan. She was wearing grey trousers and a jumper that was far too big for her. Dugdale guessed it had belonged to her husband: over the years, he had become used to bereaved people wearing their loved one's clothes.

'No,' he replied. 'I don't either. Who knew his passwords?'

'Well, anyone who went into his study,' she said. 'He kept the notebook with them in on his desk. I told him that was stupid but he was stubborn like that.'

'October the first and second were a Saturday and Sunday. Wouldn't you be at home then?'

'I work at a garden centre,' said Sarah Kernan. 'They're our busiest days. I work from eight till six.'

'Do you have secure locks?'

'I double-lock the door, if that's what you mean.' She gazed at him, her eyes dark with fear. 'Front and back. And the windows are locked. We had a break-in ten years ago and since then I've been extra careful.'

'Who else has a key?'

'A key?'

'Yes.'

'My son,' she said.

'Who was at university?'

'Yes. And my neighbour has a spare.'

'Your neighbour?'

'Eleanor Prentice. She's in her late seventies and recently widowed. She comes and waters the plants if we're away.'

'No one else?'

'No. Oh, maybe my sister does. I gave her one ages ago to use in emergency, but there haven't been any emergencies.' She gave a stifled sob.

Quarry was taking notes. He looked up, his eyes bright. 'Who did your patio?'

'The patio?' Her voice cracked.

'Yes. The last time we were here you mentioned that a man was doing it.'

She looked at Quarry dully, but didn't answer.

'This man. Did he have a key?' Dugdale leaned towards her. 'Mrs Kernan?'

'I think so.' The words came out muffled. 'I think Geoff might have given him one.'

'What's his name?'

'Barry,' said Sarah Kernan. Her voice had thickened; she sounded as though she was about to weep.

'Barry who?'

'I don't know.'

'Think.'

'I don't think I ever knew his last name.'

'Do you have his contact details?'

'No. Geoff found him.'

'How did he find him?'

'I'm not sure. Maybe there was a flier put through our door. But you don't think Barry had anything to do with this?'

'I'm not leaping to any conclusions,' said Dugdale, 'but we need to find out who was using your husband's computer after he disappeared. How long has this Barry been working for you?'

'Three weeks?' said Sarah Kernan, doubtfully. 'Or it could be less than that. He didn't come every day, just when he had spare time. It drove Geoff crazy.' Her voice had weakened. She blew her nose.

'Did you meet him?'

'A few times.'

'Can you describe him?'

'He was just ordinary.'

'White?'

'Yes.'

'Accent?'

'English. London, I think.'

'Young? Old?'

'Neither. My age, maybe. I don't know. I wasn't paying attention.'

'Colour of hair? Of eyes?'

'His hair was very short, almost shaved. Grey, perhaps?' She made it into a question.

'Eyes?'

'Eyes? I've no idea. I mean, he was just working on the patio.'

Dugdale gave a nod to Quarry, who had been tapping on his phone, and Quarry leaned towards her, holding out an image on the small screen. He could feel Dugdale beside him, very still. He could feel his own heart hammering in his chest.

'Is this Barry, Mrs Kernan?' His voice was quiet but there was a crackle of excitement in it.

Sarah Kernan looked at the photo. Without prompting, Quarry used his forefinger and thumb to zoom in.

'I don't know. It might be. Who is he?' she whispered.

'Let's not get ahead of ourselves,' said Dugdale, briskly, before Quarry could answer. 'But I think we need to get your locks changed.'

'Jesus,' hissed Quarry, under his breath, as they left the kitchen 'Fuck. Dean Reeve.'

'Don't get too excited.'

'Dean Reeve. And three murders. This is huge.'

Dugdale nodded glumly. 'The media's going to go mad. Forget about sleep for a while. Tell your wife not to expect you home.' If he saw Quarry wince he showed no sign of it. 'I'm going to call Matt Selby.'

Quarry checked the Kernans' neighbours, showing them a photograph of Dean Reeve that had been altered, so that his hair was cropped short, and asking if they recognized him. Several did, including Eleanor Prentice, the widow in her seventies who lived next door and had several times chatted to him over the fence. One couple seemed to recall a flier he had put through their door as well, but it was weeks ago and they would have thrown it in the recycling bin.

'Widen the search,' said Dugdale, though he had no hope of Reeve being traced this easily. 'And we're going to need more officers.'

Karlsson had almost got used to his feeling of distress. When he was working, when his two children were staying for the weekend, when he was with friends or alone in his flat, he was in its shadow. The only person he could have talked to about this was Frieda; she would have sat quietly and listened, her dark eyes fixed on him, hearing even the things he couldn't say out loud. But, of course, it was Frieda he was anxious about. She had disappeared. Her phone was dead. Her shutters were closed. And now Dugdale had called to say that Dean Reeve was behind the three murders and the feeling of distress had thickened into dread. 'This is becoming big,' Dugdale said. 'There'll be media. Lots of it. But I guess you've been through that before.'

'You don't get used to it,' said Karlsson.

'And there's another thing.'

'What?'

'Those computer searches. That was Dean Reeve.'

'I see.'

'Is there anything you'd like to tell me? Anything that might help the inquiry?'

'I will let you know. If I think of anything.'

Afterwards, Karlsson had thought of something. When he had heard that Dean Reeve had been doing searches on him, a part of him had felt secretly pleased: Reeve had been thinking of him as someone close to Frieda, someone she would turn to and confide in, who might know where she was. But the fact was, he didn't know where she was because she hadn't turned to him and confided in him. He found it painful to accept that she had left without saying goodbye or explaining her plans to him. Which was why, on his day off, he had found himself walking through Regent's Park and up towards Reuben's house.

Reuben McGill had the gauntness, the grey pallor that months of chemotherapy give. There were new lines and creases in his face; his hair was curlier than it used to be. He gave a sardonic grin. 'I've been half expecting you. I've got twenty minutes before I have to be at the Warehouse. Come in.'

Karlsson followed him into the kitchen. There were vodka bottles on the table, and on the floor several tools were laid out on a grubby towel. A cat – Frieda's cat – lay on one of the chairs.

'I didn't know you were coming or I'd have cleared up a bit,' said Reuben, emptying the contents of an ashtray into the bin. 'Coffee? Tea? Something stronger?'

'Coffee will be fine.'

Reuben filled the kettle, then sat opposite Karlsson at the kitchen table, propping his chin on one hand and looking at him with amused curiosity. 'You've come about Frieda.'

'Do you know where she is?' He stopped. 'I suppose if you know you wouldn't tell me. Can you at least tell me if she's all right? What is she doing? When is she coming back?'

'So many questions.' Reuben stood up and poured water over the coffee in the pot. 'No.'

'No?'

'You're right I wouldn't tell you, not if she'd asked me not to, so you might not believe this. I don't know where she is. I don't know how she is. I don't know what her plans are – something to do with Dean Reeve, I assume. I don't know when she's coming back.' He put two mugs of coffee on the table and a bottle of milk. 'Or if she's coming back.'

'She has to come back.' Karlsson spoke before he could stop himself.

There was a silence. They looked at each other; their relationship had always been a wary one, but now with Frieda gone something had shifted.

'Why?' Reuben's tone was unexpectedly kind. 'Because you miss her?'

'Because she might be in danger. I worry that she'll do something reckless.'

'Indeed,' said Reuben. Frieda's recklessness had marked both of their lives.

'And self-destructive. She wouldn't ask for help. She would think she couldn't involve anyone else. I want to tell her that she can. Involve me, I mean.'

'As a police officer?'

'As her friend.'

'Even if it's not strictly legal?'

Karlsson nodded, and Reuben looked at him with an expression that was almost pitying.

'Well,' he continued softly, 'I can't help. God knows I wish I could. But I don't know any more than you do. I don't think anyone does, though of course she might have said something to Josef. You and I just have to do the hardest thing, which is to wait.'

Twenty

'Are you going to tell me why we're here?' Lola had found an old bar of chocolate in her bag and was munching it angrily.

'See the names of the houses?' Frieda gestured. 'Shepherd's Well, Conduit House.'

'So?'

'This is the Tyburn.'

'This road?'

'There's a river underneath us.'

'I still don't get it. Is this just a tour of your hidden rivers?'

'I don't get it either,' said Frieda. 'I thought if I came here I might.' She looked around her.

Lola pushed another square of chocolate into her mouth. 'Why here? Why not some other river? Like –' She floundered, trying to remember what she'd read about Frieda's rivers.

'Because the Tyburn runs between the Fleet and the Westbourne,' Frieda replied. 'Two rivers don't make a pattern. Three would. Why would Dean miss out this one?'

Lola grimaced. 'You mean, when you put yourself in the mind of a psychopathic murderer, you'd kill someone just here.'

'Yes.'

'But Dean didn't. Where are we going now?'

'This road is the course. You can see it and feel it.'

'You may be able to. I can't.'

They walked downhill, between the tall, red-brick houses, Frieda glancing constantly from side to side.

'Are you looking for a body?' asked Lola. 'I think someone would have noticed.'

'I know you're angry,' said Frieda. 'And I can understand why. You're probably feeling scared as well. But if you're going to be with me, try to concentrate on what we're doing. Like this.'

She had stopped just before a small row of shops: a florist, a wine shop, a small café. Propped against the wall was a white-painted bike. Even its leather saddle, its handlebars, pedals and chain were white. In its basket was a shrivelled bouquet of flowers.

'There must have been a hit-and-run,' said Lola.

Frieda looked up and down the road. 'You wanted a coffee.'

The café had only four tables, two of which were occupied. Frieda ordered tea for herself and a cappuccino for Lola. 'Do you want something to eat?' she asked.

'The flan looks nice.'

'Good, and I'll have the soup.'

The woman serving came across.

'That ghost-bike outside?' Frieda asked, after she had ordered. 'What happened?'

'A hit-and-run. He was found in the early morning by a passing motorist, lying on the road with his bike beside him.'

'Who was he?'

'I don't know. Just a random cyclist.'

'When did it happen?'

'When?' She seemed rather surprised at Frieda's interest. 'I can't remember exactly. It would have been a Thursday because it was my day off and I didn't hear about it until the next day.'

'Last week? The week before? Or before that?'

'Why do you want to know?'

'We're looking into road safety,' said Lola, brightly. 'For cyclists, that is. Was he wearing a helmet?'

'It must have been October the sixth. I don't know about the helmet.'

'October the sixth,' repeated Frieda, softly. 'That would be about right.'

'About right for what?' asked Lola, once the woman had left.

'Geoffrey Kernan was found on October the third, near the source of the Fleet, Lee Samuels on October the tenth, near the source of the Westbourne. This man was found on October the sixth, by the source of the Tyburn, which lies between those two rivers.'

'I hope you don't mind me saying, but I think there's a technical term for this. In fact, I know there is because we had a lecture about it, although I can't remember the name. Aren't you doing that thing we're told never to do of looking for any evidence that will fit your theory and ignoring everything else?'

Frieda nodded at her approvingly. 'Perhaps,' she said. 'Or you could say that I have a hypothesis and I'm testing it.'

'And your hypothesis is that Dean Reeve is working his way along the rivers as a sign to you?'

'Yes.'

'There is still that question of why two bodies were found on the same river.'

'Perhaps he wanted to make quite sure they weren't missed, the way this one seems to have been. And he chose Liz Barron to make doubly certain.'

The food arrived. Lola sank her knife into the soft, wobbly flan and gave a sigh of satisfaction. 'Isn't it great that even when things are crap you always know you can have a comforting meal?'

'Gerald Hebb,' said Frieda, reading from the computer later that day. 'Forty-three. Victim of a hit-and-run and found on October the sixth.'

'So nothing we didn't already know,' said Lola.

She had insisted on stopping at the shops on the way back and was now energetically cutting up aubergines and courgettes.

'Not yet.'

'You've only got one knife for cutting and it's blunt. And you still don't have any black pepper. Black pepper is essential, don't you think? If you had to choose three spices on your desert island, what would they be? Mine would be ginger, black pepper and cinnamon.'

'The inquest is tomorrow. I need to go to that.'

Lola threw the aubergine into a pan and wiped her palms down her trousers. 'Don't you ever get tired of thinking about it?'

'Lola.' Frieda lifted her eyes from the computer screen. 'I have no choice.'

'I thought psychotherapists say that you always have a choice.'

'Usually that's true. But I ran out of them.'

'When your partner was killed?'

'Sandy wasn't my partner.'

'That must have been like a nightmare.'

'Yes.'

'Have you recovered?'

'Recovered?' Frieda turned her gaze on Lola.

'Yes,' Lola ploughed on. 'I mean, are you over it?'

'I don't think one gets over things exactly. Do you?'

'It's just an expression.'

'I think that the dead are always with us.'

'Oh,' said Lola, doubtfully. 'Well, I don't know about that.'

'My friend Josef says that his dead wife comes to him in his dreams and it is his duty to be hospitable to her.'

'I met him, I think. Sad brown eyes.'

'That's Josef.'

'Frieda.' Lola stopped chopping. 'How long is all this going to last?'

'I don't know. It won't be long.'

'How do you know?'

'I just know.'

'Don't you miss your old life?'

Frieda turned her face away, staring out of the window at the darkening sky. But she didn't speak.

Josef unlocked Frieda's front door. He switched on the light, stooped and picked up the envelopes on the mat, then unlaced his boots and slid them off. He hung his jacket on the hook next to Frieda's coat. He stood for a few seconds in the hall, listening. Then he went into the living room. The chess pieces still stood on the board where she had left them. He had twisted sheets of newspaper into tight balls, the way he had seen her do so many times, and laid them in the fireplace with kindling stacked on top, and he had fetched more logs and put them in the basket, ready for when she returned. He took the orange dahlias that he had brought into the kitchen and put them in the vase, throwing away the old flowers. He ran a cloth over the surfaces, took a dead fly from the windowsill, watered the pot of basil.

Josef came to Frieda's house several times a week. He

dusted and cleaned; he moved around the house quietly, slowly, ready to notice any change, making sure everything was ready for when she decided to come home.

But today was different. When he had performed his normal routine, he went to the kitchen and took two tumblers from one cupboard and a bottle of whisky from another. The bottle was only about a quarter full. He made a mental note to replace it, and if he was going to replace it then this needed drinking up. He poured a finger of whisky into one glass and then another finger into the second glass for himself, then looked at it and decided it wasn't enough and poured a second finger. That was more like it. He took the two drinks and the bottle through to the living room and sat in an armchair. He took a gulp and waited.

He had emptied the glass, refilled it and emptied that one by the time the doorbell rang. It was Chloë. She came in and saw the two glasses on the table.

'For you,' said Josef.

'For a moment I thought Frieda was here.'

She picked up the glass, clinked it against Josef's and had a sip. 'When you invited me here,' she said, 'my first hope was that Frieda would have come back, though of course I knew she hadn't. And my second hope was that you would tell me where she is, or what the hell she's up to.'

'I do not know.'

'If anyone knows, it's you, Josef.'

He shook his head. 'And, anyway, even to know where she is is dangerous maybe.'

'Fucking Dean Reeve.'

All of Josef's attention seemed to be focused on the problem of refilling his glass. When he was done he gestured towards Chloë's.

'No, thanks. I want to keep my thoughts clear,' she said.

'Josef, if you thought Frieda had some kind of death wish, if you thought she was going to let herself be killed by Dean Reeve as a way of getting him to stop, you'd prevent her, wouldn't you?'

Josef was looking round the room, seeming to pay no attention, but then he turned to her. 'How?'

'By telling her. By telling *us*. By protecting her. By kidnapping her, if necessary.'

'I do not know where she is.'

Chloë looked at Josef through narrow, suspicious eyes. 'So Frieda isn't here,' she said. 'And you're not going to tell me anything about her or what her plans are. So why are *we* here? To steal her whisky?'

Josef looked indignant. 'I buy new bottle. But we are not here to drink. Come.'

Chloë followed Josef as he walked up the stairs to the first floor and then to the second. He stood in front of a window in the rear wall of the house, just below the garret room in the roof. 'Look,' he said.

Chloë stepped to the window. 'At what, specifically?'

'You like view?'

The window looked out on the blank back wall of an office building. But it was only two storeys high. Above it you could see the jagged London skyline to the south, the BT Tower, church spires. 'It's all right. What about it?'

Josef pointed downwards. 'You see roof?'

It was the flat roof of the bathroom on the floor below. 'Yes.'

'It feel bad, coming here, coming here, coming here, just picking up mail and watering plants. We do a surprise for Frieda.'

'What kind of surprise?' asked Chloë, warily.

Josef waved his hands as if he were conjuring with them.

'Take window away, put door here. Make balcony there on roof. The wood decking, the railings. A place to sit in the evening, to sit, to drink.' He looked round at Chloë with an enquiring expression.

'Have you thought of running this by Frieda?' she asked.

'Is not possible.'

'Exactly.'

'I tell you it's a surprise.'

Chloë frowned. 'Why are you telling me about it?'

'You make things. Like me. We do this together.'

'All right,' said Chloë. 'Before I get into my manual-labourer role, I just want to make a couple of observations. I'm not sure that Frieda likes surprises.'

'I surprise her before. With the bath. She was happy with that.'

Josef had indeed previously rebuilt Frieda's bathroom without telling her in advance.

Chloë looked doubtful. 'She was happy in the end. I'm not sure she enjoyed the actual process so much.'

'She not here for process. Is perfect.'

There was a long pause.

'I just can't stop thinking,' Chloë said, 'about what Frieda would say if she knew we were in her house doing something like this without her permission.'

'But she is not here.'

Another pause before Chloë spoke again. 'I suppose we should check the roof. If it's strong, we can put a platform on top.'

Josef shook his head. 'We need beams.'

'Beams? That sounds like a big job.'

'No, no,' said Josef. 'Beams. Door here. Platform. Railing. All done.'

'It's easy to say the words.'
'Think of us standing there. With drink. In evening.'
Chloë thought of it but didn't reply.

Not far away, a man sat by a river in the dusk, whistling through his teeth, patiently waiting for a fish to bite.

Twenty-one

Quarry knocked at the door of 39 Launceston Crescent and waited, ID in hand. He heard a sound, faint at first but then louder. A baby was crying. No, yelling. It hurt to listen even through the closed door.

Then the door swung open and the yelling became like a fire alarm. Quarry held out his ID to a thin, exhausted-looking woman, who was holding a large baby. Its mouth was opened so wide it almost swallowed the whole of its red, angry face. Attached to one of the young mother's legs was a small boy. He'd seen the tired look that was on her face before. It reminded him of the period when the woman he'd married had become the woman he'd let down, the woman he argued with, the woman he found any excuse to avoid going home to.

'Charlotte Beck?' asked Quarry, raising his voice to be heard.

'I can't help it if she cries all night. What do they want me to do?'

'Who are they?'

'The neighbours,' Charlotte Beck crooned, rocking her slightly.

The baby looked too large for her mother's slight frame, and writhed in her arms so wildly that Quarry was scared she would fling herself to the floor. 'The neighbours haven't complained. At least not to me.'

'Then why are you here?'

'Can I come in?'

Charlotte stepped back to admit him. 'I haven't had time to clear up.'

She walked down the hall, her daughter howling over her shoulder and her son still attached to her leg so she dragged her foot along the floor, like a convict in chains. She was right that the living room was a mess – it looked as if there'd been an explosion in a toy factory, with wooden bricks and plastic figures and soft toys flung in all directions.

Charlotte Beck lowered herself into a chair with both children still stuck to her.

'I'm here about the incident in Hampstead.'

'I don't think there's anything I can add.'

The little boy was now trying to climb onto his mother's lap, pushing away his howling sister as he did so.

'I'm hungry,' the little boy said.

'In a minute.'

'I want to show you something,' said Quarry. He pulled the photograph of Dean Reeve out of his bag and held it up. The baby made a grab for it. Her crying was getting softer, full of hiccups and rasping breaths now.

'Have you seen this man before?' asked Quarry.

Charlotte Beck peered at it. 'Who is he?'

'Where have you seen him?'

'He looks like one of the people who was there. When it all happened.' She leaned closer. 'Yes, it's him.'

'You say he was there?'

'He came and talked to me after it had all calmed down. I was in a bit of a daze and there was blood all over me and he sat on the pavement beside me and told me I'd done well. I wasn't thinking straight. I was all over the place.' She looked around her. 'I mean more all over the place than usual. He helped me get home. He walked me almost to the front door. He seemed nice. Why are you asking? Who is he?'

'Did he tell you his name?'

'I don't think so. Or wait.' She frowned in concentration.

144

Her daughter had stopped crying and her eyelids were beginning to close. Her head lay heavily on Charlotte Beck's shoulder. 'Dave, I think. Or David.'

Quarry nodded. On the statement he had given, he had said his name was Dave McGill.

'Why?' asked Charlotte Beck again.

'Just someone we need to contact,' said Quarry, sliding the photo back into his pocket. 'I'll let myself out. I don't want to wake your daughter now she's asleep.'

Charlotte Beck gave a tired laugh. 'You don't need to worry about her. She'll sleep for hours and wake up all fresh and ready for the night.'

'Yes,' said Constable Darren Symons. 'That looks like one of the witnesses. I took his statement. What was his name?'

'Dave McGill?' suggested Quarry.

'That's it. He was the one who said he thought there was something odd about the whole set-up. You got to hand it to him, he was on to it before any of us were.'

'He was,' agreed Quarry. 'Way before.'

Frieda and Lola were able to walk almost the whole way to St Pancras Coroner's Court along the canal.

'Don't you ever think, sod it, I'm going to jump on a Tube?' said Lola, as they walked along the stretch in the middle of the zoo.

'Walking is how I think,' said Frieda. 'When I'm alone.'

'Am I stopping you thinking?'

'You mean at this very moment?'

'At this moment you're having to answer my questions. I mean in general. While I'm staying with you.'

'I'm not doing much thinking. I'm just waiting.'

'Maybe you're both just waiting for each other.'

'We'll see.'

Lola looked up at the giant aviary. 'I've never been to the zoo. Isn't that strange?'

'Neither have I.'

'That's insane. You only live a few minutes away. Why not?'

'I don't like seeing things in cages.'

'Maybe it's better to be in a cage than to go extinct.'

'Maybe.'

'I think that's a jackal,' Lola said. 'What if they don't let us in?'

'The zoo?'

'The coroner's court.'

'It's a public event. They have to let us in.'

It was just a few minutes' walk from the canal. The building looked almost hidden, like an afterthought bolted onto the side of St Pancras churchyard, surrounded by the railway and the canal and the road leading down to King's Cross and St Pancras stations. Inside the door there was a little lobby area. A middle-aged man was pinning a notice to the wall. He glanced round at the two women.

'We're here for the Gerald Hebb inquest,' Frieda said.

'Are you family?' said the man.

'No.'

'Press?'

'We're just members of the public.'

The man frowned and seemed to be searching for a reason to object but he waved them in the direction of what appeared to be a plain, veneered office door. When they pushed it open, it seemed as if there was something wrong, like a meeting where nobody, or almost nobody, had turned up. At the far side of the small room was a table. A man was sitting behind it, reading an open file. A rotund middle-aged woman was sitting to one side, staring down at her phone. Facing the table were three rows of plastic chairs. Only one of them was occupied.

The man behind the desk frowned at them. 'Are you family?'

'We're just here to observe,' said Frieda.

'In some official capacity?'

'No.'

He seemed puzzled, but not especially interested. 'Well, we'll be beginning soon. We're just waiting for the police to arrive. They're running late.'

Frieda and Lola sat down in the back row, away from everyone.

'So are we looking for a clue?' asked Lola, cheerfully.

'We're looking for something,' said Frieda.

Ten minutes after the inquest was due to start, the door opened and two young uniformed officers came into the room. They made their way through the chairs and sat down in the front row. When the man started to speak it was in a bored tone.

'I'm Dr Charles Mahdawi. I take it there are no family members here.' He gave a very short pause. 'For the sake of the two ladies who are here to observe the proceedings, I should say that the remit of an inquest is very narrow. We are simply here to answer four questions: who the deceased was, where they died, when they died and how they died. I don't think we'll be detaining you long.' He turned to the two officers. 'Is one of you Sergeant Grady?'

One of the officers stood up and Mahdawi gestured him into a chair next to the table. Grady took a small notebook from his pocket. 'Is it all right if I refer to this, sir?'

'We're very informal here.'

It felt like a routine middle-management meeting as

Mahdawi led the sergeant through his account of how the body of Gerald Hebb had been found beside his bike. The body was face down, half on the pavement and half off, on Downs Road near the corner with Wiltshire Gardens. As the officer spoke, Mahdawi took notes on a pad. Then he opened the file in front of him and started to read extracts aloud.

'Cause of death was a "blow to the back of the base of the skull which resulted in death by cerebral haemorrhage". That is consistent with having been struck by a vehicle. As we have heard, the call reporting the discovery of the body was made at about six twenty in the morning. The report says that the temperature of the body suggested it had been lying there for six to eight hours. All very sad, but it seems to be straightforward enough. I think we can come to a conclusion here.'

'Excuse me.'

Lola was startled, wondering who had spoken and then, with a sinking feeling, realized it was Frieda. Mahdawi looked puzzled.

'Yes?'

'Can I ask a question?'

'I'm sorry, but only properly interested people are entitled to ask questions. That means family.'

'There are no family present.'

'Exactly.'

'I would like to ask the questions that his family would ask.'

Mahdawi took a deep breath and rapped the table several times with his pen. Lola saw that the two police officers and the other man were staring at Frieda with expressions of surprise.

'All right,' Mahdawi said, in an icy tone. 'You can ask a question. First, can you identify yourself?'

'Of course. My name is Ursula –'

But then Frieda halted. She narrowed her eyes, visibly coming to a decision. Lola clutched at her arm: she had a sudden sense of foreboding.

'My name is Dr Frieda Klein.'

'What are you doing?' hissed Lola. 'Don't!' Frieda paid her no attention.

Mahdawi started to write the name down and stopped. 'That sounds familiar. Have you been in this court before?'

'No.'

'All right. What is your question?'

'I'd like to ask the police officer. The autopsy says that Gerald Hebb had been dead for over six hours. Downs Road is fairly busy, isn't it?'

The officer looked distinctly uneasy. 'It was the middle of the night.'

'Yes, but even so, is it conceivable that a body could have lain there, outstretched, in the street with no passer-by, no driver, noticing it?'

'It's what happened.'

'And did you consider what Gerald Hebb, who lives and works in South London, was doing on his bike in the middle of the night up in Hampstead?'

Before the officer could speak, Mahdawi interrupted: 'I said I'd allow you one question. I didn't say you could operate like a barrister. In any case, this is all irrelevant. As I explained, we are here with a prescribed remit. It's not some half-baked investigation.'

'I thought that one part of your remit was to establish where Hebb died,' said Frieda.

'Please don't try to instruct me about my remit. Mr Hebb's body was found in the street next to his bike. There is not the remotest suggestion of any evidence that he died anywhere else.'

'I've already made a suggestion.'

'That's enough,' said Mahdawi. He turned to the officer. 'Thank you for your evidence. The only possible conclusion is that Mr Hebb died by misadventure. That is my verdict. I hereby release the body for burial.' He closed his file and stood up. He looked across at Frieda.

'If you have any other concerns, please address them to the police.'

Twenty-two

'I don't understand why you would do that.'

Lola and Frieda were walking back along the canal. Frieda didn't reply, so Lola continued, gesturing wildly as she spoke, 'You've got another name, another identity. You've dyed your hair and cut it short. And me – I've got to leave my entire life behind. I've got to live like a secret agent. Don't use your phone. Don't contact anyone. Don't let anyone know where you are. And then you announce your identity in court in front of a couple of policemen. That other man in the court looked like he might be a reporter.'

'Yes,' said Frieda. 'He looked like that to me too.'

'Your name will probably be mentioned in the report. Or even in the papers. Dean Reeve will probably see it.'

'Probably.'

'So why did you do it? Was it some kind of rush of blood to the head, like that time you got thrown in prison?'

'Times.'

Lola laughed. 'You mean it happened more than once? Sorry, I wasn't keeping count.'

'I didn't plan to do it,' said Frieda. 'But when I heard that ridiculous account of how they found the body, I had to say something. It probably won't do any good.'

'And what if Dean Reeve sees that you were there?'

'I hope he does.'

'Why?' Lola was practically dancing on the spot, waving her hands in distress. 'I thought we were in danger.'

Frieda stopped and stared down into the water. 'Something

went wrong in staging the Gerald Hebb killing. I don't know what it was. Maybe something was taken from the scene. Maybe he was disturbed when he was dumping the body. His death, which was meant to be a sign, went unnoticed. But the body of Liz Barron was a way of rapping us over the head, telling us to pay attention.'

'You mean rapping *you* over the head.'

'Yes, that's what I mean,' said Frieda. 'And I'm telling him that I'm here, I'm listening.'

They continued walking.

'You know, in my first year, I had this really intense relationship with a guy. I mean the sex . . .' Lola turned to look at Frieda. 'You're a therapist, yes? It's all right to talk to you about sex, isn't it?'

'You can talk about anything you like.'

'Well, it felt like real sex for the first time. You know what I mean?'

'Yes, I know.'

'The problem was that we got into each other's heads. He became obsessed with what he thought I was thinking. He felt he knew me better than I knew myself. He'd be, like, explaining me to me. It may sound sweet and intimate, but it actually became claustrophobic in the end. It just couldn't continue. We still hook up occasionally but that's not the point of what I'm saying. You can see what I'm saying, can't you?'

'I can see it, but I don't think it's a helpful way of looking at it.'

'But the way you talk about him. It's like you understand his messages in a way that nobody else does. And he's doing all this just as a way of communicating with you. It sounds really strange.'

Frieda quickened her stride and spoke without looking at

Lola. 'I've had female patients who were rape victims. I've had female patients who had been stalked. Who had had their lives ruined by it. And without exception they were told by friends, by people who were close to them, by people who were trying to help, that it must have been something they did, that there was some kind of complicity.'

'I've touched a nerve,' said Lola.

'You didn't touch a nerve. You were wrong.'

'But if I think that –'

'Could you do something to help me?' said Frieda.

'Anything. I'm really glad you're asking.'

'Could you be quiet, so I can think?'

'Oh,' said Lola, crestfallen. 'If that's what you want. Although I think that it might help to talk about this.'

'Starting now.'

They walked the whole rest of the way back to the flat in silence and remained in silence as Frieda sliced bread for sandwiches.

'Can I ask a question now?' said Lola.

'What is it?'

'You think that Dean Reeve is sending you a message?'

'Yes.'

'But isn't a message meant to say something? Or is he just saying, "Here I am"?'

Frieda laid slices of cheese across the bread. 'I've been thinking about that.'

Lola brightened. 'So we're thinking alike?'

Frieda took out a pen. On the table was a pile of letters. She picked up one and looked at it. On the front of it was written: 'To the owner'. She put it face down on the table. She drew a line that looked like a snake curving down and up and down.

'That's the Thames,' she said. She drew a line straight up from it. 'That's the Fleet.' She drew another line up from the Thames to the left of the first line. 'That's the Tyburn. Two may not mean anything, but three makes a pattern.' Then she drew another line to the left. 'The Westbourne. Like three spokes on a wheel.'

'What's the next spoke?'

'Another good question.' Frieda drew a further line to the left. 'Counter's Creek.'

'Never heard of it.'

'That's the thing about these rivers. They flow through London and people sit by them and sail on them and dream beside them, and then they get built on and forgotten about. And Counter's Creek is especially forgotten. But it's there. Somewhere.'

Lola leaned over Frieda's diagram. 'So you're right that he's working his way round these secret rivers?'

'It looks that way.'

'What are you actually going to do?'

Frieda smiled and stood up.

'Oh, no,' Lola said. 'I'm feeling sore already. My blister's getting worse.'

'You can stay here.'

'Of course I can't stay here.'

Quarry met Neil Morrell near the ponds on the Heath. The whole area had been dug up and drained recently, and although the grass had grown back quickly, it was still possible to see the scars from the excavation. Morrell had a ponytail and a lined face; his clothes were spattered with mud. He took the photo of Dean Reeve and held it away from him. 'Of course.'

'What do you mean, of course?'

'I used to see him round here quite a bit. He even helped me with that bonfire. He dragged branches across. Said he had time on his hands and he liked to be useful.'

'I see.'

'Why?'

'Just following things up,' said Quarry, vaguely. Dugdale had impressed on him the importance of not mentioning Dean Reeve's name. 'Have you seen him recently?'

'Not for a bit. Who is he?'

'As I say, we're following up leads. If you do see him, please contact us.' He handed over a card.

Frieda and Lola started at the huge Kensal Green cemetery, a riot of different styles, ornamental benches, plastic Greek temples, miniature gates.

'I guess this is the cemetery where you can do anything,' said Lola.

'As long as you pay upfront,' said Frieda. 'I rather like it.' She looked around. 'The river starts somewhere here, but it crosses the canal and the railway. We'll need to walk round.' They went out of the cemetery and along the edge of Worm-wood Scrubs, past the hospital and the prison and then down through a maze of streets that led under the Westway, the traffic rumbling overhead.

'It doesn't feel much like there's a river here,' said Lola.

'You're right. It feels as if they really tried to obliterate this one. They turned it into a sewer and changed its course. Usually you can feel the river somehow. You can see the shape of it, the slopes of the old riverbank, the way it twists and winds. I don't feel Counter's Creek. I never have.'

They managed the awkward crossing of Holland Park Avenue, just by the huge, noisy roundabout. Frieda led them into a small side road and gestured up at the sign: Clearwater

Terrace. 'That name is the only faint memory of the river, the whole way, and it's not enough.'

A few minutes later she pointed out to Lola that they were walking along the side of a railway. 'It's where the river used to flow.'

Lola started to speak but Frieda just shook her head. A little while later they were in the heart of Chelsea, white-stucco houses, heavy four-wheel-drive cars, coffee shops and delicatessens. Frieda stopped and shook her head. 'I'm lost,' she said.

'You've got your phone,' said Lola.

'I don't mean that. I mean the river. I don't know where it is.'

Lola looked around. 'We're not likely to see Dean Reeve fishing anywhere near here.'

Frieda's expression hardened. 'Don't joke about it. We'll just make for the Thames.'

'Is that it?' said Lola. 'It doesn't even look like a stream.'

They were standing on the little bridge, looking down at the creek. Now, at low tide, it was mainly wet mud, with a few rivulets trickling down towards the Thames, a couple of hundred yards away. They crossed to the other side, away from the river. This stub of the creek looked abandoned and forgotten and shut away, with a builders' yard on one side, a car park on the other. They gazed down on mud, dumped tyres, rusting shopping trolleys and bikes.

'Is this what's left of Counter's Creek?' said Lola.

'Yes,' said Frieda. 'This is the place.'

Chloë arrived at the pub late and saw Josef sitting in the corner, waving her over. As she sat down, she saw that there was a man with him. He had rings in both ears, a pierced eyebrow, long hair tied in a knot on the top of his head. His short-sleeved Arsenal shirt revealed full tattoo sleeves. His face was lined and weathered.

'This is my friend Stefan,' said Josef. 'He help us.'

'I know Stefan,' said Chloë. 'You were both bouncers at that party I had.'

'That is right.'

Chloë and Stefan nodded warily at each other. Josef produced a piece of paper from his pocket and unfolded it on the table.

'The balcony,' said Chloë. 'I thought you'd forgotten about it.'

The pencil sketch showed it from above and from the side. 'So the beams go right back into the house,' she said.

'Naturally.'

'I thought it was going to be simple.'

'Simple, but also strong. And safe.'

'So these are wooden beams.'

'Steel.'

'And wooden decking.'

'Yes.'

'And wooden railings.'

'Which you can make, I think.'

'Of course. It's what I do. But have you costed this, Josef? This is expensive stuff.'

'Is not problem.'

'What is the cost of the materials? These steel beams?'

'There is no cost.'

Chloë looked at Josef, then at Stefan and back at Josef. 'Wait,' she said. 'Wait one minute.' She went to the bar and bought a pint of Hedgehog bitter and brought it to the table. She took a gulp of the beer. 'These steel beams,' she said. 'This decking. They're not actually stolen, are they?'

Josef and Stefan exchanged glances.

'They are leftovers,' said Josef.

'Leftovers?'

'Leftovers.'

Chloë looked back at the plans. 'Just tell me about the railings,' she said. 'I'll pretend I didn't ask about anything else.'

Twenty-three

Lola was playing her harmonica with gusto. Through the clamour of split notes, Frieda made out the vestiges of a tune. 'That's Christmas music.'

'I thought if I practised enough I could play it to people then. It's only two months away. Do you recognize it?'

'"Good King Wenceslas"?'

'That's it! Maybe I picked it because, in a way, it's like you and me. I mean, you're like Wenceslas and I'm like the boy who had to follow in his footsteps to keep safe when the snow lay round about. If you see what I mean.' She gave a long high blast on the harmonica. 'What do you think?'

'I think a little goes a long way.'

Lola looked at her with a hurt expression. 'At least I'm trying to keep occupied. What am I supposed to do here?'

'You could think of another idea for your dissertation.'

'The original one seems to be going all right. "In the Footsteps of Dr Klein". Or would that be violating your privacy? Honestly, if you don't want me to do it, I won't.'

'To be candid, I'm not really thinking of that at the moment.'

'I'm going to miss the deadline anyway. I think we should go and see a film.' Lola threw down her harmonica. 'I don't care what it is. Where's the nearest cinema?'

'We're not going to a cinema.'

'Let's go to a pub.'

'Lola –'

'I know what that means. *Lola.* That patient, suffering voice. *Lola. Silly Lola.*'

'It doesn't mean that at all.'

'I've had it all my life. *Oh, it's just Lola being Lola. Never mind her.*'

'All your life?'

'You'll call me "sweetheart" next.' Tears stood in Lola's eyes. 'I'm not a child. Don't talk to me as if I were one. I've been ripped out of everything I know and I'm scared and I'm confused and I'm bored and I don't know what I'm supposed to be doing. Why shouldn't we go out? You've blown our cover. Why are we safer here than anywhere else? I want to see a film. I want to do something ordinary.'

'Sit down,' said Frieda, gently.

'I don't want to.' Lola sniffed hard. 'I want to go home.'

'Where's home?'

'I don't know. Maybe I don't have a home, but if I do, it's somewhere that's not here, where you don't even have flour in the cupboard. I can't even make a cake.' She gave a hiccuping sound, halfway between a giggle and a sob.

'This isn't going to last long.'

'If we aren't going out, maybe we can play cards. I brought a pack with me. Oh, don't tell me you don't like card games. I knew it.'

'I could teach you how to play chess.'

'Chess?'

'Yes.'

'My dad used to play chess with his friend. He never taught me, though. He said it was too mathematical.'

Frieda looked at her intently. 'You could be good at it. But you have to learn to plan several moves ahead, consider all the different possibilities.'

Lola pulled a face. 'I'm not playing if it's going to be a lesson in how to be a better, wiser person.'

An hour later, when they had put away the chess set and Frieda was standing by the window, gazing out at the water as if she could see faces in it, Lola asked, 'You're always staring out of the window. What are you thinking about?'

Frieda turned. 'I was thinking about what the four victims have in common. Or, rather, the three – Liz Barron is different. But why did Dean Reeve choose the others, unless it was random?'

'Maybe they just got in his way.'

'Yes. Maybe. But I'm trying to find something that distinguishes them.'

'What kind of thing?'

'I don't know.'

'Like a birthmark, you mean, or a mysterious scar?'

'No, I don't mean that.'

'Or perhaps they're all born on a leap year, or have the same birthday.'

'They don't.'

'Or they were all born in the same tiny village. Or –'

'Lola.'

Frieda walked across and sat down close to her.

'I know,' said Lola. 'You're going to tell me to shut up.'

'No, I'm not. I'm interested.'

'But I'm just talking rubbish,' said Lola.

'Talking rubbish can be good. It can be a way of thinking.'

'All right.' Lola rubbed her head, like it was helping her to think. 'There just doesn't seem to be anything special about them. They do boring sorts of jobs. One of them is married.

One of them isn't. They live in different places. They're different ages.'

'Start with the first.'

'Why?'

'Geoffrey Kernan was killed in Barking. That's Dean Reeve's part of London, or near it, anyway. It's where he grew up, where he lived. Maybe he killed Kernan for a reason. Maybe Kernan knew him or found out something about him. But then he found out something he could use.'

There was a long, long silence.

'I don't really know what you mean,' said Lola.

The silence resumed. It was several minutes before Lola spoke again. 'He seems really ordinary and dull. The only weird thing was his name.'

'What? Kernan?'

'No. Didn't you see the report? His middle name. Udo. I read in the paper that his wife said he was very proud of it. He used to say that to most people he was Geoffrey, but there was a hidden, Udo-bit of him. *Udo* – what kind of name is that, anyway?'

'It's German,' said Frieda. 'He's probably got a German relative.'

'Like Frieda,' said Lola.

'Yes, like Frieda,' and then she stopped. She stared at Lola, unblinking.

'Udo,' she muttered. 'Udo.'

'Shall I make tea? And what are we going to have for supper? Not scrambled eggs, or poached eggs or omelettes. Something less snacky and make-do. We could cook a chicken and watch a film on my laptop, something cheerful. Then we can have chicken sandwiches tomorrow, with lots of mayonnaise and some tomatoes, which is my favourite thing. Comfort food.'

'Pass me your computer.'

Lola slid it across to her and Frieda bent over the keyboard. Lola saw how her eyes glowed darkly; she felt obscurely scared and folded her arms around herself.

'Roast chicken with garlic bread,' she murmured to herself. Her head was throbbing.

Frieda typed in names and found the website she wanted. 'Yes,' she said, after a long pause during which Lola wanted to scream.

'What?'

'Come and see.'

Together they looked at the calendar on the screen, a square for each day and several names in each square.

'This shows name days,' said Frieda. 'We're looking at October.'

'But –'

'Sssh. Look. October the third. Do you see?'

'Ewald,' read Lola. 'Paulina. Bianca. Oh.' She stopped, then said, 'Udo.'

'Yes. And the body of Geoffrey Udo Kernan was found on October the third. Now look at October the sixth, when the body of Gerald Hebb was found.'

'Bruno, Adalbero, Melanie, Brunhild, Gerald.'

'And on the tenth there's Samuel for Lee Samuels.'

'What about Liz Barron? Are we meant to look for an Elizabeth name day? Or a Barron?'

'That was different. That was what he does to people who go after him. Or think they understand him.'

'You seem to understand him,' said Lola. 'And you're going after him.'

Frieda looked at her. Lola always found that direct gaze almost unbearable. 'You think I'm going after him?' she said. 'How can I possibly?'

'But what does it mean, then? I don't get it. Is it just, I don't know, a way of showing off?'

'There's another name to look at.'

'What other name? There hasn't been anyone else.'

'Look ahead. At October the nineteenth.'

Lola read the names out: 'Isaac. Paul.' And then she saw.

'That's right. Frieda. My name day.'

'October the nineteenth. That's the day after tomorrow.'

'Yes.'

'No. *No!* We have to go to the police. We have to go *now*. This minute. We should have gone before. Please.'

Lola stood up and actually tried to tug at Frieda, but Frieda simply smiled at her and disengaged herself. 'It's OK.'

'How can it possibly be OK? This has gone far enough. You're mad.'

'This is the message I've been waiting for. Now at last I can act.'

'Act? How can you act? What can you do? All you can —' Lola stopped and her mouth hung open in shock. 'Oh, no, Frieda. Don't tell me. You can't.'

'October the nineteenth at Counter's Creek. That's what he's telling me.'

'You're crazy. I can't listen to this. I should never have listened. No.' Lola put her hands to her ears and squeezed her eyes shut. She looked like a terrified toddler, thought Frieda.

She stood and crossed to her, putting her hands on Lola's shoulders. Lola let her arms drop and opened her eyes.

'Don't you see?' said Frieda, in a soft voice. 'Dean has murdered four people in order to give me this message. Four lives wiped out. You think I shouldn't go because I don't want to lose mine?'

'Of course I think that. Any sane person would. The

police can catch him. Tell them everything you've worked out and let them do their job. You can hide until it's over.'

'It won't be over until I end it.'

'I don't believe you. I don't believe you at all. I don't want to be here. I don't want to have found you. I want to be doing a boring dissertation on recent advances in DNA fingerprinting and drinking with my friends and getting irritated because I've dyed my favourite white shirt pink in the wash.'

'You did find me.'

'Please don't go to Counter's Creek. Please, Frieda.'

Frieda took her hands off Lola's shoulders and took a step back. 'People have been killed because of me. Do you think I value my life so highly that I can let that go on happening? Do you think I'm prepared to put people in danger, people who are strangers and also people I love, just because I'm scared?'

'But I don't think you *are* scared,' said Lola. 'I think you've got a death wish.'

'I don't have a death wish.'

'You don't have a life wish.'

'I have a niece,' said Frieda, and as she spoke she saw Chloë's face in her mind: stubborn, angry, needy. 'She's about your age. We've been through many things together. Not long ago a Dean-Reeve copycat drugged and abducted her.'

'I read about that.'

'Yes. When that happened, when I understood that because of me she had been put in danger, I knew that I would do anything to stop him. There has been too much damage, too much loss. I have no intention of dying, but I'm not scared of it. I *am* scared of being the cause of other people's death.'

'But –'

'I will not.' Frieda lifted up clenched fists, then let them fall. 'Do you hear me? This has to end. I have to end it.'

'So you're just going to go there? Do you have a gun?'

'Of course I don't have a gun.'

'Can you get one? You must know people who could help you with that. Do you know how to use one?'

'Lola, I'm not going to get a gun.'

'What, then?'

'I don't know.'

'That's your plan?'

Chloë and Jack were sitting in an Italian restaurant eating spaghetti and drinking red wine; once they'd been lovers and now they were learning to be friends.

Josef and Reuben were in Reuben's house. Josef was cooking a Ukrainian lamb dish, a bottle of vodka at his elbow; he was humming something under his breath. Reuben, wearing his Moroccan dressing-gown and with spectacles perched on the end of his nose, was reading a book about contemporary forms of mourning. Every so often, he raised his head and stared into space, thinking. Upstairs, Josef's son Alexei was playing a computer game with a new friend, the first child he'd invited back since he had started school.

Chloë's mother Olivia – Frieda's sister-in-law – was on a first date with a man she had met on the bus a few days previously; she watched him as he stood at the bar, loudly ordering drinks, and wondered what on earth she was doing there, what on earth she was doing with her life.

Karlsson was reading to his daughter Bella, who leaned her head on his shoulder as he turned the pages. Her hair tickled his cheek and he could feel her warmth. He would have been happy except Frieda was gone. He wondered where she was now, what she was thinking.

It was dark and clouds obscured the moon. The wind blew in gusts. The tide rose in the Thames and soon water covered the mud of Counter's Creek. Small waves slapped against the bank.

Twenty-four

Frieda looked at her watch. 'Time to go.'

'You know the day,' said Lola. 'At least you think you know the day. But you don't know what time you're meant to go there.'

'I'll just go there and wait.'

'Can I come?' said Lola.

'Of course you can't,' said Frieda.

'I could stay at a safe distance.'

'There's no such thing as a safe distance.'

'Can't I help in some way?'

'You can stay here.'

'And what? Wait to hear about it on the news?'

'You've got the phone I gave you.'

'Yes.'

'I'll be back or I'll phone you.'

'Or?'

'If you haven't heard anything . . .' Frieda thought. 'By the time it gets dark, phone the police. Or better still –' She took a notepad from her paper, wrote on it and tore out the page, handing it to Lola. 'Ring Malcolm Karlsson. He's a detective. And he's a friend. He'll think of something.'

'Why not ring him now?'

'Enough,' said Frieda. 'Just do as I say.'

'Don't go,' said Lola. She started to cry, large tears that rolled smoothly down her cheeks. 'Don't go, Frieda.'

'Remember what I told you about Karlsson.'

Frieda would have liked to walk but for once she

decided the distance was too great and that it would take too long. Instead she walked to the main road and hailed a taxi.

DCI Dugdale was rechecking a set of witness statements when a young female officer came into his office without knocking. She was out of breath.

'There's a call for you,' she said.

'What's it about?' he said, without looking up.

'It's about the murders.'

He tossed the file aside. 'There are a thousand calls about the murders.'

'You'll want to take this one.'

During the long drive across London, Frieda didn't look out of the window. She barely even thought. She just sat with her eyes closed and felt a sort of calm, a finality. The traffic was heavy through Hyde Park and Kensington, and Frieda looked at her watch once or twice, but it didn't matter much. It would wait. He would wait. She directed the taxi to drop her on the King's Road, just a short walk up from the Chelsea Embankment. She walked down to the river and leaned for a few minutes on the railings, looking down at the water. The tide was coming in, with fierce currents and swirls. A tourist boat passed. Two small children standing at the stern of the boat gazed directly across the water at Frieda and waved. She waved back and they laughed. She turned and walked along the embankment with the river on her left, then turned away from the river, following Lots Road along the side of the creek. She reached the spot where she had stood with Lola. Now what? She knew the place, she knew the day, but she didn't know the exact time. It was just a matter of waiting.

She looked around at the plush office buildings of Chelsea Harbour. This didn't feel like Dean Reeve's territory. He belonged further east, to the London of Poplar and the River Lea and the Isle of Dogs. She might have expected somewhere more remote, more secluded, darker. But it was bright, sunlit. It wasn't crowded, but it wasn't isolated either. As she leaned over the railings, looking into the creek – now swollen with the high tide – she was passed by a woman pushing a buggy, by a man in a suit talking loudly on his phone, by two men in hard hats and visibility vests. It didn't matter. She had nowhere else to go.

She turned her back to the creek and faced the road. On the far side, a dark blue van was parked, half up on the pavement. A young man, tall, short-haired, track-suited, ran past her in a slow, loping stride. Frieda walked into Chelsea Harbour itself. Eighty years ago this would have been a place for unloading ships, with cranes and dockers and stevedores. Now it was all offices and restaurants and bars. If there was an anchor remaining, it was there as part of an artistic display. The boats were leisure craft. As Frieda turned left, she noted the people walking past: a young couple arm in arm, a woman in a pin-stripe suit. Frieda looked more closely at a man in a grey bomber jacket and a woollen cap. No, it wasn't him. Even so, something felt strange. She couldn't quite identify it but it was as if the weather were about to change, or someone in an orchestra had played a wrong note. She arrived at the final stretch of the creek, where it lost itself in the great river. So much had changed, but not that, not the endless flow to the sea and then back from it. It had contained so much, including the body of the man she had once loved.

She turned round and started to retrace her steps. She glanced at her watch. It could be hours. Perhaps she would have to wait until dark. But she didn't mind. As she walked back across the little bridge over the creek, she stopped to let the man in the tracksuit run past her. He looked like a serious runner. He was probably running along the embankment, then back. It was a rather uninspiring choice. Frieda pictured more interesting routes: along the embankment, across Chelsea Bridge, then along the south side through Battersea Park and back to the north over Wandsworth Bridge.

She leaned over and stared down into the water, the slow drifts and the currents, and fell into a kind of trance. She was thinking nothing, remembering nothing. Her mind felt empty. When she turned round, she saw something she didn't expect and it took a few seconds to process. The runner, the loping, elegant runner, wasn't running now. He was walking towards her and he was pale and agitated. His face was glowing with sweat and he was looking directly at her. Briefly, she wondered if this could be Dean Reeve but she knew at the same time that it couldn't possibly be. This man was taller and younger and wasn't anything like him. But still he was getting closer. Frieda couldn't have run away even if she wanted to and she didn't want to. This was what she was here for. The man was in front of her now. He was glassy-eyed, panting heavily and visibly trembling.

'He said a name,' the man said, his voice shaking. 'I don't remember the name.'

'Dean Reeve?'

'No. No. He said a woman's name.'

'Frieda Klein?'

'Yes. Frieda Klein.'

'That's me.'

'He said to give this to you and then I could go.'

The man held out a piece of paper and Frieda took it. It

was a page of lined paper, folded in half and roughly torn at one end. She unfolded it. There was writing on it in familiar block capitals:

I COULDN'T MAKE IT. LOOK AROUND YOU.

She didn't need to. There was a sudden bustle and shouting around her. Two men were bundling the runner to the ground. Frieda felt a moment of alarm, then everything became clear to her and she felt only anger. The couple she had seen earlier were running towards her. The man was talking on his phone. The woman looked down at the man and then at Frieda.

'Is it Dean Reeve?' she said.

'Of course it isn't Dean Reeve. What the hell are you all doing here?'

The woman took out a badge and showed it to Frieda.

'I don't need to see that. I know who you are.'

The runner was wriggling and squealing and crying out in the grasp of the two men. The third man joined them and held him on the pavement with an arm across his throat.

'Stop!' Frieda shouted. 'You'll kill him.' And when nobody paid any attention she tried to pull the last man away. She felt herself being grasped from behind and pulled back. She hit back with an elbow and there was a cry. Then she was grasped more firmly and pulled round. She was being held by two young men in suits. Another man in a rumpled suit, older than the other two, more heavily built, was facing her.

'Let her go,' he said.

One of the younger men stepped back holding a hand to his face.

'She caught me on the nose,' he said. 'It's bleeding!' He glared at Frieda.

'What's going on here?' said the older man, and moved to the human tangle on the ground that was now still. He bent down to the runner, who was under full restraint. 'We need to ask you some questions. Can we let you go?'

'Of course you can let him go,' said Frieda sharply.

Slowly the three men relaxed their grip and raised themselves up, away from the runner, who was still sprawled on the ground. Frieda thought he might be about to cry.

'Help him up,' said the older man, in a gentler tone. He looked at Frieda. 'What did he give you?'

Frieda handed him the note and he read it. 'He must have seen us,' he said.

'Yes, he must have seen you.'

'I know who you are,' he said. 'Give me a minute.' Then he turned back to the runner. 'I'm Chief Inspector Dugdale. I need to ask you some questions. What's your name?'

'Duffy,' said the man. 'Paul Duffy. I was just going for a run.'

'Who gave you this?' The runner shook his head. 'Come on, mate, you've got to tell us.'

Duffy looked at the people around him and then, with an expression of puzzlement, at Frieda.

'He took my phone,' Duffy said. 'He made me unlock it and he examined it. He said he knew my name and he knew where I lived and he knew I had children.' He started to cry.

'It's all right,' said Dugdale. 'You're safe now.'

'I'm not saying anything. I haven't said anything.'

'You're safe,' repeated Dugdale.

He motioned Frieda away from the group. 'You need to tell me about this, Dr Klein.'

'What is there to tell? You ruined everything.'

'I was thinking more about you making a statement.'

'That was my statement. Here's another one: look around you. That's what the note says. You found nothing, you achieved nothing.' She was silent for a few moments, her face sombre. 'I thought this would be the end. It could have been.'

'You need to explain yourself.'

'Do I?' On her face was an expression that Dugdale found hard to read.

'Come to the police station and tell us everything,' said Dugdale, in a kinder tone.

She looked away, and when she spoke, it wasn't to him. 'I just don't know what's going to happen now.'

'What's going to happen is that we will do our job and we will catch him. And you can leave that to us.'

'I don't want to stop you doing your job,' said Frieda. 'I'll leave now.'

'You can't just go.'

'Why not?'

'Because to do my job properly, there are things you need to tell me. Urgently. If we have just interrupted a meeting between you and Dean Reeve, you are duty-bound to give us all the help you possibly can to find him, track him down.'

'Yes,' she said. 'I will. But not now, not here. It's dangerous, don't you see?'

'You're safer if you cooperate with us. We can protect you.'

She made an impatient movement with her head. 'No, you can't. I'll come to you soon.'

'Tell me your phone number, at least.'

'I'll contact you.'

Dugdale looked at her with a fixed expression. Then he

took his wallet out and removed a card and handed it to Frieda, who put it into her pocket and then remembered something.

'If you talk to Malcolm Karlsson, tell him you saw me. Tell him I'm all right.'

'Why don't you tell him yourself?'

'If you see him.'

She took a complicated way back, jumping on a bus, taking the Underground and changing trains several times before taking another bus. It was more than an hour after leaving Counter's Creek when she let herself into the flat. Lola ran towards her and, before Frieda could do anything, threw her arms around her.

'I didn't think I'd ever see you again,' she said. 'I didn't know what to do.'

Frieda extricated herself and pushed Lola away from her.

'What?' said Lola.

'It was you,' said Frieda, slowly.

Lola stepped further back, as if she needed to get out of range. 'I had to,' she said. 'I just couldn't let you go and die like that.' Frieda didn't reply. 'You want me to say sorry. Well, I'm not sorry. I did what I did and I don't regret it.'

'Regret?' said Frieda. 'I can promise you that one day you'll want to get in a time machine, come back and stop yourself doing what you did today.'

It took Josef and Stefan and Chloë and Jack and two friends of Stefan's to get the steel beams out of the van and up the stairs of Frieda's house. While heaving the second up the stairs, one of Stefan's friends backed against a wall, dislodged a mirror that fell onto the floor and shattered. Everyone looked at it in dismay.

'So sorry,' Josef said.

'No,' said Chloë. 'Frieda once said to me, "Don't have anything you would mind losing and breaking."'

'But it's a mirror,' said Jack. 'Seven years of bad luck.'

'Frieda's already had her seven years of bad luck,' said Chloë.

Twenty-five

At first Reuben thought it was one of the homeless people from the hostel up the road. It wouldn't be the first time they'd taken shelter under the porch of the Warehouse, or huddled there to sleep. But as he got closer, he saw that the figure was lying at an unnatural angle, and then he saw a canvas backpack by his side that he recognized. And he recognized the light-brown hair tied back in a ponytail and the black boots.

He started to run towards it, and at the same time he was pulling his mobile out of his pocket, fumbling it open. He fell to his knees beside the body, and while he was calling the emergency services he tried to find a pulse, but he knew that Jonah Martin was dead. As Reuben started pumping at his young colleague's chest, he heard a faint, tinny sound and realized that Jonah was wearing headphones and music was still playing.

'Come back, Jonah,' he said, but Jonah's blue eyes stared past him, up at the sky.

He heard footsteps behind him and turned to see Paz staring at them, frozen in shock.

'It's Jonah,' he said unnecessarily, and Paz knelt beside him, her dark hair falling like a shawl over the dead man's body.

'Jonah Martin had just started work at the Warehouse Clinic,' said Dugdale to his assembled team several hours later. His face seemed pouchier than ever. His shirt had come untucked.

He looked at the men and women who had squeezed into the large meeting room, saw their bright eyes, their expressions of barely concealed excitement. They were loving this, he realized: it was the biggest case they would ever have. But he wasn't loving it. Four murders, the name of the man they were hunting – and yet he felt as far from catching him as ever. 'He was thirty-one years old and lived with his girl-friend, who is expecting their first child. He was strangled, probably as he was opening the door to the clinic. The key was under his body. He had probably been dead for under an hour when Dr McGill found him. We're awaiting the pre-liminary reports.'

He took a mouthful of water from the glass in front of him, then continued, 'Nothing seems to have been stolen. His iPod was still on him – in fact it was still playing. His wallet was in his backpack, holding seventy pounds and sev-eral credit cards. It's early days, but he seems to have had a great many friends and no obvious enemies. Dr McGill spoke very highly of him.'

'Do you think –' began a young man at the back, then stopped.

'You were about to ask if this murder is connected to the other high-profile cases on our patch,' said Dugdale. 'At first glance, there seems to be nothing to tie them together. They were planned in advance and staged with a careful delibera-tion. Jonah Martin died where he was found. That's at first glance.'

'What are you thinking?' asked Quarry.

'As you know, last night – what's the kind way of putting this? – we attempted to intercept a meeting between Frieda Klein and Dean Reeve. At any rate, we botched it. Dean Reeve never appeared, but he was there. This morning, a psychoanalyst was murdered on the doorstep of the clinic that Dr Klein is closely connected to.'

'So you're saying Dean Reeve murdered Jonah Martin.'

'That's my working hypothesis and I'd be very surprised – though happy – to discover it wasn't true. It's a message.'

'What's he saying to us?'

'To us? Nothing. The question is, what's he saying to Frieda Klein? And the answer is, fuck knows. Nothing good.'

The door opened and an officer came in and whispered something in Dugdale's ear. He stood up. 'Maybe she's about to tell me, though,' he said. 'Quarry, brief everyone.' He looked around the men and women in the room; some of them seemed like schoolchildren to him. 'One more thing: this is a national story now. An international story. A media frenzy. Everyone will be watching. Everyone will be an expert. For God's sake, keep your bloody mouths shut.'

'Please take a seat,' he said to Frieda. He was afraid she might suddenly disappear, as she had done the previous day, melting back into the greyness.

She shook her head and remained standing. He had seen many photos of Frieda Klein, when her hair was long and dark, and he had always found something about the directness of her gaze unsettling, even when she was looking into a camera. Now her eyes glowed in her pale face as if there was a flame inside her.

She took a step towards him. 'Jonah Martin,' she said.

'Had you met him?'

'Never. He was my replacement.'

'At the Warehouse?'

'Yes.'

'You mean,' said Dugdale, 'standing in for you once the meeting yesterday did not take place.'

'Yes. He is my substitute.'

'Are you saying that Reeve was going to kill you – that you were going there yesterday to be killed?'

Frieda gave an impatient shake of her head. 'That's not the point. The point is that, at the moment, Dean Reeve is in control. He is calling the shots. He killed Geoffrey Kernan. He killed Lee Samuels. He killed Gerald Hebb.'

'I've never even heard of Gerald Hebb.'

'He killed Liz Barron. And now he has killed Jonah Martin. And he's not going to stop.'

'You don't have much faith in the police.'

'You know my history. Are you surprised?'

'He's not a genius.'

'He doesn't need to be. He's obsessed. He has a single fixed purpose.'

Frieda took a large envelope from her bag and handed it across to Dugdale. 'I've written everything down,' she said. 'As clearly as I could. I believe that there is a pattern in what Dean Reeve is doing. I won't go through it now in detail, because it's in this letter, but you will see that he is placing victims on the sites of secret rivers.'

Dugdale blinked. 'That sounds far-fetched.'

'Nevertheless it's what he's doing. What's more, the reason he's killing them and then waiting before he displays them is connected with their names. You'll see when you read my explanations. It doesn't apply to Liz Barron and it doesn't apply to Jonah. Those were . . . particular messages. And, please, this is important.' She took a step forwards, fixing her gaze on him. 'I feel sure that you need to look at the first death.'

There was a pause.

'What do you mean "look at the first death"?' said Dugdale. 'What do you think we've been doing? We've been conducting an investigation into all the murders. That's our job.'

'I know, I know,' said Frieda, impatiently. 'What I mean is that the second and third murders were done to fit the pattern. Geoffrey Udo Kernan, Geoffrey *Udo* Kernan, and it's the *Udo* that's significant here. Placed at the source of the Fleet on his name day.'

'Dr Klein . . .' Dugdale began, but she held up one hand.

'You need to believe this. That's where it started. It's his murder that explains the pattern of the killings. The others follow on from it. There's more than that. There's something territorial about this. Dean Reeve grew up around Plaistow.'

'Kernan lived in Barking.'

'They're only a few minutes apart. That's his area, it's what he knows.'

'All right,' said Dugdale. 'It's his area. What follows from that? What are you suggesting?'

'I just feel that if you're going to have any chance of finding Dean Reeve, Geoffrey Kernan is where you should be looking. I know this must be irritating for you.'

'Which bit?'

'Having someone from outside the police making suggestions.'

'Why would that be irritating? We always welcome input. Just as I'm sure you welcome advice from me about how to conduct your psychological work.'

'Obviously you're free to ignore everything I've said.'

'We'll consider your views,' said Dugdale, evenly. 'As we consider all relevant opinions.'

'That's up to you.'

'Of course it's up to me. To us.' Dugdale frowned. 'There's something you should know,' he said, after a long pause. 'When we looked at Kernan's computer, we found searches that were made after his death. For DCI Karlsson.'

'Oh.' It was barely a word, more like a sigh; her eyes were very dark.

'It seems likely that Dean Reeve wanted us to find them.'

'Yes. He wants you all to know he's playing with us.'

'We'll see about that.'

'What does he say?'

'Karlsson? He's worrying about you.'

'Well.' She took a step back, half turned away. 'I want to help and I will do anything that I can. But you mustn't try to follow me, and you won't be able to find me – because if you can, so can he.' She fixed her gaze on Dugdale. 'I've got to go.'

'Hang on,' said Dugdale. 'It's not as simple as that. What is it you're actually doing?'

'Is that a question I'm required to answer?'

'I'm a police officer leading a murder investigation in which you are involved. I think you have a responsibility to cooperate.'

'I'm here. I've answered your questions. As for the rest of it, I thought I told you. I'm moving around so that Dean Reeve can't get at me.'

'And then what? Or are you going to stay in hiding for ever?'

'It won't be for ever. You can see from the information I gave to you that I don't want him to find me, but I want to find him. I have to find him and I will.'

'Dr Klein, you must understand that you need to make yourself available to the inquiry. At all times.'

'I can phone you.'

'It doesn't work that way. You are a material witness. I need to know where you are and I need a number where I can reach you.'

'I have a problem with that,' said Frieda.

'Oh, do you? And what might that be?'

'I've found that when I give information to the police it has a way of being leaked.' Dugdale's expression darkened even more. 'Don't pretend to be offended. I've seen too many of my secrets turn up in the newspapers.'

'I'm not pretending. My team do not leak.'

Frieda thought for a long time before answering. 'All right,' she said reluctantly. 'One more thing.'

'Are you bargaining with me?'

'I'm thinking of that fiasco down in Chelsea. If you're planning anything like that, you need to let me know in advance.'

Dan Quarry came into the room and started saying something, but when he caught sight of Frieda and Dugdale staring at each other he stopped and backed out of the room.

'Look at my face, Dr Klein. This is the face of someone who is known as tolerant and easy-going. You're testing it. You're testing it to the limit.' When he spoke, it was as if he were choking, as if he were suppressing a violent emotion. 'What I will agree to is, if you cooperate, which means letting me know, at all times, where you can be reached, then I will . . .' He stopped and took a few breaths. 'I will keep you informed.'

Frieda took her little notebook from her pocket, wrote the phone number and the address on it, tore it out and handed it to Dugdale. 'We need to deal with Dean Reeve,' Frieda said. 'We don't need to be best friends.'

'Neither of those seems very likely just now,' said Dugdale.

*

Reuben sat opposite Jonah Martin's partner, Maiko. She was small and slender. She bent over, weeping silently, and her long hair, black and silky, hid her face. Her hands were on her full stomach, protective.

'When's the baby due?' he asked.

She raised her face. 'Six weeks' time,' she whispered. 'He was so happy. We were so happy.'

'I know,' said Reuben. 'He shone with it.'

'And now,' she whispered, 'now it's over. It's over. Why?'

Twenty-six

Lola was roaming through the rooms of the flat. Outside, rain fell from a dull sky, dimpling the canal. Today it had never got properly light, and soon it would be dark again. She felt restless and irritable and trapped. She went to the fridge and opened it and found a carton of eggs and four tomatoes; she bit into one and juice spurted out, staining the T-shirt she was wearing. She took her harmonica out of her pocket and played a half-hearted few notes on it. She picked up Frieda's sketchbook and flicked through the pencil drawings: the cranes they could see out of their window, the glass of water, the bulb of garlic. Opening up her computer, she played a game of Tetris and then looked on Facebook, although it was horrible to read posts from friends and not join in, not even to like something. Her fingers itched as she scrolled down the comments; her eyes filled with tears.

She saw she had a direct message and she clicked on it: it was from Jess. 'There's something I need to tell you urgently. Wherever you are, come to the flat as soon as you get this. Don't tell anyone. I'm waiting. Please hurry.'

Lola frowned. She was about to reply but remembered Frieda's warnings and thought better of it. Jess was a very mellow person: if she said something was urgent, then it was. She made up her mind, and before Frieda could come back and tell her not to, she had put on her jacket, laced up her shoes and left the flat.

*

Karlsson was sitting on the sofa, eating a takeaway and watching the early-evening news on television. He had had a long day and was tired, and the news didn't do anything to lift his spirits. Sometimes it seemed that chaos and violence were swallowing everything he had once taken for granted. He picked up the remote, and at that moment, his doorbell rang.

'Hello?' he said, peering out into the gloom.

Dugdale stood on the step, a bulky shape in the murky light. The wind swirled leaves about his feet. He was wearing a tatty raincoat and his greying hair was damp from the rain. 'Sorry to disturb your evening,' he said.

'It isn't much of one. Come in.'

He opened the door wider and gestured him inside. 'Can I offer you anything? A hot drink? Whisky?'

'I wouldn't say no to the whisky.'

Karlsson turned off the television, cleared away the remains of his meal, and gestured at the chair. He poured them both whisky. 'What brings you here?'

'I met Frieda Klein today,' Dugdale said bluntly.

Karlsson froze, then slowly replaced the tumbler on the table. He thought he might drop it. 'How? Is she all right?'

'She came to see me. This afternoon. She had information for me. And as for how she is, I don't know how to answer that. She's hard to read, isn't she?'

Karlsson nodded.

'She has a theory,' he continued, and handed Karlsson Frieda's letter.

For several minutes, neither man spoke. Dugdale nursed his whisky and Karlsson read the letter with fierce concentration, hunched in his seat and shadows falling on his face. At last he folded the letter and passed it back to Dugdale and took a sip of his drink. 'What do you think?' he asked.

'I don't know. It makes sense, but that doesn't mean it's true. I have to say that it takes me out of my depth.' He gave Karlsson a smile. 'I'm not going to announce that publicly.'

'Of course.'

'I'm old-fashioned. I look at evidence, follow clues, conduct interviews. This – hidden rivers and name days and a man who's supposed to be dead stalking a woman he loves and hates and wants to possess and destroy – this is a whole new territory.'

'I know,' said Karlsson. 'I felt the same when I first came across Dean Reeve, years ago.'

'Klein says we need to concentrate on the first murder.'

'Then that's what you should do.'

'You really trust her, don't you?'

'Yes.'

'She's playing a dangerous game. She's looking for Dean Reeve and he's looking for her, and at some point one of them is going to find the other.' Dugdale gave a shrug of bafflement.

'We have to get there first,' said Karlsson.

'"There",' said Dugdale. 'Wherever that is.'

Twenty-seven

Dugdale called Quarry in. He briefly summarized his conversations with Frieda and Karlsson. 'What do you think?' he said, after he had finished.

Quarry pulled a face. 'She's probably been traumatized,' he said. 'By all she's gone through. People get obsessed.'

'Still. If we were to follow her advice and take another hard look at Kernan, where are the gaps? Klein said that he was different from others. He's from Reeve's territory. So what have we missed?'

'We could look at the people in his company,' said Quarry. 'Dig into their backgrounds a bit more.'

'Where's their office?'

'Up in Whipps Cross.'

Dugdale shook his head. 'Too far.'

'Are we doing all of this because a therapist has a theory?' said Quarry.

'Have you got a theory?'

'I'm just making enquiries and looking at evidence. The way you always say we should.'

'Well, perhaps you could make some more enquiries about Geoffrey Kernan.'

'Is it about checking the things we've already checked?' said Quarry.

His tone was so close to sarcasm that Dugdale gave him a suspicious look. 'We may get around to that. If I decide it's necessary. But what are the things we didn't look at? Where did we draw a blank?'

'Kernan's satnav. As I told you, some of the people weren't in, so we don't know why he went there.'

'I thought you were going to chase those up.'

'Yes, I am.'

Dugdale breathed deeply. 'Where were they?'

'All over the place. One was up near Coventry.'

'What about closer to home?'

'You know, there's a problem with checking his satnav.'

'And what's that?'

'Because it's the one in his own car. But when he died, he wasn't in his own car. That's the car we should be interested in.'

'No, we should be interested in that as well. If you can find out where it was kept between being stolen and set loose down Heath Street then that will be most helpful. But at the moment we're interested in Kernan.'

'Because Frieda Klein says so?'

'Because it seems like a positive line of enquiry.'

'What if we're wasting our time?'

Dugdale leaned back in his chair. 'You know, at the end of every investigation you realize that ninety per cent of it, sometimes ninety-nine per cent of it was pointless. Banging on the wrong doors, talking to people who have nothing to say. What's your better way of doing it?'

'I'll get my notes,' said Quarry. 'Shall we talk about it later?'

'Now's good,' said Dugdale, icily.

Quarry left the room and within two minutes was back with a file. 'I'm sorry,' he said. 'I should have rechecked these addresses.'

'Sorry doesn't get it done, Dan. Just give me the information.'

Quarry looked at the file. His hands were shaking. He had to steady himself. 'The closest to Kernan's address was a furniture store less than a mile away. He bought a set of shelves. I checked the receipt. The shelves are standing in their living room.'

'That's no use. What else is there?'

'There's a house in West Ham where nobody answered the door.'

'Are the occupants away?'

'I don't know.'

He had gone very red.

'Anything else?'

'There was a house in Creek Street. I talked to some people who lived there but they said they didn't know Kernan or recognize his picture.'

'He might just have been dropping someone off, or collecting someone.'

'They didn't seem like the kind of people Kernan would know. Or even work with.'

'All right,' said Dugdale. 'Go to the West Ham house first. Then swing by the other one, see if you can find anything out. Go this evening. Then you might find them at home.'

'Actually, I've got a sort of arrangement this evening. Seeing my kid.'

'Why are you telling me this?' said Dugdale. 'Can't you cancel your own arrangements?'

Quarry thought of the conversation he was about to have with his wife. 'That's all right,' he said.

The door of the house in West Ham was opened by a middle-aged man in shorts and a sweatshirt. He was a colleague of Kernan's. They weren't friends but they had been to a conference together and Kernan had come to the house to collect him.

'How was his mood?'

'I don't know,' said the man. 'He talked about sales figures and about his home-improvement plans. I didn't pay much attention.'

'You're a salesman, aren't you?' said Quarry.

'Yeah, but I don't talk about it. Not when I don't have to.'

'Does that mean you didn't like Kernan?'

'It means that he was someone in the same company who I didn't know very well.'

Back in the car, Quarry scribbled a few notes. The man hadn't liked Kernan. And Kernan had talked about DIY to him, so that gave him a motive. Quarry smiled to himself. He wouldn't repeat that to Dugdale. He was pretty sure Dugdale wouldn't find it funny. But there had been nothing in the interview that made Quarry think he could have killed Kernan.

When he got out of the car in front of the little clump of houses on Creek Street, he was immediately hit by the sour smell from the waste site. He stepped back reflexively as a huge, rusty lorry thundered past. Who the hell would choose to live here? People who don't have a choice.

He walked up to the house and rapped hard on the door. It opened, revealing the man he had met before. He was wearing the same grubby T-shirt.

'Remember me?' said Quarry.

The man sniffed. Quarry held up the picture. The man shook his head.

'But he came here,' said Quarry.

'If he did, I didn't see him.'

Quarry nodded slowly. 'What's your name?'

'Dobrinin.'

'First name?'

'Jan.'

'The thing is, Jan, this is serious. That photograph I showed you. He was murdered. Now, we don't care about you and we don't care about the people who live in the house. Maybe you're paid in cash. Not my concern. Maybe you deal a bit of weed. I couldn't care less. Maybe you're all here illegally. Good luck to you. But if you don't help me, I can make a call . . .' He stopped. 'No. Let's make it three calls. Three calls and various people will arrive and they will go through everything and they will ask about everything and they'll want the receipts and you will be fucked. But I don't want to do any of that.'

Jan blinked rapidly. 'You show me the photo. I don't know.' His voice was almost pleading. 'What should I do?'

'All right,' said Quarry. 'Let's reframe the question. That might make things easier. We know that this man came to this address. We have proof. You say you don't know him. Explain that to me in a way I can understand.'

'What proof?'

'Geoffrey Kernan's satnav said he came here. It had this postcode. Perhaps you can comment on that.'

'The postcode isn't just this house. These houses have the same postcode.'

'But there's nobody living in them.'

'There could be squatters.'

'There's no sign of that, but we'll check.'

'And there's the lock-ups. Vans keep knocking on the door trying to deliver parcels to us. It's a pain in the fucking arse.'

Quarry narrowed his eyes. 'What lock-ups?'

Jan gestured to the right. 'That alley leads round the back. There's lock-ups there.'

Quarry didn't say anything. He just left Jan on the doorstep and walked round the side of the house.

'Stupid,' he muttered to himself. 'Stupid.'

Behind the houses there was a small tarmac track with a row of eight lock-up garages on the opposite side from the houses. It was dark now but one of them was open with a car half out, bonnet raised, and an indistinct figure leaning into it. As the detective approached, the person looked up and revealed himself as a man, dark-haired, dark-skinned with a bushy beard. He was wearing navy-blue dungarees and a white T-shirt and his hands were stained with oil.

'You rent this?' asked Quarry, showing his identification. The man nodded. Quarry showed him the photograph of Kernan. 'Recognize him?'

The man shook his head.

'He drove here about three weeks ago, maybe a month.'

'Never seen him.'

Quarry took a step back and looked around. This had to be the place. It had to be. Then a thought occurred to him. He took a different picture from his pocket and showed it to the man. He looked more closely at it. Then took it from him and held it almost against his face. 'You've seen him?'

'A couple of times.'

Quarry was so taken aback that for a moment he couldn't think what to ask. His skin tingled. 'When?'

'I don't know. A week maybe. Maybe longer.'

'Does he rent one of these?'

'I don't know but he was using the one at the end.'

'Do you know what he's using it for?'

'I guess he's storing something.'

'Why do you think that?'

'Because that's what they're for. And one of the times he was here he had a van. I was working on my car. I had to move it out of the way so he could get past.'

'Can you describe the van?'

'It was white.'

'Do you know the model? The registration number?'

'I wasn't paying attention.'

'Did you see what was in it?'

'No.'

'Did you speak to him?'

'I guided him past my car. He was backing up the alley towards his lock-up so it was tight.'

'Did he speak?'

'He nodded. Like saying thanks.'

'Wait there,' said Quarry. 'Don't move.'

He turned aside and rang Dugdale.

'You need to get here, sir. And a locksmith. I'm in Creek Street. There's garages round the back. He used to rent one of them. No, not Kernan. Dean Reeve.'

Before Dugdale arrived, a green van decorated with an angel carrying a key slowly eased its way round the corner into the alley. A man in crisply pressed red overalls got out.

'I was expecting a police officer,' said Quarry.

'It's all contracted out now,' said the man. 'Don't worry, I've done all sorts. Burglaries. Pets that have got locked in. So, what have I got to deal with?'

When he saw the flimsy handle on the lock-up door, he looked almost disappointed. 'It'll take two minutes, that lock,' he said. 'You could almost do it with your bare hands.'

'Wait till our boss gets here,' said Quarry. 'You can do it when he arrives.'

'I get paid by the quarter-hour, you know,' said the man. 'Even one minute into the quarter counts as a quarter.'

It was twenty minutes before another car pulled in behind the locksmith and Dugdale got out. 'So, what have you found?' he said.

'We were waiting for you.'

'What do you think I am? The Queen opening a super-market? There could be someone in there.' He waved the locksmith forward. 'Get it open. And don't muck around with it too much. This is a crime scene.' He took white surgical gloves from his pocket and gave them to the locksmith.

It took less than two minutes before the locksmith twisted the handle in the middle of the door and pulled it towards him and up.

'There you are,' he said. 'For what it's worth.'

The space was filled not with a car but with four chest freezers, all of them with their lids raised. They weren't switched on. The cords and plugs were strewn on the floor.

'Hunting stolen freezers?' said the locksmith.

'Shut up,' said Dugdale.

The locksmith pulled a face. He went to his van and came back with a form on a clipboard and a pen. Quarry signed it.

When the locksmith had gone, Quarry stepped into the lock-up. Dugdale was crouched behind a freezer at the back.

'Have you found anything, sir?'

Dugdale stood up and brushed his trousers where he had been kneeling down. He shook his head. The two men walked outside.

'So we know where he kept them,' Dugdale said.

'Shall I call the crime-scene guys?'

'They won't find anything but, yes, you'd better call them. And get some officers down here to do house-to-house.' He sniffed. 'It's too late, though. He's done what he had to do here.' He looked at Quarry. 'Good work. But we're behind. We're too far behind.'

Twenty-eight

What would Frieda think? That was what Lola said to herself over and over again on the long bus and Underground journey. She knew the answer. That was why she hadn't even considered asking Frieda's permission. Frieda would have told her not to go. And she needed to go. She had to find out what Jess knew. She just had to be careful, that was all.

When she approached the flat, she looked around the street outside without being quite sure what she was looking for. Everything was as it always was. She had decided that if there was any sign of a disturbance, if the front door was open, if there was visible damage, she would walk past, keep on going. But there was nothing. The lamps were lit and people passed by in the gathering gloom.

She walked up to the door and took out her key. Now there was just one last thing. She had thought of it on the train. She reached into her pocket and found the pay-as-you-go phone Frieda had bought her. She tapped the number nine three times: now with just one press of the button she would call the emergency services. She turned the key in the lock and pushed the door inward. Something smelt different: Jess must have been smoking indoors, even though they had a house rule.

She stepped inside, closed the door behind her with a small click.

When Frieda returned, she expected to find Lola leaning over the computer or lying on the sofa with her headphones on. She called out. Nothing. She looked around the flat. She quickly saw that Lola had left without taking anything. Her laptop was open on the table, there were clothes scattered in the bedroom. She had probably just gone out to the shops. Frieda took out her phone and rang Lola. No answer. Again, it was probably nothing. Still, Frieda knew what she had to do. She put Lola's laptop and her own laptop into a shoulder bag. She didn't even check for anything else. She had planned this a hundred times. Everything else was dispensable. Within five minutes of arriving, she was back out on the street, striding quickly. Fifteen minutes later she was sitting in a coffee shop. Waiting.

Lola seemed to have lost the use of her fingers. Her phone felt like an object she had never seen before. She needed to phone Frieda but it felt bafflingly hard to do. Her mind wasn't working. Her breath was coming in wheezes that hurt her chest.

She had turned away from Jess's open, sightless eyes but it didn't help. There was still the smell of the blood. The room was hot and sweet with it. It was everywhere. Jess's T-shirt and sweatpants were soaked and it was pooling on the floorboards and there were Lola's own footprints. She had stepped in it and left prints on the floorboards. She could see all of it, even though she was looking away. She was trembling right through her whole body so that it felt like the whole house was shaking. Deep breaths. That's how you calm yourself. Lola breathed once, twice, three times, deeply, even though it felt like she was inhaling the blood. The smell filled the room, and the smell must contain particles of blood, so didn't that mean she was breathing in the blood itself? Stop. Stop thinking about that. She had to concentrate. She had to talk to Frieda. It was all that mattered.

197

Slowly, clumsily, she managed to find Frieda's number and call it.

'Where are you?'

'Frieda? Frieda?' Was that her voice? It didn't sound the same.

'Where are you?'

Lola sniffed and rubbed her nose with her sleeve. 'She's dead.' The words came out in a croak. For a moment, she saw Jess's face, then pushed the image away. She mustn't. She mustn't.

'Who is dead?'

'Jess. My housemate. My friend. Jess!'

Now her voice cracked. Little sobbing sounds were bubbling out of her.

'Lola. Tell me.'

'She's dead. Her throat's cut. There's blood. It's everywhere.' She could hear herself talking, a gabble of sound, squeaks and croaks. She felt sweat on her forehead and down her back. Sickness in the back of her throat. The thick smell of blood.

When Frieda's voice came, it was calmer than before, calmer than Lola had ever heard it. 'Are you sure she's dead?'

'Her eyes are open. There's blood everywhere. Her head's almost . . .' She couldn't finish the sentence.

'Are you still in the house?'

'Yes. What shall I do? What have I done?'

'Have you called the police?'

'I had to talk to you.'

'Ring the police right now. Then call me back.'

The line went dead. Lola dialled 999. A woman answered and said, 'What service?' and Lola said, 'She's dead, she's been murdered,' and started to cry again, splintering sobs. Her body felt like it was breaking apart. She still couldn't bring herself to turn and look at Jess.

She was asked for her name and for the address and she found it hard even to get the words out. As soon as the operator said the police were on their way, Lola ended the call and rang Frieda back.

'I'm so sorry, Frieda, I'm so sorry.'

'Are you all right?'

'She's lying there. She's here with me, just a few feet away. She's my friend. I got her killed.' There was a pause. 'Frieda?'

'Why did you go there?'

'She sent me a direct message. She said she had to see me. I know I should have told you. I'm so sorry.'

'That doesn't matter now.'

'What should I do? Should I run away and get back to you?'

'No. The police will be there in a minute or two. So listen carefully. Tell them everything. Be completely honest. Miss nothing out. And then ask them to put you in touch with Chief Inspector Malcolm Karlsson.'

'Why?'

'Say the name back to me.'

'Malcolm Karlsson.'

'You're in a severely stressed state. If you forget the name, just ask for the detective who worked with me. They'll know who he is or how to find him. He'll make sure you're safe.'

'I want to see you. Please. Don't leave me alone.'

'You've got to talk to the police and then you have to let Karlsson keep you safe. Do you understand?'

Lola heard the sound of sirens, distant, getting less distant.

'They're coming.'

'Good. You're safe now.'

'But how can I –'

'Stop,' said Frieda. 'I need to say something first. Lola, I am sorry about Jess. Your friend. Very sorry indeed. But you must know that it isn't your responsibility, not any of it. You wandered into his world. Once you did that, there was nothing you could do about it.'

'I want to talk to you about this. I want to see you. Please.'

'Maybe when this is over. Now, remember, trust the police and tell them everything and ask for Karlsson.'

'When will I see you?'

'Goodbye, Lola.'

And then the police started to arrive and the paramedics and then the detectives, a younger one and one who seemed to be in charge, the one she'd heard of, Dugdale. When she saw him looking across at the sprawled body, at the blood, when she saw his shocked face, she felt like she was living it all over again.

Twenty-nine

Chloë often stayed late at the joinery workshop. She spent the evening hours on her own projects. For some time she had been constructing a small table for Frieda. It was made from a golden elm tree that had somehow survived the disease that had wiped out most of the elms in the country, but had blown over in a storm and been planked up and brought to the workshop, where it had lain for months, sending out a rich, yeasty smell as it released its sap. Chloë had put aside two of the widest planks and, as soon as they were seasoned, had set about the task. She remembered Frieda saying to her, shortly after Chloë had started training to become a carpenter, that one day she should make her a table. She could almost see her aunt's face as she bent over her task.

But in recent days she had been working on Frieda's balcony. This evening she had been sanding the supporting rail smooth so that the grain in the wood almost glowed.

It was dark when she left; the days were getting shorter. Soon it would be winter, she thought. She didn't like to think of time passing, of seasons changing. When it had been only days, and then weeks, since Frieda had disappeared, she had been able to tell herself that she would be back soon. But the weeks had turned to months. The leaves had started to fall, and now lay in sodden drifts. Although it was still only October, the shops were full of Christmas things.

The little street was empty, except for a woman who was standing at the corner, under a plane tree. She had silver hair, cut short, and heavy-rimmed spectacles, and was wearing a shawl-necked grey coat and boots. As Chloë approached she turned and walked ahead of her, but slowly, so that soon they were level.

'Hello,' said the woman.

A shivery sensation passed through Chloë, as if she had suddenly been struck by a nasty bug. Her skin prickled. She turned her head towards the woman who walked beside her. 'Oh,' she said, on an out breath, the exclamation like a sigh.

'Don't say anything and keep on walking. I won't be long.'

'If you leave again I won't be able to bear it,' said Chloë.

'I will leave again, and you will bear it.'

Frieda put out her hand and held Chloë's; they walked along like that, footsteps in time.

'Are you all right? Where have you been? When are you coming home?'

'I need some help.'

'Tell me what.' Chloë remembered hurling a brick through a window and helping Frieda clamber into the building.

'I need somewhere to stay. Somewhere discreet. An empty flat.'

'Stay with me. I'll keep you safe.'

'Nobody must see me and nobody must know. I thought you might have friends, or friends of friends, who were away travelling perhaps. It won't be for long.'

Chloë thought for a moment. 'I have an idea,' she said.

'Yes?'

'One of my flatmates is looking after her mother's cats at the moment. She's on holiday. My flatmate complains about it all the time, though. She's allergic to cats and has to go halfway across London. I could get the keys off her and say I can do it. I'll say I've got work round the corner.'

'Where is it?'

'Near Cable Street.'

'Do you know the address?'

'I've been there a few times: three Vincent Street. If you come to my flat then I can get the keys and . . .'

'No. Leave them under a stone or a pot before midnight and I'll collect them.'

'Oh,' said Chloë, disappointed.

'And, Chloë . . .'

'Yes?'

'Don't visit.'

'So I know where you are and I'm not allowed to come near you?'

'That's right.'

'That's ridiculous.'

'If I can't trust you, I'll go somewhere else.'

'You can trust me.'

'Thank you.'

'But is that all you need? There must be something else.'

'That's all.'

'Don't go yet.'

'I'll walk with you to the main road.'

'It's like seeing a ghost. Olivia thinks you're dead already.'

Frieda smiled. Her hand tightened on Chloë's. 'How are you?' she asked softly. 'How's everyone?'

'We miss you. We're worried. We want to help.'

'You're helping.'

'Is this where you're going to be? If I urgently need to see you, can I find you there?'

'No. And I won't be there long. There's someone who can find me a safer place.'

'Who?'

'Someone with friends in high places. You don't need to know the name.'

'I guess not,' said Chloë. Then: 'Can I tell the others I saw you?'

'No. This is between you and me.'

Chloë saw the main road ahead. She slowed her steps. 'You're not going to die, are you?' she asked.

'Not if I can help it. Give me news.'

'Reuben seems OK,' said Chloë, dragging her feet. 'His hair's growing back all curly. And Alexei's doing well at his new school, though he's still a bit shy and Josef worries about him. Sasha isn't back yet but I think she's returning by Christmas. Jack's Jack and he's being really sweet, and don't look at me like that, no, we're not going out again, though sometimes I think – Oh, never mind that. Your cat's being looked after like it's a substitute you. Everyone buys it treats so it's getting quite chubby. Josef goes to your house almost every day and makes sure everything's all right and puts fresh flowers out and waters your plants.'

She hesitated. She felt she ought to tell Frieda what else Josef was doing. The last time she had been in the house, Josef and Stefan had been pulling up the floorboards. Was it important that Frieda knew or was it important that she didn't know? But she had to keep talking. Frieda couldn't leave as long as she was talking. 'Olivia's read a book about decluttering and has thrown about two hundred bin bags of stuff out. I haven't seen Karlsson. I'm doing well at work, I think. I like it. I wouldn't have been a good doctor but I am a good carpenter.'

They were at the main road. She stopped.

'Can you do me a favour?' she said.

'What's that?'

'When you come home, grow your hair long and dark again. I prefer it.'

Frieda laughed. 'I promise.' She gave Chloë a gentle push. 'Get the keys there by midnight. Off you go.'

'But —'

'It's our secret.'

'I won't say a word,' said Chloë, her voice wobbling. But Frieda was walking away. Chloë gazed after her. 'I'm making you a little table,' she called after her. 'For when you come home. It's made of golden elm.'

Thirty

Dugdale and Karlsson met in the commissioner's anteroom. They exchanged nervous glances.

'I feel like I'm about to go into an exam,' said Karlsson.

'I was thinking more of dental surgery,' said Dugdale. 'Root-canal work. The one where they go really deep down.'

'All right, I get it.'

A young woman came in and escorted them through to the commissioner's office. Karlsson had been there before, with a different commissioner. This time it felt equally uncomfortable. Helena Leigh, her short grey hair standing out against her dark uniform, was seated behind the familiar desk. She didn't get up. She just nodded to the two detectives to sit down.

'Geoffrey Kernan,' she said. 'Lee Samuels. Gerald Hebb.'

'Yes,' said Dugdale, in a slightly strained tone.

'Liz Barron. A journalist. We all know the consequences of a journalist being murdered.'

'Yes.'

'You know how many front pages this story has been on in the last month?'

'Quite a few, I think,' said Dugdale.

'I can't move for press. Jonah Martin, and now Jessica Colbeck. Twenty-one years old. She looks like my daughter. Like everyone's daughter. Have you met her parents?'

Dugdale saw their faces when he closed his eyes. Pale, stunned, red-eyed. 'I talked to them yesterday.'

'Did you see them on television this morning? On the sofa?'

'No, I didn't.'

'It made compelling television.'

Dugdale didn't reply. Leigh turned her attention to Karlsson. 'And you are here why?'

Karlsson coughed. 'We all know that Dean Reeve is the main suspect in this case. We believe he used Geoffrey Kernan's computer and that he used it to search for me.'

'Why?'

'His real target is a woman called Frieda Klein. He has a history with her.'

'Yes, I know about Frieda Klein. In fact, she is responsible for my being here.'

'How?' said Dugdale.

'She destroyed the career of my predecessor. I was brought in to pick up the pieces.'

'I'm not sure that's entirely fair,' said Karlsson.

'Then we'll agree to disagree on that. Meanwhile, you have Klein under surveillance?'

There was a silence.

'Not at this time,' said Dugdale.

'Why not?'

'Because it was what she wanted.'

The words hung in the air.

'Why is she doing this?'

Dugdale looked helplessly at Karlsson.

'Frieda knew that Reeve was after her,' Karlsson said. 'I think she didn't want to just wait for him to kill her. So she went off the radar.'

'You mean to hide?'

'Possibly.'

'Possibly? What else could she mean to do?'

'I'm not sure,' said Karlsson.

'I did interview her,' said Dugdale, a little desperately.

'And you let her go?'

'She hasn't committed a crime.'

'I'm not sure about that.'

There was a silence that was only broken by Leigh rapping the desktop. 'I have a press conference first thing tomorrow,' she said. 'There are camera crews from America. From China. What am I to say?'

'We're making progress,' said Dugdale. 'Steady progress.'

'That's enough,' said Leigh. 'You're coming with me. If that's all we can say, I want you to be standing next to me.'

'Are you going to say it's Reeve?' asked Dugdale.

She shook her head. 'Not yet.'

'But –'

'Don't think I haven't thought it through,' she interrupted sharply. 'I have decided, on balance, that it is better to keep this secret for the time being. Can you imagine the attention and the panic there would be if the public knew that Dean Reeve is behind all of this?'

'The public can be our best weapon sometimes,' said Dugdale.

'I've made up my mind. It's on my head. It might look different in a few hours' time. It probably will. But for the time being, not a word. Do you understand?'

'Yes.'

'Keep this leak-free.'

As the two detectives started to leave, Leigh nodded at Dugdale. 'You realize what the consequence will be if this goes wrong?'

'For Klein?'

'For you,' said Leigh. 'And for me.'

'I've considered it.'

She looked at Karlsson. 'You're sure she doesn't have some kind of a death wish?'

'She's seen a lot of death. That does something to people. If she thought she'd be saving her friends, she'd do anything.'

'I'll take that as a yes,' said Leigh.

Thirty-one

As soon as Frieda stepped through the door of the house Chloë had arranged, she was confronted with two small cat faces staring up at her, their eyes huge and round. She pushed the door shut and leaned down to stroke them. They both lifted their noses towards her hand, then suddenly streaked up the stairs with a patter of paws. She put her bag down and looked around. There was a mirror on the wall in an ornate golden frame. Next to it a key dangled from a nail. She looked at the key in her hand. It was the same. She began to explore the house. On the left of the hallway was a living room that had been knocked together from two smaller rooms. It was cosily decorated with a blue woven rug on the wooden floor, rustic landscapes on the walls. Another cat, large and black, was curled up asleep on the sofa. Frieda stroked its head gently and it shifted but didn't get up. It was old and content. She looked around, checking the exits and entrances. At the far end of the room a barred window gave onto a small backyard. Nobody could get in or out that way.

She returned to the hall and walked up the stairs. The house was tiny. There was a bedroom at the front, overlooking the street, then a small bathroom and at the back another tiny bedroom. A black and white cat was lying on the bed: there seemed to be cats in every room. It looked up at Frieda and she stroked its back as she stared out of the window onto the paved yard. Frieda noted that this row of houses didn't back onto the gardens of another row of houses. Instead there was a gate in the wall that led into an alley that ran parallel with the street. It made the house less secure than she would have liked. You can get in from the front and you can get in from the back. That was something to bear in mind.

She walked down the stairs and then along the short hallway to the kitchen at the back of the house. There were windows on two sides, all with heavy bars on. It was because the access from the alley was so easy. It wasn't very reassuring. At the end of the kitchen a door opened not into the yard but into a more basic room, with a sink and a washing-machine. There was another door, with heavy bars, that led outside. Both doors had keys in their locks. She turned one of the keys and opened the door into the yard. It was paved, edged with loose gravel. There were no plants except for one sad, straggling ivy trailing from a large pot in one of the corners. Frieda immediately thought of the pots she would have arranged, the plants that would soften the space, then smiled at the irrelevance of thoughts of that kind. That was all for another life, a life she wasn't living.

The back wall was quite high, eight feet perhaps, with a heavy grey wooden gate. Frieda turned its brass handle. Locked. She walked back into the utility room and looked around. There it was. Another key was hanging from a hook above the washing-machine. She returned to the kitchen. She had seen everything and felt she had it in her head. Nice place.

She opened some cupboards until she found a tumbler. She filled it with water and drank it in one gulp. Then she refilled it and sat at the kitchen table. She took out her phone and dialled Dugdale's direct line.

'Well?' he said. He sounded abrupt. His voice had a rough edge to it that she hadn't heard before.

'I've moved,' she said, but before she could give him the address, he had changed the subject.

'I've just met your young friend,' said Dugdale.

'How is she?'

'Shaky.'

'Did you learn anything from her?'

'There wasn't much to learn. She found the body. She was in a state of shock.'

'Of course she was.'

'She talked about you a lot. Like she's relying on you.'

'She's in a precarious situation.'

'There's something else. You'd hear it soon enough anyway.'

'What?'

'We've found where Reeve kept the bodies.'

'Where?'

'East. A lock-up in Barking, in an industrial area near the river. He had four freezers.'

'Empty?'

'Yes.'

'What now?'

'I've been talking to the commissioner. If it was up to her, we'd haul you in and put you under guard.'

'That would be a disaster,' said Frieda.

'For who? You'd be safe. Reeve couldn't get at you.'

'He'd get at someone.'

'Well, we're doing what we can. We're conducting a door-to-door both there and where young Jess Colbeck was killed. But it is pretty clear that Reeve hasn't been to the lock-up for some time – probably since Liz Barron was murdered. He didn't need it after that. OK, I've got a pen. Let me have your address.'

When the call was over, Frieda sat for a few moments, staring ahead and seeing nothing. Then she remembered what she was there to do. Boxes of cat food were piled up on one of the work surfaces. She took out four sachets and squeezed them into four feeding bowls. She put the bowls on the floor. The two young cats were already at her feet, clambering up her legs. She realized she didn't know their names.

'You can be A and B,' she said to them. She walked into the hallway and saw the cat from upstairs padding down. 'You can be C,' she said, as he, or she, walked past her into the kitchen. The remaining cat – D – was still lying asleep on the sofa.

'Old thing,' said Frieda, picking it up and carrying it through to the kitchen. She placed it on the floor in front of the food bowl but D was apparently unable to see or smell the food. Frieda had to push its head down into the bowl until it noticed and started eating.

She needed to buy some food, washing-up liquid, soap. Instead of leaving through the front door, she went out the back way, unlocking the gate in the yard and walking along the cobblestones in the alley. It led under a railway arch and then along another even narrower alley. A short walk brought her into the noise of Commercial Road.

Back in the house she ate a simple salad of tomato and avocado and a bread roll. She felt as if she had taken a wrong turning and didn't know whether to retrace her steps or to keep going.

After she had gone to bed in the front room upstairs, cats A and B appeared in the doorway, explored the room and then jumped up beside her. When she tried to stroke them, they ran away, streaking out of the door with a rattle of paws and claws on the wooden floor. But they came back and she could hear their soft breathing in the darkness.

She lay awake for hours, thinking about Jess, about the bodies in the freezer, about Lola, and then she suddenly wondered whether she had remembered to lock the back door. Surely she must have done. But she couldn't be certain. So she got up and walked downstairs in the dark. She was alert to every sound but there was nothing except a hum of traffic and a rattle of a train passing. The back door was locked. Of course she had locked it.

Chloë looked in dismay at the scene on the upper floor of Frieda's house. The floorboards were up. The back window had been removed and the wall beneath it partially dismantled. The two steel joists had replaced the wooden ones in the floor and were projecting out into the space above the backyard. Josef and Stefan were sitting in one corner drinking tea from a flask.

'Can I ask a question?' said Chloë.

Josef nodded.

'Don't you need planning permission to do something like this?'

Josef shrugged. 'Is invisible.'

'It's not in any sense invisible.'

'No. Nobody see from the road. Nobody look on it. When we finish, it is like always here. No problem.'

There was so much Chloë could have said in reply. She knew of people being prosecuted for illicit building work, of people who had had to restore the property to its original state at their own expense. There seemed little doubt in her mind that Josef and Stefan were conducting illegal building works using stolen property. But in the larger scheme of things, looking at what Frieda was up against, Josef was probably right. Frieda should have her little garden in the sky.

Thirty-two

Dugdale had never liked giving press conferences. He knew he wasn't good at them and always wished that someone else could do them for him instead. Standing next to Commissioner Leigh wasn't much better. He felt like a human shield, there to absorb as much of the blast as possible.

The hall was crammed with journalists and there was an almost palpable air of excitement in the room. Cameras flashed. Mikes were held out. He stared at the sea of faces and saw how hyped up they all were. Tiredness pressed down on him. He had been up all night, drinking coffee out of Styrofoam cups on the hour, trying to co-ordinate the two new operations. He was hungry and felt stale; his eyes throbbed and he rubbed them.

Leigh gave a brief, essentially meaningless statement. Then questions were asked in a variety of accents. Some of them were aimed at Dugdale. He was asked if there were any leads. He was asked what he had to say to the victims' families. He was asked how he felt. Afterwards he went to the bathroom and scooped cold water over his face. He saw that his shirt-collar was turned in on itself and the shave he had given himself before he went into the conference had been inadequate. He shrugged: the investigation was what mattered.

The meeting room was barely large enough for the officers who had assembled. Dugdale took off his jacket, aware of the rings of sweat round his armpits, and spoke sombrely. He felt as though someone else was doing the talking. As he dispassionately described the death of Jessica Colbeck, he recalled the scene-of-crime photos. She was so young, there was so much blood. The pathologist said the artery had been entirely severed. Like butchery. He wished she hadn't said that.

The inside of his mouth felt furry and he took a sip of water.

'Although it was a terrible day,' he continued, 'it was also a day which I feel certain will lead us to Dean Reeve.'

He looked from face to face. They were all exhausted. They knew what was happening, they realized the urgency, they didn't need him to tell them.

Afterwards, Dugdale waved Quarry over. 'Find out where those freezers came from,' he said.

'Probably Freecycle or eBay or something like that,' said Quarry. 'They were old. One of them's half rust. I'll get Phelps to do a comprehensive online search. We've got all the photos now.'

Dugdale nodded and clapped him on the shoulder. 'We're closer now than we've ever been. I feel it. I can almost smell it.'

At just after nine the next morning, when Frieda had fed the cats and was sitting in front of the computer, her mobile rang.

'Frieda. It's me.' Lola's voice was hoarse and loud, as if she had been calling for hours to Frieda across a ravine.

'I know. Tell me how you are.'

'I'm outside your door. Are you out somewhere or just not answering?'

'My door?'

'Yes.'

Frieda realized that, of course, Lola had no idea she had moved.

'Why are you there?'

'Where are you? When are you back?'

'Lola, I told you to go to Karlsson and he'd make you safe. What are you doing there?'

'I need to talk to you. I need to see you.'

'What about?'

'I don't feel safe. I don't feel safe anywhere. I need to be with you. Please. Please, Frieda. I'll go mad.' Lola started to sob wildly.

There was a long pause.

'Stay where you are. I have to think about this. I'll phone you back in a few minutes.'

Frieda sat very still, then called Lola.

'Do you remember after the inquest, when we walked on the canal past Camden Lock?'

'Yes.'

'Then listen carefully. I want you to do that again. Go to Camden Lock, get on the canal and turn right, the Regent's Park way. Keep walking until you get to the very end of the towpath. Then wait.'

'What for?'

'Just do as I say. And do it now.'

The line went dead.

Frieda stood on the bridge over the canal, but on the Regent's Park side of it, out of sight. Ahead, on both sides of the canal, was the zoo. A barge was coming towards her with a slow, chugging sound. At the rear of the boat stood a grey-haired couple, both holding mugs. The woman had her other hand on the tiller. The man looked up at Frieda. His face was impassive. He didn't smile and he didn't wave.

It was a weekday morning, but even so the towpath was busy. There were cyclists in both directions, people leading dogs, mothers or fathers or nannies with small children. And then there she was, walking more slowly than she usually did, as if her feet were heavy. Frieda felt a wave of sadness at the sight of Lola, her hands in the pockets of her short blue jacket, her eyes looking down in front of her, her hair in childish pigtails. Who was there to look out for her?

Enough of that, though. Frieda needed to concentrate. Lola passed under the bridge but Frieda didn't follow her with her gaze. Instead she looked behind. She could see a long way. There were two different cyclists, a woman and a man. There was a runner, late-middle-aged, bespectacled, balding, out of breath. There was a woman pushing a buggy. There were two women in active conversation. And that was all. Frieda forced herself to wait another couple of minutes. Three more cyclists appeared. A man with a dog. A young female runner.

Nobody was keeping Lola under observation.

She took out her phone and dialled. She saw Lola reach into her pocket

'Frieda, where are you? I'm scared.'

'Walk back the way you came,' said Frieda. 'Just before the canal turns sharply to the left, take the steps up to the right.'

Frieda stayed for a few moments watching as Lola retraced her steps. She looked at the people who had been behind the girl and were now in front of her. None of them reacted. She had done all she could.

Lola walked past the giant birdcage and then up the steps. She didn't know what to look for but then saw, across the road, a black taxi with a door open and Frieda leaning out. She ran across, stepped inside and shut the door. The cab pulled away.

Lola put her head against Frieda's shoulder. Her skin felt sore and frail and her eyes hurt. 'I'm so, so glad to see you,' she said. 'I wanted to . . .'

Frieda lifted her upright. 'Give me your phone.'

Lola handed it over. Frieda pushed the window down and threw it out.

'What are you doing? That's the second phone you've thrown away. It's only pay-as-you-go. Nobody can trace me.'

'Wait,' said Frieda. 'We'll talk soon.'

They got out of the taxi in Camden High Street, almost back where Lola had joined the canal. Frieda started walking briskly along the pavement. She led Lola into Marks & Spencer.

'We're going to get you some clothes,' she said.

'Why? What clothes?'

'Everything you need. But nothing that needs trying on for size.'

She picked out underwear, a high-necked black T-shirt and black leggings, a soft, baggy sweater the colour of aubergines, a waterproof jacket and a pair of white trainers with green laces. Frieda paid but then, instead of leaving, led Lola to a changing room, went in with her and pulled the curtain shut.

'I thought you didn't want me to try anything on.'

'Take everything off,' said Frieda.

'What's this about?' said Lola. All the bounce had gone out of her. She looked grubby and exhausted.

'If I'm going to keep you safe, then we're starting from zero. First, empty your pockets.'

There were only a few coins, the key to Lola's flat and her purse.

Lola unbuttoned her jacket, took it off and hung it on a hook. She kicked her shoes off. Then she pulled her top over her head, unclipped her bra and slipped it off. She unbuttoned her jeans and pulled them down with her knickers and stepped out of them. Teetering awkwardly, she took her little socks off. She stood naked in front of Frieda, who saw how passive she had become. There was a dazed expression on her face.

Frieda tipped the new clothes out of the bag. She examined Lola for several seconds.

'Take your watch off,' she said. 'And your earrings.'

'What are you looking for?'

'I don't know,' said Frieda. 'But if we get rid of everything, we don't need to think about it.'

Lola handed the watch and earrings to Frieda, who tossed them into the empty plastic bag. She put Lola's clothes into the bag as well.

'You can get dressed now.'

As Lola put the clothes on, Frieda searched through the wallet. She handed the small number of coins to Lola. A credit card, a driving licence, a student union card and several store cards she put into her own pocket.

'Don't you trust me with those?'

'You can't use them if you don't have them.'

Then Frieda tossed the wallet into the bag as well.

'That was a present from my parents,' said Lola.

'Is it worth dying for?'

Lola looked at herself in the full-length mirror. 'I look like someone else.'

Frieda followed her gaze. 'You don't look conspicuous. That's all that matters. Now we need to go. We've already been here too long.'

As they walked out of the shop, Frieda crammed the

shopping bag into a bin on the street. Lola started to protest. 'I suppose I'm not allowed to say that those clothes and my watch meant something to me,' she said.

Frieda looked at Lola with an expression that wasn't too far away from a smile. 'You should never own anything that you would mind losing,' she said.

Thirty-three

Lola had become used to these trips across London. This time they took the Overground east from Camden Road, then changed at Highbury and Islington and headed south. They got out at Shadwell and walked along Cable Street, then turned down a side-street lined with small houses built in the sixties, set slightly back from the road, with porches and miniature front lawns. Frieda took a key from her pocket and opened the door of number three. The hall smelt of lavender. Lola glanced at the mirror on the wall then immediately looked away: she didn't want to see her face. It didn't look like her any more.

Suddenly two pale shapes streamed past them.

'Oh!' she said, startled.

'I'm cat-sitting,' said Frieda.

Lola sat down heavily on the stairs and gazed at Frieda, standing there so calmly in this comfortable, clean little house.

'Cat-sitting?' she said. She started to laugh, a hard sound that ricocheted round the hall. Frieda stepped forward and the laughter changed to a hacking sob. Lola leaned down, her head between her knees, and her shoulders shook under the soft new jumper.

Frieda put a hand on her shoulder and waited for the sobs to subside. At last Lola lifted her head and stared at her blearily.

'Come into the kitchen,' Frieda said. 'I'll make you a hot drink.'

'How did you get this place?' asked Lola, once she was sitting at the table. There was a lava lamp on the side and on the white wall a picture of a harlequin.

'Just a contact. It's not important. You mustn't open the curtains front or back, turn on overhead lights or make any loud noises. We enter and leave as discreetly as possible – and if we're asked, we've come to feed the cats. Anything we use I must replace. This, for instance.' She dropped a ginger teabag into a large green mug. 'The people who live here are on holiday and nobody must know anyone is in here.'

Lola nodded.

'Now, we have to talk.' She passed Lola the mug of ginger tea. 'Tell me how you're feeling.'

Lola wrapped her hands round the mug and dropped her face so that Frieda couldn't see her eyes. There was a long silence. When she spoke it was in a voice straining to be steady. 'I don't know how I am. Sometimes I feel calm, like I'm looking at myself from the outside and nothing is real, like I'm on the other side of a glass door.' She looked up briefly, her face shiny from the tea's steam. Frieda nodded at her but said nothing. 'And sometimes I feel like there's a rolling sea inside me and I'm drowning in it. But whichever it is, I see it all the time. See her. When I close my eyes, I see her looking up at me. I've never seen anyone dead before. Dead eyes are different. It's hard to explain. And there was so much blood. I trod in it. They gave me new shoes at the police station, the ones you threw away. I smell it too. It's like it's coating the lining of my throat and nose.'

'I'm very sorry about your friend,' said Frieda, gently.

'She's got a name. Jess. Jessica Colbeck.'

'I'm very sorry about Jess.'

Lola swallowed and started to breathe quickly, as if she had run up several flights of stairs.

'If I hadn't had this stupid idea of writing about you and then meeting Dean Reeve on the canal and then . . .'

'And then what? You can't blame yourself.'

'I'm not blaming myself. I'm just wishing that none of this had happened. I wish I could just go back in time and none of this had ever happened. I don't want to be here.'

'What you saw was terrible. You can talk to me about it. You can say anything to me and I will listen. However, I can tell you that it will always be painful, but it will fade.'

'I don't want it to fade.' Lola's voice was fierce. Frieda, looking at her, thought how she'd grown up over the course of one terrible day. 'I feel that would be a way of forgetting Jess.'

'You won't forget her. Neither will you remember her only as you do now, with horror and guilt.'

Lola dipped her head down again. Her shoulders were hunched forward and her hair had come untied and fell in limp strands.

'Do you want to describe exactly what happened?' asked Frieda.

Lola gave a violent shake of her head. 'I can't. Not yet.'

'All right. Tell me what happened at the police station then.'

Lola gave a halting, disjointed account of her questioning by Dugdale, how he'd made her go over and over her account and made her feel guilty somehow, and a young man called Dan Something-or-other had written things down, and she'd signed a statement but her hand had shaken so much it didn't look like her signature. They'd given her tea and a sandwich but she had vomited it up in the toilet minutes later. They asked her where she would be staying and she'd given them the address of a friend, and they'd told her to keep herself available for more questioning. They wanted to give her a lift there but she said she would prefer to go alone, and then they wanted to call her parents, but she'd refused.

'They'll never understand any of this,' she said. 'They'll blame me somehow.' She gave a violent sniff and wiped her nose with the back of her hand. 'Silly Lola,' she said. 'Look at what she's got herself into now. What a bloody, bloody mess.' Her voice broke up; the words came out in harsh, separated syllables.

'No, Lola,' said Frieda. 'Nobody will blame you.'

'You don't know my parents.'

'Did you get the impression that the police are making any progress?'

'They just asked me questions,' said Lola. 'Lots and lots of questions, the same ones over and over again. They didn't tell me anything.'

'And then you went to Karlsson? Tell me about that. Wasn't he helpful? Why are you here?'

Lola took a long time to answer, and when she did, it was in a low voice. 'Don't be angry with me. If you're angry with me, I couldn't bear it. I know I've done everything wrong.'

'I won't be angry.'

'I didn't ask about him and I didn't see him. I was going to but then I didn't. I can't rely on anyone. You've taught me that. Except for you. That was all I could think of. I had to get in touch with you. Nobody else.'

'I see.' Frieda looked at her with knitted brows.

'I had this night – this awful night. It was like a terrible dream, but I was awake. I haven't slept at all. I didn't want to go to our place until it was light. I couldn't walk along the canal in the dark. So I wandered around. I went into the Underground and just rode up and down the Northern Line, and I kept thinking he'd be there. Every time the doors opened in a station I thought he'd step in. I knew I should go back to the police station. There's this Italian café near the Barbican I've been to a few times and they stay open until five a.m., and I went there and I ordered tea and a pastry and I sat there for about two hours without touching either, and then when I came to go I didn't have enough money to pay.' She gave a gulp. 'This sweet guy paid for me and then he kind of asked me on a date. The old me would have said yes – he was cute. But of course I couldn't. I walked to Liverpool Street station and I sat in this grotty waiting room and I waited until it was light and then I came to where I thought you were. I had to walk because I had no money left and I was so tired and scared I kept having to stop and hold on to things and I wanted to lie down and roll into a little ball and never move again or open my eyes. And you were gone. You were gone.'

She lifted the mug and took a large gulp of the cooling tea. Great tears rolled down her face.

'You must be completely exhausted,' said Frieda.

Lola nodded. 'I am. But how will I ever sleep again? I'll dream about it.'

'Perhaps. But you need to get some rest.'

'I know I shouldn't have gone to see Jess. I was stupid. But I got a direct message from her saying I had to go and see her. Saying it was very, very urgent.'

'Why didn't you tell me?'

'She said not to tell anyone. And you'd have told me not to go.'

Frieda looked into Lola's swollen, bloodshot eyes. 'Let's not spend time on what you think I would have done,' she said. 'We need to think about now. From now on you're not going to have a phone and you're not going to have your computer.'

'Don't you trust me?'

'It's not a matter of trust. It's very hard to be on your guard all the time – especially someone like you.'

'What am I like?'

'Naturally trusting. So if you don't have them, you can't make a mistake with them. Anyway, it doesn't matter if I trust you. What matters is that you trust me. If you think I'm unreasonable or unreliable or unsafe, you can walk out now, and find someone who will protect you. But if you decide to stay, then it's on my terms. Is that something you can manage?'

'What'll I actually do?'

'Read a book. A book won't give our location away. There are lots of books in the living room. Most of them are strange self-help books or books about cats, but there are a few novels. I think you should have a bath, the water's piping hot. And then see if you can have a nap. Tomorrow I'll buy you a sleeping bag – this once you can sleep in their sheets.'

Thirty-four

Dan Quarry was driving away from the lock-ups and trying to work out how many hours' sleep he had had in the last three days. Eight, perhaps? He had gone beyond tiredness into a kind of tipsy alertness, where everything seemed to have sharp outlines, where sounds were more vivid and where his thoughts sprang at him, like creatures that had been crouching in the undergrowth, waiting. He knew he should go home, shower, crawl into bed for a while. His skin itched. He felt as though tiny insects were crawling all over him. He wished he had changed the sheets; for a moment he let himself think of his old home, the one Maggie had thrown him out of, where the sun came in through the back windows in the evening, and where his daughter would climb on his lap when he came home tired.

He pulled over, got out of his car and lit a cigarette. It was a damp, grey afternoon, with no wind. The autumn leaves hung limply on the branches of the plane tree that stood in the centre of the tiny patch of green. He shut his eyes for a moment, but his tiredness made the world lurch beneath his feet, so he opened them again. He didn't know this area of London at all. The sun was invisible in the sky's thick grey and he couldn't work out where the river was. On either side of the road there were small shops – kebab and fish-and-chip shops, pawnbrokers, shops selling household goods, a funeral director's with dying lilies in the window. Above them were flats, but it was impossible to tell which were occupied and which deserted. Ahead was a jumble of low-rise light-industrial units, scrapyards, depots for vans. Quarry saw there was a gym as well, but its doors were boarded up and its windows shattered.

He finished his cigarette, dropped it and ground out its ember with his heel. Then he got back into the car. Much as he had expected, the forensic examination of the garage had produced almost nothing. There were no relevant human traces in the shed. Almost certainly the murders had happened elsewhere. There were multiple fingerprints but none that matched Dean Reeve's. The lane had been used by dozens of other people; the items that had been collected – the condoms, the crisps bags, the clumps of hair that turned out to belong to a dog – took them nowhere.

The lock-ups belonged to a man called George Pearsall, who ran a building company in Swindon. The individual garages were sub-let in a mass of different arrangements, off the books, for cash. They hadn't yet been able to find who Reeve had rented his from.

Phelps had trawled through online sites to see where the freezers had come from and had also drawn a blank. There was no way to track sales of second- or third-hand freezers.

As Quarry was about to drive away, his phone rang. He didn't recognize the caller's number.

'Is that Dan Quarry?'

'Who's this?'

'My name's Ellie Hannan. You don't know me. I was a colleague of Liz Barron. I came across your name in her notes.'

Quarry was thinking hard. He didn't know what to say.

'Are you still there?'

'It's not a good time,' he said.

'We're all devastated by what happened to Liz. You must be too. I thought we could talk about it.'

'I said, it's not a good time.'

'Can we talk later?'

'Yes,' Quarry said. 'Later.' Anything to get her off the line. He ended the call, turned on the engine and drove off. The grey day, the flat concrete landscape seemed to weigh down on him. That abandoned car-wash. That place selling glass. The one selling tyres, a cluster of men lurking in the interior. Or that large building piled high with the odds and ends from people's lives that no one wanted any more. On the pavement outside, there were rusting buggies, wheelbarrows, stacked chairs and two huge metal filing cabinets.

Quarry drew over and parked. Getting out, he walked back and peered in through the double doors. In front of him, a deep shelf was piled with old printers. Who on earth would buy second-hand printers? He stepped inside.

The room was massive, both wide and deep, and it was crammed with what at first sight looked like worthless junk, sorted into approximate categories. The printers were next to computers with dusty screens and trailing wires. The computers were next to the televisions, some of which reminded Quarry of his grandmother's when he was a boy. There were giant speakers, DVD players, boxes of mobile phones. To his left were the bikes, stacked against each other, and as he looked Quarry saw a young man wheel two more through the doors at the back. Another man came through carrying a large box, obviously heavy. He realized that there were several figures working in the space, half hidden behind the walls of junk.

Quarry went further into the room. There were food mixers. There were mattresses. There were plastic Christmas trees, deckchairs, pitchforks, trowels. There were two chainsaws with blunted teeth. There were chests of all shapes and sizes. Vacuum cleaners. Buckets and mops. Microwaves, ovens, hotplates. Pots and pans. Piles of chipped plates. Old doors. Wellington boots. And at the far end there were fridges. And there were freezers.

'Need help?'

Quarry turned. A man stood before him, enormous and pink-faced and bald, with blue eyes that looked like bright light would hurt them. The man was smiling, revealing small yellow teeth, but the smile disappeared when Quarry fished out his ID.

'I'm trying to find out where some freezers came from.'

'Freezers?'

Quarry pointed over the man's shoulder. 'You know what a freezer is, don't you?' He pulled the photos from his bag. 'Recognize them?'

'No.'

'You haven't even looked.'

The man slid his eyes across the photos. He pushed his plump hands into the pockets of his baggy jogging pants and waited.

'It was probably a month ago,' said Quarry. 'Maybe two.'

'I'm doing nothing wrong here. People bring stuff they don't want. Or we collect it. We're doing them a favour.'

'I am not accusing you of anything.'

'Like I said, a freezer's a freezer.'

'Or this man.' He took out the photo of Dean Reeve.

Again the man barely looked. 'Sorry,' he said.

'It's important.' Over the man's shoulder, he could see shapes moving about. All men, all young, sorting out crap, hauling stolen goods along the grimy floor. 'You don't want me to interfere with your business, do you?'

'I'm doing nothing wrong.'

'Then look at this photo. I mean *properly*. And tell me if you've seen this man. And if I think you're doing your best, as a concerned citizen, to help me, then I won't start asking more questions. And I mean questions you really won't want to answer.'

The man's pink face darkened. He took the photo and stared at it. He held it at arm's length, then drew it closer, so close he was only an inch or so away from the image. He tipped it as if something hidden might be revealed.

'Sorry. We take stuff people don't want and give them stuff they do, and they pay us for it and then I don't think about them again.'

Quarry sighed and handed him his card. 'If you remember anything,' he said.

The man slid it into his back pocket. 'Yeah,' he said, turned and walked away.

Thirty-five

Frieda woke Lola at four that afternoon. She was curled on the leather sofa in the front room with the old, blind cat lying against her shoulder.

'How long have I slept?'

'Only an hour or so. I thought I should wake you now so that you can sleep properly tonight. How are you feeling?'

'I'm fine.'

'Of course you're not fine. But in the meantime we're going to the shops. You can do an impersonation of being fine by doing something normal.'

'Will that cure me?'

'I don't know, but it will help us get supper.'

There was a family store at the end of the road. Frieda looked at the shelves and Lola glanced from side to side and back towards the entrance, her eyes flickering nervously.

'What do you want to eat tonight?' asked Frieda.

Lola turned to her with a dazed expression. 'I don't know.'

Frieda bought a cauliflower, some cheddar cheese, butter, milk and a half-baked baguette. She added a small jar of mustard to the basket, two bars of chocolate, apples, a jar of marmalade and some porridge oats.

'We can use their flour,' she said.

Then she went over to the shelves of newspapers and picked out six national ones, folding them so that their glaring headlines and their photographs of Jess smiling broadly, a dimple in each cheek, were obscured. As she was paying, she noticed something behind the counter.

'One of those,' she said, pointing to a bottle of whisky.

'I've never drunk whisky,' Lola said. 'It smells of disinfectant.'

'It's like drinking mud and fire.'

'Is that a good thing?'

When they got home Lola sat in the kitchen with a mug of tea and a book by Gerald Durrell, and Frieda went into the living room with all the papers. She opened them one by one. Each led on the murder of Jess Colbeck, twenty-one years old and brutally killed in her flat. Each linked Jess's death with the spate of London murders, which several papers called 'an epidemic'. There were pictures of Dugdale, of the other victims. There were comment pieces and interviews with friends of Jess's, not with her parents who were too distraught; she was their only child. Frieda read everything, scowling with concentration. It took her a long time, and when she had finished she took all the papers up to her room and put them out of sight.

Then she went into the kitchen and cooked a mustardy cauliflower cheese, which they ate with hunks of baguette. It was comforting, filling, and she was glad to see Lola had a second helping.

After, they went through into the living room. There were china-cat ornaments on all the shelves and a large photograph of Venice on the wall. Frieda opened the bottle of whisky and poured some into two tumblers. She handed one to Lola, who took a sip and started coughing.

'It just needs practice,' said Frieda.

Lola nodded and took another cautious sip. She screwed up her eyes and wrinkled her nose. 'It almost stings.' She put the glass on the small table. 'You've been through terrible things,' she said 'Violent things. Aren't you haunted by them?'

'You saw me at the grave. Everything that happens to you becomes part of you. It's like what you eat. You metabolize it.' Frieda took a sip of her drink and then shook her head. 'I don't have any answers. We can't make ourselves forget. We shouldn't forget. But there are ways of remembering that are helpful and ways of remembering that are not. We shouldn't go over and over bad things in our past, as if we want to polish them and harden them and preserve them.' Then she looked at Lola with a keen expression. 'It was terrible. If you think I can't understand how terrible, I can. You can acknowledge it. You must confront it. But don't give it power over you.'

Lola looked frightened. Her eyes grew huge in her round face. 'Power over me? What do you mean?'

Frieda drained her glass. 'It's just something to think about.'

Frieda was woken by a noise. Of course, this house was surrounded by noises. Cars drove past. There was the rattle of a passing train in the distance. A couple shouted, saying terrible things they would regret in the morning. But this was different: it was a high, keening sound. Frieda unzipped the sleeping bag she had bought for herself and walked out of her room and into the smaller room where Lola was. She was scrunched up in bed, her arms wrapped around her head, rocking herself to and fro and crying. Frieda sat beside her, and put a hand on her shoulder. Lola jolted as if an electric current had passed through her and turned towards Frieda, glassy-eyed.

'Oh, no,' she said. 'No, no, no. Please.'

'I'm here.'

'Frieda.'

'Tell me what you're feeling.'

'You don't want to know.'

'I do.'

Lola sat up, pulling her covers round her. 'All right. I wish I was dead. Except that wouldn't help.'

'No. It wouldn't help.'

'You don't understand,' said Lola. 'You can't understand. I don't know what to do with myself. What shall I do? I can't bear this feeling. I feel like I'm splitting open with it.'

They sat in silence for a time.

'You know, there's a theory about human beings,' said Frieda. 'We're not very fast and we're not very strong. But we had an advantage over animals. We could run or walk and just keep going and going. Animals like deer could outrun us for a bit. But we could keep after them for hour after hour and in the end the deer would just give up. It would just stop and lie down and give up and be killed.'

'I don't know who I'm meant to be in that story. Because I sound more like the deer.'

'That's what Dean Reeve wants. He wants us all to fuel his pathetic fantasy of power by giving in to him.'

'He's killed a lot of people. That doesn't sound so pathetic. Have you thought that maybe we are in his power and we're just doing what he wants us to do?'

'It's not just you,' said Frieda. 'It's the two of us. You do realize that, don't you?'

Lola gazed at her, her lower lip trembling.

'You're not alone, Lola.'

'Do you really think you can protect me?' Lola was visibly shaking. 'Could you protect Liz Barron? I read about you and Dean, remember: could you protect that policeman who was working for you? Could you protect Dean Reeve's brother? Could you protect any of the others?'

'They all made mistakes,' said Frieda. 'It wasn't their fault but they left themselves vulnerable to him. If we don't do that, he can't get at us.'

Lola turned away from Frieda and mumbled something.

'I didn't hear that,' Frieda said.

'I said, maybe we've left that too late.'

'Do you want me to stay here while you go back to sleep?'

'All right.'

Lola lay down again but her eyes were wide open. Her shoulders were tense.

'Do you want to talk about it, Lola?' There was a silence. 'You can tell me anything. Anything at all. There is nothing that would shock me or that I wouldn't understand.'

'There was so much blood,' said Lola. 'It was like an abattoir. And Jess just looked at me. She stared at me and there was blood everywhere. Oh, God.'

'She wasn't seeing you.'

'I close my eyes and I see her face. It was my fault. I don't want this.'

'Of course you don't,' said Frieda.

'I want it never to have happened. I want to go back to the way things used to be, missing deadlines and hanging out with friends and worrying about whether Ben fancied me and being overdrawn.'

'I know,' said Frieda.

'I'll never get over it.'

'You'll never be the same,' said Frieda. 'But this feeling won't last.' She waited a few moments, then said: 'If you have anything to say to me, this is a good time. It's dark. You don't need to look at me. You can just talk as if you were talking to yourself.'

'I'm the last person in the world I want to talk to.'

Lola gave a hiccupy sob and closed her eyes. Frieda sat beside her and waited until her breathing had deepened. Then she got up, returned to her room and didn't sleep for a long time.

Thirty-six

Frieda hoped that Lola would be better in the morning but she looked almost worse. Pale with dark patches around her eyes. She was subdued, almost as if she had been medicated. Frieda made tea for them both and then porridge for breakfast. Lola seemed not to notice it and Frieda had to encourage her to eat, which she did with slow mechanical movements. But she didn't speak and Frieda didn't urge her.

'We're going out,' said Frieda.

'Where?'

'You need a few more clothes.'

'It doesn't matter.'

'Just a couple of things.'

Before they left, Frieda put her laptop into a shoulder bag and laid it on the kitchen table. They walked together up towards Commercial Road and then continued for a long way, all the way up to Spitalfields. Lola hardly spoke. She seemed even worse than when they'd set out. She kept chewing her lips, muttering to herself. Frieda looked at her with concern. When they arrived in the market, Frieda felt she had to say something.

'Sometimes it's good to talk about things,' she said. 'And sometimes it's better not to talk at all. You decide. But I'm here, all right?'

'Not now.'

They went into the large Gap store.

'You just need something for the next couple of days. It doesn't matter what.'

'All right,' said Lola. 'Could you get me some knickers and socks?'

'Sure.'

Frieda found some underwear. She spotted Lola at the far end of the shop, holding a big pile of clothes, and went across.

'All of those?' she asked.

'No, but I thought I should try them on, or the trousers at least,' said Lola. She glanced down at the heap of garments she was cradling: three pairs of jeans, a denim shirt dress, a sweatshirt with a large star on its front, two plain T-shirts and a grey hoodie. 'I've lost weight since all of this. I don't know what fits me any more.' Large tears stood in her eyes. 'I'm shrinking,' she said.

'OK. Shall I take the things you're not trying on?'

Lola handed over everything but the three pairs of jeans and disappeared into the changing room. Frieda waited, feeling too hot in the crowded shop, and after several minutes Lola came out and handed over one pair of jeans.

'Most of those are in the sale but you don't need to buy everything,' she said, looking at the clothes Frieda was holding.

'It's fine,' said Frieda.

When they were done, they emerged from the market in front of the huge church.

'Shall we make our way back?' said Frieda.

'Or could we get a coffee first? I feel trapped in the house, like it's a prison. It feels better being out.'

So Frieda led her up the road to a coffee shop of artfully mismatched tables and chairs. She got a black coffee for herself and Lola some tea and they sat silently. Frieda looked across as Lola fiddled with her mug, ran her finger round the rim, picked it up and put it down again, did everything except drink it.

Finally she met Frieda's gaze. 'I don't know how you've done all this. The things you've seen, the things you've been through. I don't know how you've survived. You're strong, much stronger than me.'

'There are no easy answers,' said Frieda. 'Sometimes I think there aren't any hard answers either. You carry on because it's better than the alternative. Remember that I'm here. You can say anything to me and you can ask me anything. You don't need to hide from the things that most terrify you – hiding can be the worst thing to do. Things feel better when they're looked at.'

Lola gave her a wild look.

'Come on, time to go,' said Frieda, and they left the café.

Frieda took hold of Lola's elbow as they crossed Commercial Street in the hot roar of traffic. She looked as if she might walk into a lorry, or fall over the kerb.

'This isn't going to work,' Frieda said. 'You can't put yourself through this.'

'Later,' said Lola. 'I can't think now. I can't talk.'

'I think you should go to Karlsson and he'll find you a safe house. That would be better, Lola. You can't cope with this.'

'I don't know,' said Lola. 'I don't know anything any more.'

'Then I'm going to know for you.'

They retraced their steps, back to Cable Street, up the little road. Lola followed Frieda obediently, a few steps behind; her legs felt shaky, as though she had climbed a steep flight of stairs. Frieda unlocked the door, pushed it open and the two of them stepped inside.

As Frieda kicked the door shut behind her, she looked up

to her left and then down, expectantly, for the cats. They weren't there. She tapped Lola's shoulder.

Lola looked at Frieda and she felt, quite suddenly, as if she were in a dream, as if nothing quite made sense and she had lost all control.

Frieda's expression was entirely calm but she raised a finger and put it to her lips. What did that mean? Oh, yes. Silence. Frieda took Lola by the arm and led her through the kitchen and spoke in a tone that was very slightly strange, very slightly too loud.

'We'll just grab a tea and take it upstairs, OK?'

What did she mean? Lola had just had tea. And she hadn't even drunk it.

As they entered the kitchen Frieda picked up her shoulder bag, while still walking and still grasping Lola's arm, and led her to the end of the kitchen. She opened the door to the utility room at the back of the house. What was she doing? Hadn't she talked about going upstairs?

Then everything changed.

Frieda pushed her hard into the room. She pulled the key from the inside of the door, slammed the door shut, put the key into the lock and fumbled at it. She couldn't get it to turn.

Lola didn't just hear the sound of someone in the house, she felt it. Boots on the stairs. She looked at Frieda. The key turned. Frieda stepped across and pushed the washing-machine across the floor with a terrible scraping sound and jammed it against the door.

'Out,' Frieda said.

Lola tried to turn the handle of the outside door but couldn't get it open. Was it locked? There was a banging at the other door now. Frieda edged her aside, got the door open and dragged her out into the yard.

Frieda stopped suddenly.

She went back into the house and now everything seemed to be happening slowly, not just like a dream but like a dream where you were under water or moving in soft sand. Frieda re-emerged with a key in her hand. She ran to the gate and unlocked it and pulled it open. Lola felt like she couldn't move. Frieda came back and dragged her through into the alley. She gestured to the left.

'Just run and don't stop,' she called.

Lola ran a few steps and then looked back. Frieda was bent over, locking the gate. Lola started to run, out of breath before she had started, and before she knew it Frieda was beside her, taking her by the hand, pulling her.

'Don't think. Just run.'

Lola felt herself being dragged to the right and the left, under the railway, through a housing estate, all the time not daring to turn her head, to see what might be behind them. They reached a busy road. It was the road they had crossed just a few minutes earlier but now it felt like a different world. Everything seemed a blur of movement and in the middle of the confusion and the noise Lola saw Frieda raising her arm and a taxi pulled up beside them. Frieda pushed her inside and there was the sudden smell of leather and disinfectant.

'Mile End Tube station,' Frieda said sharply and Lola felt the cab pull away.

Frieda took her phone out. 'He was in the house,' she said. 'Dean Reeve was in the house. He knew we were there.'

'Where are you?' Dugdale's voice was urgent.

'We got away. We're in a taxi.'

'We?'

'Lola's with me.'

'How is she?'

'How do you think? But she's not hurt.'

'I'll send some people to the house.'

243

'It won't do any good.' Frieda looked across at Lola, who was staring ahead of her. 'I told you where I was and you promised to keep that information to yourself and he knew where we were.'

'I don't know what happened. I'll find out.'

'Do that.' She put the phone back in her pocket.

When they stepped out of the taxi at Mile End, Lola was in a daze.

'How are you?' Frieda asked.

Lola looked around her, then down at the bag she was still carrying.

'I brought my clothes with me,' she said. And then she leaned forward and vomited on the pavement, again and again, apologizing all the while.

'I'm sorry,' she said. 'I'm sorry.'

Frieda took a tissue, wiped Lola's mouth and put an arm round her. 'It's all right,' she said.

'It's not all right. It'll never be all right again.'

'There's been a leak,' said Dugdale, gazing round the room at the men and women in front of him. His voice, normally so calm, was quivering with rage. He bunched his fists and said again, louder, 'A leak. In any circumstances, it would be unacceptable. In this particular one, it is monstrous. Do you hear me? Dean Reeve found out where Frieda Klein and Lola Hayes were hiding. Who knew their whereabouts? We did – or a few of us. Has anyone got anything to say?'

The room was thick with silence. Not a breath could be heard.

'We are police officers. Our job is to keep people safe, to protect people from harm.' He folded his arms across his chest and glared. 'Has anyone talked to the press?'

Again, silence. A chair creaked.

'Or told anyone anything about this case that was not public?'

'We wouldn't do that,' said Quarry, but without much conviction. He knew that people did do that.

'I'll be in my office for an hour. If anyone has anything to tell me, that's where they'll find me.'

Thirty-seven

'Take my arm,' said Frieda.

Lola put her arm through Frieda's and Frieda could feel her whole body trembling. She led her along the road, then turned through a gap in the iron railing, leaving behind the bustle of people. There was grass and gravestones all around them and ahead a grey church.

'This is St Dunstan's,' she said, steering Lola towards its entrance, and now they were in a cool gloom, with the dry smell of wood and candles. 'The bells here are the ones in "Oranges and Lemons" – the bells of Stepney. There's been a place of worship on this site for over a thousand years. Sit down.'

Lola sank onto the wooden pew. Frieda put her hand into the Gap shopping bag and drew out the grey hoodie. She unzipped it and wrapped it round Lola's shoulders. 'I'm going to make a phone call,' she said. 'You just stay put.'

Lola nodded and bent over, putting her face into her hands as though she was praying. Frieda walked back towards the entrance. She fished her mobile from her pocket and made a call.

Half an hour later, she and Lola were standing in St Pancras station, near the Eurostar's departures gate. People moved in a steady line past them, some in suits and carrying briefcases, others dragging wheelie bags or with rucksacks on their shoulders. A tiny child fell over at Frieda's feet and lay on his back, staring up at her with bright surprise until his mother scooped him up.

Frieda led Lola into a vegetarian café. She ordered two teas and a bowl of bean sprouts, a Greek salad and two bread rolls.

'I'm not hungry,' said Lola. 'In the circumstances.'

'I normally say that you shouldn't force people to eat. But you need to eat. Go on.'

Frieda watched while Lola took a few tentative forkfuls of salad.

'I can't,' she said finally.

'You tried,' said Frieda. 'That's something.'

'Are we here for a reason?' said Lola.

'We're meeting someone.' Frieda looked at her watch. 'But not quite yet.'

They were sitting at a table by the window and Lola gazed at the crowds walking past, parties of schoolchildren, anxious tourists pulling their wheeled cases. But Frieda was paying no attention to any of it. Instead she just seemed to be staring at the wall in front of her. Then she turned; Lola wasn't sure whether Frieda was looking directly at her, scrutinizing her, or at something behind her head.

'So what are we doing?' asked Lola. 'Are we just waiting for the next thing Dean Reeve will do?'

'Have you got any other ideas?'

'We could wait for the police to catch him.'

'I've been waiting for years.' Frieda reached a hand out and put it on Lola's. 'You can go away,' she said. 'I can arrange it.'

Lola gave a shudder. 'I couldn't,' she said. 'He'd find me.'

'Even after what you've been through?' said Frieda. 'What you've seen?'

'Especially after that.'

Frieda took a pen from her pocket and opened up a paper napkin and started drawing on it.

'I can't believe it,' said Lola. 'We almost get caught, we

almost die and you're all calm again.' She looked at what Frieda was drawing. She recognized the shape of the radiating spokes. 'Your rivers again?'

'We've been talking about what we're going to do. The real question is what he's going to do. He almost got to us, but he didn't. He had a plan. He improvised. None of it quite worked out. So the question is: what's he going to do now?'

Lola stared dully at her. Frieda took out her phone and dialled.

'I didn't think I'd be hearing from you for a while,' said Dugdale, at the other end. 'Has something happened?'

'I've had a thought. Do you know Beverley Brook?'

'Should I know her?'

'It's not a woman. It's a stream that flows through Richmond Park.'

'I didn't know it. I'm more East London. So?'

'Reeve is working his way through the hidden rivers, like spokes on a wheel. I think the next one may be Beverley Brook.'

'Working his way through them,' said Dugdale. 'That's one way of putting it. You mean killing people.'

'That's what I mean.'

'So what do you expect us to do? Keep it under surveillance?'

'It's too long for that. It goes through Wimbledon and Richmond and Putney.'

'So why are you telling me?'

'So you'll look out for something. You may see something that doesn't get in the papers.'

'Murders always get in the papers.'

'It may not be a murder. It may not be anything. I'm just guessing.'

'I'll keep a lookout. One more thing, do you have anywhere to stay?'

'I'm about to find out.'

'Are you going to tell me where?'

Frieda looked across at Lola. Their glances met. 'We'll see,' she said. 'Not yet. There was a leak.'

'It won't happen again.'

'Not yet,' she repeated. 'Please let me know if you hear anything.' She ended the call.

'Beverley Brook?' asked Lola.

'Yes,' said Frieda.

'Is it named after a woman called Beverley?'

'I've just had this conversation with Dugdale. It's not named after a woman called Beverley. It used to have beavers. A long time ago.'

'What are the police going to do?'

'That's up to them. They know about the rivers and the name-day theory. The trouble is, it's like trying to mould water into a shape, or to hold fog in a cupped hand.'

'What do you mean?'

'Every day is a different saint's day. Dean isn't targeting a particular kind of person. He's picking people off by name and waiting for their day to fall. It's a horrible thought, but perfectly feasible, that he has already killed others and is waiting to make that known.'

'So the police can't go to Beverley Brook and wait?'

'They don't know how long they would be there for. Days. Weeks. Waiting for something that might never happen.'

'So what do we do?'

'Frieda,' said a familiar voice behind her, and she turned.

Walter Levin was dressed in a pin-stripe suit and a tie that looked as though it had been knitted with grubby string. His shoes glowed like new conkers. His eyes behind the thick glasses were like pebbles out of water.

'Thank you for this,' she said.

249

'It's better than talking on the phone, given what's happened.'

'I'm sure you're right. Lola, this is Walter Levin.'

He gripped Lola's hand so hard she gave a small yelp.

Frieda looked at her. 'I need to talk to Mr Levin about something. Is it all right if we leave you for a moment?'

Lola nodded.

'I need the toilet,' she said.

Frieda pointed to the back of the café, then took a twenty-pound note and put it on the table. She got up and she and Levin walked out onto the concourse. His jovial manner disappeared.

'Have you been compromised?' he asked.

'Dean Reeve knew where we were.'

'Do you know how he found out?'

'I'm thinking about that. In the meantime, I know that I need to be careful about who knows where I'm living.'

'I hope you feel you can trust *me*.'

'About this, at least.'

Levin looked amused. 'Did you leave anything behind?'

Frieda shook her head. 'Nothing important. I took my laptop and my phone and my wallet with me. There's nothing else except clothes and toiletries and a bit of food in the fridge. They need to be taken away before the owners return. And there are four cats that have to be fed.'

He smiled. 'Jude will love that little job. She's always complaining she doesn't get out enough.'

Frieda handed over the keys and told him the address. 'Once you've taken our things away, the front-door one has to be returned to my niece Chloë so she can give it back to her flatmate.'

'Leave that to us.'

'Do you need her address?'

'I have her address.'

'You do?'

'You forget, we've been friends for quite a long time now.'

'Friends,' Frieda said dubiously. 'So where are we to go?'

'I've written it down.' He patted his many pockets experimentally, then produced a white card. 'Jock Keegan will be there at five with the keys.'

'Where are the owners?'

'You don't need to worry about them.' He looked up at the large clock. 'And I've got a train to catch.'

The two of them walked back towards the café. They saw Lola before she saw them.

'Is she all right?' Levin asked.

'Did you read the report?'

'I know that she found the body of her friend. She narrowly escaped Dean Reeve. Not everyone can deal with something like that.'

'What's the alternative to dealing with it?'

'I mean that she might become a liability. To you.'

Frieda looked sharply at him. 'A liability? What does that mean?'

'I mean that something can always be arranged. To help you.'

'And her?'

'That goes without saying.'

'She's refusing to leave me just at the moment. Perhaps that will change. But thank you.'

He looked at Frieda with an expression of concern. 'You were lucky this time,' he said. 'Resourceful, of course. And well prepared. But he'll learn from that.'

'So it mustn't happen again.'

He held out his hand but Frieda shook her head. 'Why?' she said.

'What do you mean?'

'This is the last time we'll ever meet.'

'Don't say that,' said Levin. 'It sounds morbid.'

'However things turn out, I'm finished with all of this.'

'You mean the police stuff?'

'Yes, I mean the police stuff. So, I wanted to know: why me? Why did you choose to help me, or make use of me, or however you'd put it?'

Levin looked around. 'I feel this is the sort of thing we should be talking about over drinks in front of a fire, not in a crowded station.'

'That's all right. I didn't think you'd answer.'

'No, Frieda. I'll answer.' Levin's expression changed to one she rarely saw. Hard, shrewd, a little chilling. A glimpse of the real man. 'Some years ago I was having a drink in Whitehall.' He gave a faint smile. 'I believe it was actually in front of a log fire. And the man I was talking to, a man whose judgement I respect, said there was someone who might interest me. It was you, of course, and, as it happens, your involvement in the Dean Reeve case. We looked into you, and the tragic suicide of your father . . .'

'If you're going to say something like "What doesn't kill you, makes you stronger", then . . .'

'It's not entirely inapplicable in this case,' continued Levin. 'There was the trouble you ran into as a teenager, leaving home. I talked to various people in your past. It was quite remarkable. I started to follow your progress and I thought, That's the sort of person I should recruit.'

'But you didn't recruit me. You used me.'

'That's harsh, Frieda. I hope that we helped each other.'

Frieda held the keys up. 'I don't mean to sound ungrateful.'

Levin smiled. 'You don't,' he said. 'Even when you try to. Now . . .' he paused for a moment '. . . I'm not a person who hugs or kisses on both cheeks, so I'm just going to shake your hand, but I hope you realize it represents, connotes, a genuine regard.'

He held out his hand gravely and Frieda shook it, but then Levin didn't let go. 'On the issue of recruitment . . .' he began.

Frieda pulled her hand free. 'No,' she said.

'You'd be good at it,' he said. 'You'd find it challenging, stimulating.'

'Yes,' said Frieda. 'It's like a drug. Which is why I have to stop.'

Levin shook his head sadly. 'I thought so. But I feel I haven't done enough.'

'You've done plenty,' said Frieda. 'The last bit I have to do on my own.'

'I was afraid of that. So I've provided you with a place to stay, I've failed to recruit you, we've shaken hands. There's nothing more to be said.'

He rapped on the window of the café. Lola looked round and Levin gave a little wave, then walked away and was quickly swallowed in the stream of people. Frieda rejoined Lola inside.

'Who is he?' asked Lola.

Frieda thought for a moment. 'That's a difficult question to answer. He did me a favour once and I think I did one or two for him. Be careful when someone does you a favour. You never know where it will lead.'

'Why did he look at me like that?'

'How did he look at you?'

'Like I was something he was about to dissect in a laboratory.'

'That's his normal manner. Now, there's something I want to say to you.'

Lola shrank back, looking at her with a scared expression. 'What? You sound angry.'

'I'm not angry, but I am very serious. I don't think you're being rational, Lola. You're clinging to me like a child clings to its mother, but I'm not your mother and you're not a child. I'm no longer your place of safety.'

'No.' Lola looked at Frieda like a tragic child, her eyes and her mouth round, tears rolling once more down her cheeks. 'I'll be all right. I won't collapse. I'll help you and do everything you say, but you mustn't send me away. I won't go. Frieda?'

Frieda looked at her for several seconds, and then she nodded. 'You're absolutely sure?'

'Yes.'

'Very well. If that's the way you want it. But you are to do as I say.'

'I will.' Lola took a deep, shuddering breath, wiped her cheeks with her sleeve, then asked, 'Where are we going now?'

Frieda looked at the address written in neat copperplate on the card that Levin had pressed into her hands.

'Eighteen A Rivingdale Terrace,' she said. 'NW1.' She frowned. 'I know where that is.'

'What? Is it somewhere horrible?'

'I think you'll never have lived anywhere like this before.'

Thirty-eight

Frieda and Lola went first to a camping shop on Euston Road where they bought yet another couple of cheap sleeping bags because they didn't know what there would be in the new place. Then they walked along the canal and up towards Regent's Park. The wind blew leaves along the ground and the air was full of scraps of yellow, red and brown. Frieda thought of the message that Dean had sent her, not so long ago: *We are leaves on a tree. Autumn is coming.*

Lola, walking fast to keep up, lurched between silence and sudden torrents of speech.

'I could do with a cigarette,' she said at one point. 'I'm not really a smoker. Just at parties, you know. But now I suddenly want to be smoking, smoking really hard, the way my friend Lily does. It makes her cheeks go hollow. I want to be like that.'

'Perhaps because smoking can be a way of getting through the time, when you don't know how to endure things,' said Frieda. 'For a few minutes, that's what you're doing: you're smoking a cigarette.'

'I'd probably just feel dizzy. Why are we going here?'

'This is Rivingdale Terrace.'

'This! Wow!' For a moment, she sounded like the old, guileless Lola.

The stately white buildings were set back from the road behind iron railings, many with tall pillars and long terraces.

'It looks like a palace,' said Lola. 'Who lives here?'

'Apparently nobody,' said Frieda. 'Somebody far away probably owns it as an investment.'

'Some of the windows are the size of a small house.'

Jock Keegan was coming from the opposite direction, in the threadbare suit he had worn all the time Frieda had known him, his hair like stubble, his shoulders broad. Frieda saw how he walked heavily, trudging along beside the grand façade with his eyes on the road in front of him.

'Frieda,' he said, as he reached them. 'And this is your friend.'

'This is Lola.'

'You've been having a hard time.'

He slid his hand into his jacket and drew out two keys, one large and one smaller.

'Do we have neighbours?' asked Frieda, taking them.

'In Rivingdale Terrace no one can hear you scream,' he said. 'I don't know if that's a good or a bad thing. Most of these places are empty. Drive past them at night and no lights are on. Their owners are somewhere else, hiding the rest of their loot.'

Frieda smiled; she liked Keegan's grumpiness.

'Your apartment hasn't been lived in for over five years,' he continued. 'Do you want me to come in with you?'

'There's no need. Thank you.'

'There's something else.'

He took a small envelope and gave it to Frieda.

'Spare key?' she said.

'If you need to leave in a hurry, there's a key here and the address. It's always good to have a back-up.'

'That's very thoughtful,' said Frieda.

'Be careful,' he said, and turned on his heel.

Their apartment was a duplex on the ground and first floors. There was an entrance hall larger than Lola's flat, a laundry room, a personal gym with a punching bag and a rowing machine, a small self-contained flat that was probably meant for the servant. There were two sitting rooms, one on either level, and in the upper one there was a semi-circular bar and a bronze statue of a naked woman, while in the lower a projector and a screen occupied one wall. There was a dining room, where eight high-backed chairs upholstered in red velvet were placed around a long table, a large kitchen, a bathroom with gold taps and marble washbasins and two en-suite bedrooms, one of which had a dressing room attached and a four-poster bed hung with thick purple drapes, and both of which had safes bolted to the floor. There were vast, gaudy chandeliers hanging from ceilings, and pictures of sunsets with ornate frames. There was a garden at the back with huge earthenware pots containing ornamental trees and at the front, running the length of the first floor, a terrace. From there the park lay clear in front of them, golden in the late afternoon.

The walls were damp and mildewed and one internal wall had half collapsed, showing the joists underneath. Water dripped through the ceiling in the dining room, whose wooden floor had disintegrated, and whose walls were sodden and rotting. The velvet on the chairs was chewed; the leather sofa was obviously home to mice, or perhaps to rats, while the chaise-longue with its gilded frame lay on its side, its legs broken. The purple drapes around the four-poster bed were faded and ripped. The mattresses in the bedrooms were damp and stained. The enormous mirror in the hall was shattered into a crazy network. The wallpaper in the larger sitting room bubbled, as if there was something underneath, trying to escape. The windows were grimy with thick dirt; several were cracked. In the kitchen, Lola almost stepped on the rotting remains of a pigeon. The garden was a tangle of weeds and rubbish with a great barbecue rusting at its centre. There were mouse droppings everywhere and a smell – rank and heavy – lay across each room.

Lola pulled a face. 'It's disgusting here.'

Frieda didn't reply. Instead, she went into the kitchen, feeling the stickiness of the tiles under her feet, and turned on a tap. There was a spluttering sound and, after a few seconds, water was coughed out.

'We can clean,' she said. 'Just an area for us to live in. We won't be here long.'

She started pulling open cupboards.

'What are you looking for?'

'Buckets, mops. Here we are. These will do.' She looked at her watch. 'We've got plenty of time to buy cleaning stuff, and we'll get food for this evening.'

'Shall I go? You'd have to give me the money.'

'We'll go together. I could do with some fresh air.'

They found the locks to the windows and opened every one. They swept up grime and dust, mouse droppings and dead spiders and flies, the rotten pigeon, the bits of broken glass, the objects they couldn't even identify. They wiped surfaces, cleaned the lavatory and bath, mopped the floor, using bucket after bucket of water. They pulled all the covers off the large bed and bundled them into bin bags. Frieda looked across at Lola as she sprayed disinfectant and scrubbed at encrusted dirt. Her face was flushed; she seemed better than she had a few hours ago. It was probably good for her to do this.

By nine that evening, one bedroom, its bathroom and the kitchen were clean enough to walk into without shrinking back in revulsion.

'That'll have to do,' Frieda said.

Then she took out the food she had bought: pitta bread,

hummus, carrots already chopped into batons, a small tub of olives, a netted bag of satsumas, a packet of Digestive biscuits. They'd found a shop next to the Polish deli that sold everything – paddling pools and walking sticks, party hats and cheap mugs – and she laid the bright paper tablecloth on the floor of the living room, over the stains on the mouldering carpet. No amount of scrubbing would make the table or the floor clean and, anyway, the red velvet of the chairs was torn and rotting.

'A picnic,' she said.

'Do you think there are rats in here?'

'Perhaps.'

'I hate rats. Their tails are too thick.'

'It's just a few days. The main thing is to be safe.'

'You were all prepared,' said Lola. 'How did you know?'

'I didn't. But it's like chess. You need to think a couple of moves ahead.'

Lola nodded. She tore off a piece of pitta bread, dipped it into the hummus, but didn't eat it. 'I still feel a bit sick,' she said. 'I'm hungry, but I think I might throw up again.'

'Eat a bit and see.'

Lola put a tiny morsel in her mouth and chewed. 'Mum used to try and make me go on these diets when I was at home,' she said. 'I was quite a chubby teenager. She'd look at me and say, "I think there's a beautiful Lola waiting to come out."'

Frieda looked carefully at her. 'What did you feel when she said that?'

Lola shrugged. 'She just wanted what was good for me. They both did. I'm their only child, you know. They thought they couldn't have one so I was like their miracle, just when Mum was nearly past child-bearing age. But I don't think I was quite what they expected. They used to have this look they'd give each other when I did something stupid. They thought I didn't see it. It was their oh-Lola look. I dread to think what they'd make of all of this.'

She gave a small laugh, put some more pitta bread into her mouth. 'Oh, well.'

Frieda insisted on sleeping in the same room as Lola. It looked over what must once have been stables but were now impossibly elegant mews houses.

'I have bad dreams,' said Lola. 'I'll keep you awake.'

'I tend to keep myself awake,' said Frieda. 'For the moment we're roped together, like mountain climbers.'

'I've never liked that idea. I've always imagined one person falling and pulling the other after them.'

'Here's a first,' said Frieda. 'I'm going to be the optimistic one. One falls and the other saves them.'

In the middle of the night Frieda was listening to Lola's slow breathing and assumed she was asleep until her voice came out of the darkness.

'Are you awake?'

'Yes.'

'I'm sorry. I'm a burden to you. And on top of that, I'm stopping you sleeping.'

'You're not a burden and I wasn't asleep. But I'm going to keep on saying this. I could still arrange for you to be taken somewhere.'

'There's nowhere.'

'Couldn't you stay with your parents?'

'No!' The word came out like a howl of pain. 'I couldn't do that. They wouldn't be safe. Don't even mention them. I can't bear even to think about them.'

'We can find a way,' said Frieda. But there was no answer.

Just Lola breathing in and breathing out. She was asleep. Or pretending to be asleep.

They got up early the next morning and Frieda made coffee, cut up some fruit and insisted that Lola eat it, passing across to her the segments of orange and apple one by one. Lola was pale and barely responsive. Frieda had to steer her towards the shower, then laid out clothes for her to put on.

'Can't I just stay in my pyjamas?'

'We're going for a walk.'

'You can go. I'd just like to go back to bed.'

'You don't get to do that. If you stay in, then I stay in. And I don't want to stay in.'

Lola looked as if she wanted to argue but it was just too much effort. So she slowly pulled her clothes on and then a jacket. Frieda led her out and they walked across the road into the park. There were the usual runners and dog-walkers, and a group of young Americans was throwing a football around.

'Shouldn't we be hiding?' said Lola.

'This is hiding.'

'Are we going to meet someone?'

'No.'

'Are we going to walk along one of your rivers?'

'We'll cross one of them but that's not the point of this.'

'So what is the point?'

'Maybe not to have to ask what the point of it is.'

Lola looked at Frieda with a puzzled frown. 'I'm not one of your patients.'

'Do you need to be?'

Lola turned away from Frieda and when she spoke it was in a mutter that didn't seem directed at anyone in particular. 'Nobody can make me better.'

They didn't speak for several minutes as they made their way around the southern edge of the park, then turned up towards the north. Frieda pointed at the ponds on their right.

'That's part of the River Tyburn,' she said. 'If you want the tour.'

'I don't want the tour.'

As they approached the Regent's Park mosque, Frieda gestured across the road. 'The canal's ahead there,' she said. 'But we won't walk that way. It feels too exposed. We'll just head straight across the park.'

Lola didn't reply and they walked eastwards across the grass. Then Lola stopped.

'What?' said Frieda.

'Are you frightened of dying?'

'Why are you asking?'

'It seems kind of relevant at the moment. Can't you answer the question?'

'No,' said Frieda.

'You won't answer?'

'I mean, no, I'm not frightened of dying.'

'I was afraid of that. That's what I was thinking about in the middle of the night.'

'I'm frightened of other people dying, though. If that's a comfort.'

'Not really.'

Chloë met Jack at the entrance to Saffron Mews.

'What's this about?' he said. 'Is Frieda back?'

'Don't be stupid. You'd know if she was.'

She led him along the little cobbled street to Frieda's front door and rapped on the wood. Josef opened it. Without speaking, he stepped aside as they walked into the house.

'Upstairs,' said Chloë.

'Where are we going?' said Jack.

'Just wait and see.'

They walked up, Josef behind them. When they got to the top, Chloë looked around. Josef was right. It really did feel as if it had always been like that. Where the window had been, there was now a door.

'Bloody hell,' said Jack.

'I know,' said Chloë. 'Pretty amazing. Open the door.'

Carefully, as if he were stepping into a strange new world, Jack opened the door and stepped out onto the new, spacious balcony, more like a roof terrace. He peered down at his feet and shifted slightly, trying his weight on it. Chloë followed him, then Josef. They all stood with their hands on the railings.

'So what did you do?' Jack asked Chloë.

'Just the railings. And I've made a little table.'

Jack examined the railings. 'Beautiful.'

'Getting the posts into the top and bottom balustrades and getting them straight took for ever,' she said. 'I'm not sure if I ever quite got it. I think Josef just asked me to make me feel I was doing something.'

'No. Is good,' said Josef.

'Or maybe to share the blame when Frieda gets completely furious about this.'

Chloë and Jack looked at each other. Jack went red and turned away.

'I know what you're thinking,' Chloë said.

'No, you don't.'

'You're thinking that if Frieda were here getting angry with us about this balcony, then at least she'd be here.'

Jack turned round and leaned back on the railing, heavily, so that Chloë worried whether she'd made it strong enough.

'No, not exactly,' he said.

'What, then?'

'It's like magical thinking. You and Josef think that if you create this for Frieda, it's a way of ensuring she'll come back.'

'You make it sound childish.'

Jack smiled. 'I didn't mean to. I wish I could have built some part of this, but if I had, I wouldn't let anyone stand on it.'

They stood for a long time, staring at the lights in silence.

'What's that tall building?' Jack said.

Chloë ignored him. 'Why do you think Frieda's doing this?' she said.

Josef shrugged.

'It's partly to do with us,' Jack said. 'She's seen what's happened to the people around her. I think she feels responsible.'

'I think it's more than that. She may have had enough. I sometimes wonder whether she might want to die.'

'That's crazy,' said Jack.

Chloë turned to Josef. 'What do you think, Josef? Do you think Frieda wants to die?'

'Why ask me?'

'Because you would know, if anybody knows.'

Josef took a deep breath. 'To save somebody, she might . . . I do not know. I cannot say.'

'What about saving herself?'

In response, Josef only shrugged again.

'We can't just stand here,' Jack said. 'We should do a toast to Frieda.'

'No,' said Chloë. 'Not here. It'd be wrong. God would hear and would punish us. He'd punish Frieda.'

Jack smiled again. 'I didn't know you believed in God.'

'I'll believe in anything just at the moment.'

Thirty-nine

'What do you think? A five iron or a six iron?'

Paul Arrowsmith pretended to think about that. What he was really thinking was that it didn't matter much whether Lee Denton used a five iron or a six iron or a wood or even a putter. With other friends he would have made a joke about it, but Denton was hopelessly serious about his golf. So Arrowsmith adopted a serious tone.

'I'd go for the five,' he said. 'You might need the extra length.'

'The problem is overrunning,' said Denton.

'Then maybe you should go for the six.'

'No, I think I'll stick with the five. I'll try to hit the front of the green.'

'So as not to overrun.'

Denton looked at Arrowsmith suspiciously but Arrowsmith's face was as sober and serious as he could make it.

'Well, I'd better go for it,' Denton said. He looked at his partner, who hadn't moved. 'Are you going to stand and watch me make the shot?'

'I thought I would. If that's all right.'

'Yes, that's fine. Completely fine.'

Denton took the club out of the bag. He weighed it carefully in his hands as if he were pondering his decision. Then he placed his feet apart and carefully addressed the ball. He put the club beside the ball, then raised it once, twice and struck. The two men swerved their heads simultaneously.

Denton sighed. The ball had not reached the front of the green or the back of the green or any part of the green. He had hooked it round and it had skittered along the edge of the fairway, then disappeared from view.

'Do you think it cleared the water?'

There was a little stream that emerged from under the railway line, wound its way across the course and disappeared between houses on the far side. It was terrible luck to hit a ball into it. The chances were a hundred to one, a thousand to one.

'I don't think so.'

'I suppose that means a lost stroke.'

'Them's the rules,' said Arrowsmith, cheerfully.

'All right, all right, play your own shot, and I'll worry about finding my ball.'

Arrowsmith walked across to his ball, pulled an iron from his bag without even checking the number. He looked at the ball, looked at the green, looked at the ball again, then struck it cleanly. It landed on the green, to one side, leaving a lengthy putt. Still, a good position to have. Especially with Denton's dropped shot.

He looked across at his opponent. He expected to see him lining up his shot, or maybe on his knees retrieving his ball. But he was just standing, his head bent, his club still grasped in his hand. He shouted to him but Denton didn't look around, even when he shouted again. So Arrowsmith walked impatiently over to him. 'What's going on?' he said, as he got closer to his friend.

Denton didn't reply but pointed into the water. Arrowsmith looked down and at first couldn't make sense of what he was seeing and then: 'Oh, for fuck's sake,' he said.

It was a body lying face down in the shallow stream. The skin was very pale, almost white, and very smooth.

Arrowsmith couldn't see whether it was a man or a woman. 'Oh, for fuck's sake,' he said again.

'It wasn't in Richmond Park,' said Dugdale. 'And it wasn't Wimbledon Common. It was on a golf course just next to the Kingston bypass.'

'What are you talking about?' said Frieda.

'The body of a man was found face down in Beverley Brook earlier this morning.'

'Oh, no,' said Frieda.

'What do you mean? It's what you predicted.'

Frieda covered the phone and whispered to Lola, 'They've found a body. In Beverley Brook.'

She could see the blood leaving Lola's face, as if she might be about to faint. She took her hand from the phone. 'Yes, it's what I expected. And someone else is dead. I don't exactly feel triumphant about it. Who is the victim?'

'There's been no identification so far. The body was naked. He's a male, estimated twenty-five to thirty-five. No distin-guishing features.'

'Do you know how he died?'

'No wounds. There was some bruising on the face and torso but it's inconclusive.'

'Did anyone see anything? Was anything caught on CCTV?'

'Your Dean Reeve, if that's who it was, chose a good spot. The men who found it were having an early-morning round of golf. The body must have been dumped in the middle of the night. There's easy access from a track that goes under the bypass next to the railway. Not overlooked, no cameras.'

Frieda didn't answer.

'So?' said Dugdale.

'Thank you for telling me.'

'I wasn't asking for gratitude. I was asking what you're going to do now. Wait for him to work his way round the rivers?'

'No,' she said. 'This feels different.'

'Different how?'

'The other killings were big, they were staged. This one's smaller, quieter.'

'A naked body on a golf course doesn't seem so quiet.'

'He knew we'd be looking for it, so he didn't need to make it into a huge spectacle.'

'So what was he saying?'

'He was saying: I'm still here.'

'We know that.' He hesitated, then said, 'You should know something.'

'What?'

'In a few days, we're going to go public on our suspect being Dean Reeve. In my view, we should have done so already.'

'Why now?'

'It's the commissioner's decision.'

'Because you've run out of clues?'

'Because we feel that the public might be able to help us and because we want them to be vigilant.'

'Vigilant. Right.'

'There's going to be a press frenzy.'

'I imagine,' said Frieda, drily.

'OK. Give me your new address.'

'No.'

'What?'

'No. I am not giving you our address. I don't want you to know where we are.'

'Are you serious?'

'What do you think? He knew where we were.'

'Frieda, listen,' said Dugdale, urgently. 'You're in danger, you and the girl.'

'I know that.'

'We can help you, but only if you tell me where you are.'

'I've decided,' said Frieda. 'It might be the wrong decision but I take full responsibility for it. I'm not telling you.'

'It's not just your own life. It's Lola's. Think of that.'

'Do you believe I'm not thinking of that?'

'I won't tell anyone.'

'You won't tell anyone because you won't know. I'll be in touch.' Frieda put the phone on the table.

Lola was looking at her. 'He's done it again?'

'Yes.'

'Another person who was alive yesterday or a week ago is now dead because of this.' Lola covered her mouth with her hand. She closed her eyes and opened them again, round and blue. 'It just goes on,' she said. 'And you're not letting the police help us, is that right?'

'I don't think they were helping, not in the way we need.'

'So we're on our own?'

'We've always been on our own.'

Forty

Five days after the freezers had been found, Quarry went back to the lock-ups. He parked his car and walked up the road, staring restlessly around him as he did so. He'd got nowhere. Every time he reported back to Dugdale, he felt he was disappointing him. He'd been so sure, when they discovered the place where Dean Reeve had stored the bodies, that they'd had a breakthrough. He had allowed himself to imagine how he'd find Reeve and he'd let himself feel an anticipatory triumph, a glow of achievement at public recognition. Then Maggie would view him differently and his daughter would be proud of him.

He lit a cigarette. He was smoking too much, drinking too much Diet Coke and bitter coffee. Over the last two days, officers had interviewed everyone who worked here. A few people recognized Dean Reeve from the photos they'd been handed to look at. He'd been coming here for months; they'd missed him by days.

They'd widened the search and gone door-to-door but with no joy. And, of course, he could be anywhere. There was no reason to suppose that where he kept the bodies was close to where he lived. There were ten million people in London – and Reeve might not even be in London.

Quarry walked over to the lock-up. The lights had been removed and it stood empty and drab. Here, in this small space, four chest freezers had held four bodies, while all around people had been tinkering with their cars, making deliveries.

After a few minutes, Quarry went back to his car and drove off, feeling disconsolate. It was a familiar route by now: the down-at-heel shops, the light-industrial units, the deserted offices, the little flats with smeared windows. It was getting dark. Lights were on in windows. As he passed the building selling second-hand household stuff, including freezers, he saw two men easing a sofa out of the back of a van.

He didn't know why he stopped. Instinct, said Dugdale later, clapping him on the shoulder. Quarry sauntered up to them. He didn't pull out his ID. They glanced at him warily and continued hauling the sofa towards the doors.

'That looks like heavy work,' he said.

One of them – who looked young, probably a teenager still, and was so painfully thin it was hard to believe he wouldn't snap under the weight – appeared nonplussed. He probably couldn't speak English. The other grunted and nodded. They put the sofa on the ground a few yards from the door and stood still, looking at him. Quarry pulled out his packet of cigarettes and offered it to them. Both men took one.

'Is your boss in?' asked Quarry.

The older man snorted. 'He come and go when it suits. None of the lifting for him. Good at taking money, though.'

Quarry nodded sympathetically. 'Do you live near here?' he asked.

The man looked suspicious. 'You police, right? I saw you when you came before.'

'I've no problem with you,' said Quarry. 'Have you been here long?'

'Two years me. Him.' He jerked a shoulder towards the young man. 'Three, four weeks. Still homesick.'

'I'm sorry,' said Quarry. 'You live near here?'

'Why?'

'I'm just interested. Like I said, I'm not here to cause trouble.'

'Not just near. We live in this shithole. Down the stairs. No windows. Seven of us.'

'That's tough.'

He sat on the sofa and the older man sat beside him; the younger one turned his back to them, smoking his cigarette greedily, sucking the smoke in. Quarry pulled out the photo of Dean Reeve and handed it across. 'Your boss said he hadn't seen this man.'

The man made a derisive sound. 'Fucking liar.'

Quarry felt a spike of excitement. 'You recognize him, then?'

'Sure.'

'He was here?'

'Sure,' the man said again.

'He bought freezers from you?'

'Three, four. Came twice.'

'When was this?'

The man shrugged. 'A month. Two month.'

'Did he pay in cash?'

'Only cash here.' He spread his hands. 'And no questions.'

'How did he take them away?'

'Van. We helped lift them.'

'What was the van like?'

'Like?'

'What colour?'

'White?' It was a question.

'You didn't see the registration number, did you?' The man gave him a blank look. 'Did he tell you his name?'

'Why would he?'

'No. OK. Or where he lived?'

A slow shake of the head. The young man finished his

cigarette and let it drop to the floor. Although it was cool, he was wearing a thin T-shirt; he looked cold and hungry.

'It's important,' said Quarry. 'Very. Is there nothing you can tell me?'

'Sorry. Perhaps the other man would know.'

'Other man?'

'His friend.'

Quarry took a deep breath and spoke calmly. 'He was with someone else?'

'Len.'

'With someone called Len?'

'I think.'

'Len what?'

He shrugged once more. 'He come here with bikes. I see him often.'

'Len sells bikes?'

'Yeah. Cheap.'

'Stolen,' said Quarry, and regretted it. 'Is there anything else you can tell me about this Len? Do you know where he lives?'

'No.'

'Does he come here with a car?'

'Van. Grey van. Or white. Dirty.'

'What does he look like?'

'Big. Very big. Long hair like this.' He lifted both hands and drew them back around his face.

'Ponytail.'

'Tattoos on arms.'

'What kind of tattoos?'

'Just tattoos. Many.'

'Right.'

The young man turned and bent towards his friend, muttering something in a language Quarry didn't recognize, low and fast. 'What's he saying?'

'Saying we should go now.'

'Wait.' Quarry drew out his wallet and took out a twenty-pound note. He handed it to them with the packet of cigarettes. 'One more thing. This Len, when does he come?'

'Whenever.'

'Has he come recently?'

'A few days ago.'

'Would your boss know how to find him?'

The man sighed and looked at Quarry as if he was a foolish child. 'He know nothing, he say nothing.'

'But he might have a name, an address.'

The man shrugged a third time. Then he added, as an afterthought, 'I saw him in pub.'

'You saw Len?'

'Yes.'

'Which pub?'

'Three Feathers.'

'Where?'

'Near here. On the big road.'

'You saw him once.'

'A few times.'

Quarry stood up. 'Thank you,' he said. He handed over a second note.

'You don't tell boss I say this.'

'Don't worry.' He nodded at them both.

The Three Feathers reminded Quarry of pubs his granddad had taken him to when he was a little boy. He'd had to sit outside with a packet of crisps and a Coke, but when the door flapped open he'd glimpsed the enticing world inside. It was like that. All that was missing now was the fog of cigarette smoke. There was no freshly cooked food, no seasoned wooden floors. There was lino and an autographed photo of

Bobby Moore and a fruit machine and a chalk sign promising a stripper on Tuesday nights. A man and a woman in their sixties were sitting at a table with pints of beer.

Quarry walked to the bar. A young woman was sitting in the back looking at her phone. She had blonde hair, shaved on the sides of her head so that the pink of her scalp showed through. She had piercings in her ears, eyebrows, nose and lower lip. She had sleeve tattoos and tattoos on her neck and little dotted tattoos on her cheeks. Quarry ordered a cup of tea and it arrived the colour of mahogany.

'Quiet in here,' he said.

The woman didn't reply.

'There's a friend of mine comes in here,' he said. 'He's called Len.'

'You don't have to give your name to buy a drink,' said the woman.

'That's a good one,' said Quarry. 'You've got a sense of humour.'

He flipped open his ID, laid it on the bar, then placed the photo of Dean Reeve beside it.

'I want to know whether you've seen this man. That's all. Take a look.'

The woman leaned over the bar, looking at the photo, so close that he could smell her perfume: it was like sweet, burned rubber.

'That's Len, is it?' she said.

'No. Len's his friend. Have you seen him?'

'Maybe,' she said.

'Maybe? Is that yes or no?'

'It's an I-don't-know. He's ordinary-looking. There's loads like him.'

'OK. Do you know anyone called Len? Very big, ponytail, tattoos.'

'I know someone like that,' she replied grudgingly.

'Called Len?'

'Yeah.'

'Does he come in here often?'

'I've seen him a few times, I think. I'm not always here.'

'When was he last here?'

'I don't know.'

'Three days? A week?'

'A few days.'

He picked up the ID and the photo and gave her his card. 'If you see him, give me a call.'

Outside, he phoned Dugdale and told him what had happened. 'We should put someone in there,' he said. 'In case Len shows up. He must be easy to spot – he's a big guy with tattoos and a ponytail. Or even Reeve.'

'They can sit outside in a car. But that's good work.'

Forty-one

Frieda looked across at Lola, who was lying on the large living-room sofa looking up at the ceiling. Her hair was matted, her skin pale, her stare almost blank.

'I don't want to sound like your mother,' said Frieda.

'Then don't.'

'But we've got equipment here. You could lift some weights or have a go on the exercise bicycle. Raising your heart rate would make you feel better.'

'It's a myth,' said Lola, dully. 'They did research on it. They took a group of depressed people and some of them exercised and some of them didn't and there was no difference between them.'

'Or you could read a book or draw something.'

'You're right,' said Lola.

'What do you mean?'

'You sound like my mother.'

'Or if you want to talk, you can say anything you like. You're frightened. Of course you're frightened. But I'm going to protect you.'

'Will you protect me the way you protected your boyfriend?' Lola looked round at Frieda to observe the effect of what she had said. But Frieda's expression hadn't changed.

'It wasn't my job to protect him,' said Frieda, calmly. 'We'd separated by then.'

'How much do you think it would cost to buy this place? Five million?'

'More. Much more.'

'I'm in a place worth five million pounds or ten million pounds. It's got its own gym and I feel like I'm in prison. I can suddenly understand why people kill themselves in their cells. I know you think I'm just like a bored child on a rainy day.'

'I don't think that.'

'Anyway, you've taken my phone away and you get to go online and go on Facebook and chat with your friends.'

'I'm not on Facebook and I'm not chatting with my friends.'

'So what are you doing?'

'I'm looking at a map of the London rivers.'

'Oh, your fucking London rivers.' She noticed that Frieda was frowning. 'What is it?'

'I don't know,' said Frieda. 'I'm looking at the map and I think there's something.'

'What do you mean, something?'

'I feel like I've made a mistake.'

'What do you mean? You said he would leave a body in Beverley Brook and he did. You were right.'

'Yes,' said Frieda, slowly. 'I was right.'

Lola lay back on her sofa. Frieda took a piece of paper and a pen and, as she had done before, drew a simple map of the rivers. First she drew the curving sweep of the Thames. Then she started at the north-west and drew the Fleet, then, moving west, she drew the Tyburn, the Westbourne, Counter's Creek. South of the river, to the west, she drew Beverley Brook. Moving to the east she drew the Wandle, a river she knew all too well. Now she hesitated. Instead of continuing east, to the Falcon and the Effra, she moved her pen above the Thames again, to the west of Counter's Creek, and drew a spindly little line down towards the Thames at Hammersmith. Stamford Brook. She had forgotten that one. But what did that mean? Could it be that Stamford Brook was too insignificant for Dean Reeve to bother with? Or could there be a body somewhere that hadn't been found yet?

Frieda heard a voice. It wasn't Lola's voice. It was a voice from inside her head: 'What does it matter?' the voice said. 'You predicted what Dean Reeve would do and you were right. What is there to worry about?'

But there was something missing and there was something to worry about. Gradually the thought she had been carrying for days now took proper shape, like a blurred image, becoming clear and hard and cold.

'I hear the rats,' said Lola.

'Where do you hear them?'

'I don't know where. I just hear the scuttling and the scratching. They may be under the floor or in the walls or in the ceiling. At night I shut my eyes and I can still see them with their fur and their teeth and their red eyes and their thick tails. People drive past this house and it looks white and beautiful and elegant and inside it's rotting and falling apart and rat-infested.'

Frieda walked across, sat next to Lola on the sofa and put a hand on her brow.

'I haven't got a fever or anything, if that's what you think.'

Frieda looked at her closely, as if she were a patient. Frieda was a therapist. Her patients talked and she listened and she tried to help them find a way through their distress, their destructive thoughts and habits. But she also knew that there were limits to talk. Some patients were like a house on fire. There was no point in thinking about the decoration or the arrangement of the rooms. You had to put the fire out. Those patients might need anti-psychotic drugs just to numb them against the psychological pain for a few hours or days. They might need time in a psychiatric ward because they couldn't function in the outside world. Frieda could clearly see that at this moment Lola wouldn't be healed by talk.

'It's just going to be a few days,' she said softly. 'We're nearly at the end.'

Lola turned her head and looked at her.

Frieda continued speaking. 'I could get some medication. Something to help you sleep.'

'It's not that. It's the dead people. Don't you think of them? Don't you see them when you close your eyes? And there are going to be more of them. More and more and more.'

'No,' she said. 'There aren't going to be many more. There's going to be one more.'

'One more? Who's that going to be?'

'Me, of course.'

Now Lola sat up and faced her. 'Is that what you want? Do you want to sacrifice yourself to him?'

'It's not what I want. It's what he wants.'

'And you think, if . . .' Lola paused, and when she spoke it was with an apparent effort. 'If he killed you, you think he would stop? Stop all of this killing?'

Frieda leaned closer to Lola, raised a hand and stroked her hair, as if Lola was a small child who had woken from a nightmare. 'Yes, Lola, I think he would.' She stood up. 'I'm going to make some tea. Something herbal. Ginger, I think. Would you like some?'

'Sure.'

'It'll make you feel better.'

'I already said yes.'

So Frieda got up and walked out of the large living room into the dining room, which they hadn't used because the table and the chairs were all rotten and dirty. From there she entered the kitchen at the back of the house. She filled the kettle and switched it on. While she waited for it to boil, she looked out of the back window. There was a cobbled street where there would once have been stables, which were now those immaculate houses. Two mugs stood in the sink. She washed them up and put a ginger teabag into each one, poured the boiling water onto them, then stirred them with a teaspoon until the water turned amber. The ginger aroma was soothing in itself.

She took the two mugs through the dining room and then into the living room. Lola wasn't there. She called her name, but there was no reply. She took a sip of the ginger tea. It was still too hot and burned her lips. She walked across to the front window. There she was. Lola, jacketed, was blundering across the road. She was making her brief escape, sucking in air, weaving about as though she was drunk. She went through one of the entrances to Regent's Park and disappeared behind the boundary hedge.

Frieda looked at the mugs she was holding. She had a sudden impulse to throw them to the floor, let them smash. But then it occurred to her that the owner would never know and wouldn't care if they did. Someone else might come to stay here and they would have to deal with the mess and that wouldn't be fair. So she just put the two mugs on the floor.

When Lola arrived in the park, she looked around. Then she went swiftly towards a middle-aged woman who was walking with two dogs. She was throwing a tennis ball for them to fetch. She looked at Lola with a mixture of disapproval and alarm. Lola wondered why, then remembered her appearance, her grubby clothes and her pale, unwashed, matted hair.

'Excuse me,' said Lola. 'I'm so sorry to bother you. I've

lost my phone. I need to ring my friend to get her to pick me up. Could you lend me yours? It'll just be a minute. Less than a minute.'

The woman seemed doubtful.

'It's really important,' said Lola. Her eyes filled with tears and her voice wobbled.

'All right. If you're quick.'

And she handed Lola the phone. Lola moved a few yards away and turned her back on her, so she couldn't be overheard. She dialled the number that she had memorized. She thought she would remember it for the rest of her life.

She waited. Perhaps he wouldn't answer. Tears were rolling down her cheeks, thicker and thicker. They rolled into her mouth and she could taste the salt. There was a plane overhead, scrawling its signature into the autumn sky. Her heart was jolting so hard she thought it would break out of her body.

He answered. A thick, soft voice.

'It's Lola,' she said.

Silence at the other end, just breathing.

For a brief moment she thought she couldn't say the words. They were in her mouth, grim as stones. But then she took a deep, harsh breath that hurt her throat. 'We're at eighteen A Rivingdale Terrace . . . Yes. Rivingdale Terrace. Frieda says you're only going to kill one more person . . . Yes, of course she means herself. I've got to go.'

She didn't quite know how to walk. She had an image of herself lying down on the damp grass, among the fallen leaves, and curling into a ball and waiting there until all of this had gone away. She wanted to disappear. The ground to swallow her. Her body felt strange to her, and she felt strange to her body, as if everything was breaking up inside her. She stood quite still for a moment, trying to regain her equilibrium. The she walked back out of the park.

'Lola.'

She jolted to a stop. It was Frieda and she was holding out a hand.

'Oh. I'm sorry,' she managed to say, though her voice sounded like a blurt of sound. Surely Frieda would notice everything was wrong. 'I just had to get some air.'

Frieda smiled and took her arm. 'I know,' she said. 'It's the most expensive place I've ever stayed in. And the most unpleasant. When I saw you run across the road, I realized we need to get out of it.'

Lola looked at Frieda. She had a bag slung over each shoulder. 'Get out?' she repeated. 'You mean, now?'

'This very minute. Why wait?'

'I've got things I need to get.'

'I've got everything.'

'But . . . I'm not sure I can bear moving again, Frieda. I mean, this is horrible, but what's the next place going to be like?'

'Let's walk while we discuss it,' said Frieda, and she led a reluctant Lola back into the park and turned south. 'I don't want to play my therapist card, but when someone starts thinking about rats crawling over them while they're asleep, it's time to move.'

'But surely moving isn't a way of solving your problems. You need to deal with them where they are.' Lola stopped. Her gaze was wild. 'There'll probably be rats wherever I go. They were probably in my mind. Let's go back. Please.'

'It's the kind of thing I've said to my patients,' said Frieda. 'You can move as much as you like, but you'll still have your problems with you. However, in this case I'll make an exception. The rats were real. There are probably cock-roaches as well. '

They moved off again, Lola allowing Frieda to steer her, her feet dragging through the leaves.

'Where are we going?' she said. 'Do we have to contact one of your friends again?'

'Keegan thought something like this might happen. He gave me the key. And we can walk there. I think we both need a bit of exercise.' She tipped her head back. 'It will rain later,' she said, talking more to herself than Lola. 'Heavy rain to clear the air.'

They reached the south-east corner of the park and joined Euston Road. It was tantalizingly close to Frieda's house, almost dangerously so. Someone might recognize her. They crossed the road and left the traffic for the quieter roads that ran past the university buildings. It was a route she knew intimately from her restless night walks. She walked past the terraced houses, the stolid red apartment blocks, the small hotels, until they reached an improbable little house in the corner of a small square. Frieda unlocked the front door and they stepped inside.

It was like an imitation family house. There were etchings on the wall. There was a front room with a sofa and a couple of chairs. There was a kitchen at the rear and a small yard backed by the walls of a huge building. But there was noth-ing personal. No mail on the mat. No television and no phone.

'What is this house?' asked Lola. 'It's like a pretend house or a film set or something.'

'I think my friend uses it for people like us.'

'What are people like us like?'

'People who need to disappear for a while. There are more of them than you'd think.'

'So what does your friend do?'

'It's clearly one of those jobs that's hard to explain. Like a management consultant. But this is better, isn't it?'

Lola looked around. 'You're right,' she said. 'It's better. I'm glad we left that place behind. I wish I could have left myself behind as well.'

Forty-two

That evening, Frieda made them butternut-squash soup. The kitchen was clean and bare. There was one large saucepan and one small; a frying pan, a roasting pan. All the china – pale green – came in sets of four: four large and four small plates, four bowls. So too did the cutlery and the glasses.

She had bought some more whisky and she poured them both a slug, setting Lola's in front of her without a word and sipping at her own as she chopped the squash, tipped it into the pan to fry. While it cooked, she sliced bread, set places at the table, then opened her laptop and turned it on. All the while, Lola sat without a word, her shoulders soft and heavy, a blank look on her face.

As Frieda started scrolling through news items on her computer, she spoke without looking up: 'When you get to the endgame in chess, everything changes. There are just a few pieces left. A pawn can be as powerful as a queen. They circle around each other, blocking each other, protecting each other, even bluffing, trying to find an opening, a way through.'

'And this is the endgame?'

'It is.'

'What are you going to do?'

Frieda didn't answer. She stood up and prodded the squash with a fork, making sure it was tender.

'There's no food mixer here,' she said. 'We'll have to mash it with a fork and then add the stock. Can you do that?'

'What?'

'Can you mash the squash with a fork? Lola?'

'I guess.'

'Have some whisky.'

'It'll make me cry.'

'Crying isn't so bad.'

'No. I mustn't. I feel like I'm coming apart.' She looked at Frieda with her wide child's eyes. 'I mean, literally coming apart. My stomach's kind of unfolding itself.'

'You're scared,' said Frieda.

'Yes.'

'Here. Mash these roughly.'

Frieda tipped the squash onto a plate and pressed a fork into Lola's hand. She watched as Lola obediently sank the fork into the yellow chunks. She remembered the first time she had met Lola – how guileless she'd been, chattering away. She remembered how she had impulsively flung her arms around her and said she was so sorry for all she must have been through. Now she sat mutely at the table. She had lost a lot of weight and her skin was dull, with a cold sore at the corner of her mouth. Her hair needed washing and cutting. Her clothes were grubby. Her nails, Frieda saw, were bitten to the quick. She took the fork out of Lola's hand and pulled the plate away. 'That's enough,' she said gently. 'Thank you.'

She made the soup, adding yoghurt at the end, and ladled Lola a full bowl.

'Eat.'

Lola lowered a spoon into the thick liquid, lifted it to her mouth, hesitated. She took half the spoonful, then laid it back in the bowl.

'Starving yourself is not going to help,' said Frieda. Her tone was sterner. 'And have some of the bread.'

Lola had a few more spoonfuls, then pushed the bowl away from her. 'I feel a bit sick,' she said. 'I don't feel very well. I think I'll go to bed.'

'You can have some for lunch. I'll make you tea.'

'Thanks.' And she left the room.

Frieda cleared everything away. Then she went into the small yard with her whisky. It was just starting to rain, large drops falling from the dark sky. She stood for several minutes, relishing the rain on her face, the smell of autumn it brought. She went back inside, made tea, and took a mug to Lola who was lying curled in a foetus position in her bed, the covers over her head.

'Any better?' she asked, and put the mug on the side table.

A small, indeterminate noise came from the shape.

'OK. I'll see you in the morning. But if there's anything you need, at any time, I'm just next door.'

Lola lay quite still and heard the door click softly behind Frieda. The light on the landing went off. She drew her knees further up, put both loosely clenched fists against her face. She closed her eyes and it was dark; opened them and it was still dark. She could hear the rain falling outside, beating against the windows.

How close she had come to telling Frieda. She had felt as if the words were behind her lips and every time she opened them they might escape. She could imagine them now. She could imagine the gush of relief once she had spoken and how Frieda would listen, take the words into herself, relieve her of her terrible burden. But she hadn't spoken and she mustn't. She mustn't.

And as she did every night when she lay in the darkness and closed her eyes and listened to the sound of her own breathing, Lola let herself remember.

Receiving that message from Jess and deciding to go there, without telling Frieda – because, of course, Frieda would have prevented her, and she gave a tiny moan under her covers, thinking of how everything might have been different, if only, if only . . .

Opening the door of the flat she had shared with Jess, noticing there was a different smell. She had thought Jess had been smoking, though it was against their house rules to smoke inside their flat. But she hadn't really given it a thought. She'd run up the stairs, calling Jess's name, puzzled as to why she didn't answer at once. She was the one who'd said it was urgent, after all.

There'd been no one in the main room, nor any answer when she'd called through Jess's shut door, so she'd gone into her own bedroom to fetch some of her stuff. Now that she was here, she might as well. She got as far as taking the watch that her granny had given her when she turned eighteen and putting it on her wrist when she heard a sound. Just a small sound, but it made her turn.

'Jess,' she had called. 'Is that you?'

And she'd opened her bedroom door and stepped into the living room.

And her world had changed. At that moment, it had tipped, become something else entirely, and even now as she lay curled up in bed, she could feel the way that fear had gushed through her body like toxic chemicals.

Jess was there. She was being held upright by a man. Lola could see her eyes, her eyes that stared at her in utter terror. His hand was over her mouth; her dark hair trickled over his fingers. There was no sound in the room at all. With his other hand, he held a knife against Jess's throat, its blade against the white skin. As Lola looked, she saw one tiny bubble of blood spring up at its tip.

Nobody spoke. Nobody moved. Lola saw that the man was looking directly into her eyes, and that he was smiling at her amiably. In some corner of her consciousness, she recognized him as the man by the canal, the man on her phone. His name swam into her mind. Dean Reeve. She was standing in the living room of her flat with Dean Reeve, and he had a knife against her friend's throat and he was smiling at her, as though it was a mildly nice surprise that they had met like this.

'Hello, Lola,' he said at last. Jess gave a small jerk, and he didn't bother to look down but held her more tightly. A bead of blood worked its way down her neck. 'I'm glad you got the message.'

Lola wanted to put a hand up to steady herself but she was standing frozen in the centre of the room. She wanted to shout, but her throat was locked with terror.

'You're going to do something for me,' said Dean. 'Aren't you?'

She made herself nod, up and down and up and down, like a puppet's round wooden head jerking on a string.

'That's a good girl. But I'm going to make it easier for you. Your mum and dad, Dave and Carol. In that little village near Málaga. You wouldn't want anything to happen to them, would you?'

Now she shook her head from side to side. Her hair clipped her cheek. Jess's eyes were still staring at her.

'I know you wouldn't. And it won't, if you help me. But if you don't help, do you know what will happen?'

He was still smiling. His eyes were brown and friendly.

'Of course you don't know. Not until I've shown you. Watch carefully.'

And then, quite casually, barely glancing down, he had drawn the knife across Jess's neck and, for a moment, nothing happened and then the neck opened up and dark blood came out in gouts and he had lowered her body to the floor.

And Lola still didn't move. She didn't help. She didn't run to her friend and try to save her. She had tried to tell herself that it wouldn't have made a difference, and of course it wouldn't. But, still, she hadn't moved and she'd watched as Jess lay on the floor, like a fish on land, writhing.

'It's no use telling me where you and Frieda are now,' said Dean, taking a step back so that the blood didn't cover his shoes. 'As soon as she discovered you'd gone she would have gone as well, if I know Frieda.' He smiled. 'And I do know Frieda. But when you know your next address, you're going to call me.'

Lola couldn't say anything. She was watching Jess's eyes cloud over. She was watching her die.

'I'm going to tell you a number,' continued Dean. 'And you're going to memorize it.'

He had given her a number and made her repeat it. She had repeated it over and over again, until he was satisfied. It was the number she had called from the changing rooms when they were staying in that house full of cats. It was the number she had called from the toilets in St Pancras station, when Frieda was talking to the man with cold eyes. And it was the number she had called that morning in Regent's Park. She would remember it, she thought, until the day she died; the paired digits she had said over and over while Jess stared up at her with sightless eyes.

Now she was scared to speak in case she let the words out. Sometimes she physically put a hand across her mouth. She would feel Frieda's dark eyes rest on her and she would have to turn away, leave the room. Because every time she nearly spoke the words, she heard his voice, soft and slow, *Your mum and dad, Dave and Carol. In that little village near Málaga.*

Frieda had said it was the endgame. She just wanted it to be over. But after it was over, then what? Who would she be? What would she have done?

Forty-three

Dolan had drunk two Red Bulls, eaten a pack of salted pea-
nuts, smoked four cigarettes, and felt both jittery and sleepy.
Next time, he would bring a sandwich, a flask of coffee and
a large bottle of water, and he would stretch his legs more
often. It was too late for that now: it was pouring with rain
outside, the kind of rain that would soak him in a few seconds. But the car felt muggy so he opened the window a few
inches, and it was at that moment that a small group of men
passed him and made their way to the Three Feathers'
entrance, heads lowered, one of them in the middle uselessly
holding a small umbrella whose loose spoke flapped, direct-
ing water in a spout.

There were four of them, but it was the one on the left
who caught his attention. Quarry had said that the man they
were looking out for was big. This man was big, and broad.
And Quarry had said he had long dark hair, perhaps tied
back in a ponytail. In the light thrown by the pub as they
opened its door and went inside, Dolan saw the man's long,
dark hair was roughly pulled back into a ponytail. Quarry
had also mentioned tattoos, but for that Dolan would have
to go inside and see for himself.

He got out of the car and jogged towards the pub, feeling
the rain run down under his collar. The Three Feathers was
crowded, people sitting at tables and standing by the bar. But
it was easy to see the man who might be Len: he was head and
shoulders taller than anyone else. Dolan edged closer: yes, he
had tattoos, snaking out from the long sleeves of his shirt.

Dolan went to the entrance and pulled out his mobile. 'I think he's here,' he said to Quarry, in a low voice.

'Buy yourself a drink, keep an eye on him, but don't do anything till I get there. No sign of Reeve?'

Dolan felt a jolt of panicky excitement: it hadn't occurred to him that perhaps one of those other men with Len was Dean Reeve.

'He's with a group. I'll take a look,' he said.

'Look but don't act. I'll be there as soon as I can.'

It took Quarry half an hour. There'd been an accident and the traffic was painfully slow. As he walked into the Three Feathers, he spotted Dolan standing near the bar, nursing a ginger ale.

'Is he still here?'

'In the other room, playing darts. No sign of Reeve.'

He went through, sat to one side and watched until the end of the game. Then he stepped forward. He was quite tall himself, but he looked slight beside the other man.

'Len?' he asked.

The man looked down at him. 'What do you want?'

Quarry introduced himself. Most people became shocked or defensive when suddenly confronted with the police. Len seemed utterly indifferent.

'I heard you might be able to help us,' said Quarry.

'Who told you?'

'You are Len, then?'

'I might be.'

'Can I have your last name?'

Len gazed at him impassively, then said, 'Smith.'

'Smith?'

'It's a common name.'

Quarry glanced around at the men who were watching

293

them, feeling a prickle of unease. 'Can we talk somewhere more private?'

'Why?'

'This way, please.'

For a moment, Len didn't move and neither did any of the men surrounding them. Then he gave a shrug and went with Quarry out of the pub, Dolan following at a distance. The rain had stopped but it was still damp and blustery. They stood by the side of the pub, near the service entrance and the big metal bins. Len looked at him indifferently.

Quarry leaned towards him so that he could see his face clearly. He held up the picture of Dean Reeve. 'Do you recognize this man?'

'Not sure.'

'This isn't a joke. Do you recognize this man?'

Len gave a sigh. 'That's Barry.'

Quarry kept his face expressionless: Barry was the name Dean Reeve had used with Geoffrey Kernan, when he had paid him to build the patio.

'Do you know where he lives?'

'Why?'

'Do you have an address?'

'No.'

'Stop,' said Quarry. 'Just stop. Stop. You're boring me and you're wasting my time. This can go two ways. You give me an address and we say goodbye. Or you don't give me an address and I'll take you in and I'll promise to make your life a fucking misery to the utmost of my ability. I'll start from you giving a false name and go from there.'

'You're allowed to call yourself what you like,' said Len, in a newly uneasy tone.

'I'll be the judge of that.'

He gave an indifferent shrug. 'He's got a room above the

doner-kebab place on the high street. If he's still there.' He gave a short, hacking laugh. 'Barry doesn't like to stay in one spot for long. Restless type.'

'Which high street?'

'East Ham. Up from the park.'

'You don't have a number?'

'It's above the kebab place. There's a line of little shops, selling all sorts. Next to the kebab place is a shop selling stuffed animals. They've got a big bird in the window.'

'Do you have a mobile number for him?'

'We don't know each other like that.'

'Nothing else you want to share?'

'No.'

Quarry pointed. 'Give your details to young Dolan there. A contact number and an address. And he'll need you to stay with him for a bit.'

'Why?'

'You might feel a sudden urge to get in touch with Barry.'

'I told you. I don't have his number.'

'Yeah, right. Even so. Stay with Dolan, Len.'

Quarry called Dugdale. 'We've got a possible address.' And he told him what Len had said. He could hear the excitement in his own voice, making it husky, but Dugdale was his usual calm self.

'Park outside and stay there. Wait for back-up.'

Frieda lay in bed, knowing she wouldn't sleep. She heard cars in the distance and, later, a fox. It was still raining, but less heavily. Usually she liked the sound of wind and rain, especially when she was in her own little house in the darkness. It wasn't so far from here; she could walk there in a few minutes. She closed her eyes and let herself imagine opening the blue door, stepping into the hall that smelt of beeswax polish, into the living room, where the fire would be laid and the shutters closed against the night. Everything in its proper place. A pot of basil on the kitchen windowsill, and in her garret study a pencil sharpened and lying on the pad of grainy paper. The cat would be curled on a chair, or at the bottom of her bed, and it would open one yellow eye, then shut it again. The longing for home ached in her.

She heard a sound, a kind of groan. It was Lola, on the other side of the wall, also unable to sleep. Poor, lost Lola, she thought, sucked into the maelstrom. But it would be over soon. *We are all just leaves on a tree . . . and autumn is coming.*

Quarry found the kebab shop all right. It was just as Len had described it. But it was difficult to park outside. There was a bus stop, double yellow lines, a traffic light. Of course, he was a police detective. He could flash his badge and park anywhere but he would need to explain. It would be obtrusive.

Instead he parked the car off the high street in a residential road and walked back. He positioned himself opposite. The kebab shop was busy, with teenagers clustered around the counter. He looked above the shop at the flat. The windows were dark. On the right-hand side there was a charity shop, closed at this time, but with a stuffed squirrel visible in the window. On the left-hand side there was a mini-mart, fruit and vegetables laid on stalls on the pavement. Next to that, sportswear and then household goods, both closed for the night. After that a small cobbled alley. Quarry walked across the road and showed Reeve's picture in the kebab shop and the mini-mart. Everybody just shook their heads.

When he emerged from the mini-mart, he saw Dugdale on the other side of the road, in a dark coat, hands in the pockets. He crossed to join his boss and they walked along the road a few yards, then stopped in a doorway.

'Well?' said Dugdale.

'It's possible,' said Quarry.

'You trust your source?'

'He identified Reeve, he identified this place.'

'Anyone home?'

'The lights are off.'

'So what do you think?'

'We could keep a watch. Wait for him to arrive.'

Dugdale frowned. He didn't look happy. 'I don't know,' he said. 'He could have moved on. It could be a dead end.' Quarry could see Dugdale chewing his lower lip, thinking hard. 'I'm sorry but we don't have the time. I'm calling a squad out. We'll knock the door down. Maybe we'll find something. He might even be at home.' He reached into his pocket. 'Is there a back way?'

'I don't know.'

'Nip round and have a look. No point in letting him just walk away. If there is, we can post some guys round there just in case.'

Quarry went back across the road towards the little alley he had seen earlier. There was a small van parked there and behind it two large metal bins. He walked past them and saw that there was indeed a narrow, unlit road that ran along the back of the shops. Quarry guessed that in the past it would have been a place for horses or for coal deliveries. It looked almost abandoned. There was some cracked paving at first but then the ground became rough dirt. He counted the buildings as he passed them. The first was the hardware shop, then the mini-mart, with piles of overflowing bin bags. There was a smell of decaying food. After that the kebab shop.

Yes, thought Quarry, they would need a couple of men round here. He reached for his phone and just when it was far too late he was aware of a movement at the periphery of his vision. When the blow came, he didn't so much feel it as see it. Everything went white and there was a red flashing and pulsing. He didn't seem to be falling. Instead the ground came up to meet him and he felt the dirt prickling against his cheek and his nose. He could even taste it. It was in his mouth and on his tongue. Then there was another blow but he didn't even know where on his body this was all happening. And he thought, as he lay there and tasted blood in his mouth, that this was Dean Reeve. Dean Reeve was here with him, standing over him and kicking him. He could have caught him, could have been a hero, but now Reeve would get away and the killings would continue and he was just the fool who hadn't seen it coming and there wasn't a damn thing he could do. He heard himself groan. Is this it? he wondered. Is this what it's like to die? It didn't seem very much to be afraid of. He knew he couldn't do anything to protect himself. His body didn't seem to belong to him any more. It wasn't up to him. He just had to wait for it all to be over. None of it felt real.

Gradually it started to feel real again. Now there was pain and the pain systematically resolved itself. It came into focus. It located itself in very particular parts of his body: the right side of his face and his chest and his leg. And the dirt in his mouth made him cough and spit. Even now, though, he couldn't move and he could barely think. He tried to reach for his phone but it was impossible and he sank back. After some time he was aware of lights in the darkness and he felt himself being touched and prodded. He tried to speak in response but all he managed was a groan.

Ten minutes later everything was clearer. He was sitting

on a gurney in an ambulance in intense white light. He felt a whole spectrum of pain: aches and flashes and spasms. A paramedic was dabbing at his cheek with something that made Quarry want to cry out. He wiped tears away from his eyes and saw that Dugdale was sitting opposite him.

'Sorry,' he said, in a thick, swollen voice. His tongue felt slow and too large for his mouth. 'So sorry. Didn't see him.'

Dugdale shook his head helplessly. 'No, Dan. It's me. It's my fault. I had him,' he said. 'I had him and I let him go.'

Forty-four

'Is Reuben McGill in?' asked Karlsson.

The woman gazed up at him from her desk, which was more like a shrine, heaped with dried flowers and strange ornaments. She had curly dark hair piled on top of her head, red lips, long earrings dangling from her lobes. 'Reuben. He's in but if you want to make an appointment with him you have to . . .' She came to a halt. 'I know you.'

'That's right. And you're Paz.'

She frowned at him. 'Is he expecting you?'

'No.'

Karlsson had woken that morning early, before it was light. He had dressed and sat in his kitchen drinking coffee and looking out at his garden, where the trees were shaking leaves from their branches. It was his day off and he didn't know what to do with himself. He was restless, anxious, with an ache in his chest that didn't ease and that he had become familiar with over the past weeks. He was thinking about Frieda. He felt sure she was in great danger and it was a torment to him that he could do nothing to help her. So, on an impulse, he had walked to the Warehouse to see Reuben, knowing all the while that it was probably for nothing.

'Wait here,' said Paz, and she disappeared up the corridor, her high heels clicking on the boards. When she came back, she gave him a nod. 'He's waiting,' she said.

Reuben stood up as Karlsson entered, and they shook hands across his desk.

'Any news?' Reuben asked, before Karlsson had a chance to say anything.

'No.'

'So, let me guess.' Reuben gestured at a chair and sat himself. 'You want to know if I know anything. Like last time you came to see me.'

'Yes.' Karlsson looked away, at the tall bookcase crammed with textbooks. He let his eyes settle on one with the title *Anticipatory Mourning*. 'Sorry to disturb you,' he added. He felt unexpectedly and horribly sad and it was hard for him to speak.

'I don't.' Reuben ran a hand through his hair, newly grown back.

He looked so much older than a year ago, thought Karlsson, with new creases in his face. 'Would you tell me if you did?'

Reuben looked at him through narrowed eyes, then spoke without his habitual irony. 'If I thought it would help. Because, of course, what you're feeling is what we're all feeling. She's out there and she's in danger and we can't protect her from it, but must simply wait.'

'What about Josef?' said Karlsson, standing up.

'Do you mean does Josef know anything?'

'She confided in him when she was in hiding from the police.'

'You asked me this before. She did, and he didn't breathe a word,' said Reuben. 'Josef can keep Frieda's secrets, even after a bottle of vodka.'

'Do you think he knows something?'

'He hasn't said anything to me.'

'Maybe I should go and talk to him.'

'Good luck with that. You'll find him at Frieda's house.'

'What?'

'He's made her a roof terrace, or maybe it's a large balcony.'

'A roof terrace?'

301

'Him and Chloë. He went there this morning with some pots. Who knows what Frieda would make of it.'

'Will,' said Karlsson.

'Sorry?'

'What Frieda *will* make of it.'

'That's what I meant.'

They shook hands again. Reuben gave Karlsson a nod. 'It's hard,' he said.

Karlsson stood outside Frieda's door for several moments before knocking. It was infinitely strange to be there. In spite of himself, his heart beat harder when the door opened, and he felt a surge of absurd disappointment when it was Josef's face he saw, not Frieda's.

'What wrong?' Josef said.

'Nothing. Reuben said I'd find you here. Can I come in?'

Josef opened the door wider and Karlsson stepped inside, inhaling the familiar smell of the hall. He could see into the living room, where there was a fire laid in the grate and a vase of crimson dahlias on the mantelpiece. Everything lay waiting for Frieda's return.

'Reuben said you'd built a roof terrace.'

Josef's face brightened. 'For her surprise, yes. You want to see? Follow.'

They went up the stairs together, and out onto the balcony. There were several large terracotta pots and two hefty bags of compost to one side.

'What you think?'

Karlsson looked at the new structure, then out at the view of London; he looked into Josef's deep brown eyes. He tried to imagine Frieda coming home at last to find her precious space had been transformed in her absence. 'She'll love it,' he said carefully.

'Yes?'

'Yes.'

'Chloë making a chair to go just here.' He gestured with his broad hands. 'And a small table. Soon we go to garden centre for plants.'

'Good.'

'Lots of plants.' Josef smiled. 'Then Frieda come back.'

Karlsson waited a moment before speaking. 'Josef,' he said. 'Where is she?'

'What?'

'Where's Frieda?'

'I not know.' Josef widened his eyes, overacting sincerity. 'I know nothing.'

'I need to find her.' He waited but Josef said nothing, just stared at him with his sad brown eyes. 'I'm convinced she's in danger and I can help her.'

'Nothing.'

On his way out Karlsson met Chloë. She was carrying a plastic pot with a spindly sapling in it, more like an unpromising twig with three or four leaves attached to it.

'It's a miniature apple tree,' she said.

'For the roof terrace.'

'Yes.'

'I've just been up there with Josef.'

'Maybe we shouldn't have done it,' said Chloë, wrinkling her nose doubtfully. 'Frieda hates surprises. It was just – well, something. While we wait.'

'I understand,' said Karlsson, gently, and then added, on an impulse: 'You haven't seen her, have you?'

He expected her to shake her head, and she did, but to his surprise two bright spots appeared on her cheeks and she turned away.

'Chloë?' He took a step nearer to her. 'You've seen her?'

'She'd kill me if she knew I was telling you.'

'I want to help her. I can't help her if I don't know where she is.'

'I did see her, just the once. She came up to me as I was leaving work and we walked together for a few minutes. Her hair was cut short and dyed grey. She wanted my help to find a place to stay.'

'And could you help?'

'Yes. She went to a friend's parents' house that was standing empty while they were away on holiday. I left her the key.'

'Where is this place?' asked Karlsson.

'She's long gone.' Chloë stared up at him, her eyes brimming with tears. 'The parents came back days ago.'

'So you don't know where she went?'

'I've no idea.'

'You'd tell me.'

Chloë nodded. 'Frieda being angry is better than Frieda being dead,' she said, and tears began to roll down her cheeks.

'She didn't give you a clue where she'd go next?'

'No.'

'Nothing. No clue.'

'I know she said she wouldn't be staying in the house I found for her for that long.'

'Why?'

'Because,' said Chloë, slowly, frowning in concentration and biting her lower lip, 'I think she said about someone else being able to find her somewhere.'

'Who?'

'I don't know. She didn't say a name.'

'You're sure?'

'Yes. But she said he had friends in high places.'

'Friends in high places.'

'Or something like that. Does that mean anything to you?'

'Yes.'

Walter Levin was sitting at his desk wearing a three-piece suit. His glasses shone under the lights. He removed them and polished them with a white handkerchief.

'I need to know where she is,' said Karlsson.

'Need?' Levin gave him an amiable smile.

'I know you know where she is.'

'Really?' He sounded mildly surprised.

'Chloë told me she was going to ask you. Or, at least, ask someone with friends in high places.'

Levin laid his glasses on his desk. 'She may have meant someone else.'

'Please,' said Karlsson, impatiently. 'I don't have time for games.'

Levin's expression chilled. 'Frieda suspects someone in the police force of leaking information about her. I don't mean to insult you, but my hands are tied.'

'I'm not here as a detective. I'm here as a friend who happens to be a detective and who can help her.'

Levin put his glasses back on his nose, tapping them into place.

'I have to help her,' Karlsson continued.

'Of course I'm an outsider, but am I right in saying that she has gone into hiding precisely so that her friends won't try to help her?'

Karlsson put his hands flat on the surface of the desk and leaned forward, looking into Levin's cool eyes. 'Dean Reeve is going to kill her.'

'As it happens, I don't know where she is.'

'I don't believe you.'

Levin smiled at him. 'Of course, that's your prerogative.'

'Christ. Don't you care what happens to her?'

'My dear Karlsson. You can be as emotive as you want. The fact is, I am not going to disclose her whereabouts. If I know them, that is.'

'Even though you know she's in danger.'

'Precisely because I know she's in danger.'

At the door, Karlsson turned. 'Did you see her?'

'Just the once.'

'Was she all right?'

'I don't know.' Levin smiled at him. 'She's a code I've never quite been able to crack.'

Karlsson walked away from the little house. He didn't know what to do next. Then he heard the sound of running feet and, turning, he saw the young woman who was Levin's assistant.

'It's Jude, isn't it?' he said.

'Ask Jock Keegan,' she said. 'He knows.' And she pressed a card into his hand.

Forty-five

Josef and Alexei sat on the balcony together, side by side, wrapped up in their waterproof jackets. It was windy and chilly and the first specks of rain were starting to fall. They were eating burgers, and Josef had a bottle of beer that he swigged at between large mouthfuls. Alexei had ginger beer that was so spicy it made him want to sneeze.

'Soon we sit here with Frieda,' said Josef to his son, in an encouraging voice. He always spoke to him in English now: he wanted it to be Alexei's first language. Soon, he thought, his son would hardly remember his mother-tongue and his childhood in Ukraine would be like a dream.

Alexei glanced across at him but didn't reply.

'Have I told you story of our first meeting?' continued Josef.

He had of course, many times, but Alexei shook his head: he knew his father needed to speak about Frieda and, anyway, he liked sitting on this balcony, high up among the rooftops, looking out across London as night fell. It felt both precarious and safe.

'I crash through her ceiling,' said Josef. He laughed loudly and drank some more beer. 'Just like that. Oomph onto her floor, staring up at her in clouds of dust. She was there with a sad man who was telling her his story.'

That sad man had been Dean Reeve's twin brother and he had been killed by Dean many years since.

'They both look at me,' continued Josef, wiping his mouth with the back of his hand. 'Like this.' He opened his eyes wide and stared at Alexei. 'Frieda, she very cross with me.

Not shouting, but stern. That's how we begin, me falling through a hole in her roof. It has been eight years we are friends. She help me, I help her. Nothing I would not do. Nothing. That is friendship, Alexei. It is always here.' He knocked on his chest, as if it was a door that might open.

Alexei nodded again. Josef's eyes shone in the dusk.

'She return soon, you will see. Tomorrow, I bring her cat back. Everything is ready. She will come. She sit here like this. We do not speak. We look out together at the lights. Bad days are gone and we are safe again.'

After they had eaten a simple meal that Lola barely touched, just prodded at with her fork, Frieda laid out the chessboard. 'Come and sit down,' she said.

'I can't concentrate.'

'This won't take long.'

Lola sat at the table. She was by turns listless and jumpy.

'Why have you only put those pieces out?' she asked.

'This is the endgame,' said Frieda. 'I'll show you. This is from a game that was played by two Russians almost a hundred years ago.'

'How can you remember that?'

'There are some games that I don't forget. I play them over and over, in the winter especially.' There was a faraway expression on her face and she spoke quietly, as if to herself: 'I have a little wooden chess table, and when darkness falls, I close the shutters and I light the fire in the living room and I go through the moves. It's like meditation.'

'That and walking.'

Frieda nodded. 'Yes. Everyone finds their own way of letting go of the world.'

'I used to bake,' said Lola. 'And eat. And sit around with friends. Lolling and giggling and watching reality TV.'

'And you will again.'

Lola gazed at Frieda. 'Do you really think so?'

'Of course.'

'So who won?'

'White was winning for almost the whole game. He swapped off pieces, simplified the position. And then he did this.'

She moved a bishop. Lola wasn't looking at the board but at Frieda's face. She bit her lip. 'Was that good?'

'It wasn't good. He'd moved his bishop one square too far. He lost the game, he lost the match, and he must have thought about it for the rest of his life.'

'What are you going to do?' she asked.

'That's what I'm thinking about.'

'What's the next river?'

'Hmm?' Frieda moved another piece. 'Well, after Counter's Creek comes the Wandle, and then the Falcon.'

'So you think he'll choose the Wandle next?'

'I think so.' She picked up another piece, put it down on a different square, stared at the board through narrowed eyes. 'The question is when and where. I think I'm almost there. But I want to be ahead of him.'

'So how will you do that?'

Frieda looked at Lola across the board. 'You know me by now. When I want to think, really think, I walk, see things more clearly.'

'Now? It's cold and rainy.'

'No. Tomorrow.'

'Where will we go?'

'Not we, me. I need to be alone, Lola, for a few hours at least. You can stay here for once. It's safe, for the time being at least. I haven't told the police where we are. Only one person in the world knows, apart from us. And I trust him.'

'So where will you go?'

'I'll decide that tomorrow. Perhaps to where it all began, eight years ago.'

'I don't know what that means.'

'You don't need to know.'

Lola stood up abruptly, scraping the chair across the boards. 'I'm tired. I'm going to bed,' she said.

'Of course.'

'What time will you go for your walk?'

'Early.'

'How early?'

'I don't know.' Frieda smiled at her. 'Don't worry. You'll be all right here, I promise. I'll bring you a mug of coffee before I go, shall I?'

'Yes, please.'

'Goodnight, then.'

Lola left the room. Frieda could hear the water running upstairs, a door shutting. She imagined Lola lying in her bed, her eyes open, full of fears and gradually drifting towards sleep.

But Frieda sat at the table for many hours, her chin in her hand, listening to the wind outside and waiting for morning.

Forty-six

Frieda boiled the kettle and poured the water over the ground coffee in a jug and stirred it. While it was brewing, she chopped an apple, a nectarine and a few grapes into a bowl. Lola was sitting at the kitchen table, her face still puffy from sleep.

'I've made enough for you,' she said.

'I'm not hungry,' said Lola dully.

Frieda tipped the fruit into two smaller bowls. She took a carton of yoghurt from the fridge and spooned it over the two bowls. She pushed one of the bowls in front of Lola and placed a spoon next to it. She took the tea strainer from the sink and poured the coffee through it into two mugs. One of them she topped off with milk and gave to Lola who just shook her head.

There was silence as Frieda ate all the fruit in her bowl and drank her coffee, then refilled her mug.

'Are you still going out?' Lola asked.

'Yes.'

'Where are you going? Aren't you going to the next river?'

'Not yet.'

'You said last night you were going to where it all began. What does that mean?'

Frieda looked at her broodingly, her brow gathered in a frown. 'There's a spot where Dean Reeve killed his brother,' she said eventually. 'I want to go there.'

Lola was silent for a long time. 'It sounds as if you think it's haunted. That's not like you.'

Frieda sipped slowly at her coffee. 'I do think it's haunted. We're all haunted by our past, by things we can't forget. I walk for different reasons. Sometimes it's a way of emptying my head, getting away from things. Other times it's the opposite. When I walk in London I think of everything that's underneath, that's buried, all the voices of people who are gone.'

'Which is it this time?'

'Both. As I told you, we're nearly at the end. And as I get to the end I need to go to the place where it started and say sorry.'

'Sorry to who?'

'There are lots of people. But Alan, Dean's brother, for a start. He died because of me.'

'Sorry to a dead person? What good will that do?'

'Have you heard of Samuel Johnson?'

'Who is he?'

'He was a writer, poet, three hundred years ago. He felt he hadn't paid proper attention to his father so once, when he was grown-up, he went back to Lichfield, his home town, and to the market square and took his hat off and stood in the rain for an hour.'

'That sounds like a complete waste of time.'

'I don't agree,' said Frieda, draining her mug. 'People may be dead but we're never free of them.'

'You haven't asked me whether I want to come with you.'

'Do you want to come with me?'

'No. I can't do this any more.'

'I guessed that. But, in any case, I said yesterday that I needed to be alone today. I have to think about what I'm going to do next.' Frieda started to put on her jacket.

'Can I ask a question?' said Lola.

'Of course.'

'Dean Reeve wants to kill you.'

'That isn't a question.'

'Don't you have some kind of protection?'

'Like what?'

'Like a gun?'

Frieda shook her head. 'You know I don't have a gun. Where would I get one?' she said.

'You know some strange people.'

'I *do* know some strange people. I'm not sure that they'd trust me with a gun. And I'm not sure a gun would be much use to me.'

'Or a knife. You've used a knife before. I read about it.'

There had been a faint smile on Frieda's face at the idea of her wielding a gun but at the mention of a knife her expression turned sombre. 'Yes, I've used a knife. If I pulled a knife on Dean Reeve, I think it's more likely it would be used on *me*. Anyway, today I'm safe. I don't know where he is and he doesn't know where I am.'

Frieda walked out of the room and returned with her bag over her shoulder.

'Stand up,' she said.

'What for?'

'If nothing else, move around, get your blood flowing.'

Lola stood up.

'Here, take this.' Frieda held out several twenty-pound notes.

'Why?'

'Just to tide you over.'

'I don't understand.'

'I'm not coming back,' said Frieda.

'Why? What do you mean?'

'I can't protect you any more. You're probably not in danger now anyway. But just in case.' Frieda took a little torn-off piece of notepaper from her pocket and handed it to Lola. 'Malcolm Karlsson's number is on that. I've given it to you before and you didn't make any use of it. This time you must. He'll protect you better than anyone. Better than me.'

Frieda put up her hand and stroked Lola's cheek gently. It was so pale.

'I should say thank you,' Lola said, in a faint voice, almost a whisper. Fat tears were rolling slowly down her cheeks and her eyes were huge.

'Maybe you should and maybe you shouldn't,' Frieda said. 'There'll be a time to talk about things like that. At least, I hope there will be. If there isn't . . .' She gave a nod. 'Tell Karlsson I'm counting on him to look after you.'

Frieda turned to go but Lola clutched at her sleeve. 'Have you got some clever secret plan you're not telling me about?'

Frieda put her hand on Lola's and tapped it. 'That's what this walk is about.'

'Don't go,' said Lola, in a rush. She clutched Frieda's sleeve. Her lips were bloodless and her voice cracked. 'Please don't go.'

'I have to.'

'Frieda, please. Please don't go. You can't.'

'Can't?' Frieda smiled at her.

'Mustn't.'

'Why?'

'I can't bear it.'

'You can, Lola. You will.'

When Frieda left the house she walked towards King's Cross, but then turned left and went through the little network of streets and red-brick apartment blocks that line the south side of Euston Road. She walked past the university buildings and the hospital and across Tottenham Court Road and Fitzroy Square and, with a growing ache in her chest, arrived at Saffron Mews and her own front door.

She opened it and stepped inside and felt a rush of emotion she could hardly bear. She felt like a ghost, returning from the dead for just a few seconds. She laid her bag down. She looked around and sniffed. There was an unfamiliar smell, sawdust and something else, something industrial. Well, that was a matter for another time. She could see into the kitchen, where a vase of crimson dahlias stood on the table, and a pot of basil on the windowsill. She went into the living room. The fire was neatly laid, kindling over scrunched-up newspaper and logs stacked on the hearth. On the chess table, the pieces had been lined up. Everything was waiting.

She heard a sound, a familiar sound, a brindled cat padding across the floor towards her, the claws tapping on the wooden floor. Frieda crouched down and stroked the cat's head and along its spine. 'Hello, you,' she said. 'So you've come home at last. You've seen some things in your time, haven't you? If you could talk, what tales you'd have to tell.'

It looked at her with its yellow eyes; she could feel its body vibrating.

'I should have given you a name,' she said. 'But it's probably too late for that. You don't mind, do you?'

The cat purred and arched its back and didn't seem to mind. Frieda stood up. That was enough: more would turn the solace into a terrible homesickness. She opened the front door and stepped outside, closed the door and walked away from her house without looking back.

Forty-seven

When Frieda closed the front door, Lola lay down on the beige carpet and pulled her knees up to her chin. She stayed like that for several minutes, balled tightly and rocking slightly. Small moans escaped her. Everything hurt: her head and her heart and her stomach and her eyes. She felt as if she was turning inside out so that all the soft and hidden parts of herself were exposed.

Then she got up, although it seemed impossible that she could stand on her two feet. She looked dazedly around her, then down at the money still crumpled in her hand. She pulled on her jacket, put the key in its pocket and left the house. The sun went in and out of the clouds and the wind blew in gusts, swirling leaves around her feet. She walked across the square to Euston Road and found a shop that was little more than a booth and bought a pay-as-you-go phone, using one of the twenty-pound notes that Frieda had given her.

She didn't quite know why, but she didn't want to make the call there on the street surrounded by people. They would be able to hear her even though they would have no way of understanding what she was saying.

She walked back to the square and stood under the plane trees by the tennis court. Despite the cold, two women were playing, hitting the ball in high loops and giggling at each other. For a brief moment, she watched them. How would it feel, to be carefree like that?

Then she took out her phone and dialled the number she

knew by heart. There was a click as it was answered. She screwed up her eyes. She could hear someone breathing. Just breathing. But she remembered his face so clearly, the way he had smiled, that it was like he could see her. She thought she would be sick, and her body felt poisonous with the horror of what she was doing.

'She's gone for a walk . . . Just now. A few minutes ago . . . The place where your brother was found. I mean your brother's body . . . She said it was where it all began . . . All right.' Lola waited. 'I've done all I can. Will you leave me alone? Will you leave my family alone? . . . Hello? Hello?'

There was nobody there. Lola dropped the phone into a rubbish bin and walked back to the house on her rubbery legs and let herself in. She shut the door but didn't bother to draw the security bolts, then went into the living room and sat on the sofa.

Pushing her hand into her pocket she drew out the piece of paper Frieda had given her. *DCI Karlsson*; a phone number. Frieda had said he would help her. But that was because Frieda didn't know what she had done. She could never ask him for anything.

She dropped the piece of paper to the floor, leaned her head on her hands and shut her eyes as tightly as possible, but she could still see Dean's face, his smile. And she could see Jess, staring up at her as the life ebbed away. And then she could see Frieda, her dark, bright eyes, and that was almost worse than anything. She could almost feel her hand stroking her cheek and her soft, clear voice. She pressed her fingertips against her throbbing eyes. What should she do now? What should she ever do?

'What have I done?' she said in a whisper.

For a moment, she imagined rushing to the place to tell Frieda it was a trap – but she didn't even know where the place was, just that it was where Dean had killed his brother, Alan, and, anyway, his words came to her: *Your mum and dad, Dave and Carol. You wouldn't want anything to happen to them, would you? If you don't help, do you know what will happen? Of course you don't know. Not until I've shown you. Watch carefully.* And night after night, in her waking dreams and in her nightmares, she had watched as he had drawn the knife across Jess's throat. She leaned further forward, pressed her fingers harder against her eyelids, and still she saw Dean's smile, and she saw Frieda's dark and watching eyes. Seconds ticked past. Minutes.

At last Keegan answered his phone.

'I've been trying to call you.'

'I know. I've got twenty-two missed calls from you. I'm on holiday – you're lucky I answered this one.'

'You know where Frieda Klein is.'

'Is that what you've been calling to say?'

'I need to see her.'

There was a brief silence. Karlsson could hear that Keegan was walking. 'If I did know,' he said, 'I wouldn't tell you.'

'She's in danger.'

'When Frieda comes to me, it's because I'm the only person she can trust.'

'Christ,' said Karlsson, violently. 'She's going to get killed if we don't do anything.'

'You know there was a leak.'

'Maybe there was, maybe there wasn't. I don't know about that, I'm talking to you as her friend. You have to tell me. Please.'

Another long pause and the sound of voices.

'All right.'

*

As Quarry came into Dugdale's office and sat down, he was aware of his boss looking at him appraisingly. Quarry's face was bruised on one side and he had a plaster on his left cheek. The ribs felt worse. They hurt when he twisted or moved his arms. Or sat down.

'Are you all right to work?'

'I won't be much use in a fight,' said Quarry. 'But I'll do what I can.'

'You might want to talk to someone eventually. It does something to you, being attacked like that.'

'I'm fine.'

'I'm serious.'

'And I'm fine,' said Quarry, a bit more loudly.

'All right. I've got the soft and cuddly bit out of the way.'

Quarry suddenly felt a lurch in his stomach.

'Dean Reeve found out where Frieda Klein was hiding,' Dugdale continued. 'We knew and Frieda Klein knew and Frieda Klein didn't tell him.'

Quarry slowly shook his head. 'I didn't tell anyone,' he said.

'I've been thinking about it,' said Dugdale. 'Going over and over it in my mind. I was sure that it couldn't be us. It couldn't be my department. Not in this case. Not the Dean Reeve case. Not with the world watching. And then I thought of you and Liz Barron and I remembered that you met her.'

'Sir, I wouldn't . . .'

'Quiet,' said Dugdale, in a voice that was itself so calm that it gave Quarry a chill. 'I'm just going to say this. You are going to tell me now any and all dealings you have had with the press during this case. If I believe you have been holding anything back, I will suspend you and put you under investigation and we'll check your calls and see who you've been talking to.'

Sweat prickled on Quarry's forehead. 'I told you I met Liz Barron when I interviewed Karlsson.'

'No, I told *you* and you confirmed it. And?'

'She said she would be interested in any information I could give her. I considered it. I probably would have talked to her. But then she was murdered.'

'Did money pass hands?'

'No.'

And it hadn't, but only because of her death: it was what she had promised and what he had wanted. Guilt and shame washed through him. His mouth felt dry and it was all he could do to keep on meeting Dugdale's gaze.

'And then another journalist saw her notes and phoned me. She wanted to meet. I didn't exactly say no but we haven't met and we haven't talked.'

There was a long pause. Dugdale glanced away, then back at Quarry.

'You can see how it looks,' he said.

'I didn't tell her anything. You have to believe me.'

'I couldn't trust you then, but I can trust you now. Is that what you're saying?'

'It wasn't me.'

'Then who? It wasn't Frieda, it wasn't you. And you were in contact with a journalist.'

Quarry thought frantically. He felt like he was fighting for his life. 'Klein could have told her friends.'

'She went into hiding to protect her friends,' said Dugdale. 'The whole point was to leave them out of it.'

They stared at each other.

'There is someone else,' said Quarry, slowly.

'Who?'

'The girl. Lola Hayes.'

Dugdale lifted his hand and, very slowly, rubbed the side of his face. 'Could it be her?' he said. 'Could it?'

'She's the only person left.'

'But why? Why would she do that?'

'Maybe Reeve got some kind of hold over her. Klein was with her to protect her. She might have misjudged her.'

Dugdale jabbed his finger at Quarry. 'If you're fucking me around, Dan, if you're putting the blame on this girl to protect yourself . . .'

'I swear it. I swear it by anything.'

'Stop it. I'll consider it. I don't have a choice. But if you're right, if it's her, then Dean Reeve knows what she's going to do and we don't. So have you got a plan for that?'

They looked at each other again. They didn't have a plan.

'All right,' said the commissioner wearily to Dugdale. 'I think the time has come.'

'To go public?'

'Yes.'

She picked up the phone.

Karlsson and Yvette strode rapidly along the streets. They didn't speak until they reached the house. Then Karlsson nodded at her.

'This is it,' he said.

'The curtains are closed upstairs.'

Karlsson knocked, then knocked again. Nothing.

'What next?' asked Yvette.

He didn't answer, simply put his shoulder to the door and gave a violent push, then another. The door didn't give. He lifted his foot, with its elegant shoe, and smashed it against the lock. Yvette heard a splintering sound and the door swung open. They stepped into the hall.

'You go upstairs,' said Karlsson. 'I'll take the ground floor.'

He went into the living room and almost didn't see her,

was about to go into the kitchen when he noticed a scrap of paper on the floor. Picking it up, he saw his own name was written on it, in Frieda's unmistakable handwriting. And as he stared at it, he heard a faint sound behind him. He turned. There was a figure huddled up behind the armchair, almost out of sight. He glimpsed a pale face and terrified eyes. Her fists were held against her mouth, like she was stopping herself crying out. He yanked the chair away and she pushed herself further back against the wall, as if she was hoping it would open up and swallow her.

'Lola,' he said gently, as if she was a startled horse. 'It's all right. You're safe now.'

'Who are you?' It was a croak.

He held out a hand to help her up. 'I'm Chief Inspector Karlsson. I'm a friend of Frieda's.'

'I know. She said you would help me.'

And at this the young woman began to cry bitterly, sobs shaking her whole frame. Yvette, entering the room, put an arm round her to keep her upright.

'I need to know where she is. Has she been here?'

'Yes.'

'Where is she now?'

'She's gone.' And the sobs increased. Yvette manoeuvred her over to the sofa and sat her down.

'When did she go?' Karlsson crouched down beside Lola. 'This is urgent. You need to tell me at once.'

She raised her face, tear-stained and swollen with sobbing, her eyes red-rimmed and cold sores on the edge of her mouth. 'About half an hour ago,' she managed to say.

'When is she coming back?'

'I don't know. Never.'

'Never?'

'I don't know.'

'Where did she go?'

Lola shook her head from side to side and then buried it in her hands again.

'You don't understand,' she whispered. 'You don't understand anything.'

'Later, you can tell me everything. I promise. Now, you just need to tell me what you know about Frieda. I'm here to help her. Did she tell you where she was going?'

'Not exactly.'

'What did she say?'

Lola sat up. She pushed her hair behind her ears and took a deep, shuddering breath. He saw a new expression on her face, as if she was coming to a decision. 'All right,' she said. 'I'll tell you.'

Forty-eight

Lola had said Frieda was going to walk there, and although Karlsson knew how swiftly she walked, it gave him time. She was only forty minutes or so ahead of him. He left Yvette with Lola, though she protested, wanting to come with him, and ran onto the main thoroughfare, waving at cabs until one stopped.

Now that he knew where she was, he felt that every second counted, although perhaps Frieda was simply walking and thinking and the danger still stood far off. It was his sense that he was near her that was a torment – the gap between here and there. For the first time in all these weeks of waiting and watching and wanting, he knew where she was. The sudden hope made time into an agony and the sense of urgency something almost physical, pressing down on him, making his chest hurt. Getting out of the centre of London was painfully slow, cars and vans and buses clogging every road. Perhaps he should have gone on the Underground, or called for back-up and gone with blue lights flashing. But he knew he had to be stealthy and arrive unnoticed. He sat tense and still in the back of the cab. Every so often he thought of Lola, twitchy and blotchy with terror, and with some other emotion as well – but what? He pushed away the thought and sat forward, willing the cab through the snarled-up traffic.

And now at last they were past the worst of it and edging forward. He looked at his watch. He tried not to imagine seeing Frieda, because that would make it all the more distressing if he didn't. And he tried not to imagine her in danger. It did no good to torment himself. Instead, he focused on the moment he was in: the twenty-pound note in his fist, ready to pass to the driver as he jumped from the cab; the plans he made in his head for when they arrived. He would make sure they stopped well before they reached the spot. He would be unobtrusive and, after all, no one would be expecting him.

Frieda walked steadily through the familiar streets. She didn't need to think of where she was going: her feet led her. The day was hazy, shapes looming at her, roofs and spires, tall cranes and the tops of buildings vague in the heavy grey air. The plane trees had lost most of their leaves and she could see smoke rising out of some of the chimneys. It was 1 November: the Day of the Dead, she thought. A day to remember those who have gone, to walk with them awhile, abide with them and then let them go.

And as she walked, she felt them beside her, all those shadows: people she had loved and people she had harmed; people who had harmed her. Her mother, who had never wanted to be a mother. Her father, who all his life had carried a weight of malignant sadness and then one day had been unable to bear it and killed himself. Sandy, the man she had once loved, who had once loved her, and whose body had been found floating in the Thames. And then those others over the years, so many of them, who had been sucked into the black hole that was Dean Reeve. She could see their faces, young faces and old ones, and she could feel them beside her, inside her, some angry and some sad, some crying out for help and some at peace. All the ghosts she carried with her; and the ghost of her younger self, eager and just starting out, but the road had led to here, to now. So many dead people, a great crowd of them at her side. They walked with her; she walked with them. Would it be such a bad thing to join them? To be dead with them?

You have to forgive yourself. Who had said that to her? Probably Reuben, she thought. Or perhaps she herself had said it to patients over the years. *You have to forgive yourself.*

Did she? Perhaps there would be time for such questions later, after this was over. She knew it would be over soon. She knew it was the endgame at last, the day of the dead. She thought of that phrase. People misunderstood it. They thought of it as something scary and ghoulish, with skulls and zombies. But really it was about the dead as our companions, our friends, still alive in our memories and in our hearts. Frieda had never really understood a fear of death, still less a fear of being dead. It was just an absence, a non-being, the bit of being asleep where you're not dreaming.

It was the living we should be afraid of. For Frieda, the dead were beyond harming us, except in our minds. We should think of them with love or regret or remorse or simple sadness, but we shouldn't fear them or let them harm us. Over and over again that was what she had tried to convey to her patients. But the living were something else. For seven years now she had known, whatever else she knew, wherever she was, whatever she was doing, that Dean Reeve was thinking of her. He had planned and brutalized and killed in a trail that led to her, and now every step was taking her closer to the end of that trail. To him.

Karlsson got out of the cab and handed over the money, waving away the change. He glanced around him: a soft drizzle was beginning to fall and there was barely anyone about. Frieda wouldn't be here yet. He had time. He walked to the edge of the water that lay still in the windless air.

He knew why Frieda would come here. He looked at the iron bell and brown water, and at the row of great cranes, their tops swallowed by the mist. Then he found himself a position where he wouldn't be seen and wrapped his coat closer about him. Now he was looking in the direction that she would come from. He settled back to wait.

Chloë and Jack sat on Frieda's new balcony, drinking coffee. They had just planted several small lavender bushes in terracotta pots.

'It feels like it's waiting to rain,' said Chloë.

'I know. It's the kind of day that never quite gets light.' Jack shivered and buttoned up his jacket.

The cat came out of the door and wound its way between them, pushing its head first against their legs, asking for attention. They could hear the low rumble of its purr. Chloë ran her hand along its body.

'I wonder where Frieda is now,' she said.

Karlsson was cold and wet. He glanced at his watch: it had been more than an hour and still Frieda hadn't come. He went over in his mind what Lola had told him, but knew he had the right place. Then his mobile buzzed in his pocket and he fished it out. It was Bill Dugdale.

'Bill?' He kept his voice low.

'I tried you at work but they told me you were on annual leave.'

'Yes. What is it? Any news?'

'Not as such. Where are you?'

Karlsson looked about him; he saw a heron sitting motionless in the tree opposite. 'Well. I'm by the river.'

'I just thought I should keep you in the loop.'

'Thanks.'

'It's probably nothing. But we've been investigating the leak that led to Dean Reeve knowing where Frieda was.'

'Go on.'

'We think – don't know, mind, it's probably just a red herring, but it makes sense of things that we can't explain otherwise – that it might have been the girl.'

For a moment, Karlsson's mind went blank. 'Girl?'

'Lola Hayes.'

'Oh, fuck. Fuck fuck fuck.'

'What is it?'

But Karlsson had ended the call. He punched in Yvette's number. 'Get Lola,' he said.

'What? Where are you?'

'I'm at the mouth of the Wandle, like she said. But she might have sent me to the wrong bloody place. Yvette, find out where I should be.' He heard the despair in his voice.

'Wait.'

He could hear Yvette moving through the house. Then running. He heard her calling Lola's name.

'She's gone,' Yvette said. 'She's disappeared. Why would she do that when she was so scared?'

'Find her. Call Dugdale and tell him.'

'I will. What are you going to do?'

'I don't know. She could be anywhere at all. And where's Dean? Has Lola told him where to go?'

Frieda was getting near the spot. Her hair was damp from the drizzle, but she didn't mind that. She had always liked walking in the cold and the wet; it unknotted her thoughts and calmed her mind. Sometimes she felt that all those miles and miles of walking were lodged in her bones, like a kind of knowledge. Those nights when she couldn't sleep and slipped on her clothes, heading out into the empty darkness. The secret rivers whose courses she had followed, feeling the shape of them beneath her feet, sometimes stopping to hear them murmur through grates on the roads. All the things that lay out of sight but powerful, the secret history of a city that appalled and enthralled her.

Near here, Alan had been killed by his twin, Dean. And so it had all started. That was why she had to come to this place: back to the beginning. Brown leaves drifted through the still air to the pavement. Frieda held out her hand and caught one as it fell. It was supposed to be lucky. She didn't believe in that kind of luck, but she put it into the pocket of her coat anyway. Walked on.

While dozens of police officers were being sent out to search for Lola Hayes, Dugdale sat in his office with Dan Quarry.

'Perhaps she's gone to the next hidden river,' he said. 'You know Frieda's theory – that Reeve was killing people on hidden rivers, in order to send her a message. So what's the next one, after Counter's Creek?'

The two of them looked at the map he'd pulled up on the computer. Quarry pointed. 'The Wandle and then the Falcon.'

'They're both miles long,' Dugdale said. 'We need lots of officers – and even then it's just a guess.' He made up his mind. 'I'll send some officers to patrol them both. We need to do something.'

'This might turn out to be a panic without proper cause,' said Quarry. 'We don't know Lola is the source of the leaks, it's just a possibility. And even if she is, we don't know that she's told Reeve where Frieda's going.'

'We'll find out soon enough,' said Dugdale. 'One way or another.'

*

Karlsson put his fingers to his temples, and closed his eyes. Where would Frieda go? London was so vast and messy and complex, spreading its tentacles out like a monster, swallowing up little hamlets, invading its own edgelands, always spreading, always mutating. Frieda could be anywhere.

'Think,' he said to himself. '*Think*.'

Once he had found her by imagining her thought processes on the day of Sandy's funeral. He remembered that brief moment, when they'd sat together on Parliament Hill and she'd said her private goodbyes. So where would she be now? By Sandy's grave? Walking one of her rivers? If she needed to think, if she was in trouble, where would she go? And why, he asked himself, wouldn't she go to him?

The tide was waning and the Wandle was draining away, leaving just a trickle of water running through the mud banks. Karlsson turned and started to walk, but slowly, because he didn't know in which direction he was heading; he felt as though he was going in circles.

And at that thought, an idea struck him and he was running, hope and fear tearing at his chest.

Forty-nine

Reuben McGill was actually pulled out of a therapy session, leaving a young woman crying and Paz offering her tissues and bringing her coffee.

When Chloë's phone rang, she was in a workshop wearing noise-excluding headphones. One of her colleagues had to gesture in front of her to get her attention.

Alexei answered the phone at Reuben's house. He said his father was on site somewhere. No, he didn't know where. Nobody else knew anything either.

Professor Hal Bradshaw took off his glasses and stepped away from the lectern, leaving his text behind him. He was reaching the climax of the lecture. It was always more effective, he had found, over the years, when it was delivered as if in the inspiration of the moment.

'It's all very well to think about crime in here, here in the safety of our lecture hall, of our libraries, of our laboratories. But at a certain point, the psychologist of crime, the philosopher of crime, needs to go out into the world, to learn what a crime scene is really like, to see it, to smell it, almost to taste it.' He paused for effect. A girl in the front row had gone very white. Young people nowadays, Bradshaw thought. 'We should consider the criminal as a sort of artist and the crime scene as his work of art.' He waited for a beat. 'Or *her* work of art. Every crime is a text. It is our job to learn to read it.' Another pause to let the meaning sink in. 'That's all for this week.'

There was clattering and rustling and chattering as the students got up and collected their bags and drifted out of the lecture hall in groups. Bradshaw picked up his papers and put them into his shoulder bag. As he started to leave, he saw that there was a figure still seated at the back of the hall near the door. It was slumped over, the knees pulled up. He couldn't tell whether it was male or female or even whether it was conscious. He nudged the figure gently and a pale, stained face of a young woman looked up at him. The eyes seemed to stare through him. Year by year he found it harder and harder to tell them apart, but she was familiar.

'You're . . .' he began, but the name wouldn't come to him.

'Lola,' she said, in a croaky voice. 'Lola Hayes. I came to see you.'

'Are you all right? You don't look well.'

'I'm not well.'

Bradshaw was uncertain about what he should do. As a psychologist, he could see that this was a woman in deep distress but he wasn't her doctor. He wasn't even her teacher. He sat down next to her. 'Shall we get some help for you?'

She was shivering. He took her arm and tried to pull her to her feet but she shook him away.

'I'm taking you to the nurse,' he said. 'If you won't come, I'll have to call for help.'

Lola stood up and immediately wobbled, and Bradshaw had to reach out to stop her falling.

'Easy,' he said. 'Are you ready?' He put his arm round her and led her slowly and awkwardly out of the lecture hall into the corridor. He felt self-conscious leading Lola through the groups of students chatting or tapping on phones. Some turned to stare at them. A girl asked if everything was all right but he waved her away. He just needed to get her down-stairs, into the nurse's room, and he would have done his duty. It wasn't enough to be a teacher now. You had to be their parent and childminder and therapist rolled into one. Lola herself seemed entirely unaware of her surroundings.

Getting Lola down the stairs was a cumbersome process. At one point she stumbled, Bradshaw grabbed her, she tried to escape his grasp and, for a farcical moment, he thought the two of them might tumble down the stairs.

Finally, they arrived at the nurse's room. Bradshaw opened the door and led Lola into the waiting room. There was nobody there. He was tempted to leave her but decided not to. People got sued for things like that. Too many people had seen him leading her down there. He looked around rather desperately at all the posters advertising services for mental health and sexual health and gender issues. He sat her down on one of the plastic chairs lined against the wall. Then he knocked on the door leading into the treatment room. There was a pause and the door opened and the nurse appeared. They had met many times but Bradshaw couldn't remember her name.

She frowned at him. 'I've someone in with me,' she said. 'Terrible nosebleed.' She looked past Bradshaw at Lola. 'Is it an emergency?'

'She's in a state of distress.'

'I'll be out as soon as I can. Can you stay with her?'

'I can't really –' he began, but she interrupted him.

'You're a doctor, aren't you?'

'Of a kind. Not that kind, though.'

'I'll be as quick as I can,' she said, and slammed the door.

Bradshaw sighed. The nurse knew Lola was there, so could he leave her now? But the woman had specifically asked him to take care of her. He looked at Lola. He could imagine her wandering away, jumping off something, jumping in front of something. He could imagine the inquiry, the articles in the newspapers. He had written some of those articles. This time it would be him. He sat down in the chair next to her.

'It looks like it's just you and me for a while,' he said. She didn't answer. Instead she was sitting against the back of the chair, hitting her head lightly against a poster advertising a helpline for LGBT rights. Thump. Thump. Thump. 'Could you not do that?' he said. 'It's probably not a helpful thing.'

She stopped and instead leaned forward. He thought for a moment she might be about to vomit. He couldn't remember their previous meeting very clearly but he had a dim impression of eagerness, affability. What could have happened? Boyfriend problems, probably. Or girlfriend problems. These things happened all the time. Even so, this seemed a bit extreme. He leaned his hand forward to touch the back of her head, then stopped himself. You never knew. These things might be misunderstood.

'Is there something you want to talk about?' he said.

She gave no sign of having heard what he was saying.

'I'm a psychologist. You can tell me anything. I've heard it all before. Sometimes it helps to say things out loud.'

He felt slightly embarrassed even saying the words. He knew that sometimes it helped saying things out loud and sometimes it made it worse. But just sitting there was a torment. Did this girl need an ambulance? Was she in a psychotic state? He thought not. She looked in a bad way, a very bad way, but she seemed aware of her surroundings. She wasn't entirely unresponsive. She had been able to walk, with help. It was just this silence. He felt a need to fill it with something.

'I seem to remember that you were writing your dissertation on Frieda Klein,' he said, with an attempt at cheerfulness. 'How's that going?' She shook her head. That was some kind of a response at least, if more like a spasm than an attempt at communication. 'You were going to deconstruct her, weren't you? Strip away her façade. Sounded like a promising idea. Did you manage it? Have you punctured the Frieda Klein myth?'

At that, Lola sat slowly upright and looked him full in the face. 'I've destroyed her,' she said.

He gave a nervous little laugh. 'What do you mean?'

'I've killed her.'

He coughed and looked around. When was that nurse coming back?

'Not literally?' he said. But she didn't reply. 'What do you mean you've killed her? Is she dead?'

'I don't know.'

'Is she injured?'

'I don't know.'

'Then what do you mean?' Now he raised his voice. 'Tell me. When you say you've killed her, what do you mean?'

Still staring at him, without seeming to see him, Lola rubbed her bloodshot eyes and then blinked. 'I think she's going to be killed.'

That was it. Bradshaw took his phone out of his pocket and dialled 999. Immediately the voice asked what service he wanted. He had been going to call for an ambulance. This was a clear case of psychosis, surely. He knew case after case of students falling in love and then in hate with their teachers. Teachers and therapists attracted that kind of attention. As he well knew, Frieda Klein attracted that attention more than anyone he had encountered in his entire professional life. She had even attracted *his* attention. And this attraction could turn into a full-fledged delusion. Students could be so highly strung. There were so many pressures. They could become manic or florid like this, or they could sink into a stupor of depression. Looking at her, Bradshaw thought, as doctors so often had to, of how he would defend his action before an investigation if it all went wrong. There would be no problem. The symptoms were classic. There was no reason to think that this talk of Frieda Klein being <u>killed</u> was anything more than the fantasy of a troubled mind. But he hesitated.

'Police,' he said. 'I need the police.'

Fifty

Years earlier, when Frieda had first walked along the canals, they had been almost deserted, inhabited by the odd illegal cyclist, a few eccentric fishermen, gangs of young men you brushed past without making eye contact. Today she had walked past the new office buildings, the coffee shops, the runners, the au pairs and young mothers pushing buggies, the houseboats double-parked, their smoking chimneys reeking of coal and fragrant wood. She had walked along the side of Victoria Park and seen lines of little schoolchildren in their yellow high-visibility jackets, fitness classes. But beyond that, turning onto the River Lea, the towpath became quieter and then entirely deserted.

This was the spot. There was an old dock, off the canal, which must once have been used for unloading goods for a depot that no longer existed. Once you turned off the canal – as Frieda now did – you were completely out of sight of the main towpath, under an old bridge. This was the spot. This was where Dean's brother had died. Frieda had once thought the spot marked the end of something, but really it was the beginning of everything.

She leaned on a railing and looked down into the water. Normally she liked to look at flowing water, rivers, tides. But this water was stagnant, unmoving, cut off from the main body of the canal, which itself lurched and rippled rather than flowed. Frieda took a breath. She had a feeling of immense calm and of acceptance. She wasn't thinking of Dean, but of her father, whom she had loved a great deal and who had taken his own life when she was a teenager. She had found his body. Not a day had gone by when she hadn't remembered that moment, looking into his dead face and sightless eyes. It was the last time she had prayed, to a God she didn't believe in but whose help she had begged. She knew that the entire course of her life had been shaped by those few seconds. The knowledge that she had failed to rescue her father, or even adequately recognize his pain until it was too late, meant that over and over again she had had to recognize the pain of others and try to rescue them. As if by rescuing them, she could rescue him; rescue herself. Now, staring into the brown water, she let herself remember her father as he had been years before his death. Not sad. Not hopeless. As someone alive, full of energy and hope. She called him into her mind; she saw his face; she smiled at him. What a journey it had been.

When she heard a scuffling sound nearby, behind her, she didn't turn around. She didn't even move.

It didn't happen the way Hal Bradshaw had expected. He'd expected a policeman might arrive in an hour or two, ask a few questions, maybe take a statement. Instead he was transferred to one police officer, then to another, then patched through to a crackly mobile phone line. He was told to stay where he was and not let Lola Hayes out of his sight. Not for a second.

'Fucking follow her into the toilet, if necessary,' said a voice on the phone.

'What?' said Bradshaw, but the line was dead.

While he was still collecting his thoughts, he heard the sound of a siren, then another. He dimly thought there must be a fire somewhere. He heard the sound of heavy footsteps outside and the door opened. He saw the face of the porter, the man who sat in a little wooden lodge at the front entrance. Bradshaw had never seen the man outside his lodge. Then another person whose name he didn't quite know.

'This is the place,' said the porter, and two male and two female uniformed officers walked past him. One of the women stepped ahead.

'Are you Dr Bradshaw?'

'Yes.'

'And this is Lola Hayes?'

'Yes.'

The woman stepped away, unclipped her radio and spoke into it. There was a crackling sound. She turned back and leaned over Lola. 'Where's Frieda Klein?'

Lola looked up, glassy-eyed, and shook her head and twisted, like she was in pain, but didn't speak.

'I don't think she's in a condition to answer questions,' said Bradshaw.

The officer stepped back and spoke into her radio. 'She won't say anything. OK.'

She looked back at Bradshaw. 'You're to stay here. Both of you.'

'I think she actually needs to go to a hospital. I should have probably called an ambulance.'

'Later, maybe. You need to stay here. They're on their way.'

'The ambulance?'

'No.'

He was standing in a small recess in the wall under the bridge. As he edged slowly forward, he saw her leaning on the railing, lost in her thoughts. He wanted to hold that moment, to look at her before she looked at him, before she knew he was there. Before it happened. What was she thinking about? Was she ready? Because at last it was her time. All

339

these years, all the waiting, and they were here. Back at the beginning, at the ending.

He stepped out. He was between her and the main tow-path, cutting off any possibility of escape. At last she looked round, then raised herself from the railing and stood, facing him.

He gazed at her and felt a ripple go through him, as if he had become liquid. He had seen her so often, but obliquely, at a distance. It had been eight years since they had looked at each other in the face, their eyes meeting. Her hair was different. She had dyed it. Otherwise she had barely changed. Perhaps the lines around her eyes, at the corners of her mouth were etched a little deeper, the skin on her cheek-bones drawn a little tighter, but this was the same face that had haunted him. Now he was seeing it up close: the eyes, dark bright eyes that were almost black, whose gaze he could feel on him like something physical; the smooth aquiline nose, the full lips, slightly parted.

She stood very upright, taller than he had remembered, her hands by her sides. He looked at her body, the slope of the shoulders, the curves of her breasts in her blue shirt, her hips in the tight black jeans. She wasn't like the others. There was nothing pleading about her. There was no giveaway breathing, no widening of the gaze that signalled fear.

If this moment could just go on for ever. But it was time.

He took the knife from his pocket. He didn't raise it, just felt the heft of it, comfortable in his palm. Nine-inch blade. German steel. The dark, heavy holster, cool in his grip. It had cut the throat of Jessica Colbeck, like scissors through silk.

People always looked at the knife, hypnotized by its edge, by its gleam. But she didn't. He saw her looking into his eyes, almost with concern for him.

He thought of saying something but there was nothing to be said. They both knew. She would be grateful, really. Welcoming. She had always known this was coming.

Hal Bradshaw looked up as the door banged open and two men came in with a clatter, breathing heavily: Dugdale and Quarry. Dugdale glanced at Bradshaw, then turned to Lola.

'Remember me?' he said.

Lola let her head drop forwards but Dugdale grabbed her by the hair on her crown and pulled her head sharply up.

'You are in a world of trouble,' he said.

'You can't do that,' Bradshaw said.

Dugdale looked slowly round at him but he didn't release his grip on Lola. 'What did she tell you?'

'I told them on the phone.'

'Tell *me*.'

'She said she'd killed Frieda Klein. I think she means she's responsible. Not that she actually . . .' Bradshaw's voice faded to a mumble.

Dugdale pushed his face close to Lola's. 'You sent Karlsson to the wrong place. You knew that, didn't you?'

Lola murmured something.

'What?'

'I couldn't.'

'Listen,' said Dugdale. 'We have no time. We have a police alert across London. We've got three helicopters in the air.'

Lola shook her head and Dugdale pulled his hand away. He spoke more gently. 'Lola,' he said, 'if you think you've got some bargain with Reeve, it doesn't matter. He doesn't care. If he wants to kill someone, he'll kill them. He doesn't care what you do.'

Tears were starting to run down Lola's face.

'It's probably too late. You've done what he wanted. Just tell us where Frieda was going.'

Lola looked at Dugdale and at Quarry and at Bradshaw and at the nurse, who was now standing on the far side of the room. She swallowed, hesitated and spoke in a slow croak: 'Where his brother died.'

Dugdale looked at Quarry, then back at Lola. 'If you're lying, Lola, I swear to God I'll get you put away somewhere you'll never get out of.'

'It's true.'

The two men ran out of the room, Dugdale shouting instructions as they made their way up the stairs and out to the waiting car. 'And ring Karlsson,' he said.

Fifty-one

'What have you heard?' It was Chloë on the phone and she was weeping so hard Reuben could barely make out the words. He pictured her face, young and tragic, her mascara smudged. 'What have you heard?' she said again.

'Nothing more.'

'Oh, God. Oh, Reuben.'

Karlsson was running now, gripped by a terrible dread. His leg, the one that had been broken, was aching and he had a pain in his side. His mobile buzzed in his pocket and he pulled it out.

'She's gone to the place where Reeve killed his brother,' said Dugdale. 'Officers are on their way there. It's where the canal –'

So he'd guessed right. Excitement pumped through him. 'I know. I'm nearly there,' he said.

He pushed the mobile back into his pocket. The sun had risen higher in the sky. He ran on, into the shining mist.

'What's happening to Frieda?' asked Alexei.

Reuben looked at his anxious face; the boy had his father's doleful brown eyes. 'Let's see if we can find your dad,' he said, and held out his hand. 'We should all be together.'

A helicopter spun into view above Karlsson. It sank lower so that he could see its blades. Lower still, and now it was

343

hovering like a giant insect. Below it lay the canal, smoking in the autumn air.

Lola sat with her knees pulled up and her head lowered and her hands over her ears. Her eyes were shut and she rocked slowly back and forward, back and forward.

'Please,' she said. 'Please please please.'

Three police cars, lights flashing and sirens sounding, screeched to a halt. Twelve officers scrambled out. They ran towards the footpath that led to the canal. The road-sweeper at the end of the street could hear their feet on the ground; it was like drums beating, he thought.

Young Eli Abel was in the front. He belonged to a running club and he moved easily away from the others, arriving at the bridge first. He was only just out of college, and he was thinking to himself how amazing it was that one of his first cases involved Frieda Klein and Dean Reeve. His gran wouldn't believe him when he told her what he'd been up to today.

His feet clattered on the iron bridge. A helicopter hung above him, its noise inside his skull. Mist lay in ribbons on the brown water. Leaves fell like petals and drowned.

Eli Abel stared down. He blinked. He saw a shape in the water. He stopped, screwed up his eyes. He saw a body, face down. 'Here!' he shouted, above the roar of the helicopter. 'Here!'

Then he was running across the bridge and down the steps, onto the path. He couldn't remember his training. Should he wait for back-up? Take off his boots?

Too late. He was in the water, cold and sludgy, up to his chest. His boots sank into mud. He imagined the rats in here, swimming in the murk with their yellow teeth and thick

344

tails. Weil's disease, he thought, as he waded towards the shape.

He could hear shouts from the shore and the deafening drone of the helicopter. More sirens from the road. Wait till I tell people, he thought. Water trickled down his neck and splashed in his face. The sun was in his eyes and it was hard to see what was in front of him.

He reached the shape half submerged in the water and put out his hand. But for a brief moment he hesitated, and the sun made strange shapes on the surface of the canal, like a moving pattern. He remembered the rotating lamp he had had as a child, when he'd been afraid of the dark. All night the lamp had thrown underwater creatures onto the walls, seahorses and fish and mermaids.

He'd never seen a dead body before, never touched one. He made himself clutch an arm and the figure shifted slightly and when he'd touched it once, it was all right. He took it by its shoulders and started hauling the weight towards the bank and someone was shouting his name encouragingly, and now another officer was beside him and then there were hands reaching down and the object was lifted clear and he was scrambling onto the path and as he stood up, water dripping from him, he realized it had only taken seconds after all.

'Turn it,' said a voice.

Eli looked down as the sodden shape was rolled over, and with a sickening lurch he saw the head seem almost to detach itself from the body: the throat was cut from ear to ear. The bloodless face stared at him. It looked like it was smiling.

Horrified, he looked away and that was when he saw her. She was in the shadows, sitting with her back against a young ash tree. Her legs were folded under her and she was absolutely still, so that, for a moment, he thought she was part of the tangled undergrowth. A trick of the misty light, he thought. But no. She was real. Her face was very pale; her eyes were very dark. She was staring straight ahead, but not at anything or anybody. Just staring.

For a moment, Eli Abel stood transfixed. And then behind him he heard a cry and turned to see a tall man with dark hair running with a limp towards them, on his face an expression of such anguish that it seemed wrong to look. He stopped briefly at the body of the man lying on the path and his face changed, contorted, like he might weep. He straightened up, though, and walked towards the silent figure, halting a few steps away; waiting.

At last she moved slightly, as though some spell had been broken. She looked up at the tall man and she didn't smile and neither did he, but he took another step forward and held out his hand, and after a few seconds she took it.

She stood up. Her clothes were soaked through. There was blood on her neck and on her cheek. Her hair was wet.

'Karlsson,' she said. Her voice was low and clear.

He didn't let go of her hand. 'Frieda,' he said. 'It's over. You're free.'

At this moment, more officers ran down the steps. At their rear, overweight and out of breath, was DCI Dugdale. He stopped and surveyed the scene, his eyes taking in the body laid out on the path, then Frieda standing a few yards away.

'Bloody hell,' he said.

Events moved quickly after that, like they were choreographed. Ambulances arrived, and more police cars. Tapes and barriers were put up. The SOC arrived. The public were turned away. Some of the press managed to get through, but by then there was a tent over the body; the only pictures anyone managed to get were of dozens of officers beside the canal, some in uniform and others wearing white overalls.

In the midst of this speed and efficiency was the speech-less figure of Frieda. When Dugdale asked her what had happened, she simply stared at him.

'It's all right,' he said, unnerved by her gaze and by the splashes of blood on her cheek. 'Take your time. You must be in shock. But just tell me this. How did he die?'

She looked away from him, over the canal.

'Frieda?'

'He had a knife,' she said. 'A long, sharp knife.'

She went up the steps with an officer and Karlsson. Some-one from the crowd of people behind the barriers called her name but she didn't look up. Cameras flashed. Soon the whole country, the whole world, would know that Dean Reeve was dead.

A paramedic tried to put a blanket round her shoulders but she pushed it away and climbed into the waiting car. Karlsson followed her.

They sat side by side but not touching. As he looked at her, blood slid from her hairline, down her forehead.

'You're hurt,' he said.

She put up a hand and wiped away the thread of watery blood. 'It's not mine.'

He wanted to put his hand on hers, but he didn't dare. There was a quality to her stillness that felt dangerous, as if she might burst into flames.

Fifty-two

A television van was parked at the entrance to Saffron Mews and there were journalists milling around. Josef, carrying several heavy shopping bags, pushed past them all and let himself into Frieda's house. He went first into the kitchen where he fed the cat, watered the basil plant and put fresh flowers in the vase. Then he took milk, butter, yoghurt and coffee beans out of the bags and stacked them in the fridge.

He went into the living room and checked that the fire was ready to be lit, minutely shifting the chair so that it was in the right position.

He went upstairs, stopping to check that there were towels in the bathroom, then proceeded to the balcony. He opened the door, noting with approval how it swung smoothly on its hinges, and stepped outside. There were several lavender bushes, a tub of herbs, the small ornamental tree and a long container where Chloë had planted bulbs for the spring. There was a clematis with bronze foliage that they had told him at the garden centre would have creamy white flowers in the winter months. There was a single wooden chair and Chloë's table made of golden elm.

He sat on the chair and looked out over the rooftops. The fog had thickened again; everything was shrouded in soft greyness. Josef lit a cigarette; he pulled a bottle of vodka from his coat pocket and took a gulp. He gave a heavy sigh and closed his eyes.

*

Dr Jane Franklin, consultant pathologist, looked down at the body of Dean Reeve and then across at a group of students, masked and gowned in green.

'Put out of your mind who this is,' she said sternly. 'This is a body. Our job is to establish the cause of death.'

She pointed at the neck with her scalpel. 'You,' she said. 'What do you see?'

'A lateral incision, cutting through . . . well, almost everything, really. The jugular vein, the carotid artery. The trachea looks damaged.'

'Cause of death?'

'He'd have bled out in about a minute, less maybe.'

Dr Franklin lifted Reeve's right hand.

'What about this?' She looked at one young man. 'You.'

'He's got short fingernails.'

'No, no. Wounds, incisions.'

'I can't see any.'

She reached across the body and raised the other arm.

'What about here?'

'I can't see anything.'

'Exactly. When people are stabbed, you normally find defence wounds on their hands and arms. They hold their hands up to protect themselves, like so.' She raised her two arms in front of her face. 'So what does that suggest?'

'I don't know.'

'Look at the wound again. What's it like? Rough? Jagged?'

'No, it's smooth. Like surgery.'

'How could that happen? On a towpath?'

'He could have been restrained?'

'It's possible,' said Dr Franklin. 'But there's no sign of bruising. No scratch marks. There is no other sign of injury, except here.' And she pointed at the knee. 'From which we removed this.' She held up a little metal dish. On it was a little bullet or, rather, what looked like a bullet with the tip removed. 'From this side, the knee looks intact. But this soft-point bullet entered from the rear. The soft point caused it to expand on impact causing catastrophic damage. He would have been immediately disabled.'

'It looks like an execution,' said another male student. 'You shoot him, then cut his throat.'

'Only one weapon was found at the scene,' said Dr Franklin. 'A German knife. Very sharp, the kind you would use to butcher an animal. And the kind that was used to murder Jessica Colbeck.'

'So what do we do?'

'What we do is describe the state of the body.'

When the students had moved away, Dr Franklin looked at the body again: stocky, with tattoos on the muscled arms, a soft pale stomach. That gaping wound. The face was ghastly, like white putty; the eyes were open, brown. She put a gloved thumb on their lids. It was foolish, she knew, but even when he was dead, she didn't want Dean Reeve staring at her.

There were officers searching the scrubby undergrowth and there were police divers back in the canal. They had found the knife in the first dive, but now Quarry was telling them to look for a gun as well.

'It must be somewhere,' he said.

The three divers moved inch by inch along the soft grey mud of the canal floor, picking up all the things that people threw into the water – even the carcass of a bicycle – and all the creatures that had died in there and decayed. The officers combed through the brambles and the scrubby bushes. Hours passed. There was no gun.

*

Frieda had showered and put on the clothes they had given her at the police station: a white cotton shirt and some dark trousers, slip-on shoes that were slightly too large for her. She sat in front of Dugdale and Quarry, her hands folded in her lap, a mug of tea untouched on the table.

'Frieda,' said Dugdale, leaning towards her. 'You do understand you're not in trouble.'

'Yes, I understand that. Thank you.'

'If anything, we should be celebrating. You got Dean Reeve. You beat him.'

'I'm not quite in the mood for celebrating,' said Frieda. 'Too many people have died for that. Including Dean Reeve.'

'Yes, of course, I see that. And you realize that we'll need to take a statement. If you don't feel ready for it, then we could do it at a later date.'

'Now is fine.'

'Also . . .' Dugdale stopped for a moment '. . . I'm required to say that you're entitled to legal advice.'

'Thank you, but that won't be necessary.'

Quarry switched on the recorder and identified the date and the place and everybody present.

'We can go over this briefly,' said Dugdale. 'If necessary, we can take a more detailed statement later. First, can you tell us how Dean Reeve died?'

Frieda looked at Dugdale directly. She was pale, seemed tired, but calm.

'I'm sorry. It's a bit of a fog. I remember approaching the spot where it happened and then I remember the police arriving. Everything else is a blur.'

'This must have been traumatic for you.'

'I don't know,' said Frieda.

'So you can't tell us how Dean Reeve died.'

'No.'

Quarry frowned at the answer. It seemed out of character – though, of course, he had no idea what the character of Frieda Klein actually was. He had heard so much about her and now here she was, composed and severe, and even Dugdale, who was never flustered by anything, seemed slightly unnerved.

'Were you expecting him? Did you know he would be there?'

'I went for a walk along the canal. I was thinking.'

'But he knew that *you*'d be there,' said Dugdale. 'Lola Hayes told him. Your friend betrayed you. What do you say to that?'

'If that's true,' Frieda said impassively, 'then she was acting under duress. She can't be blamed for it.'

'Did you know that Lola had been in communication with him?'

Frieda looked out of the window for a few moments. Quarry saw her clench and unclench her hands.

'She should never have got involved with me,' she said softly. 'I warned her.'

'That's not an answer,' said Dugdale, grimly.

'Have you heard of moral luck?'

'I don't care about moral luck just now. There's no point in your trying to defend Lola Hayes. She's confessed. We know what she did.'

Frieda shook her head. 'I disagree. There is a point in trying to defend her.'

'Look,' said Dugdale, who was now sounding exasperated. 'We're on your side and you're treating us like the enemy. Think of it from my point of view. We have to present a version of what happened. Dean Reeve was found floating in the canal with his throat cut and a bullet in his leg. We found the knife in the canal but we haven't found the gun. This suggests that there was at least one other person at the scene.'

'I can't tell you anything about that.'

'You mean you won't. Frieda, I completely understand the wish to revenge yourself against Dean Reeve, after all he's done to you and so many other people.'

Finally, Dugdale saw he'd provoked a response. Frieda gave a slight start and looked at everyone present. 'You think I wanted revenge?' she said in disbelief. 'You think I wanted to be a part of his sick game? What I wanted was for him to be arrested and put on trial. Clearly it didn't work out that way.'

'Why didn't it?'

'I wish I could help you.'

'Did you see him die?'

'I was there, clearly.'

'You were more than there. When you were found, you had been in the water. His blood was on your clothes, on your skin. In your hair.'

She blinked twice, like a camera lens clicking. Quarry, watching her intently, could have sworn she was reliving Reeve's death.

'There was a lot of blood,' she said.

'You're not giving us anything,' said Dugdale, helplessly.

'You've got Dean Reeve's body. What else do you need?'

Karlsson was waiting for her. They walked out of the police station together. Out on the front steps it was blustery with a few drops of rain.

'Dugdale doesn't look happy,' he said. 'He's got that look I've seen before when police try to interview you.'

'Will you do something for me?' she asked.

'Yes.'

'You don't know what it is yet.'

He shrugged.

'Will you make sure Lola isn't charged?'

'You know what she did? She almost got you killed. When she had a chance to save you, she sent me to the wrong place.'

'Lola had terrible, terrible luck. She's just another of Reeve's victims.'

'It's not really up to me. Dugdale will give a file to the Crown Prosecution Service. They'll decide.'

'But you'll do it anyway.'

Karlsson laughed. 'In your next life, you're going to be an attack dog. The sort that bites you and never lets go.'

'Come to Frieda's, Mum,' said Chloë.

'What? *What?* Oh, my God. Why?'

'Just come to Frieda's.'

'Sorry,' said Jack, to the woman with pink hair. 'We're finishing early today. The till is closed.'

'But I need cheese for my dinner party!'

'Here.'

He wrapped a slab of Brie for her, then a large wedge of crumbly blue, and handed them both across.

'How much do I owe you?'

'Nothing at all.'

'Come on,' said Reuben to Alexei. 'You can do your homework another day. Put on your shoes.'

'Where are we going?'

'To Frieda's house.'

Fifty-three

Yvette opened the door of the boxy little room. One window high in the wall let in the last of the day's mild sun, and Frieda entered.

Lola was at the table, her head resting on her arms, her hair spread out. At the sound of the door, she lifted her head. Her face was smeared with weeping and her eyes red. At the sight of Frieda, she gave a small moan and shrank back.

Frieda pulled up a chair and sat opposite her. 'Well, Lola,' she said. 'It's over.'

'Do you know?' whispered Lola. 'About me?'

'Yes. I've known for some time.'

There was silence in the small room. Lola gazed at her, pupils dilated. 'What do you mean?'

'I knew Dean had got to you,' said Frieda, steadily.

'But – but I don't understand. How did you know? When? And if you knew . . .' She trailed off.

'You don't really need to know the details,' said Frieda. 'That's not what matters.'

'It is what matters,' said Lola, helplessly. 'I'm going to spend the rest of my life going over every moment of what happened in the time I spent with you. What I did, what you did. I need to know everything.'

Frieda thought. Which were the moments when Lola had given herself away?

'Living in the world is hard enough,' Frieda began, 'but lying is harder. It's like trying to assemble a whole new world, but the bits don't fit together properly. Holes start appearing.

For someone like Dean Reeve, that isn't a problem. He lived in his lies and fabulations. But for someone like you, a good person, lying is hard.'

'Stop it with the lecture,' said Lola, in a bleak tone. 'How did you know?'

'It was different things. When I saw you after Jess died, you were wearing a watch, the watch you told me earlier you'd left there. That didn't fit with your account of finding Jess dead. So something else must have happened.'

'What a stupid mistake.'

'If it hadn't been that, it would have been something else. Then I knew because each time that Dean nearly got to us, it was after you had managed to have a few moments on your own. I assume you borrowed a phone or something and called him. I knew because you hated that Regent's Park place and yet, after you'd briefly gone out into the park, you didn't want to leave it.'

'So you were watching me?'

'Of course I was watching you. I watch everybody. I only knew for sure after I made a mistake. I told you where the next body was found. But I'd made a mistake. I missed out a river. Beverley Brook was the wrong place, but Dean Reeve put the body there anyway. He was acting on the information you gave him.'

Lola was staring at her with her mouth very slightly open. Her face was working, and she seemed to be trying to say something, but no words came from her.

'Above all, I knew from your behaviour. It wasn't just that you were terrified. You often seemed terrified of *me* – or, at least, of being with me. Sometimes you clung to me and sometimes you avoided me. Sometimes you talked incessantly, as though trying to cover up what you were unable to say. You were scared of silence and of what you might inadvertently reveal. And at other times you were mute. It was very clear to me you were hiding something. Or trying to hide something, at least. Secrets are very hard to carry. They can destroy you.'

'You knew and you didn't tell me. All that time.'

'Yes.'

'I was in *hell*,' said Lola. 'And all the time you knew. You *used* me.'

'I told you many times that there was nothing you couldn't say to me. I watched you decide, over and over again, to say nothing. But you're right. In the end, I used you to tell Dean Reeve where I was going to be.'

'I came to you and you used me. Does that make you feel good about yourself?'

'We're not put on this earth to feel good about ourselves. And don't think of yourself as the main victim in this case. There were a lot of them ahead of you in the queue, and most of them are dead.' She looked steadily at Lola. 'Even at the end, when Karlsson found you, you continued to lie.'

'I had to.'

'You really think that?'

'They're going to arrest me. I'll be in all the papers. It'll be, like, Dean Reeve and Lola Hayes. I'll be in court and everyone will know what I did and hate me.' She started to sob in earnest, wretched jerky sounds of distress. 'What about my parents? I'll go to prison. How will I ever – ever – ever –' Her frame shook with weeping.

Frieda leaned forward and put a hand over Lola's, seeing the bitten nails, the rash at the wrist. 'Lola, you've got a difficult journey ahead of you, but that won't be a part of it. You won't be charged.'

Lola wiped the back of her hand across her streaming, snotty face. 'What do you mean?'

357

'Just that.'

'Why?'

'I assume they don't think you'd be convicted.'

'Did you have anything to do with it?'

'I shared my personal opinion with them.'

'So you understand?' Lola sat up straighter and pushed her lank hair behind her ears. 'You understand why I did it?'

'I do.'

Lola took both of Frieda's hands and gripped them tightly. Her face was wild. 'He killed Jess in front of me. I watched her die.'

Frieda gazed into Lola's face, waiting.

'And I didn't even try to stop him. I just watched as she died.'

'You could have told me, Lola.'

'He said he would kill my parents. He was showing me what he would do to them. Don't you see? I had no choice.'

'Is that what you say to yourself, that you had no choice?'

'I don't know what I say to myself,' Lola said desperately. 'I don't know. I don't want to be who I am. What shall I do? How shall I ever bear it?'

'I don't know. But this is where you start: with looking at what you have been through and what you have done without self-deception. You tell yourself the truth.'

'I hate the truth!'

'You don't need to like it. It's something we live with, like water or light.'

'Can you ever forgive me?'

'That's the wrong question.'

'What's the right one?'

'Can you forgive yourself?'

Frieda stood up. She put a hand on Lola's bent head and

Lola stared at her, her eyes wet. She looked like an abandoned child. For a moment, Frieda remembered her at their first meeting, when she had wrapped her arms around Frieda and tried to comfort her for all she had been through. 'You were pulled into a terrible story,' she said. 'You've been through things that nobody should have to go through. But, though it might not seem like it now, this is also a kind of gift, if you use it courageously. You know yourself in a way that few people are ever able to. You know what you're capable of.'

She opened the door but Lola scrambled to her feet.

'Frieda!'

'Yes.'

'Will I see you again?'

'I don't think so.'

'Please don't go. Don't leave me.'

'You should go and see your parents. And you should find someone to talk to about all of this.'

'Can't I talk to you? You're the only person who can understand and make it better.'

'No, Lola. Our story together is done.'

'Karlsson?'

'What?'

'Have you ever killed anyone?'

'No, of course not.'

She nodded. 'Me neither.'

Fifty-four

Sarah Kernan put down the phone and turned to her sister.

'That was the police,' she said, in a stifled voice. 'They got him. The man who killed Geoff. They got him.'

Standing in the middle of the kitchen, in her slippers, a tea-towel over her shoulder, she started to cry. She didn't lift her hands to her face, or bend her body. Her shoulders shook and tears rolled down her cheeks. Her sister went to her awkwardly and put her arms around her; they'd never been a family for hugging.

After the call from the police, Jonah Martin's girlfriend Maiko went softly through the house in her bare feet and sat at the computer. She typed in Dean Reeve's name and stared for a long time at the image there. Then she entered the name 'Frieda Klein'. She looked at the stern face, almost feeling that it was looking back at her.

After a few minutes she turned away, laying one hand on the great dome of her belly. The baby often kicked. Sometimes it hiccuped. Now she felt it move under her palm. She imagined it with Jonah's face.

'So,' said Walter Levin to Jock Keegan. 'She did it.'

Keegan lifted his head. 'Reeve?'

'Found floating in the canal with his throat cut. And a bullet in his leg.'

'A bullet? What's that about?'

'Yet to be established,' said Levin.

Keegan shook his head and smiled. 'I didn't think she'd get away with this one,' he said. 'I thought she'd pushed her luck too far.'

Levin looked pensive. 'I put her chances at about fifty–fifty. A little less, maybe, with that girl in tow. We should have known better.'

'Is she all right?'

'Apparently.'

Keegan remembered her as he had last seen her, outside those monster houses in Rivingdale Terrace. She had been composed enough, but there'd been an intensity about her that had unsettled him.

'I don't know,' he said.

'So do you think we can lure her back to help out here?'

'Of course not.'

Levin gave Keegan a quizzical look. 'You sound very certain.'

'As certain as I am of anything. She'll never come back here, and she'll never go back to the police. She's done with all of that.'

'Oh, not at once, of course. Give her time to recover. But –'

'No. Don't you see? Dean Reeve is dead. She's done.'

Carrie Dekker, wife of Alan, Dean Reeve's twin, bent down and put her arms round her dog for comfort. The man who had killed her husband, who had impersonated him for a day and a night, was gone. But too late for her, childless and alone.

Matthew Faraday, sitting in front of the computer, heard the front door open and then bang shut.

'Matthew! Matthew!' It was his mother, calling up the

stairs in a voice that sent a prickle of dread through him. 'Come and see this.'

Eight years ago – red-haired, freckled, gap-toothed – he had become the most famous child in the country when Dean Reeve had kidnapped him. He remembered it in nightmarish snatches – a locked room, a boot in his face, a homesickness that had been so fierce and bitter it seemed to have entered his bones. Even today he would often wake up crying. But he remembered Frieda Klein like a bright image, unanchored from the events that surrounded her. She had stood beneath his window with snowflakes in her hair; she had pulled him out of the tomb, back into life.

Charlotte Beck, exhausted, sank onto the sofa with her daughter, who had at last fallen asleep. She knew there was a bottle of wine in the door of the fridge. But to get it she would have to stand up and that suddenly felt like too much effort. She picked up the remote control and flicked through the channels. Suddenly she glimpsed a face and halted, turning up the volume.

It was him, the man who had sat on the pavement beside her, who had told her she had done well and helped her home, and whom the police had asked her about later. She listened to the report, trying to make sense of it. She saw the face of a woman called Frieda Klein and realized she had met her too.

She sat dazed, her little daughter's head warm and heavy on her shoulder: for a few moments she had been caught up in the story of Dean Reeve and Frieda Klein.

She pressed her lips to the top of her baby's silky head. 'Well,' she said. 'Who would have dreamed it?'

Fifty-five

Frieda would have preferred to return to her house alone. She had imagined it so many times over the past weeks – opening the door and stepping into the clean and silent space. She had even rehearsed it that very morning, getting as far as the hall, stroking the cat and feeling the rooms empty and waiting for her like a promise.

Instead, she got a welcome party. As the car nosed its way past the press into the mews, she saw the lights downstairs were on behind the closed shutters. As she made her way to the house with Karlsson, the blue door swung open and she saw Chloë framed there, her face almost tragic with emotion.

'Frieda,' she said. 'Oh, thank God.'

'Hello,' said Frieda, stepping in and closing the door on the small crowd in the mews.

'Frieda!' shrieked a voice, and there was Olivia, aiming a champagne bottle at her and struggling with the cork that soon enough shot past Frieda's ear with a loud noise, while spumes of white froth splattered the floor. Behind her, Frieda saw the little cat streak up the stairs.

'Frieda,' said Reuben, emerging from the kitchen. He was wearing his dandiest waistcoat. 'You had us all worried.'

Jack's head appeared over Reuben's shoulder. He was smiling and bobbing his head and running his hand through his wild hair. He was wearing an orange shirt and striped trousers and had a narrow moustache that gave him a slightly comical air.

'Let her through,' said Karlsson.

'Perhaps you'd like a bath,' said Chloë. 'We bought you some foam.'

It felt to Frieda like the house didn't belong to her yet; she was its guest. She looked at all the shining faces, smiled or tried to smile, took a glass from Olivia's outstretched hand, though she didn't like champagne much.

'Thank you,' she said. Her voice rasped slightly and she looked away from them all. 'Where's Josef?'

'Josef here,' he said, coming down the stairs, Alexei just behind him.

'Hello,' she said.

He made an unsteady bow and Frieda saw he had been drinking. His brown eyes burned at her and he put a hand on his heart; for one moment she thought he would burst into song.

'Something smells different,' she said suspiciously.

'Ah, yes,' said Chloë, behind her.

'What have you done?'

'We do it together, me and Chloë and my friend.'

'It was his idea,' said Chloë. 'I said you didn't like surprises.'

'I don't.'

'You like this,' said Josef, triumphantly. 'Follow.' He gestured grandly at them all. 'All follow. Jack, bring glasses. We toast Frieda.'

They trooped up the stairs.

'Close eyes,' said Josef, as they reached the first floor.

'Oh, please!'

'Close and I say when.'

Frieda sighed and closed her eyes, feeling her way up the next flight of stairs, still holding her champagne.

'Stop now. Look!'

364

She opened her eyes. There was a silence: everyone was looking at her, Chloë with great anxiety. She saw how exhausted Karlsson was, almost grey with it.

'Is good?' Josef was gazing at her expectantly.

She put a finger to her lips. 'Wait,' she said.

She opened the door and stepped outside into the darkness. The air was cool on her face and London glittered all around her. She turned.

'It's wonderful,' she said.

Josef beamed.

'Really?' said Chloë. 'You like it? You don't mind?'

'It's a gift,' said Frieda.

They jostled through the door to join her.

'It feels solid enough,' Frieda said. 'But will it take all of us?'

Josef looked offended. 'It take twenty people. Fifty. You drive a car out here.'

'I'm just worried about seven adults and a child for the moment.'

She walked across to the railing. It seemed solid enough. She looked around. The evening sky was a mess of oranges and reds and streaks of jet plume. There were lights from the BT Tower close at hand and from Canary Wharf far away. Josef stood beside her.

'Don't you trust Josef?' Reuben said, pouring wine into glasses.

Frieda looked round with a faint smile. 'You know how I first met Josef?'

'You mean when he fell through the ceiling?'

'I thought he was dead.'

'English builders,' said Josef, with a contemptuous sniff.

Frieda looked around, at the seasoned decking they were standing on, at the new table and chairs. 'Josef, I've got to pay you for this.'

'Is my present.'

'I can at least pay you for the materials. For the planks and this table and the chairs. They're beautiful. They must have cost a fortune.'

'They cost nothing,' said Josef, with a shrug.

Frieda looked at Josef, then at Karlsson and then back at Josef. 'I'd ask more questions,' she said. 'But we've got a policeman present.'

'I'm not on duty,' said Karlsson.

'To Frieda,' said Reuben.

Everyone clinked glasses.

'You look done in,' said Jack.

'I'm all right. Perhaps it all feels unreal still.'

'We've missed you so much,' said Chloë, her voice trembling.

Frieda looked at each of them in turn. She wanted to tell them that she had missed them all, but in the end she simply lifted her glass to them.

'You must have been through hell,' said Olivia. 'I don't know where to begin. What to ask.'

'Don't ask anything.'

'But don't you want to tell us?'

'No.'

At last only Karlsson and Josef were left on the balcony, with a smudge of a moon above them. Karlsson produced a whisky bottle and Josef went inside and reappeared with three tumblers and a jug of water. Karlsson took a handkerchief from his pocket and wiped the whisky bottle. 'I've had this in a cupboard for years,' he said. 'I was given it as a present. I was saving it for something special. This feels like the time.'

He removed the cap and poured some into the three glasses. Each of them sipped it reflectively.

'Is good,' said Josef.

'Yes, it's good,' said Karlsson.

There was silence for a long time. Karlsson refilled the glasses. Frieda seemed to be lost in thought. Suddenly she looked at Karlsson. 'Go on, then,' she said.

'What?'

'Ask what you want to ask.'

Karlsson looked at Josef. 'Is that OK?'

'Is OK.'

'Because I've got a feeling that you were involved.'

'Is OK.'

Karlsson slowly put his glass on the table. 'All right, Frieda. What happened?'

When Frieda started to speak, it felt like she was talking to herself. 'Reeve wanted to tell me to go somewhere so that he could kill me.'

'Why would you do that?' said Karlsson.

'I considered it. I thought I could sacrifice myself and then he might stop. I was thinking that when I went to Counter's Creek – but, of course, the police intercepted him. I had no plan then for what I would do, beyond meeting him.'

Karlsson looked across at Josef, who was refilling his glass. 'So when did you give up that ridiculous plan?'

'Ridiculous?' said Frieda.

'I mean, ridiculous if you didn't want to be murdered.'

'I knew Lola was in contact with him.'

'You knew?'

'Yes.'

'How?'

Frieda told them, in a more dispassionate way, what she had told Lola.

'So instead of him controlling you, you could control him?'

Frieda's expression was entirely impassive. Karlsson wasn't even sure if she was listening to him.

'You could have collaborated with the police,' he said. 'You could have lured him into a trap.'

She shook her head. 'The police had already tried that and it was a disaster. And there was only going to be one chance. I thought that if Reeve knew I was going to be at the spot where he killed his brother, he wouldn't be able to resist that.'

'And you'd have someone there waiting.'

'Not just someone. Josef and Stefan. A friend of his.'

Karlsson looked at Josef, who seemed to be lost in contemplation of his whisky glass.

'How could you be sure that Reeve wouldn't get there first? That he wouldn't spot them?'

'Because when I told Lola, they were already in place. And I didn't think he would spot them because I trust Josef.' She glanced across at Josef. 'I trust him in every way, apart from doing building work in my house without permission.'

Karlsson finished his drink, then refilled the three glasses. 'So what happened?'

As Frieda started to speak, she suddenly felt outside herself. She was still talking but she could somehow listen to herself talking. At the same time, part of her self, her real self, was not just remembering and narrating but was back there on the River Lea, leaning over the railings and looking into the water. She heard the faint sound of footsteps and still waited, letting the image of her father recede. She took a slow breath, then another. She felt a sense of great calm. Peace, perhaps. She turned and looked at him. She had last seen him eight years earlier in a police interview room. He looked much the same, thinner maybe, streaks of grey in his short hair. He was wearing scuffed brown shoes, blue jeans, a black zip-up jacket with a brown shirt visible underneath.

She saw something flash in his right hand, suspended at his side: the blade of a knife. There was an expression in his brown eyes that she found difficult to read. It wasn't hatred or rage. It was more like curiosity, fascination, even a kind of yearning. He breathed deeply. Frieda thought of someone in a garden, breathing in the scents. He looked like a man who was where he wanted to be.

Frieda's main feeling was: is that it? Is this what had caused so much death, so much suffering, so many lives ruined? All for what? Something twisted, a crossed wire, in a man's mind.

'We're done,' said Frieda. 'It's over.'

'I'm not done, Frieda,' said Dean Reeve. 'Not yet. Soon. It is your time.'

'No,' she said.

There was another sound from behind him and Reeve looked round. There was a gap where part of the towpath had collapsed and not been repaired. Two men stepped out on the path. Frieda just saw that one of them, Josef, was holding a wooden club. The other, Stefan, was half hidden behind Reeve. She couldn't make him out fully. Reeve turned back towards Frieda and a slow smile started to form on his face.

And from that moment, when she looked back, she could never quite remember the sequence of events. Even then, everything seemed to be happening at the same time. Reeve leaped towards her. They were perhaps ten yards apart. While Frieda was wondering if this was how it was going to end for her and whether it would hurt, he suddenly fell to his knees and there was a noise that was so loud she could feel it as well as hear it. She could almost see it. It had a purple-black colour.

Reeve made an effort to raise himself but couldn't move

beyond his knees. He still had the knife in his right hand but Frieda and Josef and Stefan were out of reach and Reeve couldn't move and a dark red patch was growing on his trousers, just below the knee. Frieda took out her phone and as she did so she looked at Stefan, who was now behind Reeve, holding his gun at the back of his head.

'Stop,' she said. 'That's enough. You should go right now. I'm calling the police. You don't want to be caught with that.'

Stefan's eyes were flashing. Frieda wasn't sure he could hear what she was saying.

'What he did to Alexei,' he said. 'What he did to all of them.'

'No,' said Frieda, more sharply, and Stefan looked at her and then at Josef, who nodded at him.

'You've won,' said Frieda, more softly. 'Just walk away.'

Stefan put the gun into the pocket of his jacket. He raised his hand, gave a funny sort of salute to Frieda and walked quickly away.

'So now?' said Josef.

They both looked at Reeve, who was staring at Frieda, his eyes fixed on her, still with that expression of longing, yearning.

'You . . .' he began. 'Frieda. Frieda Klein . . .'

Frieda ignored him. She had no interest in anything he had to say. She was about to key in the number on her phone. Then she saw a movement: Dean Reeve's hand lifted a knife with a long and shining blade. He placed the tip in the soft hollow under his left ear and drew it along his neck with a flash of silver. For a second or so, there was nothing there, and then it was bubbling red. He gazed at her for a few seconds, the smile on his face still and the great gaping wound just below it, and then he tipped sideways, like a tree toppling, sideways and slightly forward into the canal. He slid

370

into the dark water almost without a splash and disappeared. Only the knife was left on the towpath.

Frieda threw the phone aside and jumped into the water and felt a shock of cold. She took a breath and dived under, pushing herself down with her hands. Her eyes were open but she saw nothing. She felt around with her hands. Nothing, nothing. Just mud and grit and the slimy trail of weeds. And then she was grasping something. She pulled at it and raised it slowly. She broke the surface and she saw she was holding Dean Reeve, his face down in the water. Josef was beside her.

'Turn him,' she said.

'Why? You want to save him? This man?'

'Turn him.'

With a great effort, Josef pulled on one side of the body and Dean Reeve's face appeared, pale and staring. His eyes were open and his mouth was open and the wound in his throat was open. Frieda could see the tendons and the damaged windpipe and the bubbles of water and blood. Suddenly she felt a hand on her. Reeve's hand was gripping her jacket, holding it tight, pulling, tugging at her, drawing her to him and drawing her down with him. She turned her head to look at it and slowly the grip relaxed and the hand fell away and when she looked back at Dean Reeve's face, the eyes were glassy and unseeing.

Frieda and Josef scrambled towards the towpath and clambered up. Josef picked up the knife and tossed it into the water. They stood facing each other.

'You've got to go,' said Frieda.

'I stay with you.'

Frieda looked at the body, which had rotated once more and was face down, the arms spread.

'You can't be found here. You've done everything. You've done more than everything. Now go.'

371

Josef shrugged helplessly. 'All right. I go.'

'Now,' said Frieda. 'And don't look back.'

He nodded and then, very suddenly, he put his hands on her shoulders and his forehead against hers. When he let her go, she saw his eyes were full of tears.

'Thank you, my friend,' she said, and he put his hand on his heart and gave that small bow he had given her the first day they had met. Then he turned and left.

When he was gone, Frieda felt suddenly empty, without relief or gladness. She sat down with her back against a tree. She saw her phone, lying on the towpath, but she didn't reach for it. What was the hurry? For a few seconds she closed her eyes but opened them again when she heard a sound getting louder and louder, a roar she couldn't make sense of.

When Frieda had finished her account, none of them spoke for a long time.

'Thank you,' Karlsson said finally.

'Thank you?' said Frieda. 'For what?'

'For just telling me,' he said.

'What else would I do?'

'You could have said, "I'll only tell you if you promise to keep it secret." '

'I don't like telling people what to do.'

In response to that, Karlsson managed a slight smile. 'Now that,' he said, 'is not true.'

He raised his glass to Josef. 'And thank you too,' he said. Josef gave a slight inclination of the head. 'And tell your friend to get rid of his gun.'

Josef shook his head. 'He is Russian. You cannot tell him nothing.'

Karlsson poured more whisky into their glasses.

'Perhaps you can be working together once more,' said Josef, lifting his drink.

Frieda turned to Karlsson. 'You know I'll never work with you again, don't you?'

'I know,' he said.

'Good. Never ask me.'

'I promise.'

Josef lit a cigarette. 'But we are still a team.' His words were slightly slurred. 'Team Frieda.'

Frieda snorted. She set the glass down on the small table with a click. 'I was thinking I should have a plant out here that gives out scent in the evening.'

'Jasmine?'

'Something like that.'

The three of them sat on the balcony, slowly sipping the good whisky, not speaking.

'Time for home,' said Josef at last, and the three of them went downstairs.

Josef left first, pausing on the threshold to make his small bow. Karlsson and Frieda watched him walk away.

When he was out of sight, Karlsson turned towards her. 'Frieda,' he said. 'There is something I need to say and –'

But she stopped him. 'No,' she said. 'Not tonight.'

'But –'

'Not tonight, Karlsson. We can talk tomorrow.'

He looked into her face. He couldn't read her, although he knew that she could read him. She knew it all.

Fifty-six

Karlsson left and Frieda washed up the glasses and put water into the cat's bowl. It was late but she knew she wouldn't sleep tonight. She didn't want to. She went back up the stairs onto the terrace once more, into the misty softness of the night. The cat padded out to join her, rubbing itself against her legs, telling her she was home.

Tomorrow she would think of what the future held. Tonight was for the past, a time for memories and for ghosts. She closed her eyes and in the darker darkness saw Dean Reeve's face – smiling at her, smiling even as he died. With an effort that felt physical, she made that face become the face of his brother Alan, who had been the identical reverse-image of Dean. Now the brown eyes looking at her out of the self's night were not sinister, but sad.

Other figures came towards her, more than just memories, dead but still here, vividly absent. She held their faces in her mind: men, women, girls; a mad woman in a cell muttering her own name over and over again. *I am here.* She saw Sandy among them, and he was no longer a body swollen by the river: he was strong and hopeful and he had eyes that saw her again.

No one is ever like anyone else. No one can be replaced. Every death is the end of a world. And they're gone, and yet they remain. They walk with us along the secret rivers.

Frieda followed those rivers, covered over, forgotten, but still there. She heard their trickle under the grating, felt their course beneath her feet. She peeled back the bricks and concrete and sludge of years and sat beside them. There were pebbles shining on their beds, small brown fish in their currents, and water flowers, and weeds that looked like human hair.

They flowed past her, ceaseless, and she remembered all of the stories that had ended.

She didn't know how long she sat there for. Hours, perhaps. The sky was lightening to the east and the cat had gone.

She stood up and went inside. She closed the door.